South Street

SOUTH STREET

David Bradley, 1950—

GROSSMAN PUBLISHERS
A DIVISION OF THE VIKING PRESS
NEW YORK 1975

Library of Congress Cataloging in Publication Data
Bradley, David, 1950-
    South Street.
    I. Title.
PZ4.B7996So   [PS3552.R226]   813'.5'4   75-14343
ISBN 0-670-65935-5

Dedicated to my father, Reverend David H. Bradley, and to my mother, Harriette Jackson Bradley, with special thanks to Ian Mowatt and to Hiram Haydn.

South Street

South Street runs from the eastern river
To the western river's farther shore—
Flees the slimy-stinking water,
Slides through dark dead-ended days,
Skulks through black thief-pleasing nights,
Silent in the city-roar.

South Street's pavement is cracked and broken,
Choked with beer bottle litter from a hundred bars.
It bruises and batters the feet that walk there,
And sucks at the tires of the passing cars.
South Street's shit-clogged sewers carry
The salt-sweaty liquor of men made wild—
Puke-flavored blood from a barroom battle,
The diamond tears of a hungry child.

South Street crawls for thirty blocks—
Concrete links in an urban chain
Shackling long-simmered hatreds;
Or an obese burgher's bulging belt,
Dividing the staleurine pubic ghetto
From the skyscrapers' overhanging paunch—
Watches the intrigues of bums and junkies,
The assignations of loud-mouthed whores,
Sees them fight love fuck and die,
Crosses the river and changes its
Name.

                                        —Brown

1
Lightnin' Ed's

The street lay like a snake sleeping; dull-dusty, gray-black in the dingy darkness. At the three-way intersection of Twenty-second Street, Grays Ferry Avenue, and South Street a fountain, erected once-upon-a-year by a ladies' guild in fond remembrance of some dear departed altruist, stood cracked and dry, full of dead leaves and cigarette butts and bent beer cans, forgotten by the city and the ladies' guild, functionless, except as a minor memorial to how They Won't Take Care Of Nice Things. On one side of South Street a chain food market displayed neat packages of precooked food sequestered behind thick plate glass—a nose-thumbing temptation to the undernourished. On the other side of South Street the State Liquor Store showed back-lit bottles to tantalizing advantage and proclaimed, on a sign pasted to the inside of the window, just behind the heavy wire screening, that state lottery tickets were on sale, and that you had to play to win.

There was no one on the corner where Grays Ferry met Twenty-second and Twenty-second met South: the police, spying any of the local citizens, assumed they were there to rob the liquor store or the food market, and ran the duly convicted offender away. But a little way downtown, near the junction of a nameless alley and South Street, was a dim entranceway, a hole in the wall with a thick wooden door hanging open, and out of it came belches of heavy-beating jukebox music and stale tobacco smoke.

The traffic light at the intersection changed. A flood of cars accelerated away from the corner, their lowered headlights reflecting in pools of the soft tar of the street. One set of headlamps, undimmed, lanced ahead, raking over the fronts of dingy brown-brick buildings and glinting in the eyes of a big black alley cat, scruffed and scarred from a thousand battles-royal. Blinded, the cat darted into the street and was caught beneath the rear wheel of the last car in the string. The car swerved slightly and pulled over to the curb and the driver, a balding man dressed in baggy gray slacks and a blue coat-sweater, got out. "What on earth did I hit?" he muttered, looking around.

"Oh, God, George!" said the woman in the right front seat. "It was probably just a bump in the street. There's enough of them, Lord knows. Why don't they *do* something about the streets in this neighborhood?"

"It couldn't have been a bump in the street," George said. "The front wheel didn't hit it and the back wheel did. I just hope it wasn't a child."

"A child? At this time of night? It was probably just a dog or a cat. Or a rat," she added, looking around with a shudder.

"What's wrong?" demanded a sleepy voice from the back seat.

"Your father's trying to convince himself he's a murderer because he ran over a dog or something."

"Daddy, did you kill a dog?"

"Be quiet, Stacey," said George. "If it was a dog or something, then I want to make sure it isn't lying injured somewhere to go mad."

"*You're* mad, George. Here we are sitting in the middle of this . . . this . . . *place*, about to be robbed or knifed or . . . worse, and all you're worried about is a stray dog."

"Cat," said George, who had walked around to the back of the car, where he could see the mangled body dripping red blood and yellowish intestines on the pavement.

"Good God!" exclaimed the woman, leaning out her window and staring at the mutilated mass. "Did it scratch the paint?"

"Daddy," Stacey said accusingly, "you *are* a murderer."

"George, let's get out of here. That cat smells terrible. This whole neighborhood smells terrible. It's giving me the willies." George looked up and down the street, hands on hips. Then he turned and began to walk toward the open doorway beside the alley. "George? George! Where are you going? Don't you dare leave us alone."

"Just right here, Martha. Somebody may want to do something." He walked on. Behind him he heard the windows being rolled up and door locks being engaged. He smiled to himself. Then he looked around at the dilapidated buildings and the overflowing garbage cans and the dark shadows, and he stopped smiling.

Leo, the two-hundred-and-fifty-eight-pound owner-bartender-cashier-bouncer of Lightnin' Ed's Bar and Grill, looked up from the glass he was polishing to see a one-hundred-and-fifty-eight-pound white man walk into his bar. Leo's mouth fell open and he almost dropped the glass. One by one the faces along the bar turned to stare at the single pale face, shining in the dimness. "Yes, sir, cap'n," Leo said uneasily, "what can we be doin' for you?"

George looked around nervously. "I, ah, had a little accident. I, ah, ran over a cat in the street, and I, uh, don't know what to do about it."

"Whad he say?" a wino at the far end of the bar, who claimed to be hard of hearing, whispered loudly.

The jukebox ran out and fell silent just as somebody yelled to him, "Paddy says he run over some cat out in the street." The sound echoed throughout the bar. Conversation died.

"Goddamn!" said the wino.

Leo leaned over the bar, letting his gigantic belly rest on the polished wood. "Yeah?" he said to George. "Didja kill him?"

"Oh yes," George assured him. "I made certain of that."

"Whad he say?" demanded the deaf wino.

Leo stared at George. "You pullin' ma leg?"

"Of course not," George snapped. "I ran over a cat in the street. Right outside."

"Well," said Leo, "there's a pay phone over there you can use to call the cops. But listen, was it right out in front a here?"

George nodded.

"Well, listen, cap'n, seein' as you're in trouble anyways, you think you could maybe drag him down the street a ways 'fore the cops get here? All that fuzz hangin' 'round out front, bad for business, you know what I mean?"

"Whad he say?" demanded the wino.

"Look," George said, "I don't want to call the po . . . the cops. There's no need for that. The car wasn't damaged. All I wanted was I ran over this cat and it's all smashed and it's lying right next to the sidewalk and I wanted a shovel or something to move it and put it in a garbage can or something."

Lightnin' Ed's knew a rare phenomenon—complete silence. It lasted for a long ten seconds before Leo sighed. "Whad he say?" demanded the deaf wino.

The answer was a multivoiced rumble. "He says he killed this cat on the street an' he wants a shovel so's he can hide him in a garbage can."

"Ain't that just like a fuckin' paddy?" said Big Betsy the whore.

"Look a here, cap'n," said Leo, "I don't want no trouble. This ain't like Alabama, you can't just go around hittin' an' runnin' an' tossin' bodies into garbage cans."

"Solid!" said a rat-faced man who clutched at a beer bottle. "You tell this sucker somethin', Leo, 'fore I lay this bottle upside his head."

"Look," George said, spreading his hands and looking down the long row of hostile faces, "it was just one stray al—"

"Will you listen to the honky muthafucka," snapped a dark-skinned man wearing a black beret. "Listen to him! Cocksucker probly cheered when they offed Malcolm an' cried buckets over Bobby Kennedy. We oughta waste the muthafucka, that's what I say."

"You got it, brother," said the rat-faced man, brandishing the beer bottle.

"Whad he·say?" demanded the deaf wino.

"Buddy," said Leo, "if I was you, I'd split."

George looked at him in confusion. "But it was only an alley cat."

"Look," Leo said, "I'd just as soon kick the shit outa you maself, but I got ma business to be thinkin' about an' I can't . . . Whad you say?"

"I said it was just an alley cat."

"We oughta string the muthafucka up an' cut his pasty balls off," the man in the black beret was saying. "That'd teach 'em they can't be comin' 'round here runnin' the People down in the street like we was animals."

"Amen, brother," said the rat-faced man.

"Hold it, people," Leo said, waving his big arm. "It wasn't nothin' but an alley cat."

"An *alley* cat?" said Big Betsy the whore. "Then what the hell'd he wanna go makin' out like he done killed somebody for?"

"He's crazy," Leo said.

"Shit," said the man in the black beret, "he's a goddamn muthafuckin' pale-faced honky."

"That's what I said," Leo snapped, and went back to polishing glasses.

George stood by the bar, looking around and realizing that nobody was paying any attention to him any more except for the man in the black beret, who looked up from his gin occasionally to glare and snarl and mutter something under his breath. "Hey," George said finally.

Leo looked up at him. "What you want now?"

"What should I do about the cat?"

"Damn if I know," said Leo. "It ain't ma cat."

"It's in front of your bar."

Leo regarded him sourly. "You drinkin' somethin', cap'n, or you just causin' trouble?"

George looked at him for two seconds and then backed hastily out of the bar. When he reached the car he had to tap on the window four times before his wife would let him in.

"George, where have you *been?* Why, Stacey and I could have been raped five times while you were in there! Let me smell your breath."

"I thought they were going to kill me," George said softly, staring through the windshield at the street. Suddenly he came to life, twisted his head, stared at Martha. "For a minute I honestly thought they were going to kill me." He shook his head as if to clear it and began fumbling with his seat belt, trying to buckle it with shaking hands.

"Of course they were," Martha told him. "They'd do it in a minute and think nothing of it. They aren't normal. Look at this neighborhood. Just *look* at it! I don't know why they live like this, I swear I don't."

George started the car and pulled away from the curb. As the car accelerated, turned the corner, vanished into the night, the bloody remains of the cat dropped off the fender and onto the street.

Leo corked the bottle of Old Colony gin and set the shot glass in front of the man with the black beret. "Rayburn, your woman ain't gonna let you 'lone when you gets home half dead," Leo warned.

"Shit," said Rayburn, adjusting his beret so that it hung down over his eye. "Shit. That bitch ain't gonna be messin' wid me. She knows who the man is. You gimme some beer to chase this here down with, an' quit mindin' ma wife."

"There's enough people mindin' your wife that one more ain't gonna make no difference," said the rat-faced man.

"You take that back, you little piece of pigeon shit," shouted Rayburn, hauling himself off the bar stool and pulling his beret lower on his head.

"Look out," warned Big Betsy. "Rayburn's clearin' for action."

"Why?" said the rat-faced man, spreading his hands innocently. "I was only sayin' what everybody knows."

Metal flashed in the dimness. "You clean your mouth," Rayburn said dangerously, "or I'ma clean your throat."

"You ain't gonna do shit," said Leo, brandishing the carving knife he used to slice thick slabs of ham and beef for sandwiches. "You put that blade away, Rayburn, or I'ma haul off an' let you alone. An' Elmo, you keep your shitty mouth shut, or you get the hell outa ma bar."

Rayburn slipped the razor back to wherever it had come from and sank onto the stool. "I'ma cut that mutha yet," he muttered.

"*You* cut, Elmo," Leo said. "Cut the hell outa here. You know damn well Rayburn could slice you three times while you was gettin' up enough nerve to say shit to a monkey."

Elmo gulped the rest of his beer and left quickly. Leo watched until he was out the door, then he stuck the knife savagely into a roast of beef. Rayburn glared at the empty doorway. "I could slice that mutha any time," Rayburn said.

"I know it," Leo told him, "but that simple nigger ain't even worth the time it takes to hate him."

"Humph," said Rayburn, returning to his gin.

"He's right about your woman, you know, Rayburn," Leo said softly.

Rayburn looked up at Leo's sagging jowls and clear soft eyes. "Yeah, Leo," he said finally, "I know it. Fill me up again, hey?"

"Yeah," Leo said, "sure." He uncorked the bottle and poured the shot glass full. He looked down at Rayburn's slumped shoulders, shrugged, and left the bottle standing uncorked on the bar.

Big Betsy the whore laughed loudly, and Leo glanced down at her. "Hey, Leo," yelled Big Betsy, "this dude wants to know can he buy me a drink."

Leo scrutinized the young man who sat next to Big Betsy. Leo had never seen him before. "What'll it be?" Leo asked.

"The usual," said Big Betsy.

"What's the usual?" asked the young man.

"Scotch and milk," said Big Betsy.

The young man made a face, looked at Leo. Leo shrugged silently. The young man smiled tightly. "Okay. One scotch and milk for the lady, and one plain scotch for me."

"Water on the side?" Leo asked as he poured Big Betsy's "scotch and milk" from the gallon carton that contained her private stock. The young man shook his head. Leo set up a shot glass full of scotch and Big Betsy's drink and accepted a five-dollar bill. He went to the register and rang up one fifty, returned, and laid the change on the bar. The young man glanced at it, smiled, reached over and took a sip of Big Betsy's drink.

"I got this ulcer," Big Betsy explained. The young man mumbled something. Big Betsy's loud laugh echoed over the blare of the jukebox.

"Hey, Leo, didja hear that?" she guffawed, wiping greasy tears from her rheumy eyes.

"Nope," said Leo disinterestedly.

"Whad he say?" asked the deaf wino.

"He said it musta been a plaid cow, 'cause there ain't no other way there's any scotch in this here glass. Haw, haw, haw."

Leo looked uncomfortably at the young man, who gave him another tight smile. Leo went back to polishing glasses.

Rayburn reached out and poured himself another drink without looking at the bottle or the glass or Leo. He pushed a dollar bill across the bar in the general direction of the cash register. "Last drink," he mumbled. Leo moved his bulk down behind the bar.

"It's all right, Rayburn. Last drink's on the house."

Rayburn raised his head. His eyes sparkled behind a misty alcohol veil. "I pays for what I drinks," he said.

"Sure, Rayburn, sure," Leo said. He scooped the crumpled bill up in his hammy hand, went to the register, and rang up NO SALE. Rayburn, lost in his liquor, did not see that, and gathered up the dollar's change Leo laid on the bar, dropping it into his pocket without looking at it.

"Haw, haw, haw," bellowed Big Betsy the whore, "didja hear that, Leo?"

"Nope," said Leo.

"He says he can fuck for free, but he'll pay to talk."

"That's crazy," Leo said.

"I'll tell you what," Big Betsy said to the young man, "you can talk all you want so long as you're buyin' drinks."

"Okay," said the young man.

"That's crazy," Leo said.

"Damn straight," said Big Betsy. "Gimme some gin, Leo."

"No more milk?" said the young man.

"Milk," Big Betsy informed him, "is for babies. To shut up."

Leo poured the gin and refilled the shot glass with scotch. He took a dollar fifty from the change on the bar and went to the register to ring it up. On the way he noticed Rayburn's vacated stool and paused briefly to remove the used glasses, recork the bottle, and wipe a few drops of moisture from the bar top with his side towel.

"Haw, haw, haw," laughed Big Betsy the whore from down the bar. "Haw, haw, haw, haw, haw."

The street lay empty in the wee-hours-of-the-morning darkness. There was a chill in the air, and Rayburn pulled his jacket close about him, shuddering, shaking in alcoholic tremens. He had trouble standing, so he hauled himself over to a graffiti-covered wall and leaned against it, trying to hold his head up and his vomit in. The light on the corner changed, but there was no rush of rubber-tired wheels; there was no traffic. Just as the light was changing from yellow to red one lone car, a long pink Cadillac, careened through the intersection, raking its high beams across Rayburn's slumping form, and vanished in a rush of wind and a blare of radioed soul music mingled with drunken voices. Rayburn watched it go, then he tottered into the alley and retched laboriously over some garbage cans.

When he had vomited he felt better. He fumbled in his pocket and found change, pulled it out, counted it, unbelieving. There was a dollar there. A dollar. He considered going back in for another drink but shook his head, shoved the money back into his pocket, and struggled back out to the curb. His flat nose wrinkled at an unfamiliar stench, and his eyes darted around erratically until they focused on the body of the cat, lying in the gutter. Rayburn fought down the urge to vomit again, turned right, and began to walk. Every few steps his sense of direction would give out, and he would stagger into a wall and bounce away, half spinning from the impact. He mumbled loudly as he struggled along, conversing with the grimy walls, the light poles, the cars parked at infrequent intervals along the curb. "I ain't too anxious to be goin' home," he informed a dented Ford, " 'cause you see, if I goes home, that bitch gonna give me a hard time for sure. I can hear it now. 'Rayburn, you done gone an' spent up all the money an' didn't give me nothin'.' As if to say she wouldn't a spent up all the money. Bitch." He nodded for emphasis, stumbled on to a garbage can. "But," he elaborated, "it's possible, it is definitely possible, that the bitch ain't gonna be there at all. I mean, it's hard to know, you know? I don't know. I don't even know if I want the bitch to be there. I mean, it's bad if she do be there, but it's bad if she ain't there, too, 'cause then I gotta wait for her to get back, an' you know I think it all the time, maybe this time she ain't gonna be comin' back. Maybe she gone for good. Or maybe she done gone off with somebody an' she'll come tippin' on in tomorrow with some shit about how she was out with that bitch sister a hers an' she was too tired to come home. Lyin' her damn head off. She knows I know she's lyin'. Knows I ain't gonna call her on it, 'cause if I do she's liable to go right on an' tell me all about it. Then what the hell am I gonna do? I mean, I *know*, but so long as she ain't tole me nothin' I don't got to be believin' it, you know?" The garbage can declined to reply. Rayburn launched an uncoordinated kick that did more harm to him than to the can, then hobbled, cursing, on down the street. Dark empty windows gazed at him blankly. Rayburn bounced off a wall, gyrated like a tightrope walker along the edge of the curb. "She'll be back though," he told the street. "Oh yeah, she be back, switchin' her ass around like it was a goddamn flyswatter, wavin' money in ma face. She say, 'You ain't got no money, baby? Workin' in that damn bank, place where they *keeps* that money, an' you ain't got none yourself? What's the matter with you? You ain't much of a man, that's all I got to say.' An' then by Jesus I'll take the bitch in an' fuck the hell right out of her. Make her forget whoever that bastard was, make her forget his damn name. Fuck him right out of her. Make her climb the damn walls. I can do it too, by God. Only"—Rayburn stopped and addressed the cluttered windows of a long-condemned junk shop—"only you wonder, you know what I mean? You got to be wonderin' if she even knows who's doin' it to her. Maybe it don't make no difference. Does it make a difference?" Rayburn got no answer and, after a few minutes, forgetting the question, turned east once again and moved on, feet scuffing the cracked sidewalk, past the deserted Salvation Army Mission Post, past the tobacco-juice-stained steps of tubercular rowhouses, his eyes glassed over and tired-looking. He shoved his hands into his pants pockets and held himself for a minute, then tottered into the next alleyway and urinated inaccurately, watching the clear stream splash on the cobblestones and spatter droplets back on his legs, not moving, not reacting at all when the pressure diminished and the stream shortened and the urine dribbled onto his shoes. He zipped his pants and staggered out onto the street again, but now he had forgotten where he was going, so he just kept on walking, past the glittering facade of The Word of Life Church, with its fluorescent cross and flood-lit marquee assuring all and sundry that Jesus saved, past decaying houses and dilapidated stores, past the shadowy entrance beside one burned-out store that led to the apartment he called home. The light from the sign of the Elysium Hotel fell like a wide white bar across the street and the sidewalk in front of him; he moved close to the walls, trying to avoid the harsh light, moving on to the corner, across the street. And then he looked up and stopped, seeing the spire of the bank building rising, shining, puncturing the night sky. He stared up at it, swaying back and forth, then looked down suddenly to see a bus standing in front of him, door open, engine rumbling.

"C'mon, buddy," shouted the driver. "I ain't got all night. You gonna ride or you gonna piss in your pants?" Rayburn stared a second longer, then climbed aboard totteringly, hanging onto the handrail like a tired old lady. "C'mon, for Chrissakes. Ain't you got a quarter?" Rayburn obediently fished out a quarter and dropped it into the fare box, fumbling for a minute as his erratic coordination made it difficult for him to get his hand over the slot. "Shees," said the bus driver. "What the hell am I, crazy? Runnin' around here with nuttin' but drunks. Take a seat, buddy, before you fall on your ass. Shees!" Rayburn grasped one of the chromium stanchions and eased himself into a seat running lengthwise along the side of the bus. The light changed and the driver pulled away from the curb, working at the big steering wheel, grunting with effort. His stomach hung over the edge of the wheel like a pouting child's lower lip. "Shees," he muttered, "shees. One friggin' fare all friggin' night. Crazy." Rayburn stared out the window at the swiftly passing panorama of alleys and bars and darkened storefronts with dim lights glowing in the windows above them, all dingy from the years of smog and dirt and people. "I bet this joker's soused," muttered the driver. "Hey, buddy, you drunk?"

"Say what?" said Rayburn.

"You drunk? If you're drunk you gotta get offa here. Regulations."

"Nah, shit," said Rayburn, "I ain't drunk."

"Yeah?" said the driver, peering suspiciously in his rearview mirror. "You sure?"

"Yeah," said Rayburn.

"I dunno, you look kinda beat."

"I ain't drunk, muthafucka," Rayburn snarled. "If you thought I was drunk, whad you let me on for in the first place?"

"I gotta let you on," the driver said. "It's the law. An' if you're drunk, I gotta kick you off. That's the law too."

Rayburn looked at him. "Shit." He went back to staring out the window.

"All right, okay, buddy, take it easy, take it easy, I was just astin'. Regulations. Hell, I don't give a damn if a fella wants to get himself a little one tied on on Saturday night. Hell, I'd be tyin' one on myself if I wasn't out tryin' to pick up a little spare change, you know what I mean?" Rayburn stared out the window. The driver stared in his mirror at the reflection of the side of Rayburn's head. "I got this wife, see," said the driver, waving one arm in the air and peeking in the mirror to see if Rayburn were paying any attention. "Chrissakes, I don't know what I ever wanted to go an' get married for. All she does is holler. I mean all the time. *All* the friggin' time. A man works his fingers down to the knuckles an' all he hears is, 'O'Brien, I need a new vacuum cleaner.' Shees, I just bought her a new vacuum cleaner. Or, 'O'Brien, the kid needs new shoes.' That kid must have fifteen pair a shoes already. You know what I mean?" He peered into the mirror, but Rayburn's eyes were on the passing street. "Yeah," said the driver, "an' then here I am, ridin' around in the middle of the night. An' you know what *she's* doin'? *She's* havin' Mrs. Casey in to look at TV. While I'm out here bouncin' bruises on my backside, she's watchin' TV an' drinkin' up my beer. I don't know what I ever wanted to get married for, I swear I don't. I was free and easy, I was, an' then she comes along an' gives me that, 'No, no, not until we're married.' Okay, I says, so I married her. Come to find out I wasn't even the first one. Can you beat that? Hey, buddy, can you beat that?" The driver stopped for a red light, turned in his seat to stare at Rayburn. "Shees. Saturday night. Nuttin' but drunks what can't even carry on an intelligent conversation. Shees!" He turned back and stamped on the accelerator in disgust.

ᵂ

"Haw, haw, haw," laughed Big Betsy the whore. "Hey, Leo, didja hear that?"

"Nope," said Leo, looking up at her fat face from below the bar, where he was bent over, connecting a fresh keg to one of the taps.

"I ast him who was he an' he said he don't know, did I ever see him before?"

"Ha," said Leo, bending back to the keg.

"You beats everything, you know it?" said Big Betsy, slamming her fist into the young man's shoulder and almost knocking him off the stool. "You beats hell outa everything. Hey, Leo, he's buyin' me another drink. Get off your knees an' gimme another shot."

"Shut up a minute, willya, Betsy," said Leo, without looking up. He grimaced as he felt for the connection.

"Haw, haw, haw," laughed Big Betsy. "Didja hear that?" she said to the young man. She suddenly looked old and worn out and very ugly. "Leo, you black bastard, I wants a drink. You quit suckin' yourself off down there an' get me one."

Leo straightened up to his full six two and shoved out his jaw. "In a minute," he said.

Betsy was about to open her mouth when the young man reached over and laid his hand on her arm. "Take it easy. He's getting it."

"Fuckin' A, he's gettin' it," grumbled Big Betsy. "He just better be gettin' it." She scowled fiercely. Leo looked at her with distaste. He bent down again and completed the connection, stood up, tested the tap, then poured her shot glass full, looked at her, glared at the young man. "Thanks, Leo," said Big Betsy mildly.

"Shit," said Leo.

"Hey, barkeep," said a voice at the far end of the bar.

Leo looked up, quickly concealing a frown. "What can I do for you, Leroy?"

"Mr. Briggs," said a fat, dark-chocolate-skinned man. He was wearing a bottle-green suit and a pink wide-collared shirt with a matching tie and highly polished black boots. His eyes were protected from the bar's dim light by heavy dark glasses.

Big Betsy gave her companion a gentle nudge that could have broken ribs. "Niggers is all alike," she said. "They think they're big shit if they sits around all day like a white man an' has folks linin' up to kiss their ass, an' at night they comes around, all dressed up like it was Halloween, to shit on all the other niggers. They don't get to be mister until they done had a pint a gin."

"What you mumblin' around about down there, piglady?" said Leroy.

"Nothin'," said Big Betsy sullenly.

"Yeah, well, it better be nothin'."

Big Betsy kept her mouth shut, but her cheeks puffed out and her eyes were fixed straight ahead. Leroy watched her for a minute. "Gimme a couple sixes," he said to Leo out of the corner of his mouth.

"Hey, Leroy," somebody called out of the darkness. "What you got out there in that car?"

Leroy shifted his glance into the darkness and smiled broadly, showing gold-filled teeth. "Oh, just a couple ladies wanted to do a little ridin', take in the evenin' air, you know what I mean."

"Yeah," mumbled Big Betsy, "so how come you don't bring 'em in?"

Leroy glared at her. "I said they was ladies, not fat-assed old bar bait."

Leo set two six-packs of beer on the bar, one on top of the other, slipped a paper bag over the stack, grasped the bag at the bottom and flipped the whole thing over with a snap, rolled the top of the bag down, opened his mouth, and froze into immobility, unable to believe his ears.

"What's that mean?" Betsy's young man was saying, without looking up from his scotch. "They cost more'n two dollars?"

"Whad he say?" whispered the wino. No one told him. The bar was silent.

"Well, well," said Leroy. "What have we here? A funny man? Ha, ha. Very funny, funny man."

"Glad you liked it."

"No," Leroy said, "I didn't like it. And I don't like you, either."

"Damn," said the young man, still not raising his eyes.

"Hey, blood," said Leo, grimacing and shaking his head.

"You let him be now, Leo," Leroy said. "Sonny, I don't think I ever seen you around here."

"I haven't seen you, either," said the young man.

"Well," said Leroy, "let me introduce maself. I'm—"

"You're Leroy Briggs," the young man said.

"Why, yes. Seein' as you knows ma name, I guess you knows who I am."

"Sure," said the young man, his eyes still lowered to his glass. "You're the big bad muthafucka that hasn't got anything better to do than give rides to cheap whores and call old ladies names and try to make the rest of the world crap in their pants at the sight of you."

Leroy's face darkened. "Like I said, I ain't seen you around here before, an' I better not be seein' you again. If I do, it might be the last time anybody ever sees you."

The young man raised his eyes and looked at the bottles on the backbar. "There might be some folks that wouldn't like that."

"There is, huh?" said Leroy, unimpressed.

"Yeah," said the young man. He turned his head very slowly and stared Leroy straight in the eye.

Leroy looked at him for a moment, and then his expression changed ever so slightly. "There is, huh?" he repeated. The young man turned back and sipped at his scotch, then he looked at Leroy and smiled, nodding slightly. "You work for Gino?" Leroy whispered hoarsely.

"I don't know any Gino," the young man said, turning back to his glass.

"You works for Gino," said Leroy, with conviction.

"If you say so."

"Well, you listen here. I don't give a damn 'bout no Gino. I ain't scared a no Gino. This here's *ma* territory."

"Sure," said the young man in a bored tone of voice. He looked at his nearly empty glass. "About dry here, Leo."

"You tell Gino," said Leroy, shaking his finger, "or whoever you works for, you tell 'em I don't give a shit 'bout no pasty-faced wops. An' if I ever see your ass around here again you gonna be wishin' I hadn't. Where's ma beer, Leo?"

"Right here," said Leo promptly.

Leroy picked up the paper bag and turned to go. "Hey there, Mr. Briggs," said the young man without looking up, "you forgot to pay for that beer."

Leroy whirled around. "That's all right," Leo said quickly, "it's on the house." But nobody was paying any attention to Leo. Leroy stared at the young man for a long time, then reached slowly into his pocket and pulled out a five-dollar bill and laid it on the bar. Leo looked back and forth between the two men, then he picked up the bill, took it to the register, rang up the sale, made change, and extended it toward Leroy.

The young man looked at Leroy. "Keep the change," he said softly. Leo stood confused, eyes wide. The cords stood out on Leroy's neck, and he trembled slightly with anger. "Keep it," the young man said. He smiled at Leroy. Leroy held his ground a moment longer, then whirled and barged out into the night.

Leo stared after him, stared at the change in his hand, shrugged, turned to the register, and rang up a sale in the amount. The cash drawer banged and the sound, like a signal, unstopped a flood of conversation, whispers, nervous laughter. "Haw, haw, haw," bellowed Big Betsy the whore. "Didja hear that, Leo?"

"Naw," said Leo, wiping sweat from his brow and eyeing the young man nervously.

"Haw, haw, haw," laughed Big Betsy. "I ast him who Gino was an' he says he don't know, he don't even *like* hamburgers. Haw, haw, haw."

Leo stared at the young man for a long minute, the expression on his face a mixture of admiration, disbelief, and fear. He picked up a bottle of scotch, uncorked it, and poured the shot glass full, setting it and the uncorked bottle on the bar in front of the young man. The young man reached for his wallet, but Leo waved a hand. "On the house," he said.

The young man looked at him, shook his head. "I pay."

Leo smiled. "It seems to me that Mr. Leroy Briggs done already paid for you," he said, and walked away.

Fifth Street: an uneven lane of cobblestones and trolley tracks that dated from sometime before the Civil War. There had been little traffic then, and there was no traffic now except for the dump trucks trundling away loads of rubble from the buildings being razed in an urban-redevelopment project. Rayburn walked along a weedy path that passed for a sidewalk, his shoes darkening as they absorbed moisture from the tall stalks of dandelion and Queen Anne's Lace. Halfway down the block, on the nether edge of Society Hill—the point at which demolition had been halted—the side of a rowhouse clearly displayed the outlines of the rooms of the building that had once stood next to it. Now a giant wrecking crane stood there, its heavy leaded ball threatening the remaining structure. Rayburn stared at the scene as he passed, thinking he saw a picture still hanging from the plaster that clung desperately to the side of the building. Behind him, on the far side of the street, a door swung in the wind, banged loudly; Rayburn spun too quickly, nearly falling.

Beyond the hulks of houses was a pit where a high-rise apartment building would one day stand. Rayburn paused outside the white board fence that surrounded the site, peered down into the empty hole. He opened his pants and tried to urinate in order to watch the water fall, but nothing would come. He had just turned away from the fence when he saw the police car turn into the block, and he straightened quickly and tried to walk steadily as he moved farther north. Beside the walls of restored brick he told his troubles to stars made invisible by the glow of the city's lights: "We as good as dead, her an' me; good as dead 'cept it ain't over an' she still keeps comin' back. An' it used to be so fine. But that was when it started. Things is always good when they starts, an' ends up shit. I'd be comin' home from the bank an' she'd be settin' up there waitin' for me, prettied up an' lookin' fine. It wasn't gonna last. They tole me that. They said, 'Rayburn, she's just like the rest of 'em in that damn family. Every one of 'em wild an' crazy.' Well, hell, I wasn't gonna be listenin' to that shit. It was good for a while, an' maybe sometime it's gonna be good again. Sure it will be. I'll get things for her some damn way, an' she'll be happy. Only, she useta be happy with just me home from work; two in the mornin' an' us settin' up in the front room eatin' ice cream an' listenin' to that little transistor radio, maybe drinkin' a little beer. An' she'd come over an' set up on ma lap just like she was a little girl, an' I'd hug her an' pull her hair an' tease her an' love her up. If she frowned even, all I ever had to do was say, 'Hey now, baby,' an' she'd cut it right out. They all tole me, they said, 'She's just like the rest of 'em, just like her sister, sleepin' in fifty-cent ho-tels an' screwin' anything that moves.' I tried to tell 'em she wouldn'ta been doin' none a that, 'cept she was hungry. Lord knows, nobody oughta have to pay for what they done when they was hungry. An' she wasn't nothin' but seventeen. But they wasn't gonna listen to me. Well, they was right. Pretty soon she wasn't happy just havin' her belly full an' some clothes on her back. It had to be new. She say, 'Rayburn, I wants a new dress.' But I didn't have no money for a dress like she wanted, an' I told her so. Only then I come in an' seen it hangin' there . . . ." Rayburn stumbled in a pothole, fell heavily against the side of a building, pushed himself away from it, staggered on.

"WATCHITYOUSTUPIDASSHOLE!!" yelled the taxi driver as his speeding cab missed Rayburn by inches. Market Street, six lanes wide and lit up like day, lay before him like a moat, sequestering another world: Independence Mall, stores, restaurants, offices. Rayburn stepped back on the curb, realizing in a flash of lucidity that he would have to be careful here. He straightened up and realized also that he was almost sober now, almost sober and feeling tired. It was late. The air smelled chilly and stale: late-night city, left over from the day before. He turned left and walked west, the jars as his feet struck the even pavement shaking his bones painfully. His bladder was full, but the street was far too bright for him to do anything about it. Pissing in the middle of South Street was a misdemeanor, pissing in the middle of Market Street was a major crime. The plate-glass department store windows, full of clothes and appliances and half-dressed dummies, reflected his image. It was morning now; outside Gimbels a vendor hawked the Sunday papers. Rayburn shoved his hands deep into his jacket pockets, felt the lining of the left pocket tear a little with a tiny rasping sound. Suddenly he knew where he was going, and his feet moved more quickly. He jingled the change in his right pocket as he walked—seventy-five cents.

He moved through the archway into the courtyard of City Hall and out the other side, feeling a strange urgency. The bank was at Sixteenth Street, but he stopped before he reached it, at the door of a cafeteria of the east side of Sixteenth where many of the bank's lesser daytime employees ate lunch. The place was still open; Rayburn could see the waitress lounging behind the counter, looking bored. He put his hand on the door, pushed it open, went in. The waitress looked up unhappily. "We're closin' in fifteen minutes," she said. Rayburn ignored her and took a seat at the counter. She shrugged, picked up a damp side towel, wiped the Formica in front of him. "What'll it be?" she said resignedly.

"A hamburger," Rayburn said.

"Ain't got no hamburgers."

"What you mean? It's right there on the sign."

"That's for daytime. We ain't gonna keep the grill warmed up this time of night."

"Well, what do you got?"

"Pie, donuts, toast—stuff like that."

"I'll have a piece a blueberry pie."

"Ain't got no blueberry pie."

"I guess I'll have to have me a piece a somethin' else."

The waitress looked at him uneasily.

"What kind a pie do you got?" Rayburn said.

"Onliest kind we ever got is cherry an' apple, an' we're outa cherry."

Rayburn gave her an amused look. She flushed. "Apple pie an' some coffee," Rayburn said.

"Black?" asked the waitress, writing it on her pad before he had a chance to answer.

"No," Rayburn snarled, "I wants it light. An' sweet." He glared at her, but she wasn't looking at him. Wordlessly, she crossed out "blk" and wrote in "C&S."

"We're closin' in ten minutes," she said.

"Yeah," Rayburn said sourly, "so I heard." She looked at him, shrugged her shoulders, and went to get the pie, stuffing the order pad into her apron pocket.

Rayburn watched her waddle away, thinking how bad she looked. Part of it was the uniform, but she was fat and greasy-looking anyway. Rayburn hated her. She came waddling back and slapped an almost-clean plate with a painfully thin sliver of pie on it in front of him. She laid a paper napkin beside the plate, held it down with a spoon and a fork that had obviously been used for someone's eggs. "You want that coffee black?"

"What the hell didja write it down for?"

The waitress frowned and started digging through her pocket for the order pad. Rayburn waited until her fingers closed over it and then said, "I wants cream an' sugar." The waitress let the pad fall back into her pocket and gave Rayburn a look of pure hatred.

"Look," she said, "I didn't ast to work on Saturday night."

"I wasn't the one made you," Rayburn said indifferently.

"Can't you hurry up with that pie? We're closin'—"

"I can't hurry nothin' till I gets ma coffee."

"Oh," she said nervously, "yeah." She turned to the urn and drew him a cup, poured in cream, set the cracked china in front of him with a tall sugar dispenser. Rayburn finished cleaning the fork with his napkin. The girl looked at him. "You, ah, gonna want more coffee? If you're not, I can start cleaning the urn."

"Go ahead," Rayburn said. She flashed him a yellow-toothed smile and opened the spigot, letting the muddy-brown liquid dribble into the drain.

"You got the last piece a pie," she said, looking over her shoulder.

"Tastes like it," Rayburn said. "You work here in the daytime?"

"I got a boyfriend," the girl said. "He's probably waiting outside."

"What the hell do I care?" Rayburn said. "I just asted if you worked here in the daytime."

"No," she said, "just at night on the weekends."

"Night on the weekends," Rayburn repeated. "Figures." He finished up the last of the pie, picked up the coffee cup, blew over the edge.

"My boyfriend, he plays football and wrestles. He knows judo and karate, too. They threw him outa school for beatin' somebody up real bad oncet."

"How come he don't wait for you inside? Ain't he house-broke?"

The girl looked at him. Rayburn smiled and leaned back. She turned her face away, blushing. "You about finished?"

" 'Bout," Rayburn said. "I'm tryin' to decide if maybe I better not stick around to see your boyfriend." The girl kept her head turned away. Rayburn drank the rest of his coffee. It was cold now, and it tasted like dishwater. He drank it down defiantly, not bothering to make a face when he got to the dregs. He wiped his lips with the paper napkin. "How 'bout the check?"

She stood as far away from him as she could, on the far side of the counter, back pressed tightly against the coffee urn, and kept one eye on him as she laboriously added the bill, found the tax on a printed table scotch-taped to the back of the order pad, wrote down the total, circled it. "Thirty-seven cents," she said. Rayburn pulled out two quarters, held them out in the palm of his hand. She waited for a moment, then realized that he was not going to lay them down on the counter, that she was going to have to take them from his hand. She looked at him. Rayburn smiled. Slowly she extended her hand until it hung trembling over his, then her fingers darted like a drunken hawk and snatched the coins away. She went quickly to the register to make change. Rayburn followed her, stood easily across the counter as she punched the keys. "We ain't got much cash this time of night," she said.

"What's the matter?" said Rayburn. "Ain't you got change for a quarter?"

The girl glared at him, punched a button, and, as the cash drawer sprang out, snatched at the money, finding the dime easily but fumbling for an instant for the three pennies, whirling awkwardly and slamming the drawer shut with her hip. "I gotta close up now," she said.

"Ain't nothin' to me," said Rayburn. He held his hand out. The girl dropped the change into it from high altitude. Rayburn turned toward the door. "I sure hope your boyfriend can get his judo workin' on some a them nasty folks out there in the street. Why, while we was in here safe together he coulda got killed three times, deadern hell." He smiled at her acidly. "Here," he said, tossing her the dime, "put it in your piggy bank."

Rayburn walked across the street to the bank, stood by the concrete pillars, staring through the broad plate-glass windows at the carpeted floors and the tellers' stations and the leather chairs for people to sit in while they waited for assistant managers to discuss loans for cars and homes and color TV sets. Rayburn thought about the money inside, behind the doors, behind the heavy cover of the vault. He would have liked to have seen it, to see what all that money looked like. Just once. Rayburn stepped back, out from under the pillar-supported overhang, looked up at the building, at the glass windows mounting higher, growing smaller, stretching his neck until he could see the executive suites at the top. Rayburn's job was to clean those suites, and he often stood in the carpeted, wood-paneled, leather-upholstered chambers and looked out over the city. Looking down through the dark and the smog, he could sometimes make out the row of dim lights that was his own block. Rayburn dropped his head because looking up at the tall spire was beginning to hurt his neck. He was tired. It was late. He wanted to go home.

He turned toward the corner, feeling his pocket for the dime and the three nickels. He did not want to walk, although it was not far. He stood on the corner, tapping the sidewalk with the toe of his shoe, staring down into the gutter. He looked up and peered down the street. He felt an insistent tugging at his sleeve, turned to see a fat old woman with a dark moon face looking up at him. Her skin had a strange cast in the light spilling through the windows of the bank. "Won't you give to the Indian children?" she said, holding up a tin can covered with paper and shaking it in front of his nose. Coins rattled flatly.

"No," Rayburn said.

"Please, sir, they need your help so much. They're hungry. Some of them are starving. Won't you give to the Indian children?"

"Go to hell," Rayburn said.

"Please," said the woman, catching hold of his arm. "Have you no children? Can you imagine what it means to be a child, hungry and alone?"

Rayburn whirled around and threw his change against the bank's glass windows, where it struck with a ringing sound of metal on glass and fell tinkling to the pavement. "Pick it up!" he shouted. "You wants it so goddamn bad, you pick it up!" He shoved the woman away from him and stalked away.

It was closing time at Lightnin' Ed's. "Buy it now," yelled Leo, "bar's closin' down."

"Aw, shit," muttered Big Betsy.

"Whad he say?" asked the deaf wino.

"He says you gotta get the hell outa here," Big Betsy told him.

"Like hell I do," said the wino. "It's Saturday."

"Shit," said Big Betsy to the young man. "Leo's tries to let on like he's tough, but Jake's been sleepin' in that back room every Saturday night for the last fifteen years. Leo's got a soft heart behind his soft gut. Ain't that right, Leo?"

"Shut up, Betsy," said Leo amiably.

"Hey, Leo," said a small voice.

Leo turned. "I thought I told you to clear outa here, Elmo. Now what the hell you want?"

"Just one more little drinkee," said Elmo, squinting up into Leo's face and grinning.

"All right," Leo sighed. "One more beer an' then you get your ass outa here. An' you better hope you don't run into Rayburn."

"Rayburn, shit!" spat Elmo, reaching a hand out hungrily for the beer. Leo took his money as though it were not quite clean. "That's one crazy nigger."

"That's one nigger would just as soon slice your balls off as look at you. Can't say I blame him. Only I'd aim for your throat. Your balls is too small a target."

"That nigger's crazy," Elmo said, slurping the head off his beer. "He's awful fast to start slicin' on folks that's doin' the talkin', but he ain't so quick to be slicin' at the ones that's doin' all the doin'." Elmo slammed the half-full beer glass down on the bar for emphasis.

"Maybe he would be if he knowed who they was," Leo said.

"Maybe he wouldn't be, seein' as it's Leroy Briggs," said Elmo triumphantly.

"Leroy?" said Leo softly.

"Yeah, sure, it's Leroy. That bitch is always hangin' around the Elysium, gettin' Leroy to take her for rides an' shit."

"You 'bout finished with that beer, Elmo? Then you get outa ma bar, right now." Elmo scowled, gulped the rest of the beer, and shuffled toward the door.

"And Elmo," Leo called after him.

"What?"

"You open your stinkin' mouth to Rayburn, an' I swear to Jesus I'll cut your throat maself."

Elmo smiled, but the smile faded as he realized that Leo meant exactly what he said. He turned and almost ran through the door.

"Haw, haw, haw," roared Big Betsy the whore, heading for the door, "didja hear what he said?"

"Naw," said Leo.

"Said I reminded him of his mother. Haw, haw, haw. G'night Leo. Haw, haw, haw, haw, haw."

Leo turned to the young man. "Yeah, well. Lemme tell you somethin'. You'd best not be playin' with Leroy Briggs. I don't know what kinda friends you got, an' I don't care, but you be careful a Leroy. He's got lotsa friends, too. Even folks that hates his guts has to kiss his ass, if you know what I mean."

The young man looked at Leo. "I know what you mean," he said. He got up and vanished through the door.

When the bar was empty, Leo made sure the old wino was bedded down comfortably in the back room. Then he opened the cash register and pocketed the money without bothering to count it and slipped his revolver into his jacket pocket. He took out a bottle of cheap red wine and put it up on the bar where the wino could find it easily. He turned out the last of the lights and stepped out into the darkness. He locked the door and turned to see the young man standing a few feet away. "What you want?" said Leo, easing his hand toward his revolver.

"To ask you a question."

"What?" said Leo suspiciously.

"I forgot."

"What are you, crazy?"

"Kinda," said the young man, and smiled.

"Shit," said Leo, fighting the urge to smile himself. He kept his face serious, but his hand moved away from the gun. "You listen here . . . whad you say your name was?"

"Brown."

Leo looked skeptical, shrugged. "Well, you listen, Brown. Don't you forget what I said about Leroy. He's a mean bastard, an' he don't forget. Now which way you headin'?"

"West."

"Well, I'm goin' the other way, so I'll be seein' you."

Brown stood and watched Leo move off down the street. He smiled to himself and stepped into the alley and relieved the pressure in his bladder. He came out onto the street again, wrinkling his nose at the stench of a dead cat lying in the gutter. He moved away. His feet made hollow sounds on the pavement as he moved westward toward Twenty-ninth Street, the river, and the bridge to the other side.

🏴

A slow-moving shadow sliding south along the sides of concrete towers. Nineteenth Street, one way south, lined with tiny shops: a violin dealer and a deli here, a children's boutique and a tiny, mob-monied café there. Outside the Rittenhouse Plaza, standing on the awning-covered, weather-stained carpet, the doorman watches without suspicion as the thin figure moves along, feet shuffling from fatigue and alcohol. The doorman shoves his hands into his uniform pockets and whistles tunelessly.

Walnut Street and then the Square, where in the daylight children play and bony spinsters walk marcelled dogs, where when night falls the part-time hippies swarm—female typists and high-school girls decked out in store-bought poor-boy clothes and pretattered bell-bottom blue jeans, sitting on the walls and waiting for real life to wander over and proposition them; and the boys: white boys with guitars and joints and jugs of warm cheap wine, black boys costumed in knitted shirts and beads and wide hats, looking for a gray chick to rap to, jive a little, scare a little, excitate and titillate, and maybe hold her hand.

Past the apartment houses where the D.A. lives, shadow floating down the street, past townhouses and the pizza joint where the cop cars congregate like sinners at a revival meeting, past the hospital that ministers to God-knows-who, finally to South Street, silent and dark, with even the rats asleep, the street people gone to wherever street people go when the street itself finally sleeps. Up the steps, rotten wood, spattered with paint from when someone poured his passion on the wall with great scrawling letters in obscene red; finally to his door, standing before it, key in hand, hand trembling, knowing now that he wanted her there, needed her to be there, frightened that she would not be there and would never be there again; pushing through the door and shutting it behind him, slipping through the littered living room to the bedroom, keeping his eyes turned away and closed for fear of what he might not see; carefully laying his keys on the dresser before turning his head and opening his eyes and seeing her form lying there in the broken-down bed beneath the threadbare blanket. Slipping his clothes off, letting them drop in an untidy pile on the splintering floor, the forgotten pennies fall and roll and rattle on unfinished wood, and then beside her, breathing deep, placing his hand gingerly on her side, feeling the bulge of a little fat, recalling when her body was all bone-hard and her ribs showed plainly through her skin, feeling her responding to his touch, and kissing her; running his tongue inside her mouth, beneath her tongue, along her teeth, feeling her body warm and moist and open; and hearing, just as he goes to her, her sleep-husky voice in his ear, "Give it to me, baby, oh, yes, give it to me again," and knowing, when almost beyond the point of knowing anything, or of caring, that she was not speaking to him.

2 The Word of Life

The Reverend Mr. J. Peter Sloan stood sweating into his custom-tailored clerical collar on the already burning sidewalk in front of The Word of Life Church. The Reverend Mr. Sloan was a dark-skinned man with a carefully maintained body and a head the same shape and color, and covered with about the same amount of hair, as an eight ball. The Reverend was slightly uncomfortable; he had thought the sidewalk would be cool after an exceptionally cool night and in what Mr. Sloan considered to be an early hour of the day, and he had therefore rejected thick-soled shoes in favor of thin-soled kid boots. Now, his feet burned. Despite his current discomfort, the Reverend Mr. Sloan was quite pleased with his situation; he did most of his work on Sunday, but although it was Sunday, he had very little to do. One of his four assistant ministers was to deliver the sermon, and the other three were perfectly capable of handling the other aspects of the service. All the Reverend Mr. Sloan had to do was to greet the faithful and handle one very pleasant item of business.

The Word of Life Church had been founded in a storefront some fifteen years earlier. When the Reverend Mr. Sloan had taken it over it had been a minor eyesore in the denominational district, boasting, or rather, admitting to, some thirty-even members, a rickety piano, and a perennial deficit. Now The Word of Life utilized the original storefront as a mission and for Sunday School classes, the actual sanctuary having moved next door to the abandoned Laconia Cinema building, which Reverend Sloan had, as he was fond of saying, picked up for a spiritual. The rolls had swelled to some five hundred members, an improvement due mainly to what Reverend Sloan termed his "Enlightened Reformation," which involved trading in the rickety piano for a new one, adding an organ, two trombones, a saxophone, amplified bass and guitar, a set of drums and a few tambourines, offering cut-rate subscriptions to professional sports events and charter bus trips to members of the flock, and substituting good grain punch for the watered-down Welch's previously served at communion. The deficit had been erased thanks to Mr. Sloan's highly lucrative, rather complicated, and slightly illegal fund-raising activities. These reforms had resulted in the loss of the church's denominational affiliation, a side effect neither unwelcome to nor uncalculated by the Reverend J. Peter Sloan, who had found the regulations, doctrines, and discipline of the denomination uncongenial to his *modus operandi*.

On this particular Sunday morning the Reverend Mr. Sloan found that he was particularly alert. The street swam before his benevolent eye as he reflected contentedly on the recently compiled statistics which showed offerings, gifts, attendance, and the Dow-Jones Industrial Averages up sharply, while backsliding was at an all-time low of three and one-half souls per hundred. There had been some problems with the church's liquidity, and for a while it had seemed as though Mr. Sloan's long-prophesied fact-finding tour to the West Indies would have to be postponed indefinitely, but Mr. Sloan had, with an accustomed stroke of brilliant chicanery, found a solution; the one item of business on his schedule this Sunday morning would produce sufficient cold cash to insure that the people walking in the darkness of the Caribbean would not be deprived of the opportunity of seeing the Reverend Mr. Sloan flashing before them like a neon pillar.

From time to time Mr. Sloan paused in his reverie to greet a matron with her brood of scrubbed, uncomfortable-looking children in tow—little brown-skinned boys with scraped knees and black eyes, little girls in pigtails and pastel frocks. The Reverend Mr. Sloan was careful to pat each child on the head and to kiss each babe in arms and to give each of the ladies a wink of a size in direct proportion to her age and homeliness. Sister Lavernia Thompson rated a large smile and three separate winks because she had been known, at the age of twenty, as the ugliest female north of hell, and her looks had not improved in the forty-nine intervening years. After Sister Lavernia had passed, Mr. Sloan joyously embraced the duty of greeting Sister Fundidia Larson, a twenty-three-year-old bombshell with the bombs clearly visible. The fervor of Mr. Sloan's embraces varied inversely as the magnitude of his winks; in the case of Sister Fundidia, he grasped her by the shoulders and drew her to him with fatherly firmness, lowered his face to hers with godlike benevolence, pressed his lips against hers with saintly candor, and explored her mouth with his tongue with a tremendous amount of Christian zeal. Having ascertained that all of Sister Fundidia's teeth were firmly rooted, the Reverend Mr. Sloan released her. "Mornin', Reverend," said Sister Fundidia with a sigh, her eyes misting slightly at the giving of the gift of tongue.

"How do you do, Sister?" said the Reverend Mr. Sloan. "No," he went on, raising a restraining hand, "don't answer. I can see you're just fine."

"Yes," said Sister Fundidia dreamily, "God has been good to me this week."

"God was good to you from the very beginning," murmured the Reverend Mr. Sloan, pondering the bust of Sister Fundidia.

"Yes," said Sister Fundidia, clasping her hands over her cleavage and rolling her eyes heavenward, "but this week he has been extra good. I met the most marvelous man!"

The Reverend Mr. Sloan snapped to like a recruit at boot camp. "Sister," he said sternly, shaking his head in fatherly disapproval, "we must beware of yielding up to the pleasures of the flesh."

Sister Fundidia turned slightly darker. "Oh, Reverend," she cried, laying cool fingertips on his arm, "it's nothing like *that*. I met him at the hospital when I was doing the visiting. I've been back to visit him several times. He's just the most *peaceful* person I've ever known!"

The Reverend Mr. Sloan adopted a look of Christian concern. "Still waters are Satan's workshop," Mr. Sloan said. "Have you spoken to him concerning his soul?"

"No," said Sister Fundidia unhappily, "that's the trouble. You see, he's deaf."

"I see. Well, have you given him any of our inspirational leaflets? A back issue of *Parables in Sloan?*"

"N-n-no," said Sister Fundidia, biting her lower lip, "you see, he's blind, too."

"Well, you can take him for inspirational walks."

Sister Fundidia shook her head.

"Paralyzed?" said Mr. Sloan.

"From the neck down," confirmed Sister Fundidia. "But he's so *restful.*"

The Reverend Mr. Sloan sighed in relief, perceiving that Sister Fundidia was in no danger of coming to what few senses she possessed. "Is he dumb as well? Never mind. I suggest you get the organist to play a special hymn for him. 'Oh, for a Thousand Tongues to Sing' should do nicely, especially the fourth stanza."

Sister Fundidia's eyes sparkled with admiration. "Oh, Reverend, I *knew* you'd think of something." The Reverend Mr. Sloan smiled as he watched Sister Fundidia's fundament bounce off in search of the organist.

He licked his lips.

He did not sit up quickly; he was much too wise for that. Instead he raised himself from the army cot with great care, pushing with his hands on the wooden frame and avoiding any motion that would use his stomach muscles. When he was sitting up he turned his head slowly from side to side once or twice to get the juices flowing before he opened his eyes. When he did look around, the room was as calm and steady as anyone could have wished. His eyes took in the familiar cases of liquor on their wooden shelves, the empty beer kegs stacked against one wall. He shook his head just once, hard, to see what would happen. The room stayed steady. He tensed his stomach muscles experimentally, and feeling only a little queasiness he shrugged and went ahead and swung his feet to the floor and sat on the edge of the cot for an instant before pushing himself the rest of the way up. He stood beside the cot for a minute, shivering and swaying slowly, before shuffling across the storeroom and out into the bar.

The barroom was empty and silent, ashtrays overflowing, the floor littered with empty cigarette packs and butts, with the dirt from a hundred or so pairs of feet that had stepped across it in search of Saturday-night oblivion. He walked through the litter to the men's room, pushing open the wooden door and stepping into the pungent interior. He opened his fly and stood before the urinal, waiting for his aged bladder to build up pressure and then staring reflectively at the wall as the medicinal stench from the water-activated deodorant cake rose about him. He shook himself carefully and closed his pants and went to the sink, brushing a few locks of tightly curled hair out of the bowl before running it full of water. He removed his ragged suit coat, sweater, shirt, and undershirt and looked at himself in the cracked mirror, seeing the tight bands of muscle across his shrunken chest, watching his image mist over as the steam rose up and clouded the glass. He dipped his hands into the water, swore softly, and then again, a little louder, and ran in more cold. He jiggled the lever of the soap dispenser and swore again. He left the restroom, retraced his steps back across the barroom and returned, carrying a box of powder from which he refilled the dispenser. He shook soap into his hands, mixed it with water to make a greasy white paste, and began to wash the upper part of his body. He rinsed with a handful of wet paper towels, dried with another handful. He opened his belt and undid his fly and washed the lower part of his body, staring up at the ceiling as he did so. He rinsed and dried in the same manner, wincing as the rough brown paper abraded his tender parts.

When he had completed his toilette, he pulled his stained, smelly clothes back on and returned to the storeroom. From a corner he took a mop and pail and carried them to a heavy porcelain sink attached to the far wall. He poured a large amount of a strong industrial detergent into the pail, then filled it with hot water. Grasping the handle with both hands, clutching the mop handle against his body with one elbow, he hauled the bucket out into the bar and set it in the middle of the floor. As he straightened he felt a twinge in his stomach that rapidly became nausea. His face contorted and he grasped the hard wood of the bar to keep himself from falling. In a few minutes the wave of illness passed. He straightened up gingerly and slowly shuffled back into the storeroom for a handful of rags. He set the rags on a bar stool and caught sight of the bottle of red wine that Leo had left. He smiled grimly, rubbing his stomach. He picked up the mop and dipped it into the steaming bucket, bent his back, and began to swab the floor with long, steady practiced strokes. From time to time he raised his head to gaze longingly at the bottle, but after a moment he would close his eyes and bend back to his work.

As he came up the street Leo could see the Reverend Mr. J. Peter Sloan standing in front of The Word of Life. Leo did not like the Reverend Mr. Sloan, placing him in the same reprehensible category as rats, roaches, taxes, and the last-place finishes of the Philadelphia Phillies. Every Sunday morning, when he went to let Jake out of Lightnin' Ed's, Leo came face to face with the Reverend Mr. Sloan. Leo had come to accept this philosophically; he had never known anything good to happen on Sunday anyway. Or anything bad, for that matter, except for funerals and doubleheaders, which, for a Phillies fan, were much the same thing.

The Reverend Mr. Sloan observed Leo's approach with apprehension and anticipation. Mr. Sloan always anticipated the Sunday encounter, welcoming the chance to put Leo down. The apprehension resulted from the fact that he had never quite managed to do it. But Mr. Sloan was certain that one day he would get Leo, a triumph he considered crucial. Mr.

Sloan viewed every situation in terms of "me" and "them"; there were rich people, and then there were poor people. There were the strong and the meek. There were lions and there were Christians. There was the Reverend J. Peter Sloan and there was anybody else on South Street who had a following. Leo, to Mr. Sloan's mind, had a dangerous following indeed. Some of Mr. Sloan's best members spent their hard-earned money in Leo's bar, money they could instead be giving to the church in any of the forty-nine ways Mr. Sloan had painstakingly devised, from buying weekly copies of *Parables in Sloan* to purchasing The Word of Life's special pecan pies. And so the Reverend Mr. Sloan vigorously attacked Leo and Lightnin' Ed's whenever possible, carefully implying that the bar was no better than a whorehouse and that Leo was a principal acolyte of the Prince of Darkness. The matrons of the church took heed and swung their frying pans twice as hard against the skulls of husbands who confessed to drinking in Lightnin' Ed's.

"Good morning, Brother Leo," said the Reverend Mr. Sloan, as Leo came in range.

"Mornin', Rev," said Leo.

The Reverend Mr. Sloan bristled at the familiarity but swallowed his pride in the interest of Spreading the Gospel Into All The World. "Hasn't God given us a fine morning?"

Leo looked up at the sky and considered the proposition. "Sure has. Looks like the ball game ain't gonna get rained out."

"Ah, yes," said the Reverend Mr. Sloan, searching Leo's diction for a trap. "I assume you are on your way to worship."

"Go right ahead," Leo said amiably. "I assumes I'm on ma way to let Jake outa ma bar 'fore he drinks up all the profit, an' then I assumes I'ma go on home an' take a nap an' watch the ball game."

"Ah, yes," said the Reverend Mr. Sloan. "The ball game." He clasped his hands behind his back and rocked back onto his heels. "Ah, Brother Leo, I've been meaning to speak with you about, well, spiritual affairs."

"Yeah," said Leo, with a sigh.

"Now I know a man like you doesn't always consider his soul—"

"That's for sure," said Leo.

"But," continued the Reverend, ignoring the interruption, "it is a matter deserving of your greatest attention." At this point Leo realized that it would be useless to say anything and that the less he interrupted the sooner the ordeal would be over. "Now," said the Reverend Mr. Sloan, "I know you are a good businessman. And, as a good businessman, you have insurance on your bar so that, in case of fire or theft or vandalism, you are protected from material loss. I'm sure you have life insurance, too. But have you ever paused to think how silly life insurance is? You yourself can never collect. You pay the premiums, but only others can glean the fruit of the vineyard. Now, what I offer you is the kind of life insurance that only you can collect. 'Lay not up for yourself treasures on earth, where moth and dust doth corrupt and where thieves break through and steal, but lay up for yourself treasures in heaven, where neither moth nor dust doth corrupt and where thieves do not break through and steal.' Why, Brother Leo, it is sheer folly for you to neglect to insure your eternal life just as you insure your worldly business." The Reverend Mr. Sloan assumed a pose of appeal: knees slightly bent so that he could look up into Leo's eyes, neck stretched, eyes wide, jaw dropped, hands spread with the palms facing upward and slightly outward. He had practiced it for hours.

"I ain't got no insurance on ma bar," Leo said softly, trying to sound apologetic.

The Reverend Mr. Sloan stiffened, dropped his hands, and let his mouth go slack. "No insurance?" he croaked disbelievingly.

Leo shook his head.

"None at all?"

"Nope," said Leo.

"B-b-but what it, I mean, what if—?"

" 'Consider the lilies of the field,' " thundered Leo, folding his hands over his breastbone and staring up into the smog, " 'how they grows; they toils not, neither does they spin. Yet Solomon, in *aaall* his glory, was not arrayed as one of these. Therefore I says unto you, take no thought as to what y'all shall eat, or what y'all shall wear, or where y'all shall drink—"

"That's . . . crazy!" the Reverend Mr. Sloan whispered hoarsely.

"Ah," said Leo, shaking his forefinger in Mr. Sloan's face, "that's the gospel. Good mornin' to you, Reverend."

The Reverend Mr. J. Peter Sloan watched Leo amble away. Anyone who was not aware of Mr. Sloan's gentle nature and Christian principles would have sworn the look on his saintly visage was one of pure, malevolent hatred.

Leo opened the door of Lightnin' Ed's and stepped off the hot sidewalk into the dark coolness. It took his eyes a second or two to adjust to the dimness, and when they did he looked around at the neatly arranged stools, the freshly scrubbed floor, the well-dusted woodwork, the wino sitting, glass in hand, in front of the bottle of wine in which the cork was still firmly planted. Leo lifted the gate and went behind the bar and got out another glass. "Mornin', Jake," he said.

"Mornin', Leo."

"You done a real nice job on the place, Jake, an' I thank you."

"Why," said Jake, "it's ma pleasure. Man oughta earn his keep."

"Well, I want you to know I appreciates it. How 'bout a drink?"

"Why, all right," said Jake, "I don't mind if I do."

He pulled the cork out of the bottle and poured both glasses full to the brim, first Leo's, then his own. Leo lifted his glass slowly and sipped. Jake downed his in one shot. "Have another?" Jake said.

"I'm fine," Leo said, "but you go ahead." Jake nodded and poured again, drinking more slowly this time. "Woulda been here sooner," Leo said, "only I got cornered by the preacher."

"Sloan?" growled Jake. Leo nodded. "That sonofabitch."

"Now, Jake," Leo admonished, "you gotta show more respect."

"Shit," said Jake. "You know what the sonofabitch done? I'll tell you what he done. Useta be churches was open. Anytime you got to feelin' the spirit you could go in an' pray a while, long as you wanted. I tell you, I done prayed maself the night away many a time, 'specially in the winter. But then 'long comes this Sloan an' he says, 'We can't be havin' this riff-raft sleepin' in the church. It don't look good.' Guess Jesus wouldn't like it. Anyways, he locked the place right up. No warnin' an' in the dead a winter. Sloan! Piece a goddamn shit, if you ast me." Jake tossed off the rest of his wine and slammed his glass down on the bar. Leo reached out calmly and poured it full again. "You know what you oughta do?" Jake said. "You oughta open up on Sundays an' get every one a that bastard's deacons so blind drunk they'll shit in the collection plate."

"Yeah, well," said Leo, trying not to grin.

Jake finished off his third glass of wine and smiled. "Real nice stuff."

"Same as always," Leo said absentmindedly. "Jake, I wants you to do me a favor."

"Sure," said Jake.

"You recall the fella was in here last night? One talkin' to Betsy?"

"I remember anybody can stand talkin' to Betsy," Jake said.

"I want you to ast around. Find out who he is."

"Okay."

"Name's Brown," Leo said. "I ain't seen him before, but somebody musta. He's gotta come from somewheres."

"Leroy Briggs is sure gonna take somethin' outa that nigger's hide," Jake predicted. "What you want him for?"

"I don't want him," Leo said, "I just want to know where he is so I can stay the hell outa the way. Fool's got to be crazy."

"Ain't that the truth."

Leo nodded grimly. "You want some money for, uh, expenses?"

"Naw," said Jake, "I don't need money. There's enough niggers that owes me a favor. 'Bout time I started collectin'. Course . . ."

"Course, what?" Leo said.

"It might be helpful," Jake said, "if I could kinda bring somebody in an' buy 'em a drink. While I was remindin' them a all the favors they owed me."

"Sure," said Leo.

"Okay," said Jake. "Now I better be gettin' ma ass to work."

"You still shinin' shoes over to the train station?"

Jake nodded. "Tips is gettin' to be pretty good, with them startin' that Metroliner thing."

"Guess they ain't payin' you much."

Jake didn't answer.

Leo looked at him. "They payin' you anything?"

Jake remained silent.

"What you do it for, Jake?"

Jake shrugged. "Man's gotta be doin' somethin' 'sides drink. I shines shoes." He looked at Leo for a minute, smiled, and shuffled out. Leo watched him totter through the door, then picked up his glass and washed it. Then he picked up his own, sniffed it, wrinkled his nose, and poured the wine back into the bottle.

The Reverend Mr. Sloan looked down with great satisfaction upon the sanctuary of The Word of Life Church. The theater seats were three-quarters full, and the seating capacity was one thousand. Mr. Sloan mentally converted the attendance figures into dollar signs and sighed blissfully. On stage one of the assistant ministers was doing a wild Watusi, while the elders, deacons, and trustees, seated on the right side of the aisle in the first five rows, stamped their feet and shouted amen. The congregation was waking from its lethargy and beginning to shout, too. As Mr. Sloan watched, Sister Fundidia Larson rose from her seat in the choir and let loose a long, pious wail, while clasping her hands above her head and rotating her body in ecstasy. The dancing minister stared openly at her bouncing bosom without missing a single beat and allowed attention to wander to Sister Fundidia's glorious example of Christian fervor. Then, as

Sister Fundidia began to tire, he deftly drew the focus of the service back to himself with a couple of loud shouts and a few slaps on his tambourine. The Reverend Mr. Sloan made mental notes to commend the assistant for his handling of the service and to have him warned to keep his hands off Sister Fundidia.

Mr. Sloan's vantage point was what had once been the projection booth at the rear of the theater. He had had it transformed into a rather cozy office: air-conditioned, carpeted, wood paneled. A massive ebony-finished desk occupied one corner. The desk chair had been carefully constructed to make the occupant—and Mr. Sloan made sure there was never any occupant but himself—look like a giant. In fact, the dimensions of the entire room tapered slightly, so that Mr. Sloan, when seated behind the desk, looked slightly larger than life.

The intercom buzzed, and Mr. Sloan bent to speak into it. His eyes glinted with anticipation, but he was careful to keep his voice calm and even. "Yes?" The intercom buzzed and squawked. "Of course," said the Reverend Mr. Sloan, "send him right up." The intercom squawked once. Mr. Sloan flipped it off and looked around, giving careful thought as to the most advantageous pose in which to receive his visitor. He straightened the frames of the certificates that hung on the wall, above his trophy shelf, his hands lingering lovingly over his D.D. diploma, of which he was quite proud. The Reverend Mr. Sloan had, so he told everyone who inquired, received his doctorate from Berkeley. He never found it necessary to add that the campus was a post-office box, and tuition was always remitted in cashier's checks or money orders or, occasionally, in stamps. He tried posing with a hand on the diploma but changed his mind and leaped into his chair. He reached out to the complex control panel set into a drawer of his desk and activated an amplifier circuit; sound from the sanctuary flowed into the room through concealed speakers—the mellow voice of the first assistant minister issuing the call to worship. Mr. Sloan spun the chair around so that he faced the wall, the chair's high back rising behind him. When the door opened, nothing of Mr. Sloan was at all visible.

Mr. Sloan listened in excitement, hearing the footsteps hesitate. Mr. Sloan imagined, with great satisfaction, his visitor looking around the empty room, peering into corners, shrugging with self-conscious nonchalance for the benefit of a hidden observer and, when the eeriness of the assistant minister's disembodied voice began to have its effect, shivering a little. At that point the Reverend Mr. Sloan spun his chair around and smiled broadly. "Why, Brother Leroy," said the Reverend Mr. Sloan, "it's so nice to see you."

Leroy turned quickly from examining the display of Mr. Sloan's certificates, awards, and trophies. "Huh?" he said.

"Oh," said Mr. Sloan, spreading his hands and putting a look of horrified contrition on his face, "did I startle you? I's so sorry."

"Nope," said Leroy, adjusting his purple-and-gold-checked silk tie, "I was just lookin'."

"Yes," said the Reverend Mr. Sloan, rising, smiling, and coming out from behind the desk. Leroy gave ground. Mr. Sloan's smile broadened. "Let me point a few of them out for you," Mr. Sloan offered. "This is the loving cup given me by the North American Racial Congress for my work in combatting the drug problem. This certificate was presented to me at a testimonial given in my honor by the Federation of Biblical Interpreters for my translation of Saint Paul's letter to the church at Milkigaarde. That's Constantinople, you know. Very difficult translation. I expect an honorary degree from my alma mater for it, possibly from Harvard as well. Well. This next one is the certificate from the Council of Introspective Atheists, and, last but not least, the big gold plaque is the Centennial Award from the double-A triple-E N."

"Da who?" said Leroy, looking at the plaque.

"You know," said Mr. Sloan modestly, "the American Association for the Enlightenment, Education, and Elevation of Negroes."

"Well," said Leroy, "them enlightened, educated, elevated niggers done gypped you. That there's brass."

Mr. Sloan's face clouded but he kept himself from looking at the plaque. "It's the thought that counts," Mr. Sloan said stiffly. He turned and stepped back behind the desk, seating himself precisely in his chair. "Won't you have a seat?"

Leroy nodded amiably and lowered himself into the visitor's chair, which was cunningly designed to sink until the head of the occupant was on a level well below that of the exalted pate of the Reverend Mr. Sloan. The air wheezed out of the cushion, and Leroy saw Mr. Sloan's head rear above him like the summit of Mount Kilimanjaro. Leroy pushed himself out of the chair. "I think I'll just stand," he said.

The Reverend Mr. Sloan sat helplessly looking up at Leroy. "Is the chair *that* uncomfortable?" Mr. Sloan demanded testily.

"Ain't that," Leroy said.

"Well," said Mr. Sloan, bouncing to his feet, "I've been sitting all morning." His nose was on the same level as the intricate knotting of Leroy's tie. Staring at it, the Reverend Mr. Sloan felt a little ill. "Now then, Brother Leroy—" he began.

"Mr. Briggs," said Leroy.

"Ah, Brother Briggs," said Mr. Sloan.

"*Mr.* Briggs," said Leroy.

"Mr. Briggs," said Reverend Sloan. "I hope this is only the first in a long series of transactions between us." He smiled winningly.

"I hope so, too," said Leroy.

Mr. Sloan's smile faded slightly. "You do?"

"Why shore," said Leroy, grinning broadly. "Oh, I know what you been thinkin'. You was thinkin', 'That there Leroy Briggs, he ain't gonna like payin' off all that there money.' But you know what?"

"No," said the Reverend Mr. Sloan, feeling slightly sicker, "what?"

"You," said Leroy, "was wrong. See, I look at it from a business point a view. Get the big picture, you dig? Now I runs a game. The more folks plays, the more money I makes. An' folks only plays to win. Ain't nobody gonna play if nobody never wins nothin'. After a while they gonna say, 'We ain't never won shit playin' along, we better get us a new deal.' A man ain't gonna keep on puttin' out his quarter every day if he ain't never won nothin' an' if he don't know nobody who ever won nothin'. So somebody *has* to win. Now, truth is folks don't win all that often. So sometimes I has to go an' pay somebody to tell folks that they done won. Ain't that a bitch? Course, every once in a while some lucky jackass does hit, but that can cause all kinds a trouble. I mean the man *has* to be a fool, otherwise he wouldn't be playin' in the first damn place, an' so he takes the money an' goes out an' buys a lot a crap, or worse, he puts it in the bank. Now if he buys stuff with it, sooner or later somebody's gonna want to know where this poor nigger got his eight-track stereo an' his color TV an' that starts a whole mess a shit with the po-lice comin' around astin' questions an' sometimes you gotta do things that ain't—businesslike. An' if the fool goes an' puts the money in the bank, come income tax time he's gotta report it or else the guvment computer's gonna blow a fuse or somethin', an' either way you get Tres'ry people runnin' aroun', astin' more questions, causin' more trouble. Once ain't too bad, but it just keeps on happenin' every time some fool hits big. I mean, cops is hard to get rid of, but them federal agents is runnin' the market sky high. I can't afford to be buyin' one or two every damn year, an' you don't dare kill 'em. That's where you comes in, Rev."

Reverend Sloan grimaced. Leroy didn't seem to notice. "This here's a church," Leroy said. "Churches ain't got to pay taxes an' they don't got to report shit to nobody." Leroy paused to grin. The Reverend Mr. Sloan did not grin. "I must say, Rev," Leroy continued, "the idea was a dandy. Get

the horses from that fool out to the track, figure out the number, an' get all
the deacons to hit for a dollar. But it musta cost you some bread, gettin' to
the man who knows an' all. You ain't got to be goin' through all that shit.
You wants to hit, just call on Leroy, he'll 'range everything. All you got to
do is to make sure folks finds out where you got the money. You don't have
to let on like you was playin'; just tell 'em Leroy Briggs done made a
contribution to the cause, they'll know what you mean."

The Reverend Mr. Sloan had sunk slowly into his chair, a flabbergasted
look on his face. "You don't mind about the—"

"Five thou? Hell, no. Like I said, somebody's got to win, best if it's you.
After the word gets around you Christians done hit for number one every
nigger in the world's gonna be throwin' away his dream book an' readin' the
Bible an' puttin' a quarter on the Twenty-third Psalm or some such shit.
They gonna be thinkin' all they got to do is pray an' the number'll come to
'em in a dream, like you tole them deacons a yours." Leroy reached into an
inner pocket and produced two thick envelopes, tossed them on the desk.
"Here's the jack, Jack. I woulda give you a check, but I figured you might
wanna make it look like it come in the collection plate. Just for
appearances, you dig?"

Mr. Sloan sat silently in his chair, beads of frustrated perspiration
dribbled off his head, through his eyebrows, and into his eyes.

"Ain't you gonna count it?" Leroy said gently.

"You wouldn't cheat," Mr. Sloan sighed.

Leroy smiled. "Always pays in full. Only way to do business. Now, in a
few months when things cools off, we'll just pump you out a little more
cash. After you done had one a your di-vine dreams, a course. That'll make
the market go up like a shot. Course, you ain't gonna be gettin' no five
thou, but I ain't gonna be cheap." He smiled toothily. "It's been a pleasure,
Rev, but now I got to be goin'. I got some other business that needs tendin'
to."

Mr. Sloan raised his head. "Having a meeting with Gino, Brother
Leroy?" he said, smiling.

Leroy stopped short. "Mr. Briggs," he said automatically. "What about
Gino?"

"Oh, nothing," said Mr. Sloan. "The acquaintance you mentioned, at
the track. He said perhaps you had some dealings with a friend of his named
Gino. I just thought it might be he you were going to see."

"No," said Leroy. "No, it ain't 'he. It ain't none a your damn business
who it is." He glared at Mr. Sloan for a moment, then his features relaxed.
"But, speakin' of acquaintances, I met somebody who says he knew you a

few years ago when you had an, ah, *position* in California? I believe he said you were involved with the California state penal system in some, ah, capacity?"

"Chaplain," said Mr. Sloan.

"Of course," said Leroy. "What else would a preacher be doin' in San Q." Leroy smiled and adjusted his belt over his ample belly. "You take it easy now, Rev, you hear?" He winked and turned for the door. Mr. Sloan watched it close after him, reached out and opened one of the envelopes, stared listlessly at the wad of bills, let the envelope drop.

"Now, Brothers and Sisters," came the voice of Brother Fletcher, the assistant, from the hidden speakers, "the time has come for us to worship with our tithes and offerings. . . ." Mr. Sloan snapped his head up as the door opened and Leroy's big head showed around the jamb.

"One more thing," Leroy said. "I was talkin' to this associate a mine an' he said he might be comin' around to talk to you pretty soon. Somethin' about you havin' a pretty big operation here an' gonna be needin' some insurance. Fire, theft, vandalism, you know what I mean. I tell you, Rev, these vandals is gettin' to be a real pain in the ass. I don't know what these kids is comin' to. Gettin' to be actin' like a regular bunch a hoodlums. Anyways, don't you forget about that insurance. The fella'll be around. Name's Willie T. You all oughta get along real good, you both bein' so intellectual. Willie T.'s been to night school, took all kinds a correspondence courses." He winked again, retracted his head, and closed the door with a soft click.

"Lay not up for yourselves—," said the speaker, but the sound of Brother Fletcher's voice ceased abruptly as the Reverend Mr. J. Peter Sloan turned off the amplifier, using, instead of the switch on his control panel, a heavy lead paper weight that had been given to him by the Association of Organized Pacifists.

"Goddamn your lazy ass! Why can't I have it?"

"We ain't got the money for it."

"We would if you wasn't some simple ass-kissin' janitor."

"We ain't got the money," Rayburn said again.

"All I know is, Charlene's walkin' around in a brand new dress, an' I'll be goddamned if I'ma let her be turnin' her nose up at me just 'cause you ain't got no better sense than to clean toilets for a livin'."

Rayburn sighed. "I does what I does."

"Well, I'll tell you what you better be doin'. You better be findin' some money from someplace, or I'ma get it maself."

"You ain't gonna do nothin' like that," said Rayburn, wishing he believed it.

"You don't tell me what to do. I got along just fine without—"

"Damn straight," Rayburn snarled. He slammed his beer can down on the kitchen counter, and the Formica strip around the edges burst from the restraint of the cheap glue, exposing termite-infested wood. "Damn straight. You was doin' fine, drinkin' like a goddamn wino, shootin' shit into your arms, noddin' out in doorways, cryin' an' screamin' in some damn alley where some damn pusher left you after you tried to suck his cock for a hit. Yeah, you was doin' fine. You was in great shape."

"Fuck you," Leslie said.

Rayburn picked up his beer and went into the living room. He reached over and snapped on a small transistor radio, turned it up as loud as it would go. Tinny soul music sliced into his ears, and then the self-consciously black hip voice of the deejay. Rayburn kicked at the wall.

"You act just like a baby," she said, coming out and standing in the doorway to the kitchen.

"*I* acts like a baby? *Me?* Shit."

"You do."

"So what's that make you?" She didn't answer. "Well, what's that make you? 'I gotta have a new dress just like Charlene.' Next thing you want's three fuckin' bastards that belongs to God knows who, just like Charlene."

"Maybe I would," she said sweetly. She came out of the kitchen, smiled at him, moved toward him, her robe hanging open. "What you gonna do if I does get pregnant, *baby?* Least you'd know it wasn't yours. Your little piece a limp licorice couldn't knock up a mosquito."

"Shut up," Rayburn said tiredly.

"Some folks gots cocks, Rayburn. Sometimes I even feel—"

"Shut up."

"Oh, don't you like to hear about it? You might learn somethin'."

"I don't want to learn nothin'," Rayburn said.

"You're right. You ain't never gonna learn nothin', you ain't never gonna be nothin'. You ain't never gonna get nowhere. You're too fuckin' old."

He came across the room and knocked her flying with his closed fist. She picked herself up, spitting blood, but there was a soft look in her eyes. "Janitor," she said. He struck her again, full on the mouth, and he felt blood hot in his mouth from her cut tongue as she pulled him down and kissed him. He struggled to rise, to get away from her, but she clung stubbornly to his neck. He struck out at her weakly. Her lips were against his, soft and cool-warm, like the breeze flowing down the corridors between the buildings on a night buried deep in July. Her eyes opened, wide and brown, her teeth digging into his ear as his tongue clumsily battered at her throat. He felt frightened, moving his hands over her, avoided her eyes for fear of what he might or might not see. Her body tensed and arched against him as his hand found one tender spot. She gripped him with her wiry arms. She tugged at his clothing.

Then he looked into her eyes and saw them soften as he stroked her skillfully, harden terribly when, in his excitement, he fumbled. Her hand reached for him, hard and dry, hurting him. She moistened it with her own juices, grasped him once again. Suddenly he realized that, far, far too soon, he was coming. He saw her smile of contempt, of triumph. He wanted to scream and cry. He tried to stop himself, to twist out of her grasp, but her hand moved swiftly and knowingly. He closed his eyes.

When he opened them she was smiling at him, taunting. He lifted his hand and brought it flat across her face, seeing as he did so her eyes soften and mist over. He slapped her again, feeling something inside him rip and tear like a great white sheet. But her eyes were closing, slowly, in some strange ecstasy, and he felt a glow of power somewhere inside him as he slapped her again and again.

Somebody was dying.

In the vast deserted depths of Franklin Field agonized gasps echoed faintly but clearly, a death rattle, or a ragged orgasm. But the gasps were rhythmic, accompanied by the sound of pounding feet that approached, swept past, receded. The sun beat down out of a sky that was hard and high and very blue and exceptionally clean, even for a Sunday. It was hot. It was too hot to be running. Brown knew it. He had known it as soon as he had entered the stadium and stood looking at the immense and empty stands, imagining them filled with people, hearing dead echoes, feeling the hangover lurking like a sponge behind his nose and eyes. He had felt the heat bouncing off the concrete hidden beneath the artificial turf, and he had known that the most sensible thing would be to go home and go back to bed. But he had made a pile of his sweat suit and towel and water bottle and he had set out for one slow lap on the track. With the first spring of perspiration coating his skin, with his muscles just loosening up, Brown had felt full of optimism, and so he had settled down to run in earnest. Now, hearing his own gasps echo as he punched out his fourth lap, he felt fear. It sounded like he was dying for sure; the pain that managed to penetrate his fogged-over brain scared him, and the flat track, stretching and curling back on itself and stretching again, the track scared him. He considered stopping. But Brown had long before made a rule that, once he had begun, he would not stop until he had completed the distance. It had made him feel virtuous at the time. Just now, rounding the west turn and rolling into the stretch, it was making him feel sick.

The stands watched him, and Brown kept himself going by thinking of the people that had occupied them at one time or another to watch powerhouse football games in the good old days when the University of Pennsylvania defeated Penn State instead of being confused with it. Brown labored before gathered ghosts, smiling coeds, Ivy Leaguers waving pennants, wearing boaters. Brown ran past old alumni with white hair and ten thousand dollars to contribute to the building fund. Brown ran them down.

The track got harder and the sun got harder. A little man with a hot ice pick floated down from the sky and took up a station over Brown's belly button, poked his ice pick through Brown's side, and teased. Brown kept going. The little man grew slightly more insistent. Brown got the message, kept on.

The ninth lap was always the hardest. The little man replaced his ice pick with a brace and bit, and turned away merrily. Brown felt his hip tighten and gave up. The little man smiled as Brown slowed and let his legs stretch out. Nine laps wasn't bad, Brown told himself. Not for a hot morning after a heavy drunk. Nine laps was okay. The little man snorted and floated away. Brown forced his aching back muscles to keep his torso erect, his head up as he moved down the backstretch, past the ranked hordes. Benjamin Franklin, George Washington, Abe Lincoln. Brown kept his dignity, kept his hands loose, kept his breathing in precise cadence with his footfalls. He swept down a backstretch filled with giggling ghosts, into the east turn.

Every black schoolboy runner on the East Coast dreams of the east turn of Franklin Field, dreams of rolling down the straight and pouring on the coal through that final turn and streaming on to a victory in the Penn Relays. The black faces mass in that turn, black voices clot. A last-place runner will save something for that turn. The second-place runner will make his move in that turn. Everything beyond that turn is downhill drag. Brown, defeated, years beyond high-school spirit and schoolboy fervor, rolled into that turn and heard dark murmurings of disappointment. Brown cursed and started pulling himself back together again, floated into the straight, and let himself go.

The little man reappeared, clucking sadly, unlimbered a buzz saw, and set to work, humming. Brown's face twisted in agony as his body protested. He pounded through the west turn, no longer running easily, and laboring, came up on the south stands, spitting on the track as he moved through the ghostly glares. The east turn came up. Brown shortened his stride and kicked into the straight, hearing no cheers beyond his own gasps, almost but not quite catching up to his own shadow as he powered across the finish line, head up, back straight, legs and hands outstretched and grasping.

Twenty feet beyond the line Brown fell apart like a puppet with its strings suddenly sliced, his breath coming in irregular gasps, his arms and legs going in all directions. He slowed, stopped, his head hung, sweat poured from him. He would have thought he were dead, except he hurt too much. He let his head hang but started moving again, fighting the urge to lie down on the track and turn into a knot. By the time he had completed one slow circuit he had his body under some semblance of control. At the end of the second lap he decided he had begun to think he was going to live after all. By the time he had finished a third lap he had decided he might as well. He bent over and pulled on the sweat suit, allowed himself a small swallow of water, picked up the towel, and left the stadium.

His hangover was gone. He walked to the corner of Thirty-third, contemplating an accident of the city's geography: on his left was South Street; on his right, the same street was Spruce. Brown looked to his left. Then he turned the other way and began to move west on Spruce, breaking into a jog as if he were in a rush to get away from the intersection. The street was deserted except for parked cars. Brown dodged construction sites, made his way toward a trio of high-rise apartment buildings that erupted from the asphalt like acne blemishes. Brown slowed as he approached one of the buildings, fished in the pocket of his sweat suit for his keys, but the door opened before he got to it. Brown let the keys fall clinking back into his pocket. "Mornin', Speedy," he said to the doorman.

Speedy grinned up at him from his bucket seat behind the electronic security console. "Hey, Adlai," Speedy said. "Seen you comin' on the TV."

Brown peered over the console. "What the hell?"

"Brand new," Speedy said proudly. "With this here contraption, all I got to be doin' is watchin' TV. See, you switches the channels just like a reglar TV, an' you can see in the garage an' in the elevators an' everywhere. I had ma eye on you a long time, so you be careful, nigger, or I'll have the Man on your black ass."

Brown chuckled. "The Man lives on ma ass. You see into bedrooms with that thing?"

"Don't need to," Speedy said. "Hell, I can imagine a lot bettern most a these here white folks can fuck. Course there's exceptions, like that there blond bitch, what's her name . . ."

"I know who you mean," Brown said.

Speedy gave him an appraising look. "Oh yeah? You been into that, too?"

"What you mean, 'too'?"

"Oh, nothin'. Just that, way I hears it, when her husband ain't home, which, just 'tween you an' me, is mostly, she don't like nothin' bettern to go out huntin' for some black—"

"No thanks," Brown said. "It's all yours."

"Hell, I'm too old for that," Speedy said.

"So am I," Brown said. "By about three hundred an' fifty years."

"Yeah, well," Speedy said. "Anyways, I can imagine what goes on."

"Well, you keep on imaginin' an' keep that damn TV set outa ma bedroom."

"Course, ma man," Speedy said. "Wouldn't spy on a brother. Now the super—"

"Shit," Brown said, and turned to push the button for the elevator.

"Your woman lookin' for you again last night," Speedy said. "I said I didn't know where you was."

"Umph," Brown said. "How come it takes this elevator all damn day to get nowhere?"

"South Street again?"

"Shit," Brown said, stabbing at the button again.

"Man," Speedy said, "if I was you I'd stay the hell away from there. That street's a stone bitch. I 'member once upon a time the city was gonna fix it up. Turn the whole damn place into a what you call garden spot. Townhouses, playgrounds, good schools, all that shit. So they went to work an' condemned all the buildin's, drove out all the business. Makin' way for the white folks. That whole street turned into a cemetery. Everybody was livin' on borrowed time. Then the city changed its mind. Wasn't nothin' left but sorry-ass niggers that couldn't afford nothin' else."

Brown looked at him. "It's an old story. It happens everywhere."

"Sure do," Speedy agreed. "Every day in every way. Trouble with niggers is they gets old 'fore they gets tired."

The elevator door slid open and Brown stepped inside, punched a button. "You watch that bitch," Speedy said. "She'll get a hold on you, turn you every way but a-loose."

"Which bitch?" Brown asked, as the door slid shut. The car boosted him upward, the doors opened again, Brown stepped out into a carpeted corridor. Walking down the hallway, Brown self-consciously wiped his face, patted his hair. He went to a door halfway along the hall, inserted his key, stepped inside, shivering at the sudden chill; the air-conditioning in the lobby and corridor had been reasonable, but the apartment unit was turned up too high. Brown hated air-conditioning. He longed to cut the unit off, but it wasn't his air-conditioner. It wasn't his apartment either.

Brown crossed the carpeted livng room, entered the bedroom, shucked off his sweat suit and shorts, slipping into an ancient blue terry-cloth robe that was ripped out under both arms, moving quietly so as not to disturb the woman who lay on the bed, her body concealed by the white sheet. Brown looked at her for a few moments, watching the rise and fall of the sheet as she breathed, then he picked up his soggy running clothes and carried them back through the living room and out onto the balcony. He didn't feel tired any more. He felt strong and quick and he giggled softly as the carpet rubbed against the bottom of his feet. A small spark of electricity arced from his hand to the metal handle of the sliding door; Brown winced, slid the door open, stepped out onto the tile, and stood in the hot sunshine while he draped his wet clothing over the rail. He squinted up into the sun, lowered his eyes to look out over the city, the ugly refineries in the south, the treed jungle of Fairmount Park to the north, and, to the east, the spires of Center City. Brown's eyes wandered slightly south, along Spruce Street until it reached the Schuylkill. He snorted and turned away.

Brown sat in the living room, in a big white beanbag chair, feeling bored. He got up, went back into the bedroom. The woman slept on beneath the sheet. Brown looked at her for a while, then slipped out of his robe and moved around to the far side of the bed. He started to lift the sheet and ease in beside her but hesitated. He drew his hand back. Then he set his jaw and slid onto the bed. He lay there, his still-sweaty skin sticking to the sheet, pulling slightly as he moved, sending a hand sliding out, laying it across her, his fingers brushing the tuft of hair at the base of her belly. Brown felt his body start to hum, felt strength flow into him. The hesitation vanished, he began to move with almost infinite patience. Carefully, slowly, he moved his hand over her, lightly stroking the flesh between her navel and the swell of her breasts. He raised himself up on his elbow and waited, almost bored. She moaned sleepily and turned away; Brown, unperturbed, stroked her haunch. His hand moved slowly. His thoughts were elsewhere.

The Reverend Mr. J. Peter Sloan watched as the matron cleaned up the smashed glass and smashed parts of the demolished amplifier. The sight of her bent over, sweeping, giving a panoramic view of her broad white-uniformed rear end, with fleshy legs squeezed and a roll of blubber pushed out over the top of her support stockings like toothpaste out of a tube, was enough to make Mr. Sloan faint. The matron finished her sweeping and laid her broom aside. Groaning and creaking, she eased herself down onto one knee and began to wipe the carpet with a damp cloth.

"That will do, Sister," said the Reverend Mr. Sloan.

"Gotta get this here glass up," she said in no uncertain terms. "Can't have people cuttin' they feet."

"It's carpet," Mr. Sloan said. "That won't help."

The matron continued to wipe.

"That will do," said the Reverend Mr. Sloan sharply.

The matron looked back over her shoulder and scowled at him, her face above her ponderous posterior making her look like a misformed snowman. "All right," she said, "but if you cuts your foot open, don't you come cryin' to me."

"I'm not likely to cut my foot unless I go walking around barefoot, now am I?" snapped the Reverend Mr. Sloan.

The matron looked at him, then at the studio couch at the other end of the office. "Yeah," she said, "I 'spect you'll be all right so long as you keep everythin' on all the time." The Reverend Mr. Sloan glared at her. She unconcernedly levered herself to her feet, gathered up her cloth, broom, and dust pan, and departed. Mr. Sloan cursed in a most un-Christian manner and went back behind his desk, stabbed a button on his panel. Thirty seconds later his first assistant stood before him. The Reverend Mr. Sloan looked up from his watch. "Getting a bit slow in our old age, aren't we, Fletcher?" said the Reverend Mr. Sloan.

"Sorry," said Brother Fletcher.

"Never mind," said Mr. Sloan graciously. "You have important responsibilities today. Have you prepared the sermon?"

Brother Fletcher nodded silently. His jaw muscles bulged slightly as he clenched his teeth.

"Good, good," said Mr. Sloan jovially. "No, no need to show it to me. I have complete faith in your abilities."

"Thank you," Brother Fletcher replied stiffly.

"Sit down, Brother, sit down. You won't be on again for another twenty minutes."

Brother Fletcher looked doubtfully at the chair.

"Sit, Fletcher," said the Reverend Mr. Sloan.

Brother Fletcher sat, accepting the seat that Leroy had declined.

"There," said the Reverend Mr. Sloan in a voice that dripped rancid honey and machine oil, as Brother Fletcher's body sank into the depths of the chair. "I've been meaning to speak to you."

Brother Fletcher's Adam's apple bobbed expectantly.

"Turnbull did an excellent job warming them up this morning," Mr. Sloan observed. "I'd appreciate it if you'd convey my compliments."

"Certainly," said Brother Fletcher.

"Tut, tut, tut," said the Reverend Mr. Sloan, shaking his head. "Such a shame about that young man. Promising future, good mind. Such a waste."

"Waste?" said Brother Fletcher.

"Indeed," said Mr. Sloan. "I'm afraid he is much too concerned with the pleasures of the flesh. I regret to say it, but I fear he must go."

Brother Fletcher looked shocked. "I know Turnbull has a girl friend, but don't you think that at his age that's only nat—"

"He's queer," said Mr. Sloan.

"Upl?" said Brother Fletcher.

"Queer," repeated Mr. Sloan. "Faggot. Sissy. Punk. Homosexual." He raised a hand. "I know, I know, Fletcher, you were fooled. So was I for a time. Turnbull puts on a good show. I've noticed him making advances toward Sister Fundidia, trying to confuse us. But I know. I can tell." Mr. Sloan leaned back in his chair and languidly placed a hand on the back of his neck, patting his bald head as if it were covered with a lush growth. He smiled winningly at Brother Fletcher. "If there's anything I hate," he said, "it's a closet queen." Brother Fletcher's Adam's apple bobbed rapidly. Mr. Sloan dropped his hand. His face hardened. "Really, Fletcher, we couldn't have him leading a troop of boy scouts, now could we?"

"I, ah, hadn't thought of it quite that way," Brother Fletcher conceded.

Mr. Sloan smiled. "Of course you hadn't. A man like you would not think of such things, coming as you do from an, uh, rural area. But I have seen the world, Brother, and I know. It's my job to keep an eye out for such things. Anyone else would have missed it, but I could see he was concealing his dirty, unholy tendencies. But you needn't worry about it. I'll handle Turnbull. I wouldn't have mentioned it, but it seems that I will be able to make that fact-finding tour after all. I just wanted to tell you that I feel perfectly confident in your abilities and intend to leave you in complete charge. I plan to leave in about two weeks. For the next month you will be in charge."

Brother Fletcher smiled slightly. "I hope you'll be pleased when you return."

"I'm sure I will be," Mr. Sloan said. "I know you've had churches of your own, but those were in, ah, rural areas. I think you'll find this quite different, but you'll be able to handle it. For a month. Now, Brother, I know you must prepare yourself, so I won't hold you." Brother Fletcher rose and turned toward the door. "Oh, Fletcher," said Mr. Sloan. "One more thing."

"Yes?"

"I met Leo on the street this morning. News has reached me that last night, in Leo's bar, there was some trouble between Leroy Briggs and a young man no one seems to have ever seen before. It seems that the young man forced Leroy Briggs to back down by saying he worked for Gino. The matter requires investigation. This young man could be quite useful. Now I don't care how you do it, Brother, but I want you to find out about this young man. Infiltrate Lightnin' Ed's and interrogate Leo if necessary."

Brother Fletcher looked shocked. "Infilt—you mean, go *inside?* But it's a *beer* garden."

Mr. Sloan looked at him with distaste. "If God condescends to come to South Street, he won't mind a little alcohol. Now get out of here."

Brother Fletcher looked at Mr. Sloan uncertainly, and wobbled out the door.

When he awoke he was alone in the bed. He lay there for a few minutes pulling himself together and then he threw the sheet off him and rolled out. He stood beside the bed and stretched, then glanced at the clock. It was mid-afternoon. He left the bedroom and went into the kitchen. There was a used juice glass on the counter, a half-empty coffee mug on the table, and a note on the refrigerator, attached with a magnetic clamp in the shape of a ladybug. The note said that she had gone to get a paper and it was nice that they could still do *something* together. "Bitch," Brown said, balling the note between his fingers and throwing it toward the garbage can. He missed.

Brown felt the sides of the percolator and found the coffee was still warm. He filled a cup, added milk and four spoons of sugar, and sat down to contemplate his naked navel. The apartment was silent except for the whisper of the air-conditioning. "Shit," Brown said suddenly. He got up from the table, carried the coffee into the bathroom. He set the cup on the sink, flipped on the shower, climbed in.

Spinning slowly beneath the stream of water, turned on as hard as it would go and as hot as he could stand, Brown let his mind go wandering back to dark alleys, dark nights, dark faces. He picked up the soap and scrubbed in a sudden frenzy. Lather covered him, soap stung his eyes. Brown rinsed himself off. His thoughts turned to Alicia, and he swore softly, soaped himself three times, shampooed twice. When he stepped out of the shower he felt clean and empty. He picked up the coffee cup and drained it, went out into the living room without bothering to dry himself, dripping on the carpet. He shivered in the machined cold, marched to the control, and defiantly cut off the air-conditioning. He threw open the sliding door and breathed in the hot polluted air. Finally he closed the door, went back to the bathroom and got a towel, and proceeded to dry himself off, then he went into the kitchen, took ice and a bottle of scotch from the refrigerator, and constructed himself a drink. He went back into the living room, sank down on the sofa, and slurped it. When the ice melted, despite the chilled whiskey, Brown got up and strengthened the drink from a second bottle sitting on the bar in the corner of the living room. On the way back to the sofa he picked up a yellow legal pad and a pen.

Feet propped up on the lacquered coffee table, drink in one hand and pen in the other, Brown scribbled busily, writing words, scratching them out, tearing leaves from the pad, looking at them, cursing, balling them up. He managed eventually to fill a whole sheet. He sighed, rose, and went to refill his glass. He did a few deep-knee bends. He cleared his throat. He walked around the room three times. Then he went back and looked at the pad. A sour expression crossed his face. He picked up a red pencil, made a few languid marks, sighed, dropped the pencil, balled up the final sheet of paper and threw it, like the others, across the room at the trash can. The paper teetered for an instant on the edge, then tottered and fell outside, joining all the other yellow balls in a tidy heap. Brown got up and went to the bar. He brought the bottle back with him.

Brown roused as the door opened, coming off the couch as if someone had stuck him with a pin, taking the coffee table with him onto the floor as he hit the carpet in a low dive, sending a splash of diluted whiskey and half-melted ice against the wall. The glass and ice were scattered all over the floor. Brown ended up on his feet, poised in a crouch against the far wall.

"Adlai?"

Brown relaxed, straightened. "I wish you wouldn't do that," Brown said. He came back across the room, pausing to retrieve the bottle, glass, and what was left of the ice cubes. He did not look up.

"Do what? What are *you* doing?" She stared at him. "Oh," she said, drawing her lips tight, "I should have known."

Brown straightened up and looked at her. "Should have known what?"

She laid her purse on a low table, put the paper on top of it. She removed her sunglasses and laid them on top the paper. "Should have known that when I got home I'd find you wrapped around a bottle like an alcoholic boa constrictor."

"Hmmm," Brown said. " 'Alcoholic boa constrictor.' Not bad. Mind if I use it sometime? You know any words that rhyme with constrictor?"

"For you to use it, it couldn't have more than four letters."

Brown sighed and dropped onto the sofa. "You know, it's getting so there's only two things we do together any more, and they both start with *f*."

"Fight and what else?" she said, and walked through to the bedroom.

"Ouch," Brown said. He got up and went to stand in the bedroom doorway.

She stepped out of her panties and raised her head. "If you're thinking that now is a good time to take issue with that slur on your heavy-hung black male virility, forget it."

"God forbid," Brown said. "God for*bid* I should touch your million-dollar Westchester County black middle-class ass, and that even rhymes, and do we *have* to do this?"

"Do you *have* to account for half the annual revenue of the local State Store?"

"It sounds," Brown said carefully, "like you are informing me, in your oh-so-subtle *Ebony* Magazine's Most Eligible Female way, that I drink too fucking much. I *know* I drink too fucking much."

"And you say 'fuck' too much."

"All right," Brown said. "I say *fuck* too fucking much. Anything else?"

"You're insensitive."

Brown opened his mouth, closed it. "Jesus," he muttered softly. "Jesus muthafuckin' Christ."

"Don't you know any other words?" she demanded.

"How 'bout 'cunt'?" She glared at him. "Sorry, missy," Brown said. "Us darkies has got a limited vocabulary."

"Don't you start that," she said. "I'm just as black as you are."

"That," Brown said, "is what frightens me." He spun on his heel and went back into the living room.

She followed, wrapping a robe around her. "Are you clean?"

"What?" Brown said.

"Clean. Did you have a shower afterwards?"

"After what?" Brown said, smiling maliciously.

"After that ritual self-torture you put yourself through every morning," she said.

"It ain't every morning," Brown said. "Lately it's been about once a month. Or did you mean the running?"

"I meant the running."

"Oh," Brown said. "Yeah, I took a shower after *that*." He smiled. "Answer your question?"

"Maybe you'd better take another one," she suggested.

"Why?"

"You'll smell."

"If I smell I got the smell from you. And Jesus knows *you* don't smell. Hell, you got more damn sprays than the Agriculture Department." Brown whirled and stalked back into the bathroom, jerked open the medicine cabinet. "Fuck, will you look at this shit. Perfume. Powder. Cream sachet. Underarm spray, foot spray, nose spray, ear spray, pussy spray, *and* douche. Strawberry flavored. Bet that would taste fine, 'cept anybody that tried to eat that oversprayed pussy a yours would probly die from DDT poisonin' or somethin'. . . ."

"Do you *have*—"

" 'Do you *have* to talk that way?' " Brown mimicked. "No, I don't have to talk that way. I know how to talk like nice people. Nice *white* people that wouldn't be caught dead callin' a spade a spade, 'less it happened to be a nigger."

"Negro."

"Black. Afro-American. Jungle bunny. Bullshit." Brown slammed the medicine cabinet shut. "Missy, ah sho' is sorry if ah smells a little musky. But that's life. Now y'all up there to the big house wid Massa . . ."

"You had your share of the big house," she snapped. "You're still having it."

"Wrong, baby," Brown snapped. "I had more than my share. I had my fill."

She looked at him speculatively. Brown stood rigidly against the sink, his jaw set. "Well," she said calmly. "Anyway. You'd better get ready."

"Ready for what?" Brown snapped.

"Earl's party," she said.

Brown looked at her.

"Massa's gonna be there," she said. "An' he runs a poetry magazine. Were you drunk when I told you, or did you just forget?"

"I tried," Brown said. He relaxed, sank down on the edge of the tub, buried his face in his hands for a minute, looked up at her. "I hate this," Brown said. "Why do we do this?"

"Why do you do it?"

"Oh, fuck," Brown said, and took cover in the shower.

Brother Fletcher stood on the stage of The Word of Life Church, looking out over the rows of empty theater seats. It had been a long Sunday, but now it was well into Monday morning, and Brother Fletcher longed for home, his wife, a glass of iced tea. Everyone else had gone to his home happy, renewed, his sins freshly forgiven, the soil prepared for a new crop. Brother Fletcher had stayed behind, tired, happy, and strangely confused. His thoughts were scattered. He had a slight headache. The Word of Life was to be his church, even if only temporarily. Someone had told him that the Phillies had lost both games of their doubleheader. He felt sorry for Brother Turnbull, who would soon be banished from The Word of Life. Brother Fletcher did not like that. He did not like the Reverend Mr. Sloan either. That wasn't really a problem—the problem lay in keeping his mouth shut about it. Brother Turnbull was not a homosexual, and Brother Fletcher knew that. He wondered why he had not called Mr. Sloan a liar and marched out of The Word of Life himself. He didn't know why he hadn't done that, but he knew that he hadn't, and he felt slightly dirty. And yet the church was before him, empty, quiet, peaceful, and Brother Fletcher, looking at it, felt equally quiet, equally peaceful.

Brother Fletcher closed the hymnbooks on the rostrum, picked up a program that had fallen to the floor. He stepped off the platform and walked slowly down the aisle, looking at the littered floor, the chewing gum stuck to the underside of seats that had flipped up when the occupants had departed. He leaned over to pick up a tiny pink glove that some little girl had forgotten.

At the rear of the church Brother Fletcher paused and turned around, gazing back along the aisle, across the backs of the vacant seats to the vacant pulpit. In the dimly lit recess behind the pulpit a large bronze cross gleamed dully. Brother Fletcher reached out his hand and extinguished the lights. The sanctuary sank into darkness except for one stream of light that shone down from the balcony onto the cross. In his mind Brother Fletcher heard again the shouts of Amen, amen, and Preach on, boy, preach on, that had been superimposed on his sermon. He thought of Sister Lavernia Thompson's ugly face seeming almost beautiful as he had laid his hands on her shoulders and prayed for her health. Slowly he raised his arms, stretching them out toward the front of the sanctuary. "May . . ." he said softly. He stopped, began again. "May the Lord bless you and keep you," he intoned, and his deep voice rolled across the empty seats and echoed back from the walls. "May the Lord lift the light of his countenance upon you, and give you peace. Amen."

Brother Fletcher held his arms up for a moment longer, then let them drop to his sides. He turned quickly and pushed through the swinging doors into the lobby. The custodian, whose job it was to lock up, was standing in the front doorway, kicking at something. "G'wan, get 'way fum here."

"What is it?" said Brother Fletcher.

"Oh, Bro' Fletcher," said the custodian, "it's just some shifless wino on da steps."

"Let him stay," said Brother Fletcher.

"All right," said the custodian doubtfully, "but Reverend Sloan tole me—"

"Reverend Sloan is not here," Brother Fletcher said. "Let the man stay. Where is he?" Brother Fletcher moved over to the door and looked down at the old man huddled in the corner of the vestibule. "Are you cold?" said Brother Fletcher. The old man just looked at him, his eyes glassy. The night was warm, but the old man had his arms wrapped around himself. He was shivering. "Let him inside," said Brother Fletcher.

"What?" said the custodian.

"Inside. They can let him out when they come in the morning to clean."

"But Mr. Sloan . . ."

Brother Fletcher glared at the custodian, his jaw set. "I said let him in. Now do it."

"Yassuh," said the custodian. The old man looked up uncomprehendingly.

"Come on in," said Brother Fletcher.

The old man's face assumed a look of grateful disbelief. Brother Fletcher leaned over and helped him up. He staggered on into the church.

"Mr. Sloan sure would be upset," said the custodian.

Brother Fletcher watched the old man shuffle on into the sanctuary. He went to the door and looked in while the wino settled himself on one of the rear seats, drooping his head on his chest like a chicken going to roost.

"Reverend Sloan—" began the custodian.

"Damn Reverend Sloan," snapped Brother Fletcher.

3 The Elysium

"I wants to know who he is," said Vanessa, slipping her long red-painted fingernail into the corner of her lipsticked mouth. "Yes, indeed, I wants to see him. He must be some kinda man."

"I spose so," said Charlene, sipping her Budweiser. The glass, leaving her lips, showed tiny smudges on its rim, and a few flecks of dark make-up floated on the beer's white foam. "All I knows is what I heard."

"Tell me again," said Vanessa. She reached out one graceful arm to the chair beside her and found her purse. With a languid motion of thumb and forefinger she opened the clasp and extracted a cigarette. With her other hand she snapped a small silver lighter; flame appeared as if from her fingertips. She lit the cigarette with a quick pass of her lighter and a well-timed inhalation and exhaled a double column of gray smoke.

"Ain't much to tell," said Charlene. "Leroy stops the car an' goes walkin' into Ed's to get us some beer, an' he comes out a while later swearin' up an' down that he's gone get that muthafucka someday, an' me an' Les knowed bettern to be astin' him what was goin' down. Anyways, Leroy says he wants to fuck, an' Les says she wants to go up to her place, so they could do it in Rayburn's bed." Charlene stopped and looked at Vanessa. "You know that sister a yours is kinda *weird* sometimes, you know what I mean? Anyways, I went on back down to Ed's to see if I could maybe find out what was happenin' an' on the way I run into that simple nigger Elmo, you know the one's always hangin' around here tryin' to turn some little piece a bullshit into a glass a wine? He was goin' on about how *he's* gonna cut the nigger someday, an' it looks to me that somebody sure has managed to get a whole shitload a folks pissed off. Anyway, I ast Elmo who he was gonna cut, an' he says Rayburn, so I got to thinkin' maybe Rayburn done got drunk an' said somethin' to Leroy, you know?"

"Wait a minute," Vanessa said, "I thought you said—"

"I'ma get to it," Charlene said, "you gotta give me some space. Anyways, that Elmo, he's always claimin' he knows all the shit, so I ast him."

"Elmo don't know nothin'," Vanessa snapped.

"I found that out," Charlene said. Vanessa glared at her. Charlene sighed and adjusted the straps on her overworked bra. "Anyways, I went on down an' hung around outside a Ed's—you know I don't be goin' in there no more, ever since Leo made some crack about me goin' into labor—an' pretty soon Betsy comes out, so I ast her. She says Leroy come in an' wants some beer an' was walkin' out 'thout payin' for it like he owned the place; you know how Leroy is. Anyways, the dude stops him an' tells him to pay for it. Leroy, he says, 'Yeah, an' who's gonna make me pay? YOU?' " Charlene turned her head quickly to the side, presenting her left profile. "So this dude says, 'I got friends.' " She twisted her head around the other way and put a tough expression on her face. " 'Yeah?' says Leroy, 'well I'd just as soon piss on your friends as look at 'em. An' I'ma kick your ass.' So the dude smiles at him"—Charlene smiled—"an' says, 'Okay, baby, but Gino ain't gonna like that.' Well, boys, when Leroy hears *that* he just turns around an' hightails it outa here, only before he makes it to the door the dude tells him to pay for the beer. An' Leroy done it. An' the dude tells him to leave a tip. An' Leroy done that, too. An' that," Charlene pronounced, "was that."

"Whooee!" said Vanessa softly. "I gotta find out who this cat is. He must be somethin'! What else did Betsy say? Whad he look like?"

Charlene shrugged. "Betsy said he wasn't much to look at. Said he was skinny."

"Comin' from Betsy that could mean he's the size of an elephant."

Charlene snorted. "You break me right up sometimes. I'll tell you one thing, the dude had to be crazy, movin' on Leroy like that."

"He's gotta be somethin'," Vanessa said.

"He shows up around here he's gonna be ruined," predicted Charlene.

"Don't sound that way to me. Sounds to me like Leroy might be the one haulin' ass outa Dodge."

"I ain't gonna be haulin' nothin' outa noplace, 'cept maybe some blood outa your black hide," said Leroy, coming up behind Vanessa. He put his hand on her shoulder and squeezed, digging his thumb into the tender hollow between her collarbone and shoulder socket. "Where's ma woman?" he asked Charlene, ignoring Vanessa's efforts to squirm away.

"Ain't here yet," said Charlene.

Vanessa twisted her head over and sank her teeth into the meat of Leroy's palm. "Ow, bitch!" shouted Leroy, jerking his hand away and slapping her in the same motion.

Vanessa readjusted her glasses unconcernedly. The imprint of Leroy's hand showed purple against her dark skin. She sipped her Singapore Sling and stubbed out her cigarette. "Ain't your woman," she said. "She's married to Rayburn. You just borrows her."

"Ain't none a your business," said Leroy. "You bite me again, bitch, an' I'll take your simple head off." He smiled at her.

Vanessa twisted around in her chair and looked up at him, smiling too. "All right, then, I won't bite. I'll spit."

Leroy stopped smiling. "Don't you forget who's payin' for what."

Vanessa sniffed. "I ain't for sale. I do exactly what I wants to do when I wants to do it."

"Too bad you ain't no good at it," Leroy said. "Looks like we gonna have to find some way to get rid a you. Maybe we'll have a raffle, an' you can be the turkey."

"French kiss ma ass," Vanessa said.

"Where is she?" Leroy demanded, looking at Charlene but keeping a wary eye on Vanessa.

"Maybe she's out lookin' for a man," said Vanessa. "A real one."

"Now I'm tired a your shit, 'Nessa," Leroy said. "You keep your mouth shut or I'ma sick Cotton on you. He handles all ma light work."

Vanessa looked up at him. "Leroy, don't you *ever* make the mistake a thinkin' I'm light work." She held his gaze for a few seconds. Leroy dropped his eyes.

"Hi, people," said Leslie, removing Vanessa's purse and slipping into the vacant seat.

"Where the hell have you been?" demanded Leroy. "I had to stand around here wastin' time with this bitch sister a yours."

"Well, I gotta clean up after ma *husband*," Leslie said, "long as I'm still livin' with him." She gave Leroy a calculating look.

"Husband," said Charlene in disgust.

"Well now, I got some business to attend to," Leroy said. "Y'all drink whatever you wants; tell Nemo I said to put it on ma tab." He looked down at the top of Vanessa's head. "I'm buyin' you a drink, bitch."

"I don't want nothin'," Vanessa said.

"Shit. The day one a you bitches don't want somethin' is the day I gets elected President." He spun and walked off across the room.

"Sonofabitch," muttered Vanessa, waiting carefully until he had disappeared through a door marked OFFICE before she began massaging her shoulder.

"You better quit messin' with Leroy," said Charlene. "When you was goin' with him, that was one thing, but you ain't goin' with him no more."

"Damn right, I ain't," said Vanessa.

"I ain't gonna be able to stop him if he decides to mess you up," said Leslie.

"Listen here, honey. Don't you be forgettin' who is whose big sister. I don't need nobody to protect me from Leroy Briggs. Leroy ain't gonna do nothin' to me until he gets me back so he can dump me on ma ass. He can't quite figure out why I ain't cryin' after him."

"What *did* happen with you an' Leroy?" Charlene said.

Leslie looked at Vanessa, giving her a secret smile.

"You listen to me, Les," said Vanessa, "you get somethin' on Leroy so when he gets ready to dump you he can't do it as quick as he wants."

"He ain't never gonna want to get rid a me."

"He always does," said Charlene. "Look at 'Nessa."

"I'm different," said Leslie. "Ain't I, 'Nessa?"

"You knows it all, don't you?" said Vanessa. "Now she's gonna tell me how she can take care of herself."

"Where *you* gonna sleep tonight?" asked Leslie sweetly. She screwed up her face in surprise when Vanessa slapped her. "What you do that for?"

"Just so's you wouldn't get so cute you got to thinkin' cute was all there was."

"Hey," said Charlene brightly, "let's all have another drink."

Leslie looked at Vanessa, her eyelids low. Vanessa gazed back at her steadily. "Don't try an' teach your big sister to suck eggs," she said. "I was hungry long 'fore you was."

"You was lots a things 'fore I was," said Leslie.

"I was smart 'fore you was."

"You got so smart you got dumped."

"Hey, let's have another drink, y'all." Charlene waved to the bartender.

"Leroy Briggs is gonna beat you out an' use you up, an' then he's gonna send you on back to that broken-down janitor a yours. If you're lucky."

"You're jealous is all," Leslie said. "You wishes you still had him."

"He wasn't no prize."

"What you want, Les?" asked Charlene. Leslie said nothing. "I'll have another beer. What about you, Les?" Leslie glared at Vanessa in silence. "Bring her a Seven-and-Seven," Charlene said. "She always drinks Seven-and-Seven, don't you, Les? Seven-and-Seven?"

"I got him," Leslie said. "You wants him, an' I got him."

"Bring her a Seven-and-Seven. An' another one a them things for 'Nessa, a whatchemacallit. Put it on Leroy's tab."

"You can have him," said Vanessa.

"I got him."

"Oh, Jesus, will you stop it," said Charlene.

"He's gonna kick your ass."

"He kicked *your* ass. It don't have nothin' to do with mine."

The bartender arrived with the drinks, plopped them down on the table. "No, no, Nemo," said Charlene, "I get the beer. She gets the Seven-and-Seven. An' *she* gets that other thing. Leroy's payin' for it."

"Leroy ain't payin' for me," snapped Vanessa, whipping a dollar bill out of her purse. "I buy ma own drinks."

The whisk broom made staccato rustlings on the leather couch. Rayburn carefully brushed out the accumulation of dust and dirt, bending to the floor to scoop up a few pieces of change that had fallen from some businessman's pocket into the crack behind the cushions. He carefully scraped chewing gum from a quarter, dipping the coin for an instant in the bucket of greenchemical-smelling water beside him to loosen the gum and then rubbing it until only a few sticky vestiges remained at the nape of George Washington's neck, under his nose, and around his eyes. Dropping the quarter into his pocket he glanced around the reception area approvingly. The carpet still had to be vacuumed, but he would do that on the way out. Rayburn turned, accidentally kicking the bucket. A drop of cleaning fluid spattered onto the carpet. Rayburn cursed softly. He bent quickly, searching for a rag, but, finding none that was dry enough to suit him, he pulled off one of his gloves and rummaged in the pocket of his baggy green trousers for his own handkerchief. He wiped up the stuff, smiling when he saw that it had not had time to stain the carpet. He got to his feet, reached for the keys hanging at his side, found the right one by feel, opened the door to the private secretary's office, turned to get his bucket.

There was a cart for the bucket and brooms and vacuum cleaner, but Rayburn never brought the cart into the executive suite; it made marks on the carpet that he could never get out. Instead he lugged the bucket around and carried the big canister vacuum cleaner so he would not have to roll it on its casters, and kept the whisk broom and rags and furniture polish in his pockets. He hauled the bucket into the secretary's office and began to wipe down the furniture, working clockwise around the room, wiping everything that could take the strength of the cleaner without corroding. After he had wiped the desk and carefully replaced everything in the same position, he went around again with the dry rag, dusting the lampshades and the magazines on the table next to the soft chair where the VIPs got to wait, the metal file cabinet, and even the framed picture of the secretary's husband? son? boyfriend? on top of it. Rayburn had often wondered about that picture of a young white boy in an Army uniform, his head shaved clean so that his ears seemed to stick out, a broad smile on his face. Rayburn wondered where the soldier was now, what he was doing. The uniform was the same style as the one Rayburn had worn in the Korean war. Maybe they had been in the same company, he and the soldier. They might have fought in the same battles, perhaps saved each other's life. The secretary, Rayburn decided, was the soldier's mother, and she would have white hair, be plump and jolly, still wear seamed stockings. The soldier would be married now. Rayburn wondered where he would live. Maybe he had moved to California. Or maybe he would live in the city somewhere. Maybe in the rowhouses in South Philly, maybe on Christian Street, near the Italian market, just a few blocks from South Street. He'd work in a factory or drive a truck or a taxi. No, he'd work in a gas station, own a piece of it, maybe. Be a partner. The best mechanic around. He'd go in in the morning and sit around the office, and folks would bring in their cars and try to get him to work on 'em, an' he'd just set there drinkin' a Coke an' smilin', talk to 'em all about the weather until 'bout 'leven o'clock, an' then he'd get up an' eat his sandwiches an' go to work. Man, he'd run them cars outa there like they was on a conveyor belt. Folks that didn't even own a car would stand around just to watch him work. They'd ast where he learned to fix cars like that, but he wouldn't say anything; he'd be too busy fixin' to bother. So they'd ast each other, Hey, where'd this nigger learn to fix cars like that? An' somebody'd tell 'em, Aw, he fixed tanks in the Ko-reen war. Man knows how to fix a tank ain't gonna be worryin' 'bout no Ford long. Goddamn! folks'd say, that cat sure do work! 'Long about four o'clock, after he'd done fixed half a dozen cars, he'd quit an' go in an' set around the office for a while, drinkin' a little more Coke an' listenin' to the bell ring every time a car ran over the hose in front of the pumps. He wouldn't pump no gas, though—he'd have a boy to do that. 'Long about five-thirty the phone'd ring an' the boy'd answer it an' say there was somebody needed a tow, an' Rayburn'd tell him to go on out an' bring it on in, an' the boy'd go off in the wrecker. After a while he'd be back, haulin' a long pink Caddy. Rayburn'd take one look at the Caddy an' tell the boy to take it on down the street to the next station. There'd be this big man settin' up next to the boy an' he'd say, I thought you was gonna fix ma car. Rayburn'd spit on the sidewalk an' look at him an' say, I don't fix no Caddys. The dude'd say, But, goddammit, I got a date an' I'ma be needin' ma car, an' Rayburn'd tell him, Walk. If she really loves you she's gonna want to see you, car or no car. Now, boy, take the man on down the street. Tow's free. After a while the boy'd come back an' ast could he get off early. The boy'd say he had a date with his girl. Rayburn'd say sure, only go on home now an' clean up an' come back by a minute 'fore he left. Then he'd just set there, smilin' an' thinkin' while the boy run off, smokin' a cigar an' maybe drinkin' a beer now that he wasn't gonna have to be workin' much longer. Pretty soon the boy'd come back, all turned out in his knits an' a leather, an' Rayburn'd smile an' tell him he looked real fine. Then he'd say, Gone, now, an' take ma car. I ain't gonna be needin' it tonight. The boy'd look at him like he didn't think he heard right. Rayburn'd watch the boy pick up the keys an' go walkin' around the back like he was scared he might wake up, an' pretty soon he'd be back with the car. Rayburn'd wave at him an' the boy'd say he was gonna be careful, an' Rayburn'd tell him he better be careful or he'd end up married an' the boy'd grin an' get it in gear, an' Rayburn'd chuckle when the kid gunned it at the light an' caught rubber in second.

"Shit, nigger, you dreamin'! You ain't never gonna make that."

Cotton turned his massive head on his short thick neck and glared at Willie T.'s smooth coffee-colored face. "I'd make it if you was to let me alone long enough to get it lined up."

"Listen to him," crowed Willie T. " 'Lined up,' shit. Nigger can't shoot no pool."

"Let him shoot now, Willie," said Leroy absentmindedly. He pulled a cigar from his breast pocket, stuck it in his mouth, and inclined his head toward Willie T., who produced a match as if he had been waiting for the opportunity.

"He ain't gonna make it," said Willie T.

"That's ma business," said Cotton. "You gots to let me shoot ma shot."

"Why?" said Willie T. "You ain't gonna make it anyway."

"Sho' am," Cotton said. "I'ma cut a combination on the six ball an' just slide that fifteen in down there, an' then I'll be all set up for the eight ball in the side, an' that'll be your ass."

"Damn," said Willie T., "don't you know nothin' 'bout geometry? You ain't gonna do nothin' 'cept maybe knock ma six in for me, then *I'll* be set up for the eight ball."

"I'ma eight ball your ass if you don't let me shoot the damn thing," said Cotton.

"You stop fuckin' on Cotton now, Willie," said Leroy. He puffed on his cigar, filled the air with gray clouds.

Willie T. smiled slyly. "Gone now, Cotton, an' shoot you shot. Course, if I was you, I'd just shoot safety."

"Don't tell Cotton how to play his game," said Leroy.

"That's right," said Cotton, making a face at Willie T.

"All right," said Willie T., raising his hands in a gesture of surrender. "I was just tryin' to be helpful, maybe speed things up. This nigger's attemptin' to take all night losin' one damn game."

"Let him be," said Leroy. "I been thinkin' an' we gots more important things to worry about."

"Like what?" said Willie T.

"Like Gino movin' in on me."

"Shit," said Willie T. "Ain't no Gino gonna be movin' in on *us*. Gino don't want nothin' to do with no niggers. He don't like nobody that ain't Italian."

"Willie T., we're talkin' about money. Gino likes money moren he don't like anything."

"Gino ain't interested in takin' over our street—" Willie T. began.

"Whose street?" Leroy interrupted.

"Your street," said Willie T. "There's no way he *can* do it. We'd know the minute one a his muthafuckin' fools come around."

"All right," said Leroy, "*how* we gonna know? We gonna smell the spaghetti on his breath?"

"What you want me to say?" said Willie T.

"He's gonna be *white*," said Cotton.

"So what we got to worry about then?" said Willie T. "Maybe we oughta get rid a black shoe polish so we don't get faked."

"Sposin' they ain't white," said Cotton.

"You mean a black man?" said Willie T. incredulously. "A *nigger*? Workin' for *Gino*? Ain't nobody on this street crazy enough to work for Gino. An' he wouldn't have 'em anyways."

"There's niggers that don't live on the street," Leroy said. "Maybe he'd have one a them."

"That's what the paper said," said Cotton.

"What?" demanded Willie T. "You gonna shoot that shot or ain't you?"

"In a minute. The paper said all the big time wops is into hirin' niggers now. They all turnin' into Equal Opportunity Employers. Got the brothers sellin' dope, runnin' numbers, hustlin' broads, even turnin' 'em on to real heavy shit, contracts an' stuff. Got brothers comin' back from Vietnam that kills baddern any damn wop in the *world*. It was in the *Philadelphia Inquirer*."

"More likely the *National Inquirer*," said Willie T.

"Gone, Cotton," said Leroy, "everybody knows you can't read."

"I can hear," said Cotton in wounded tones. "Fella stands on the corner peddlin' his papers, shouts everythin' in 'em. I ain't got to read. I just stands there, pretty soon I done heard it all."

"Dog," said Leroy.

"Dog, shit," said Willie T. "I don't care what the paper says. I don't trust no damn *Inquirer* anyways."

"Willie T.'s a college boy," said Cotton. "He don't believe the sky's blue 'less he reads it in the *Temple Free Press*."

"Shit," said Willie T. "That ain't nothin' but a load a shit."

"I run into one the other night," Leroy said.

"What?"

"In Lightnin' Ed's. Muthafucka said he worked for Gino. I damn near choked on the spot."

"Heard about that," said Willie T.

"Yeah?" snarled Leroy. "Just what did you hear?"

"Oh, ah, nothin', you know, nothin'," said Willie T.

"Yeah, well," said Leroy. "You get that smile off your face while you still got a face."

Willie T. stopped smiling.

"An' don't believe everything you hear."

"Never do," said Willie T.

"Whooeee," said Cotton. Willie T. and Leroy turned to see the six ball cut gently off the edge of the fifteen and send it into the corner pocket. Cotton smiled, looked at Willie T. "I'ma eight ball you ass," he said.

"Where the hell is he?" muttered Leslie.

"He be along," said Charlene. There were now seven beer bottles in echelon before her. "He be along. Leroy's always 'long sooner or later." She giggled tipsily.

"How you know?" said Leslie quickly. Charlene ignored her. Leslie looked at her watch. "I gotta be gettin' home."

"Why?" said Vanessa. "To go to bed with the janitor?"

"Like I said before, where you gonna sleep tonight, big sister?"

"At *ma* place, in *ma* bed, by *ma* self, an' don't let none a these simple niggers tell you different."

"Tut, tut, tut," said Leslie. "Poor 'Nessa's gotta sleep by herself one time. Can't you find nobody to tuck you in, 'Nessa? Well, Leroy did say you was a lousy fuck."

"Leroy says lots a things. He thinks he's the biggest dick on the street, an' all he is is the fattest prick. Tell me somethin', little sister, just what makes you think you're such a hot piece, just 'cause you married some old janitor you had to learn how to fuck?"

"Don't you mess on ma Rayburn, now," said Leslie. "He does what little he can."

"I don't know what you don't let that poor man alone," said Charlene. "There ain't no harm in him."

"An' what the hell good is a man ain't got no harm in him?" snapped Vanessa. "A *real* man's always got some kinda harm in him."

"Listen to her," said Leslie, " 'A real man.' Shit! The only real man she ever had left her high and dry like an old whore on a bar stool."

"I know more 'bout men than you'll ever know," Vanessa said, taking a swallow from her glass.

"You know more than I ever *want* to know," Leslie said.

Charlene looked around quickly. "No sign a Leroy, we better have another drink."

"She's had enough," said Leslie.

"Don't you try an' take care a me," said Vanessa. "I can take care a maself. I was hustlin' in bars when you was still suckin' titty."

Leslie sighed. "C'mon now, 'Nessa, everybody knows you ain't but four years oldern me."

"All right," said Vanessa. "You think you seen shit, an' you ain't seen no shit no way. You wasn't there when he come home."

"Oh, Christ, 'Nessa, don't be startin' that again."

"Who?" said Charlene.

"Don't you Christ me. You wasn't there, an' he wasn't neither. I was there—"

"You're drunk."

"Me an' Lindalee." Vanessa leaned forward, smiled drunkenly. "We was just settin' there, talkin' an' laughin'. She was talkin' 'bout some boy. I wasn't nothin' but 'leven, I didn't know nothin' 'bout no boys. I guess Lindalee didn't neither. God, she was pretty. I guess them boys was busy tryin' to find out all 'bout her. We was settin' there, an' then we heard him comin' up the stairs, you know, slow an' draggy, like he always done. He ain't been back in five year, but we knowed it was him, 'cause he always walked just like that. He come right in the door an' he looks at Lindalee an' me, an' he says, 'Get me somethin' t'eat.' After five years! I was too damn scared to do anything, but Lindalee, she looks him straight in the eye an' tells him to get out. Said we wasn't gonna be givin' him nothin'. She stood right up to him. Only then he hauled off an' hit her upside the head, knocked her right up against the wall, an' she hit it with her face. Lord Jesus, I never had to look, I could *hear* things bustin'. She never even made a sound, just slid right down like she was made outa rubber, an' there was blood all over the wall."

"Jesus, 'Nessa—"

"Shut up," said Vanessa. "Shut up." Her voice was dull, her body limp. "He said 'Jesus' just like you done. Only there wasn't no Jesus there. Then he set down on the chair an' looked at her lyin' on the damn floor, bleedin'. An' then that fat piece a shit started to cry! There was big, fat tears rollin' down his cheeks an' he was sobbin' like a damn baby an' he kept sayin' over an' over, 'I didn't mean no harm, I didn't mean no harm.' An' all the sudden I wasn't scared no more, an' I got me the butcher knife an' I put it up against his throat. I just laid it up against him an' cut him, just a little. An' then he stopped cryin' an' looked up at me. He had little beady eyes, just like a rat. I told him I was gonna cut his throat, an' all he says was, 'I didn't mean no harm.' I told him I was gonna let him bleed to death so slow it was gonna take forever. An' he started beggin' an' blubberin'. Beggin' a little girl wouldn't she please let him live! I couldn't cut him after that. I just told him to get outa there." Vanessa stopped suddenly. Her eyes were closed.

"You shoulda killed him," Leslie said. "I woulda killed him."

"Let's have another drink," said Charlene, motioning for the bartender.

"I don't want no more," said Vanessa. Her eyes were soft, misty. "I don't want no more." She rose unsteadily and picked up her handbag. Her body swayed gracefully. Without a word she turned and walked out.

Charlene motioned for the bartender again. "She tellin' the truth?"

"I don't know," Leslie said, staring at her glass. "Mama had took me to prayer meetin' or some fool thing. When we got back, 'Nessa was settin' in the middle a the floor holdin' a butcher knife, had Lindalee's head in her lap. Lindalee was all messed up. Never did look right afterwards. Wasn't right in the head, neither. They finally put her away."

Charlene looked at the door. "You sure she's gonna be all right?"

"Shit," said Leslie. "Ain't none of us never gonna be all right."

Jake shuffled along Eighteenth Street, his mismatched Salvation Army surplus brogans making scraping sounds on the pavement. He turned the corner and headed west toward Lightnin' Ed's. Just beyond Nineteenth he ran head-on into Elmo. "Hey there," said Elmo.

"Hey," said Jake unenthusiastically, moving to go by.

Elmo moved to block. "Where you headed in such a hurry?"

"What say?" said Jake, trying to cut by on the inside.

Elmo stuck out a scrawny arm and barred the way. "Don't give me that deaf shit, you ain't any deafer than you wants to be."

"I ain't goin' nowheres," Jake said.

"You goin' nowheres in a mighty hurry. You got somethin' goin', you can't fool me. You got some money?"

"I works for ma money," Jake snapped.

"I don't care how you gets it, shinin' shoes or pissin' in the air, either you got money to buy wine with, or you got the wine, an' I wants some wine."

"I ain't got no wine," Jake said. He blew his breath at Elmo. Elmo made a face.

"I know you're holdin' out on me."

"I said, I ain't got no damn wine."

"I know what you said. An' I know when I see some wino goin' hell for leather and lickety-split, either his underwear's on fire or he's chasin' somethin', which in your case has *got* to be wine, 'cause you're too damn old for women."

"I'm busy," Jake said. "Lemme be."

"I'll let you be, all right. I'm goin' with you."

"I ain't goin' nowheres," Jake said.

"Fine," said Elmo. "I wasn't goin' nowheres, neither. We can go nowheres together. Pretty soon you gonna figure out you can't have no wine without me havin' some too."

"I ain't after no wine, I'm just doin' a friendly favor for somebody."

"Friendly favor, ma black ass. Winos ain't got no friends, 'cept a glass a wine. Or maybe a beer. That's it, you black bastard, you got a line on some beer!"

"Shit," Jake sighed. "All right. C'mon."

The two of them started off down the street. Jake kept pulling ahead. "Take it easy," panted Elmo.

"I'm in a hurry," said Jake.

"How far we goin'?"

"Lightnin' Ed's. There's somethin' I got to tell Leo."

"What?"

"All 'bout layovers to catch meddlers," Jake said.

"Say," said Elmo, stopping in his tracks, "did you ever find that dude you been lookin' for?"

"What dude?" said Jake.

"Don't give me that shit. I heard this mornin' 'bout you runnin' around offerin' everybody free wine if they could tell you anything 'bout that dude that backed down Leroy. Looks like somebody wants to know that dude's name. Now you runnin' to see Leo like he was on his deathbed or somethin'. Now where is a wino gonna be gettin' free wine? Why, from a bar. An' who's got a bar? Leo. So who wants to know the dude's name? Leo."

"We already knows his name," Jake said.

"Yeah. It's Jackson."

Jake snorted. "I ain't fell for that kinda shit in forty years, Elmo. Quit tryin' to pump me. Now come on, we got to get to Ed's."

"Wait a minute," said Elmo. "You don't want me to go along with you. How come?"

"You got bad breath," Jake said.

"Shit," said Elmo. "I don't much want to go up there neither."

"How come?" Jake said innocently. "You 'fraid maybe you might run into Rayburn?"

"I ain't scared a no Rayburn," Elmo said. "I just don't want to be walkin' that far." Jake smiled. "I'll make you a deal," Elmo said. "I won't go with you if you tell me what the dude's name was."

Jake considered the proposition. "Okay," he said. "Name's Brown."

"Shit," said Elmo. "i coulda thought up a better one than that. Everybody's name's Brown."

"I done told you the dude's name," Jake said.

"You ain't told me nothin'."

Jake sighed. "C'mon then. Maybe we can get in an' out 'fore Rayburn comes by. Be a shame if he was to find you when he was between you an' the door."

"Dude's name really Brown?"

"I done said so."

"All right," Elmo said.

Jake turned and hurried on up the street, glancing back to make sure Elmo wasn't following. He ducked through the door of Lightnin' Ed's, waved to a few people seated along the bar, and took a stool at the far end. Leo came trundling over like a white-aproned cement truck. "How you doin', Jake? What'll it be?"

"Glass a wine," Jake said. He fumbled in his pocket, found some change, pushed it across the bar. Leo poured him a glass of muscatel and took a nickel. "I ain't been too good, Leo," Jake said. "Stomach again. But listen, you remember that dude was in here Saturday?" Leo nodded. "Yeah, well, I found out he was around today, an' he was lookin' for a place."

"Jesus," said Leo softly. "I hope Leroy don't find out."

"That ain't all. The place he was lookin' at was right across from the Elysium. Same place as Rayburn."

"Jesus!" said Leo.

Jake nodded agreement. "You think maybe him an' Rayburn—"

"Naw," said Leo. "Rayburn don't know nothin' 'bout Leroy messin' with his woman."

"That's good," Jake said.

"Yeah, well," said Leo, "let's just hope it stays that way." He reached down and pulled up the half-full bottle of muscatel. "Here," he said. "You done earned it."

"Why, thank you," Jake said solemnly.

"I gotta be doin' some work," Leo said, glancing at the television screen which showed a batter in a Philadelphia uniform missing a pitch by several feet. "Gone an' help yourself. An' let me know if you hear anything else."

"Sure, Leo, sure," said Jake. Leo trundled away. Jake sipped at the wine for a minute, then hungrily gulped the rest. He reached out a trembling hand and poured the glass full again. He gazed in awe at the immense quantity of wine remaining in the bottle and moved his lips silently as if in private prayer. Then he raised the glass with all the reverence due the Holy Grail, extended his lower lip, and poured the wine in in a slow, tantalizing dribble. He rolled it around in his mouth as if he were a French wine taster evaluating some rare and costly vintage, swallowed, and then, smiling contentedly, he poured the glass full again.

"Who the hell is it?" roared Leroy. He put his hands on Leslie's thin shoulders and pushed her head away from his body. She moaned and wriggled on top of him.

"It's me, Willie."

"I told you I didn't want no interruptions!" shouted Leroy. "Cut that out," he said to Leslie, who was nibbling at his left nipple. He pushed her head away again, but she wriggled her hips again, too.

"Cotton says it's important."

"What the hell does he know," yelled Leroy. Leslie drew back and then let her body fall full upon him. "Jesus, stop that," said Leroy. "Don't be in such a hurry for everything. You're always in such a goddamn hurry."

"You comin', Leroy?" yelled Willie T.

"He's comin'," giggled Leslie, "he's comin' all right."

"Oh Jesus, boss," said Willie T., "I didn't know you was still . . ."

Leroy rolled over on top of Leslie and proceeded to do an imitation of a runaway pile driver.

"Ahhh," said Leslie.

"Oh, Jesus," muttered Willie T. He stepped away from the door, then he stepped back and put his ear right up against it. "Maybe it wasn't all that important, boss," he yelled. "I'll tell Cotton to handle it hisself." He listened carefully but no sound came through the door except a couple of moans, assorted gasps, and the creakings of the bed.

"Ahhhh," Leslie said again, biting at the fist she held to her mouth.

"Thank God," muttered Leroy. "Christ, you like to kill a man. You're worse than the goddamn Internal Revenue."

"Ummm," said Leslie, biting at him.

Leroy pulled away and climbed out of bed.

"Maybe it ain't all that important," yelled Willie T.

Leroy pulled on his pants and headed for the door with his purple-and-turquoise shirt dangling over his arm. He opened the door and charged out, running full tilt into the side of Willie T.'s head. "Oww!" said Leroy, clutching at his groin. "What the hell was you doin' down there?"

"I was just tryin'—"

"Yeah, well you keep on tryin' an' I'ma roast your ass for Thanksgivin'. Now what's all this shit about?"

"I dunno," said Willie T., trailing Leroy down the hall. "Cotton just said to come get you, somethin' was poppin'."

Leroy grunted. On the way down the stairs he slipped his arms into the sleeves of his shirt, and he entered the barroom of the Elysium with his belly showing like a wide brown necktie. He stopped at the bar and slapped sharply on the wood. The bartender left the customer he had been waiting on and hurried over. "The usual," said Leroy. While he waited, Leroy looked at Willie T. "That gal is like to kill a man."

"Yeah," said Willie T. "Either that, or get him kilt."

"Shit," said Leroy. He accepted his drink from the bartender and marched off into the office.

Cotton was standing by the pool table, his hands folded, Buddha-like, across his belly. "Sorry to drag you away," Cotton said, "but to tell you the truth I was thinkin' maybe you'd be dyin' for a break."

"You tryin' to say I might be tired?"

Cotton smiled. "Well," he said tactfully, "let's just say ain't nobody can fill up the 'Lantic Ocean spittin'. 'Sides, this here might be important. I was settin' up to the bar when in comes this dude an' asts for you."

"Whad he look like?" Leroy snapped.

"He was just a wino, I seen him around a million times. Don't get so damn jumpy."

"I ain't jumpy, nigger," shouted Leroy.

"No," Cotton said. "You ain't jumpy. You just in a hurry to get back upstairs an' see if you really can fuck yourself to death."

"C'mon," said Leroy, " 'fore I bashes your face in."

Cotton smiled enigmatically. "Anyways, this here wino, he says he's got some information for you."

"What kinda information."

"He said it was a name."

"A name? Shit, I already got a name. Where is this fool?"

"Willie T.," said Cotton. "Go get that wino I left out there with Charlene." Willie T. went out. "I left him with Charlene," Cotton explained, " 'cause he looked like he might run."

"That was on account a Charlene," Leroy said. "That bitch litters every time some fool winks at her."

In a minute Willie T. returned with Elmo in tow. "Hi there, Mr. Briggs," said Elmo.

"What's this shit about a name?"

"It's a name," Elmo said. "Ain't no shit. Everybody's got a name."

Leroy looked at Cotton. "You hauled me outa bed so's I could play games with some simple wino?"

"Even fellas in bars that makes other fellas in bars eat shit got names," Elmo said.

"What?" said Leroy, spinning around.

"I said—"

"I know what you said," said Leroy

"An' you better not say it again," said Willie T.

"Or you ain't gonna have no face to say it with," finished Cotton.

"I didn't mean no harm."

"Yeah, well," said Willie T.

"Never mind," said Leroy. "I think I know what you're talkin' about, an' I think I know who you're talkin' about, so cut the shit an' start talkin' about 'em."

"I can't," said Elmo. "Ma throat's too dry."

"I see," said Leroy. "Willie. Get the man a drink." Willie T. vanished and returned a minute later with a glass of red wine. Elmo snatched it out of his hands and tossed it off. "Fine," said Leroy. "Now talk."

"All right," said Elmo. "But I wants more outa this than just one lil' drinkee. Why, in order to tell you what you want to know I gots to betray the secrets of a friend." Elmo held the empty glass over his breast and looked sorrowful. "That don't come cheap."

"Cotton," Leroy said, "soon as this gentleman betrays this great secret, you tell Nemo to give him wine for a week."

"Why that's mighty nice a yeaugh—" said Elmo as Leroy grasped him by his skinny throat and hoisted him high in the air.

"What's his name?" demanded Leroy, his eyes burning.

"Yeaugh," said Elmo.

"Talk, damn you!" shouted Leroy.

"He can't talk," said Cotton.

"What?" shouted Leroy.

"You're chokin' him, Leroy," said Cotton. "He can't hardly talk while you're chokin' him."

"Oh," said Leroy. "Oh." He looked at Elmo, whose tongue was beginning to hang out, seeming surprised to find him there on the end of his arm. "Oh." He dropped Elmo. Elmo sagged against the pool table. Cotton held him up. Elmo gulped like a beached catfish.

"What's his name?" said Cotton.

"Breghn," said Elmo.

"Whad he say?" said Leroy.

"Beats me," said Willie T.

"Christ, Leroy," said Cotton. "You gotta be more careful. You like to killed him."

"He ain't gonna die," said Leroy. "Ain't no wino gonna be dyin' when he's got all that free drinkin' comin', soon as he tells me . . ."

"Bra—Brah, Brahn," said Elmo, with difficulty.

"Brown," said Cotton.

"Braghn," said Elmo.

"Brown?" said Willie T.

"Brown," said Elmo, swallowing heavily.

"Shit," said Leroy. "That's a lot a help."

"Yeah," said Cotton disgustedly. "Let's get him outa here."

"What about ma wine?" said Elmo, recovering rapidly.

"Cotton," said Leroy, "tell Nemo this fool can have three drinks. Tonight. That ain't worth no damn week."

"That ain't right," protested Elmo. "You ain't keepin' your word."

"Nobody ever keeps promises to niggers," snarled Leroy. "Ain't you heard? You find out some more an' we'll see about the week. Now beat it."

Willie T. took his cue and propelled a still-protesting Elmo through the door.

"Everybody's named Brown," said Cotton. "We sure as hell ain't gonna be lookin' him up in no phone book."

"You ain't," said Willie T. "You can't read."

"Fuck you," said Cotton, "an' fuck the duck that laid you."

"Least I can get laid," said Willie T. "You just roll."

"Shut up," said Leroy, who was staring at the wall with a look on his face that would have done credit to Genghis Khan. His eyebrows were pulled down low. His mouth was twisted. Little beads of sweat stood out on his forehead. "I wanna know who he is. An' I wanna know where he is. An' I wanna know now. You get on it. Take the damn Street apart if you have to."

"Ah, can't it wait until mornin'?" Cotton said. "It's nearly two."

"What the hell's that got to do with it?"

"Folks don't generally hang out in bars after closin' time. It's kinda dark."

Leroy glared at him. "I don't care about that. I want results." He stared into space and smiled thinly. "Results. You all get to work. You find me this Brown fucker. Fast."

PART TWO

Shadow-spoor on a city street
Tells a tale of the aching time
When hate and anger and sorrow meet
Merging in a soundless cry
And I have walked the line.

Brown bloodstain on a peeling wall
Trace of violent proud despair,
Of stumbles with noplace left to fall,
Of an old man's empty wine-breath sigh,
And I have seen him crawl.

Will You look down from on high
Upon the lives You have forsaken?
And when You come again to find
Your ass is butchered and Your manger's taken
By some black barking whorebitch's bastard babe
Squalling and shitting on Your hay
Will You smile, will You sigh,
Or will You loose Your righteous wrath
And call for the Judgment Day?

And I have walked, armed with ear and eye, through the
dark mysterious unmapped streets, stalked the wild wailing
wino in his lair of yesterday's paper and last week's puke,
observed the exotic mating dance of that vanishing species,
the two-buck whore, witnessed the march of the great gray
rat. . . .
And LIVED! To write the memoirs that the National Geographic
would not buy.

And I have seen an old man die,
Felt his fingers stiffen in my hand
As his spirit returned to the Motherland,
Walking onward without fear,
Knowing that Hell was only here,
That there could be no worse.

Men fight men in a jungle dance with violent steps.
And in the bleachers clapping hands cast the vote of who goes free:
White thumbs turn, white fingers twitch
The strings of lives, and cut the threads.

But white ears seldom hear the cries,
For all the shouts, screams, sobs, and sighs
Are drowned out by the roaring gears
And covered by the rolling years,
As the City passes by.

                              —Brown

4 Tuesday

"Haw, haw, haw," laughed Big Betsy the whore, "haw, haw, haw. Pour me another one, Leo. Haw, haw, haw."

Leo glanced up from the sink. "Ain't you 'bout had enough?"

"Yeah," said Big Betsy. "Of you."

"I ain't got time to be carryin' you home tonight," Leo warned.

"I wouldn't go home with a piece a shit like you. I got standards."

"Shit," said Leo, "what you got is a welfare check."

"Some folks is lucky," said Big Betsy, "an' can afford to have standards all the time. I has standards when I can afford to. Now pour me another drink or by God I'll drink someplace else."

Leo chuckled to himself and poured Betsy another drink. She fumbled in her purse and fished out a bill, shoving it aimlessly across the bar. Leo saw the hand come out toward him, the fingers fat, sweating, tiny hairs growing out from the knuckles. Round metal bracelets on Betsy's arms jangled musically for an instant before the sound was smothered in rolls of flesh. Leo closed his eyes. "It's on the house," he said.

Betsy shoved her lower lip out, laid her head on her shoulder. "You ain't tryin' to—"

"Betsy, c'mon now, you know me bettern that. We been friends a long time."

"That's true," said Big Betsy. "An' that's just why I asked. I don't want

79

you to be gettin' no wrong ideas. I mean, I like you an' all, but you just ain't my type, you know what I mean?"

"Yeah, sure," said Leo, looking at Big Betsy's bouncing chins and breathing a sigh of relief.

"You ain't mad, are you?" said Big Betsy. "I wasn't tryin' to hurt your feelin's."

"No, sure, I understand," said Leo. "Drink up, huh? It's gettin' late."

"Sure," said Big Betsy. As she raised her gin she looked around. "By Jesus, we got the whole damn place to ourselves."

"Yeah," said Leo. "Tuesday night, ain't never much business."

"Tuesday's a real crock a shit," agreed Big Betsy.

Leo drew himself a glass of beer and downed it in slow, reflective swallows.

"Hey, Leo," said Big Betsy.

"What?" said Leo absentmindedly.

"We spent a lot a time in here together, you an' me. Seems like we're always the last ones here."

"Yeah," said Leo.

"You know, Leo, bein' a hooker is a crock a shit. Can't hardly make a decent buck no more."

"It's rough," Leo agreed.

"Damn right, it's rough. An' you know what's doin' it? It's the goddamn Pill, that's what. Useta be, a dude wanted a good time an' no worries, he'd go find hisself a hooker. Now they got these teen-age pieces a ass layin' for free, ain't got nothin' to lose on account a that damn Pill. But that ain't the worse part of it. You know what the worst part of it is?" She paused to glance at Leo, who was looking at the wall, his eyes flat and abstracted. "The hell of it is," Big Betsy continued, "you know they ain't no damn good. You know them little teen-age pieces a shit don't do nothin' but wiggle their ass an' call it a fuck. Ain't that right? Leo?"

"Yeah, yeah, sure, right." He looked at her, his eyes focusing slowly. "Yeah."

"Damn right," said Big Betsy. She tipped her glass back and drained it. "These girls nowadays ain't got no notion what a man's all about. Not like I do. I seen enough to know. You know somethin', Leo? Men is gettin' scarce. Somebody must be killin' 'em off or somethin'. Most a these dudes around here is little pieces a ape shit, two beers an' they're under the table, come one time an' they done shot their wad. Rest of 'em's fags. A real man, that's what I want. Like that dude was in here the other night. Or like you," she said, batting her eyes.

Leo stood holding his empty glass. Betsy's words went in his ear and banged around for a while before they began to penetrate the fatigue fog over his brain. Awareness stole over him. He looked at Big Betsy. Big Betsy smiled. Reactions chased themselves across Leo's features: disbelief, amazement, terror. He closed his eyes and blindly drew a beer from the tap and swallowed it in two very rapid gulps. He waited until the beer had descended the full length of his esophagus. Then he opened his eyes. "I think it's time to close up," Leo said.

Big Betsy drew back as if she had been slapped. "Yeah, sure." She removed herself from the stool by leaning over and allowing gravity to clutch at the sagging mountains of her breasts and belly and drag her down. She caught herself with her feet on the floor and one hand on the edge of the bar, the wood creaking as it took her weight. Her purse swung, open, from her free hand. She sighed, squinted, sniffed, giggled a little.

"You need help?" said Leo.

Big Betsy's head had sunk down onto her chest, her chin resting on her bosom. She turned it slowly, without raising it, and looked at Leo. "Shit," she said. Slowly she straightened her spine against the pull of gravity. She squared her shoulders. She closed her purse with a snap. "Shit," she said again. With measured steps she marched toward the door. In the opening she turned and looked at Leo. "You been a bartender too long, Leo," she said with great dignity. "You done pickled your prick in alcohol." She turned and advanced on the darkness.

Leo shook his head, bent over, and quickly finished washing the glasses. Then he went to the door and locked it, removed his apron, checked the booths to make sure no butt smoldered in the ashtrays or on the floor. He looked around and decided he would clean up in the morning. He went back behind the bar and took the money out of the register, put it in a zippered pouch. He put on his jacket, checked his gun, and went to the door. Before turning off the last light he paused and looked over the darkened bar, smiling tiredly into the shadows. Then he flipped off the light, checked the street carefully with one hand on his gun, closed and locked the door, and began the walk home.

Speedy came down the street cursing. He passed the State Store with its screened windows and locked doors and his cursing became louder. He reached the entrance to Lightnin' Ed's Bar and Grill, paused hopefully to pull on the handle, but the door refused to budge. Sadly he turned and walked on, peering through the windows and trying the doors of every bar he passed. The entire street was empty except for an occasional car and the subtle motion of shadows where, a block ahead of him, someone wandered through the darkness. At the corner of Seventeenth and South Speedy stopped and waited while a red-and-white police cruiser pulled through the intersection. The car slowed while one of the officers took a good long, slow, thorough, look at Speedy. Speedy grinned widely and waved. The car accelerated and turned the corner. "Muthafucka," Speedy muttered, letting the grin dissolve.

He walked despondently onward, no longer bothering to peer in windows. The Street was shut—tight. Suddenly, at the mouth of an alley, he stopped and sniffed the air. "Naw," he said softly. "Naw, it couldn't be." He sniffed again, shrugged, and ventured cautiously in. His feet moved carefully and slowly, skillfully avoiding the litter and garbage that covered the cobblestones. His breath came in short, quick snorts. His body was a taut bow of expectation. He peered into the gloom.

"Christ, quit breathin' so goddamn loud," came a voice from the dark depths. "Jesus, you wanna wake up the world?"

"Jake? That you?"

"Didn't I tell you to keep it down? Course it's me. This is ma damn alley, ain't it? Come on in."

Speedy moved to the back of the alley and found Jake sitting comfortably propped against two garbage cans. As his eyes adjusted to the darkness Speedy was able to make out the shape of an empty wine bottle beside Jake's leg. Cradled against Jake's stomach was a second bottle that Speedy's intuition told him was not half-empty. Sticking out of Jake's jacket pocket was something that might have been the neck of a third bottle. Speedy's mouth watered. "Hiya, Jake," he said. "How you been?"

"Not too good," Jake said. "Ma stomach's been botherin' me again. All that rotgut I been drinkin' I figure. So I treated maself to some good stuff." He nodded at the empty bottle.

Speedy accepted the implied invitation and picked up the empty bottle. "Hell," he said, as he attempted to read the label, "it's too dark in here to see shit."

"Don't need to see it," Jake said, "there's plenty a shit in here."

"Humph," Speedy said. His adjusted eyes could make out the label. "Damn!" he exclaimed, "this *is* good stuff. Musta cost a fortune."

"Well," said Jake modestly, "it wasn't 'zactly cheap."

"How much?"

"Ah, buck an' a quarter."

"A *bottle?* Jesus!"

Jake shook his head. "I just can't take too much a that cheap shit no more. I figure, a man oughta treat hisself to some comfort in his last years. I ain't as young as I useta be."

"That's true," said Speedy, his natural tact dulled by lust.

"What you mean by that?" Jake snapped.

"What, well, I mean, damn, Jake, there ain't nobody as young as they used to be."

"Humph," Jake said, somewhat mollified. "I guess there ain't. I guess if there was somebody as young as he useta be, I guess that would be pretty goddamn perculiar."

"You're right, there," Speedy said.

"Hell," Jake snapped, "you don't need to be tellin' me that. You youngbloods ain't as smart as you thinks."

"Oh, I definitely agree with that," Speedy said. "Course we does the best we can without havin' the experience. . . ."

"Have a drink," Jake said, proffering the bottle. Speedy, touched, reached out and took the bottle, raised it quickly to his lips. Rich aroma filled his nostrils. He took a swallow and managed to get the bottle away from his mouth before Jake's hand closed around it.

"Thanks," Speedy said.

"Damn near drank the whole bottle," grumbled Jake. "You young-bloods don't know how to 'preciate good wine. Y'aint sposed to guzzle it. You—sips it." He held the bottle up to the sky and peered at it. There were about four ounces remaining. Jake shook his head sadly, tipped the bottle to his mouth, swallowed twice. "Dead," he pronounced, and interred the carcass reverently beside its brother. He leaned back against the garbage cans and folded his hands over his stomach. "Ahhh," he said. Speedy ascertained that the object in Jake's pocket was definitely a third bottle.

"Those goddamn honkies," Speedy said. "Kept me up there doin' simple ass shit till after closin' time. Here I sits, money in ma damn pocket, an' all the damn bars is closed."

"Money?" Jake said. "What from?"

"Tips. Helpin' little old white ladies with their groceries. Shit like that."

"Humph. What you gonna do with it?"

"Can't do nothin' with it if all the bars is closed. What else you gonna do with money, 'sides buy wine?"

"That's true," said Jake.

"Shit," Speedy continued. "Man works all damn day, openin' the door, closin' the door—heavy damn door, too—bowin' an' scrapin' to them white folks; after a day a that shit, a man needs his pleasure. Why if somebody was to walk up to me an' say, 'Speedy, I know where you can get your ass a nice bottle a wine,' why I'd wanna kiss that dude an' call him Jesus for sure."

"I know what you mean," Jake said. "I felt that way maself, many a time."

"Sure," Speedy said. "Everybody do. Time like this, you don't care how much you gotta be payin' for a bottle."

"Sure you would," Jake said, peering at Speedy from under half-closed eyelids. "I bet you wouldn't pay a dollar an' a half."

"Bet I would, if it was good wine. If a man wants to drink after the bars is closed, he's gotta expect to pay for it, an' he can't be gettin' too particular. But for a dollar an' a half, wine'd have to be pretty good."

"How 'bout that stuff I had?"

"That was good stuff," Speedy admitted. "Shame there ain't no more."

"Well, I'll tell you," Jake said. "Just so happens I got a bottle left." He pulled it out of his pocket and handed it over.

Speedy accepted it reverently. "Why, thank you," Speedy said. "You gonna be lettin' me pay you for this, I know."

Jake stiffened and sat up. "Pay?" he said in outraged tones. "Course not. We friends. You'll be doin' the same for me one day."

"Why, thank you," said Speedy. "I sure will be. You ma main man." He examined the bottle, fished out his pocket knife, opened the corkscrew blade, and set to work. "You know," he said between grunts, "maybe what I oughta do is to give you some money now, just in case I wasn't handy when you was needin' me to return the favor. I mean, you got your steady place here, but I move around."

Jake closed his eyes to consider the suggestion.

"Now look," Speedy continued. "You take tomorrow for instance. You might wake up an' decide you wanted some wine, an' you be reachin' for it, but you done already give it to me. An' where am I? God knows. You're stuck. But if I was to leave you some money, when you reaches for the bottle you be findin' some change. Now that's even bettern wine, 'cause you can go on down to the State Store an' drink what you is in the mood for then 'stead a havin' to drink what you was in the mood for before."

"You done convinced me," Jake said.

The cork emerged with a loud pop. Speedy fished into his pocket and came up with a handful of change. Bending low, he counted out a dollar fifty in dimes and quarters and dumped it into Jake's outstretched palm. Jake wrapped the money up in a corner of his handkerchief. "Thank you, Speedy," he said solemnly, and blew his nose.

Speedy tilted the bottle to his lips. He took two big swallows with his eyes closed, feeling the wine course down his parched throat. Then he placed his tongue against the mouth of the bottle and swallowed three or four times without actually drinking anything. He opened his eyes slightly. Jake sat with his handkerchief against his nose, his red eyes gazing passionately at the bottle. With each bob of Speedy's Adam's apple Jake clenched his hands, licked his lips nervously, and shook a little. Speedy took one more real swallow and lowered the bottle. "That's fine stuff," he said.

Jake stared straight ahead. "It's all right," he said.

"Here," said Speedy, handing the bottle over. Jake gaped at him, grabbed the bottle, and took two small sips. "Go on," said Speedy. "Christ, if it wasn't for you, I'd be dry."

Jake took one big gulp, rolled his eyes, lowered the bottle. "You're one fine youngblood, youngblood," Jake said.

Speedy smiled and took the bottle. He held it for a moment, feeling its odd shape. "You know somethin'?"

"I knows lotsa things," Jake said. "Which one you speakin' of?"

"Wine," Speedy said. "Funny how it comes in all different shaped bottles when you get away from the cheap stuff."

"Yeah," Jake said. "I guess rich folks is into variety."

"Yeah," Speedy said. "You know, I been thinkin' 'bout women."

"I don't know nothin' 'bout women," Jake said. "It's easier."

"Yeah," said Speedy. He sighed, drank, lowered the bottle, and handed it to Jake. "All the same . . . You know, Jake, sometimes I wishes I had me a woman. Don't you?"

Jake peered at him over the top of the bottle. "Hell no," he said. "What the hell would I be wantin' a woman for? I'm damn near seventy-five."

"I didn't know you was that old," Speedy said.

"That ain't old," Jake said, "that's just outa childhood. Just old enough to know bettern to be messin' with women."

Speedy chuckled and accepted the bottle, sipped at it, held it in his lap. "I useta have me a woman, when I lived up to Fifty-second Street. She was all right."

"What happened?" Jake said.

"Aw, she run off. Said I drank too much."

"They all say that," Jake said. "Wine an' women mixes like niggers an' white folks. Me, I'll take niggers an' wine, let them white folks an' women be. That how come you moved down here?" Speedy did not notice. He was staring into the darkness deeper in the alley. Jake reached for the bottle, but Speedy did not move. Jake pulled it away from him.

"Yeah," Speedy said finally, "that's when I moved down here."

Jake drank and looked over at Speedy without lowering the bottle. Speedy did not seem interested, so Jake took his turn for him. Then he took his own next turn. Then he handed the bottle back. Speedy roused, accepted it, took a long drink. "How come you be thinkin' 'bout women all the sudden?"

"Got this friend," Speedy said. "He's havin' woman problems." Speedy raised the bottle, drank, and extended it.

"Hold it a second," Jake said. He groaned, tried to get up. "Shit," he said. He rolled over onto his side, unzipped his fly, and urinated. He zipped his fly quickly.

"Hey, Jake?" Speedy said, handing the bottle over.

"What?" said Jake, raising it.

"You ever have a woman?"

Jake lowered the bottle without drinking. He swallowed dry. "Yeah," he said slowly. "A long time ago."

"Real long time?"

"Forty year."

"Aw, hell, you had women since then."

"Yeah, sure," Jake said, "I had women, but I ain't had no woman."

"Oh," Speedy said. "How come?"

"Humph," Jake said, raising the bottle. "Ain't one enough?" He swallowed, lowered the bottle, examined it. "Ain't much left."

"Gone an' finish it," Speedy said, lowering his head to his chest. Jake shrugged and poured the rest of the wine down his throat. He looked at the empty bottle and shrugged again. He laid it down in a row with the others, then eased himself down on the pavement beside Speedy and put his hands behind his head. Wincing slightly, he freed a hand and massaged his stomach. He put his hand back behind his head, closed his eyes, and in a few minutes he began to snore, first quietly, then louder and louder.

The lobby was in almost total darkness, the only light coming from the desk where the light-skinned desk clerk sat reading a copy of the Koran and mumbling to himself in Philadelphia-accented Arabic. Leroy came out of the office, crossed the deserted bar, and walked toward the stairway. He nodded to the desk clerk and stepped on the first step, but then he saw a pair of female legs protruding out of the shadows, and he changed course abruptly. "Hey, good-lookin'," said Leroy, with a sharkey smile. "How's ma honey?"

"I ain't your honey."

"Oh," said Leroy, ceasing to smile, "it's you."

"Yeah, it's me," said Vanessa. She raised her cigarette to her lips and took a drag, holding the smoke in for a long time before she exhaled. Leroy looked down at her legs.

"What you doin' out here?" said Leroy.

"Settin'."

"Settin'? What you hatchin'?" He cackled at his own joke.

Vanessa took a drag from her cigarette.

"How come you settin'?"

"This here's a public hotel. I can set in it if I wants to."

"Yeah," agreed Leroy, "you can set in it. But it's a place where folks goes to sleep too. In beds." He smiled, and teeth flashed in his dark face.

"Umph," said Vanessa.

"Bar's closed," said Leroy. "Otherwise I'd buy you a drink."

"Thanks for nothin'," said Vanessa. She took another drag on her cigarette, caressing the filter with her tongue and leaving a smear of rich red lipstick on the white paper. Leroy stared at it. He licked his lips. Then he sat down beside her, his left knee brushing her leg. Vanessa did not look at him.

"Well," said Leroy, "even if the bar is closed, it don't matter. I got a bottle up to ma room."

"Yeah?" said Vanessa. She turned her head and looked at him for a minute, then turned back to her cigarette.

"Yeah," said Leroy. He placed his left hand on her thigh at the point where her skirt stopped. A few beads of sweat appeared on his forehead.

Vanessa raised her cigarette again, sucked in smoke. She closed her eyes and rolled her head back on her shoulders, smiling. She rolled her head to the right, opened her eyes, smiled at Leroy, still holding the smoke in. Leroy leaned forward, smiling too. Vanessa blew the smoke out in a long plume, directly into his face. Leroy did not retreat an inch. His fingers tightened their grip on Vanessa's thigh. "You know what I think?" Vanessa said, smiling.

"What do you think?" said Leroy, wiggling his fingers slightly.

"I think we oughta go on up to your room so you can pour me a drink."

"Yeah," said Leroy.

"Wait," said Vanessa, raising her hand, "that ain't all."

"No?" said Leroy.

"No," said Vanessa. She slowly crossed her legs, capturing Leroy's fingers between her thighs.

"Well, ah, what else did you have in mind?" said Leroy.

"Well," said Vanessa, "after you pours me a drink, we can turn down the bed."

"Um hum?" said Leroy, leaning forward.

"Um hum," said Vanessa, rubbing her legs together.

"What then?" said Leroy, as he leaned farther forward and began to pucker his lips.

"Then I'll watch for a while," said Vanessa.

"Watch what?" said Leroy, closing his eyes and moving in.

"Watch you, while you fuck yourself," snapped Vanessa as she brought the back of her hand across Leroy's puckered lips.

"Cunt!" Leroy shouted. He tried to pull his hand out from between Vanessa's thighs, but she chopped down on his wrist.

"You lay a hand on me, nigger, an' you gonna be sorry."

Leroy pulled his hand out and stood up. "Someday I'ma kill you," he said.

"Sure," said Vanessa. "An' the next day the world's gonna be findin' out where a whole lot of bodies is buried. You'll be cuttin' your own throat."

"It might just be worth it," Leroy said. "But I'll find some way. I'll make you do anything I want."

"Almost anything," Vanessa said. "There's one thing you could never make me do."

"Almost anything'll be good enough," Leroy said.

"Not for you," Vanessa said.

"How's it feel," said Leroy, "knowin' your baby sister's a better woman than you are?"

"Why's she better?" said Vanessa. "Just 'cause she don't care how stupid you are?"

"Shit," said Leroy.

"You," said Vanessa, stubbing out her cigarette, "are stupid. If you wasn't so stupid, you wouldn't have to be worryin' 'bout every street nigger that comes along tryin' to steal a piece of your action."

"Nobody moves on Leroy," snapped Leroy.

"Way I hears it, somebody done already moved."

"Your ears is big. An' crooked."

"Humph," said Vanessa. "An' even if it ain't happenin' now, it'll be happenin' sooner or later. An' when it does, when somebody does move on you, you ain't gonna be able to stop 'em, 'cause you so stupid."

"If I'm so stupid," demanded Leroy, "how come you been settin' out here waitin' on me?"

Vanessa got up and walked to the door. "If you wasn't so stupid," she said, "you wouldn't need to be askin'."

He never went straight home. At midnight he would descend from the executive suite into the lower regions of the bank, where the locker room was, change his clothes and find his card and check out. He would do it quickly, before the other cleaners came down to change and punch out and go home, talking in their loud, weary voices. He would hurry in and out and back to the elevator, let it punch him back up through the building to the executive suite, where he would stow his tools and sit for a while in the president's chair, smoking a cigarette and gazing out over the city. After he was sure the others would be gone he would descend again and go out. And then he would walk.

The city glowed quietly at night, and his feet scraped along, the lonely echo whispering back from concrete walls. Rayburn crossed Market Street and walked along the north side, past the bowling alley, stopping for a minute to look through the glass and watch the pins' quiet falling and the silent faces before walking on past the row of hacks standing in front of the bus station, on into the station itself. He descended the short flight of steps inside the double doors and stood looking up at the big bulletin board that listed departures and arrivals. He read the names of the cities, moving his lips. The disembodied voice of the P.A. system announced an arrival from New York City. Rayburn read the names and departure times over again. He was tired, his head ached, and it was hard to keep it tilted back to see the board. Rayburn dropped his head and looked around. The waiting room was almost empty. In the far corner a fat white woman, ugly veins showing like purple spiderwebs on her grayish legs, sat surrounded by cardboard boxes and beat-up suitcases. Her jaws worked slowly on a wad of gum. Rayburn moved toward her. She saw him coming and placed a protective hand on one of the cardboard boxes. Rayburn walked past her to the water fountain, took a drink, and then started back toward the door. "Hey," she said as he passed.

"Wahuh?" said Rayburn.

"You got a match?"

"Sure," said Rayburn, reaching into his pocket. As his fingers closed on his matches he looked at her. She had placed a cigarette in the corner of her mouth, where it dangled precariously. She gazed absently out through the plate-glass windows at the closed coffee shop across the street, waiting for Rayburn to light her cigarette for her. "Thought I had some," Rayburn said. "Musta lost 'em."

She wrested her attention away from the closed coffee shop, looked at him. "You ain't got no matches?" Rayburn shook his head. She looked him over, from the top of his head to the bottom of his feet, and made a face. "Figures," she said.

He left the bus station and walked west on Market Street, waiting for two o'clock when the bars would close and she would have to go home. He moved quickly along the deserted hulk of the street. He always walked fast going away so that when he was tired and turned back he would be as far away as possible, and it would take him a long time to get back. He left Center City and crossed the river, passed the Post Office and the train station and the squatting headquarters of the *Evening Bulletin*. A few blocks further on he began to tire, and he looked around for someplace to rest. But he was in the strip of no man's land along Market Street the buffer created after the riots in '64—all the buildings torn down, leaving only bottle-and-brick-strewn fields. He turned off the sidewalk, stepped through a broken white board fence, walked across ruptured earth and scraggly grass, and urinated while looking up at the sky, oblivious to the cars that occasionally passed, raking their headlights across his back. And then he turned to walk home.

He picked his way across the bare ground, kicking cans, stumbling over a bottle discarded by a wino days before, reached the sidewalk, stumbled on across the street. He turned east until he reached Thirty-fourth Street, and then turned south. He began to feel acid in his stomach. He began to wonder about her: where she'd been, who she'd seen. He turned left when he reached the University Hospital. He crossed Thirty-third Street. South Street began.

Rayburn moved through the city's shadows, hands in pockets, shoulders slumped, footsteps tapping an ancient rhythm, slowing down to give her time. South Street stretched out dark before him, and from the river a foul mist rose, chemical fog in the summer heat. Rayburn stopped, leaned out over the water. "Damn," he said. He listened to the whisper of the cars on the Expressway, the rumble of a freight train heading south. "Man," he said to the river, "that's where I oughta be goin'. South. On down to D.C. I oughta take ma goddamn paycheck an' walk into that goddamn bus station an' buy a goddamn ticket. Far as the money's gonna take me, one damn way." He gazed at the river, the idea whirling in his foggy brain. It didn't matter where he went: D.C., Boston, Chicago, L.A. He wondered what it was like in L.A., if things were better there, or worse, or even different. "Shit," Rayburn said, turning away from the silent river. Suddenly he didn't want to go to L.A. or anywhere anymore, because he was afraid that he would get there, step off the bus, and find that he hadn't gone anywhere at all, that everything was exactly the same.

His feet knew where to stop. He stood at a door beside a store's dry carcass. He looked up at the second-floor window. There was no light. He felt panic rise, thinking that perhaps he had read the time wrong, that it was still early. But the dark and silent street around him belied that. He calmed himself. She was in bed, had just forgotten, or neglected, to leave a light on for him. He pushed open the lower door, climbed to the landing, stood before the door. His key snicked in the lock, and he stepped inside. And then his heart was pounding again as he thought perhaps the light was off because she wasn't there, hadn't come back, would never be back. He stood, breathing sharply, in the darkness of the living room. He took a deep breath and stepped forward to where he could peer into the bedroom. His foot struck a glass; it rolled away into the darkness, clattering.

"That you, Rayburn?" a voice said sleepily.

"Yeah," said Rayburn. "It's me."

Brother Fletcher slept the sleep of the dead. His chest rose and fell, rose and fell. Mrs. Fletcher looked in at him sleeping and smiled to herself. He had been ordered, he had confided, to infiltrate Lightnin' Ed's Bar and Grill, and Mrs. Fletcher knew he was thrilled with his assignment. Mrs. Fletcher nursed the suspicion that it was not intrigue alone that fascinated him, that many times he had yearned to enter one of the dark, inviting doorways that lined South Street. Now, given his excuse, he approached the project with the passion of a zealot. He had spent all Monday and Tuesday preparing himself: making covert excursions to bookstores to purchase paperbacks on wines and liquors, listening carefully to beer commercials on the radio so that when he entered the lion's den he would be armed, at least, with knowledge. He had gone out at nine o'clock, disguised in tee shirt, slacks, and holey sneakers and looking exactly like a preacher dressed in a tee shirt, slacks, and holey sneakers. Two hours later he had returned, to confess that he had not had the courage even to enter Lightnin' Ed's, to eat the bacon sandwiches and to drink the iced tea that Mrs. Fletcher had prepared for him, and to go to bed, leaving Mrs. Fletcher to clean up the kitchen and to listen to his gentle snoring and to smile. Men, thought Mrs. Fletcher, are so silly. She cared nothing about Brother Fletcher's mission, but if it made him happy to sneak around playing spy, she was willing to go along. She looked at him snoring and resolved to provide him with a more imaginative disguise.

Mrs. Fletcher went into the kitchen and finished washing the dishes. She turned away from the sink just as the kettle began to boil. She pulled it off the heat before the strident whistle awakened Brother Fletcher, and made herself a cup of instant coffee. She sat down at the table and gazed out the window at the darkened street. In the living room the clock struck twelve. It was suddenly tomorrow. Mrs. Fletcher sighed. She had never understood midnight. She rarely saw it anyway; usually after listening to the eleven o'clock news and weather she roused a snoring Brother Fletcher so that he could hear the baseball scores, while she removed her teeth and put on her nightgown for bed. Occasionally she would wait up to watch the first half of the late show (she was almost always too sleepy to wait for the rest) or to see if there was going to be anyone interesting on the *Tonight Show.* But when she was watching TV, or dozing as she pretended to watch TV, midnight came and went with no more fanfare than a station break and five commercials. Those were almost the only times she saw midnight, except, of course, on New Year's Eve when she and Brother Fletcher had always watched the ball slide down the pole on the Times Building until they had torn it down and built the Allied Chemical Building for the ball to slide down, and danced an awkward waltz in the confines of their living room to the music of Guy Lombardo. Mrs. Fletcher did not mind New Year's Eve because the new year obviously had to start sometime. But midnight came every single day, and to Mrs. Fletcher a day was just different, not new like a year. It seemed reasonable that once a year she should be suddenly older, that she should have been married one year longer, but every day was too often, especially when she sat in the kitchen with a cup of coffee in her hand, looking at the street and listening to Brother Fletcher gently snoring down the hall. The clock would chime twelve times, like some awful army tramping heavily through her life. Midnight meant it was tomorrow already, and that meant it was morning already, which to Mrs. Fletcher seemed silly. Morning was light and the winos lining up in front of the State Store and shoppers lining up in front of the supermarkets, waiting for them to open, and Mrs. Fletcher watching them line up, through her window. Mrs. Fletcher did not approve of winos or of State Stores. She had no feelings about supermarkets beyond a vague distrust. Mrs. Fletcher reminded herself that she would have to go shopping tomorrow. No—today. Mrs. Fletcher hated to go shopping. Brother Fletcher had once offered to do it for her, but the result had been a minor disaster. Someday, thought Mrs. Fletcher, I'll have somebody to go shopping for me. And to clean up after I make Fletcher his midnight snacks. And, thought Mrs. Fletcher, Harriette Fletcher is every bit as crazy as her husband. She smiled at the thought of a maid. She grinned at the thought of her ever having a maid. She chuckled softly at the thought of her thinking she would ever have a maid. It was, thought Mrs. Fletcher, a shame she couldn't mention it to Brother

Fletcher. But he wouldn't understand. He was a man. He could never see her little daydreams as simple daydreams, understand that they didn't mean that she was unhappy or uncontent. He would resent the imagined implication that he was not a good provider. He would feel ashamed and guilty. He would apologize for not giving her what she deserved. He would go out and mortgage everything they didn't own to get her a maid or some other silly thing that she had never even thought about, to make it all up to her. God, thought Mrs. Fletcher, why do men take everything so seriously? If God made man in his own image, no wonder the world is in such a mess. Mrs. Fletcher smiled to herself. That bit of witty sacrilege was another little something she could never share with Brother Fletcher. He didn't take himself as seriously as some people, but he took God more seriously than anybody, probably even God. Mrs. Fletcher smiled to herself once again.

Sighing, Mrs. Fletcher got up from the table and put her cup in the sink. She went into the bathroom and slipped her plate out and placed it in the pink plastic container next to Brother Fletcher's blue one. She pulled her dress over her head and removed her underclothes, feeling her body sag comfortably. She slipped into her nightgown, turned off the light, crept softly into the darkened bedroom. She paused at the foot of the bed and looked at Brother Fletcher. He had kicked the sheet off him. Mrs. Fletcher readjusted it. Such a baby when he sleeps, she thought, looking down at Brother Fletcher's face, soft in slumber, lips pursed, head pillowed on hands clasped as if in prayer—Mrs. Fletcher imagined him in a pair of light-blue sleepers. Mrs. Fletcher knew something was bothering Brother Fletcher. She wondered if it had anything to do with the Reverend Mr. Sloan. Mrs. Fletcher gritted her teeth at the thought of the Reverend Mr. J. Peter Sloan. Mrs. Fletcher considered Mr. Sloan to be the chief conductor on the express train to hell, and she refused to go near The Word of Life except when she absolutely had to. Reverend Mr. Sloan, thought Mrs. Fletcher, ought to be hung. She imagined the greasy little man, resplendent in his rich purple robes, swinging by his neck from the balcony of The Word of Life. Brother Fletcher would be in charge. Fletcher would like having his own church again; he hadn't wanted to leave North Carolina. She'd have to help him of course. Fletcher had no head for business or for making money. But he could preach. God, could he preach!

Mrs. Fletcher thought back to the first time she had seen him, at a Sunday School convention in a little dusty town called Swann Station. He had been fresh out of the seminary, the spiritual shepherd of four tiny churches on an obscure circuit. Nobody had paid any attention to him, but somebody had failed to show up to preach, and all of the older ministers had wanted the chance but none of them had been willing to see the honor fall to any of the others. So they had asked Brother Fletcher, who was too young and obscure and mild mannered to frighten anybody. Mrs. Fletcher had been in her second year at the Normal School, and was very proud of being in charge of the convention choir. She had been sitting in the front row of the choir that hot night, flailing at the air with a paper fan provided by a local mortuary, when suddenly Brother Fletcher stood up before her. He was extremely tall and frighteningly thin. His neck was bony, his shoulders slumped, and his pants had stopped just above the tops of his socks. All the girls in the choir had tittered a little, including Mrs. Fletcher, but she had stopped tittering, or even thinking about it, when Brother Fletcher had started to speak. She had sat immobile, her fan forgotten, the heat ignored, the hymnbook clasped tightly in her fingers, knuckles gone pale, listening as Brother Fletcher's voice flowed out like a river, a flood springing from a well so deep it did not seem possible that it had been contained by Brother Fletcher's bony body. Mrs. Fletcher had felt herself begin to drown. All through that summer and fall and winter she had managed to be in the vicinity of Brother Fletcher as often as possible. Not that he noticed. Her girl friends had noticed and said she was crazy. Her mother thought she was crazy, too. But Mrs. Fletcher could only hear his voice and think of the richness that had to lie behind it. God, could he preach!

South Street slept, slumbering in alleyways and apartments and furnished rooms and burned-out storefronts and in the steamy boudoirs upstairs in the Elysium Hotel, snoring peacefully in a vast choral blend of soprano, alto, tenor, bass; in the light snores of children, in the heavy exhalations of fat, drunken men. The police route car made its leisurely tour, trolling slowly eastward, turning at the river, and speeding back along Pine Street to the all-night pizza joint that was only too happy to treat cops to free coffee and Cokes, out of civic appreciation and a desire for additional protection. Except for the squad car nothing much moved on South Street; the stumbling winos had found their homes for the night, and the whores had long since gone off duty and sent their customers home or out to be mugged and, occasionally, murdered in a secluded side street. But one shadow did move, steadily, slowly, east, toward the Delaware and the lightening sky.

Brown crossed the asphalt expanse of Broad Street against the light, plunging through the strip of commercial prosperity, gratefully regaining the quiet rotting of South Street. He had hurried crossing Broad; now he resumed his heavy, plodding pace. He had been walking for hours, ever since the intimate lighting of Frankie's Place on Rittenhouse Square had gone up, signaling closing time, pushing Brown out onto the street like toothpaste out of a tube. He had walked west at first, crossing the Schuylkill by the Walnut Street Bridge, then, on the west bank, turning north to walk up past the walls of the zoo, to cross the idle tracks of the Penn Central. Then he had walked south on Fortieth Street and through the never-locked gate of the Woodland Cemetery to sit on a tombstone and stare for a while at the stars and the river, while sobriety sneaked up on him. He had walked past the Veterans Hospital, across the University Avenue Bridge, up Grays Ferry Avenue, and finally to South Street. It had felt strangely comforting, as if he had given in to the pull of gravity. Stepping onto South Street Brown had been tense and expectant, anticipating some magic transformation of the night and of himself; walking eastward he reached out around him with his fatigue- and alcohol-dulled senses, searching in the silence for some half-remembered rhythm, some dimly recalled melody, sniffing the air for an aromatic blend of all the odors of the night. But the silence had remained dull and random, and the smells of sweat and garbage and gasoline and wine and grease and asphalt had hung as separate and distinct stenches. Brown walked on, growing more and more sad, more and more sober. Finally he reached the end of South Street and still there was nothing beyond the simple realities of night and street and buildings and Delaware River. In a few minutes the delivery trucks would begin to move and the taxis would start to stream out of the Grays Ferry lot and the busses like mechanical cows would trundle forth from their barns and it would be morning.

Brown turned away from the river, walked back along South as far as Seventh Street, then walked north to Market and on west to the donut shop between the Reading Terminal and City Hall. He sat at the counter and consumed half a dozen donuts, three cups of coffee, rose, paid, and despondently descended the concrete stairway to the Market Street subway. He sat on a slatted wooden bench and waited, his eyelids drooping. The train came. Brown stepped on, took a seat amid the curious mixture of people riding to early-morning jobs. It was far too early for office workers—these were maids bound for Thirtieth Street Station to take the Penn Central commuter trains to the big expensive houses in the tiny expensive towns along the Main Line, or for Sixty-ninth Street and the busses to Delaware County. Brown relaxed, content to let the train carry him westward, beneath the Schuylkill. He left the subway at Fortieth and Market, climbing the steps to the denuded corner that already burned in the heat. He crossed Market and headed south. He reached the tall building, passed beneath the broad awning, opened the heavy door, crossed the luxurious lobby, entered the elevator, and rose effortlessly upward. He opened and closed the apartment door with great care and headed directly for the bar. He picked up a nearly full bottle of scotch and carried it out onto the balcony.

Brown stood looking out over the city, drinking from the bottle. His eyes followed a bus as it moved down Spruce Street, crawling an inch, stopping while it swallowed a few small dots and spit out a few others, then crawling on an inch, two inches, before stopping again. Brown wondered about the bus's destination: either it was a forty-two, bound for Independence Hall, or it was a forty, bound for Front and South. When the bus reached Thirty-third and Spruce it did not turn but continued on across the river. Brown's eyes followed it as it creeped across the bridge and dipped down onto South Street. Brown stared after it as it gradually lost itself in traffic, stood gazing into the smog long after the bus was lost to sight. Suddenly the whiskey he had drunk turned to acid in his stomach. He dropped the bottle and spun toward the living room, losing his footing and falling to his knees on the carpet. Lips pressed tightly together, Brown struggled to his feet, hung on the railing of the balcony, trying to decide if he could make it to the bathroom or should simply stay there, waiting for the sour vomit to rise. But as suddenly as it had come, the spasm passed, and Brown hung on the railing gulping at the clotted air. Gradually he stopped trembling. Brown took a deep breath and bent over carefully and picked up the bottle. It was almost empty—the liquid was on the balcony concrete, vanishing before the sun. Brown looked at the bottle. Then he leaned over the railing, opened his fingers, and let the bottle fall away, twenty-four stories, to shatter beyond recognition in the street below.

The sun burned down into his reddened eyes, and Jake squinted. His eyes were permanently blurred—from sleep, from wine, from years, from countless mornings' wakings with the sun in his eyes. He blinked and groaned, rubbed his stomach, groaned again. His head, which rested against two rusting garbage cans full to overflowing with rotting refuse, rolled forward, then back. The rusted metal emitted a dry crunching sound.

He rolled to one side, moaned, grabbed the rim of the can, and tried to haul himself to his feet, but the metal, weakened by wind and rain and the acid from decaying garbage, crumbled beneath his fingers. The can caved in, and he fell to the cobblestones, lay there, panting. A black-and-tan tom cat came prancing down the alley toward him, and he watched it come without moving anything but his eyes. The cat stopped ten feet away, sniffed, mewed, and moved on, giving Jake a wide berth. He smiled bitterly, shoved himself along to the building that made a dead end of the alley. He put his back against the wall and, using his hands and friction, got to his feet. He groaned with the effort, and sweat appeared on his brow, but he was standing. He swayed slightly but kept his feet. Slowly he walked out of the alley; passing his fingers through his grizzled hair, patting his clothes into some semblance of order, he emerged onto the street.

South Street at 9 a.m.: the last of the cars from the daily traffic jam emptying off the expressway and speeding blue-suited businessmen through the gauntlet of crumbling tenements on their way to the steel-and-concrete central city, past Jake standing at the mouth of his alley, the drivers' faces white blurs as they forced their cars through steaming streets, emotions torn, worrying, wondering what might be said about their late arrival. Two children, their clothes grimy from an hour's play, rolled past on skates, calling to him to get the fuck out of the way. Jake smiled after them, then suddenly doubled over in agony. He needed a drink, and he started to turn back into the alley, where he kept a bottle hidden for emergencies. The pain stabbed at him again, but it wasn't so bad this time, and he decided to save the emergency bottle. He started walking. It took him twenty minutes to cover the four blocks to the liquor store.

Jake stood before the wire-screened glass and looked inside. The store was empty except for two clerks who stood behind the counter and stared boredly out at the street. Jake looked up and down but found no sign of the other regulars and breathed a sigh of relief; he was in no mood to share. He squared his shoulders and pushed open the door. One of the clerks roused himself. The other gave Jake an amused sneer and returned to his perusal of the street. Jake stood shivering in the chill from the air-conditioning. Then he approached the first clerk.

"What'll it be?" said the clerk, automatically reaching down beneath the counter to where the cheap spirits were kept. Jake looked at him, eyes slightly glazed. The drops of sweat on his brow, chilled by the air-conditioning, dribbled into his grizzled eyebrows and were absorbed for a moment before reappearing at the corners of his eyes, trickling along the wrinkles in his face like rainwater running along the cracks in a field of sun-dried mud. The clerk shifted impatiently; his hand danced over the bottles, his other hand drummed on the counter. "C'mon, c'mon," he said, "what's it gonna be? Bali Hai? Ripple? C'mon, old man, I ain't got all day."

Jake looked at him. "You ain't got nobody else to wait on."

The clerk glared. "I ain't gonna be spendin' the whole mornin' waitin' for some old wino to make up his mind does he want the seventy-cent rotgut or the seventy-five-cent rotgut, neither."

The other clerk chuckled without taking his eyes from the street. "Maybe this cat's a big spender. Maybe he gonna be wantin' the eighty-cent rotgut."

The first clerk chuckled in his turn. "Okay, pops, what's it gonna be?"

Jake glared at him. He reached out and grasped the price book which lay on the counter, encased in a worn black binder. Ignoring the clerks' snorts, he leafed through it.

"Domestic shit's in the front, pops," said the second clerk, still not looking away from the window. He smiled at the street outside, his pink gums and strong white teeth shining in his dark face. "Or maybe you got your mind set on some French champagne to impress your, ah, *girl friend?*" Both clerks chuckled.

Jake thumbed the book, found the page he wanted, ran his forefinger down the list of unpronounceable names in Italian, French, German, Spanish, and Portuguese while his eyes went down the list of prices until he found one he could afford. He twisted the book around so that it faced the clerk. He pointed, thumping his finger heavily beside the name.

The clerk's eyebrows rose slightly. "That there's a dollar forty-five."

"I know it," Jake snapped.

"That ain't a half gallon, now, that ain't nothin' but a bottle."

"I know that," Jake said. "While ago you was in such a rush to get me outa here, now you keep stickin' your black nose in ma business. You gonna give me ma wine, or you gonna fuck around all damn day?"

The other clerk looked over. "What's the number on that?" The first clerk peered at the book. Jake rattled the number off without looking, as if he bought Portuguese wine every day. The second clerk looked at the first clerk. The first clerk closed his mouth and headed for the stockroom. "Let's see your money," said the second clerk.

"I ain't seen no wine yet," Jake said.

"How come a wino like you got a dollar fifty to spend on one bottle?"

"How come a fat nigger like you wants to be knowin' all ma business? You just gimme ma wine, I'm doin' fine." Jake reached into his pocket and produced the collection of change that Speedy had given him. He counted out a dollar forty-five, laid it on the counter. The first clerk returned bearing an oddly shaped bottle, glanced at the money, started putting the bottle into a paper bag. The second clerk reached for the coins, but Jake grabbed his wrist, held it fast until he had the bag in his hands. Then he let go. Smiling, holding back a grimace of pain, he turned and left the store.

The door closed softly behind him. He turned and walked past the window, not glancing at the clerks inside. Once he was out of their sight his shoulders slumped and he rubbed his stomach. Clutching the bag, he turned off South Street into a shady, garbage-strewn alley and disappeared from view.

5 Thursday

Behind the bar of Lightnin' Ed's Bar and Grill Leo stood contentedly chomping on a ham-and-turkey sandwich of his own design and construction. Leo had never encountered anyone besides himself who was capable of making a sandwich that even came close to pleasing him. Leo hated sandwiches made with cold butter, which either caused the bread to rip or stuck to it in greasy lumps. He despised sandwiches which were made without sufficient meat, cheese, and mayonnaise. Salad dressing was beneath his notice; none of his sandwiches ever included either salad dressing or margarine. They did, however, include at least six ounces of lean meat. Leo's sandwiches were famous the length of South Street. But while Leo liked his sandwiches fat, he had become disgusted with sandwiches from which the filling would squirt out on one side as he bit down on the other—Leo liked his sandwiches smothered sloppily with mustard and ketchup in addition to butter and mayonnaise. The sandwich that Leo held in his hand was of a special design which, Leo's instinct toward culinary engineering assured him, should encourage all the critical fluids to remain within the confines of the bread. Leo belonged to the old school of engineers who work by trial and error. This was his sixteenth special design of the day, and as he stood behind the bar waiting for the meager Thursday-evening trade to meander through Lightnin' Ed's dark inviting doorway, Leo reflected that the best part of scientific experimentation was

100

disposing of the failures. He raised the sandwich to his mouth and bit down as firmly as his Poligrip would permit. Ketchup, mustard, and mayonnaise oozed over the sides of the sandwich and down onto the front of Leo's big white butcher's apron, staining it disgustingly. "Shfut!" exclaimed Leo, chewing his mouthful. He was disposing of the remains and contemplating his next attempt when the first customer of the evening entered Lightnin' Ed's.

In forty-three years of tending bar Leo had developed a theory that the evening's first customer was an important indicator of what the evening itself would be like. In his younger days Leo had welcomed the entrance of the occasional oddball, which usually signaled the advent of an interesting evening. Lately, however, Leo had most enjoyed the nights when his first customer was a regular—a nice, polite wino like Jake, or a reasonably well-behaved whore like Big Betsy, or a quiet, melancholy loser like Rayburn. Lately, Leo was not into shocks. Saturday night had been a tremendous strain, what with crazy white men and crazier black men named Brown running around all over the place. Sunday, Monday, and Tuesday had all been fairly quiet, and Wednesday had been so quiet Leo had almost gone to sleep. He had looked forward to an equally quiet Thursday in which to prepare himself for the weekend. When he raised his eyes and looked over the hard brown crust of the pumpernickel bread of his leaky sandwich and saw his first customer, Leo wanted to close the bar down right then and there and go straight home to bed.

It was the strangest customer that Leo had ever seen. It was about six feet long, but it could not have weighed more than a hundred and fifty pounds. It had an epiglottis that bounded up and down a long bony neck like a berserk elevator. The rest of it was a jumble of knees, elbows, feet, hands, and ears. The chest was concealed behind a pink-and-purple-striped shirt and a light-brown-and-blue tie. The lower part of the body was hidden inside a pair of green-and-orange-checked trousers. The feet were encased in purple-and-yellow argyle socks inside a pair of sandals, and the eyes were obscured by large green shades with purple frames. The head supported a broad-brimmed yellow hat with a tartan hatband. The customer smiled at Leo and sat down on a stool. Leo beat a hasty retreat behind the roast beef and tried to regain some of his composure. He took a deep breath. "Evenin', bro," said Leo. "What'll it be?"

The customer opened his mouth, closed it, opened it again, closed it, and went on opening and closing it like a beached catfish. Leo stared at him. The customer closed his mouth, fumbled in his pocket and drew out a piece of paper, looked at it, and returned it to his pocket. "Löwenbräu," he said in a quavering but surprisingly rich basso profundo.

"A lewd what?" said Leo.

"A Löwenbräu," repeated the customer.

Leo shook his head, thought for a minute. "Oh," he said, "I getcha. Sorry, brother, we ain't had none a that foreign shit in a long time. No call for it; folks can't hardly pronounce it, let alone drink it. Now we got your Schmidt's an' your Ortlieb's an' your Readin' dark an'—"

The customer had pulled out the paper again. "Tequila," he said.

Leo stopped his recitation. "Tequila?"

"You don't have tequila?"

"What? Oh, yeah, man, yeah, we got some tequila someplace here. You just hold on right there. Don't get excited or nothin', nothin' now. . . ." Leo hurriedly lowered himself to his hands and knees behind the bar and, while pretending to search for the tequila, checked the positioning of his thirty-eight, his billy club, his sap, his brass knuckles, and his genuine Louisville Slugger baseball bat that had been personally autographed by Richie Allen when he had stumbled into Lightnin' Ed's one night to ask directions. Reassured, Leo got to his feet and located a dusty bottle of José Cuervo Especial on the back bar. "You, ah, drink this stuff straight?" Leo inquired, pouring out a shot and maintaining a discreet distance between himself and the customer, as if the customer might be catching.

The customer consulted his paper. "With lemon and salt."

Leo wordlessly quartered a lemon and put it on a plate. He set the plate and a salt shaker on the bar. He pushed them both toward the customer, using the extreme tips of his fingers. The customer nodded. "Could I see the bottle?" he asked.

Leo put one hand on his billy club and handed the bottle over. Leo wasn't afraid of anything but mad dogs and psychos, and he wasn't sure if he had one or the other or a combination of both. Either way he wasn't taking chances. The customer gave the bottle a minute examination. "Where's the worm?" he said finally.

"The whahuh?" Leo retorted.

The customer looked upset. "You mean there wasn't any worm?"

"Oh yeah," Leo said quickly. "Oh yeah, there was a worm all right." Beneath the bar he shifted his hand from the billy club to the thirty-eight. "Yeah," he said, "there was a worm. A pink an' purple an' brown an' blue an' green an' orange worm. Yeah, he was here all right." Leo stopped suddenly and stared at the customer. "What the fuck are you talkin' about, a goddamn worm?"

"I, ah, thought there was supposed to be a worm in the bottle. Or maybe that was mescal. Never mind. Where is everybody?"

Leo decided that he had been drinking too much beer. He broke a forty-two-and-one-half-year-old rule and poured himself a double slug of rye, which he downed in one gulp. When he opened his eyes the first thing he saw was the pink-and-purple body shirt, and he closed his eyes again. He turned his head to the side and discovered that he could talk to the man without undue discomfort so long as he didn't actually *look* at him. "Well," Leo said, "it's still early. Most ʎolks don't come in till 'bout eight, eight-thirty, maybe a little earlier if there's a ball game on."

"You have a regular crowd in here, don't you?" asked the customer.

Leo tried to reconcile the voice with the rest of the customer but failed. "Yeah," he admitted, "there's a few folks that comes in all the time. Some folks come an' go. You, you ain't never been here before."

The customer leaned over the bar, nearly upsetting the tequila, which, Leo noticed, he had not touched. "You remember everyone who comes in?" the customer asked excitedly.

"No," said Leo, "but I'da remembered you sure."

The customer sighed and settled back on his stool.

Leo let a few seconds of silence pass. "Why? You lookin' for somebody?"

"Well, in a way."

"Yeah," muttered Leo, stealing a glance at his wristwatch to see if he could turn on the ball game and have an excuse to ignore the man, "a worm."

"What?"

"Nothin'," Leo said quickly. "You want a refill?"

The customer lowered his head as if he were looking at the drink before him. His hand fished the piece of paper out of his pocket and he looked at it while he carefully licked the back of his left hand and sprinkled salt on it. Leo watched, fascinated. His eyes still on the paper, the customer picked up the glass of tequila in his left hand, took the wedge of lemon in his right hand, licked the salt, downed the tequila in one gulp, and bit quickly into the lemon. He took the lemon away from his face. His mouth hung open for a solid fifteen seconds. The rest of him seemed to go limp. "Humm," he said. "Hummmm." He reached up and removed the dark glasses. His eyes were slightly crossed.

"You do that real well," Leo said, pouring out another shot.

"Hummm," the customer said again. He shook his head, then, as if suddenly realizing what Leo had said, added, "Oh. I've been practicing. But only with iced tea."

"Jesus," muttered Leo. He checked on the placement of the billy club once again. Then he switched on the TV. He was determined not to talk to the customer any more, even if it meant watching the *CBS Evening News*.

Leo hated the news, but he glued his eyes to the screen. He muttered, reached up, and reduced the color tone to make Cronkite a mulatto.

"Hummm," said the customer. Leo looked over. The man licked the salt off his hand, gulped the tequila, chewed at the lemon. "Hummm," he said. Leo reached over and refilled his glass and turned quickly back to the TV, just in time for the body counts.

"Hummmm," said the customer.

"Jesus," muttered Leo. "Jesus H. Christ."

Brown shucked off his apron, hung it on a hook, and slid out from behind the bar. The night bartender replaced him in oily, disapproving silence, a look of suspicion on his swarthy face. Brown watched wordlessly as he ignored several waiting customers and went to the cash register and pointedly began to count the money. Brown chuckled and shook his head.

"Hey, Adlai, c'mere," came a voice from behind a wall of greenery growing out of a trellis affair that formed a partial divider between the barroom and a small, dimly lit dining room. Brown walked around the divider and sat down on a chair that shot out toward him, propelled by a small, almost dainty foot on the end of a large, almost elephantine leg. "You done real good back there. Too bad we can't teacha youse ta talka good."

Brown grinned into the heavy-jowled Italian face across from him. "Whut's wrang wid da way ah tawks, Mistuh Frankie, suh?" Brown said. "An' I don't think Alonzo thinks I'm doin' too good back there."

Frankie chuckled, and his broad black tie bounced up and down on the tightly stretched front of his white shirt. "Alonzo's mother was a Sicilian. You know how they are. Hate you people. Think you're devils. Almost as bad as Protestants."

"What was your mother?" Brown said.

"A Sicilian. You devil. Anyways, it sure was lucky for me, you comin' in like that. I was goin' nuts back there. I can't keep on my feet all day no more."

"Get arch supports," Brown suggested.

"Get a new bartender, you mean. Either that or get a smaller stomach."

"What happened to Louie anyway?" Brown said.

"Aw, that stupid . . . I come in this mornin' like usual about one in the afternoon an' they tell me we ain't got no bartender. I come out to the bar an' there's this note from Louie sayin' he run off with that bony Jewish bitch, that Lena Bernstein or Goldblum or whatever, one that useta sit down at the end a the bar drinkin' Rollin' Rock outa martini glasses."

"Yeah," Brown said, "I know who you mean. But bony? Jesus, she musta weighed a hundred and eighty."

"Right," Frankie said. "That's her. Bony. Anyways, the note said it was true love. All I know is, it was a pain in the ass, an' I had to work all goddamn day, until you come in. I just wish I could get my hands on that stupid wop. . . ."

"Why don't you put a contract out on him?" Brown suggested.

"Heh, heh, heh," said Frankie. "We don't do that kinda thing no more, Adlai, ain'tcha heard? That's minor league stuff; for Puerto Ricans an' dinges. Us wops is into big business—corporate finance, politics. We're through with petty larceny an' movin' into grand theft."

"Yeah, that's right," Brown said. "I remember readin' all about the opportunities openin' up. I think it was in my complimentary copy of *Black Enterprise*."

"What's that?" said Frankie suspiciously. "One a them radical papers?"

"Kinda," Brown said.

"Humph," Frankie said. "Bein' serious now, Adlai, that's what was wrong with that King fella. He didn't understand big business. He thought he was all right with God on his side, but he forgot that even God could get overruled by a majority vote a the board a directors."

Brown stared at Frankie for a minute, then laughed.

"What's so funny?" Frankie demanded.

"Nothin'," Brown said, wiping tears from his eyes.

"Humph," Frankie said. "Anyways, where'd you learn to tend bar?"

"Place called Roger's," Brown said. "In Poughkeepsie."

"Poughkeepsie? What the hell was you doin' in Poughkeepsie? There ain't nothin' there."

"Only Vassar," Brown sighed.

Frankie chuckled deep in the back of his throat.

"Don't laugh," Brown said seriously. "It was true love."

"You know, Adlai, that's what I like about you. You can take any four-letter word and make it sound like 'fuck.' Listen, I'm an old man that don't like eatin' alone. You wanna call up that gal a yours an' see does she wanna come down an' we'll all have dinner?"

Brown looked unhappy. "I don't think she'd come. But I'll stay."

Frankie regarded Brown with a look of curiosity, then shrugged and motioned to the waitress. "Hey, Maria. We want some dinner." Maria was a tall Italian girl, plump and pretty, with long black hair teased up and held with too much spray, and deep black eyes surrounded by an alarming smear of silver eye make-up. Her tight uniform barely contained her. She pulled an order pad out of her apron pocket and stood, pencil poised. "Adlai wants a steak," Frankie said, " 'cause he's been workin' hard. Only one in the whole place been doin' anything."

"Don't blame me," Maria said, "I been off since Monday."

"You're off everyday," grumbled Frankie. "If you wasn't my daughter-in-law I'd a fired you long ago."

"If I wasn't your daughter-in-law you'd have to pay me decent. I'm too good a waitress to be workin' for peanuts in a—"

"Okay, okay," said Frankie. "You get a raise. Now, Miss Super Smart-Ass Waitress, we want some steak. Rare. Tossed salad, an' you make sure you tell that Vito ta keep the goddamn chickpeas outa mine. An' baked potatoes on the side, butter on mine, butter an' sour cream with chives for Adlai. I don't know how he stands the stuff, but dinges is strange."

"Yes, sir," said Maria, tossing off a mock salute. "And what dressing would you like on your salad? Italian?"

"Shit, no," said Frankie. "Russian. I don't want none a that oily wop stuff on *my* salad. Adlai just wants oil. His folks is still tryin' to imitate the wops, but they ain't figured out what vinegar is yet."

Brown snorted. "Thank you, sir," said Maria, snapping her pad shut and heading for the kitchen.

Frankie grinned wolfishly. "She forgot the drinks. I been tryin' to catch her makin' a mistake for months. She's never gonna hear the end of it." He eased his bulk back against the wall. "All right, now, Adlai, what the hell's the matter with you? You been in here a good four hours, an' you ain't started no fights. I ain't heard you say 'fuck' moren ten times, an' you ain't insulted a single one a my customers. It's been so quiet I damn near went to sleep."

"They didn't insult me," Brown snapped.

"That ain't never stopped you before."

Brown opened his mouth, closed it, and grinned ruefully.

"You ain't as touchy. You sick?"

"Could be," Brown said.

"You have a fight with what's her name?"

"Not exactly," Brown said. He took a deep breath. "I left."

"Left? Just like that?"

"Yeah," Brown said. "I just couldn't stay there any more. It was . . . ruinin' me, you know?"

Frankie nodded. "Yeah. Tell me about it. Women is the funniest damn things in the world. Sometimes you wish you could get rid a every damn one of 'em. You say 'blue'; some woman'll give you fifteen perfectly good nonsensical reasons why blue has got to be somethin' else—turquoise or aqua or some such crap. You know, I was married for thirty-seven goddamn years. To the same woman. She never liked me ownin' a bar. She'd say, 'Frankie, you gotta serve some food so respectable folk'll come in.' I'd say, 'I run a bar, not a bingo game.' I mean, hell, who wants respectable folks in a bar? Next thing you know you'll have the priest in there. She wouldn't listen, she had to come down. Not here, I had a place over on Christian Street then. She'd come down an' start makin' sandwiches, an' then she got a hot plate and started makin' pasta, an' she had bread, an' salad, an' every other goddamn thing, an' pretty soon everybody was comin' in to eat an' wasn't nobody buyin' nothin' from the bar 'cept bottled beer an' red wine, an' I damn near went bankrupt. Hell, I didn't care. We wasn't starvin' an' she was happy an' I was happy, an' who gives a damn if the banks is happy? So I said the hell with it an' turned the place into a restaurant. She useta have a hell of a time, bein' everybody's mama an' givin' away half my profit. After she died, I couldn't stay down there. All them folks would come in an' sit around drinkin' wine an' lookin' sad. It was like a goddamn funeral. Fool woman never understood a thing about business. Everybody loved her an' she loved everybody an' we damn near starved to death. Them was the days."

Brown had watched, silent and motionless, while the stream of emotions had flowed across Frankie's battered features. His right hand, almost invisible against the stained wood of the table, moved out toward Frankie, drew back, and moved out again, stopping short of Frankie's arm, suddenly becoming starkly visible as the palm turned upward before the hand balled into a fist and drew slowly back again.

"Now," said Maria. Brown and Frankie looked up quickly, almost guiltily. "I got the steaks on first. Figured if I did it that way you wouldn't get through moren three rounds a drinks."

"Moren three!" Frankie said indignantly. "Him, maybe. Not me. *He's* the lush."

"Right," said Maria. "You're the drunk."

"Listen to her, willya, Adlai! My own daughter-in-law, my own flesh an' olive oil, callin' me a drunk."

"You know what the doctor said," warned Maria.

"Yeah. He said the way I smoke an' drink I shoulda been dead five years ago. Goddamn good thing I didn't listen to him. Now bring us some booze. I want—"

"You want a Rusty Nail an' Adlai wants a scotch-rocks."

"Right," said Frankie.

"Wrong," said Brown. "I'll just have a beer."

Maria stopped dead in her tracks and her mouth fell open. "What?"

Frankie sighed. "It sounded like he said beer, but I'm gettin' old an' my hearin' ain't so good no more an' I can't believe that."

"Adlai, you been comin' in here for years an' you ain't never had anything but scotch-rocks."

"I'm on the cart," Brown said.

"Oh yeah," Maria said. "The cart. What in hell's the cart?"

"Halfway to the wagon," Brown told her.

Maria gave Brown a concerned look. "He ain't kiddin', Frankie. He means it. He's sick. Come to think of it, he didn't even ask me once to go to bed with him when he ordered. Somethin's wrong. Adlai, you in love or somethin'?"

"Or somethin'," Brown said.

"Beer?" said Maria.

"Beer," said Brown.

Maria shook her head, wrote it down, and headed for the bar.

"That girl musta done a real job on you," Frankie observed.

"Nothin' to do with her," Brown snapped.

"Okay," said Frankie. "I'm too old to argue. Let's change the subject. So you moved out. Where you livin' now?"

"I found this place over on South Street," Brown said.

"That was fast."

"There isn't exactly a waiting list," Brown said.

Maria returned with Frankie's Rusty Nail and Brown's beer. "Look, Adlai," she said, "I don't mind if you're turnin' over a new leaf or whatever it is you're doin', but if guys stop makin' passes at her a girl starts to worry. Why not pinch me or somethin', just for old time's sake?"

"I'm scared to," Brown said. "That husband a yours would kill me when he got out."

"He is out, an' that never stopped you before."

Brown sighed, reached out and patted her behind. She slapped his hand and scampered off to the kitchen.

"You sure change quick," Frankie said.

"I haven't changed. I just moved."

Maria returned with a full tray. "There you go, there's the tossed. I'll be back with the steak and baked. You do still eat steak, don't you, Adlai? Or did you give up meat?"

"Well," Brown said, "I like it better on the hoof."

"Hey, he's soundin' better, Frankie. Quick, talk some sense into him before he has a relapse."

"Jesus," said Brown, "just let a man decide he wants to cut down on his drinking and not make passes at other people's wives and you make him sound like he's a candidate for the psycho ward."

Maria grinned. "Only if it's you, sweetheart, only if it's you." She turned and wiggled her bottom pleasantly as she walked away. Brown leaned back in his chair and sighed.

Frankie grinned. "Eat your salad." They ate in silence. In a few minutes Maria delivered the meat and potatoes, tapping Brown playfully on the cheek as she went away. The bar slowly filled with the bodies of business people and professionals stopping off for a drink or two or three. Many of them lived nearby—Frankie's was on a side street just off Rittenhouse Square. At the bar men in business suits with briefcases at their feet told lies to expensive-looking women with high, hollow cheeks and thin, unadorned arms. Chatter made a dull hum, as if a giant machine idled somewhere nearby. From time to time Frankie rose to greet someone, calling them by name and waving. Brown gradually slumped lower in his seat, so that his hand traveled less and less distance conveying slivers of red meat and lumps of potato to his mouth. From time to time his left hand reached out and pulled his glass of beer toward him, and he took a few big swallows. Maria, bustling past, dropped off a full bottle. Brown nodded and smiled and kept on eating, his mouth working easily. The last bite vanished down his throat. He wiped his lips, swallowed the rest of the beer. Frankie grinned as he mopped up his plate with a piece of Italian bread. "She ain't killed you appetite, anyways." Brown smiled tightly and wiped his lips again. "Hey, Maria," Frankie yelled, "how 'bout some dessert?"

Maria appeared with her pad. "How about it?"

"Just coffee for me," Brown said.

"I want some ice cream an' pie," said Frankie.

"I'll bring you some sliced pineapple," Maria told him. "Did you take your pills?"

"The hell with the pills an' the pineapple. I want some ice cream, goddammit."

"It's not on your diet."

"You ain't my mother."

"Your mother's dead, an' she'd a lived a lot longer if she'd stayed on her diet an' taken her pills."

"All right, all right," sighed Frankie. "Sliced pineapple. Now don't just stand there. Jump!" Maria shot him a look of mock terror and moved away.

"She's a nice girl," said Frankie. "Too bad she married that kid a mine. He ain't been outa jail but three, four weeks, an' he already beat her up half-a-dozen times."

"Why doesn't she beat him back?" Brown said.

"Ask her. She'll give you some goddamn crap about how it's just his way a showin' how much he loves her. I musta not loved his mother then, 'cause I never raised a hand to that woman. Not that I wasn't tempted."

"That explains it," Brown said seriously. "If a kid doesn't see love demonstrated in the home it screws him up."

"Yeah," Frankie agreed, "that must be it."

He leaned back and loosened his belt just as Maria arrived with his pineapple and Brown's coffee. As she turned away Brown reached out absentmindedly and patted her. She smiled at him. "Never mind, doll, your heart ain't in it." Brown snorted, heaved himself erect, and shoveled sugar into his cup.

"How'd you end up in Poughkeepsie?" Frankie asked around the ring of pineapple he was stuffing into his mouth.

Brown shrugged and sipped his coffee. "I met A—this girl in New York. We had a good time for a couple a weeks, but she was going back to school. So I went up there with her and found this job at a bar, workin' behind on busy nights an' bein' bouncer on Tuesdays when the regular guy had off."

"You was a bouncer? That where you got so mean?"

"Only on Tuesdays," Brown said. "The regular dude had everybody so scared all I had to do was sit in the corner and read. That bouncer was plain crazy. He'd sit up in the corner just praying somebody'd start something, only everybody was too scared of him. So he started hiding so people would think he wasn't around. You ever see a two-hundred-and-forty-pound bar bouncer tryin' to hide behind a begonia?"

"Heh," said Frankie. "Sounds crazy to me." He pushed the last piece of pineapple into his mouth, chewed, swallowed. "Goddamn," he said, "I hate pineapple. What happened to the girl?"

Brown took a deep breath. "We came to a parting of the ways. She wanted me to work for her father. I said I preferred the bar."

"Whad her father do?"

"He ran a vanilla factory, and he worked part time as a personnel consultant for Nabisco."

"You know, sometimes I don't know when you're kiddin' an' when you're not."

"Neither do I," Brown said. "Actually, he was tne regional director of the NAACP, but it amounts to the same thing."

Frankie looked at Brown uncomprehendingly. Brown smiled tightly behind his coffee cup. "Well," Frankie said, "I'll say this for you: in six years you never brought a woman in here didn't have real class, you know? Class. Not like that damn Louie an' his bony Jewish bitch. I hope he runs outa gas in the middle of a goddamn Death Valley, an' he has ta listen ta her yammerin' until he dies a thirst. Speakin' a that, you, ah, wouldn't maybe be lookin' for a job, would ya? I mean I know you been to fourteen different colleges an', aw shit."

"Yeah," Brown said. "I'm lookin' for a job. What do I call you, Massa or Don?"

"Shut up," said Frankie. "You work good for me an' I'll treat you almost like you was Italian. Only difference is you get vacation in the winter 'cause you don't need no suntan."

"That's just as well," Brown said, " 'cause I burn real easy."

"You know, Adlai, that's what I like about you: you're smart. 'Specially your ass. You know, I got a bunch of goddamn fools workin' for me. You take that Vito out in the kitchen. The other night they brings in a whole truckload a booze. I was busy, so I says to Vito I says, 'Check them bottles an' make sure them bastards ain't cheatin' me.' Next mornin' I looked an' we was short three bottles a good red. So I calls Vito over to ask him what happened, an' he says he don't know, but he checked, just like I said, an' every bottle was full." Brown chuckled. Frankie sighed. "You want another beer?"

"No thanks," Brown said. "I gotta go clean up my apartment. If you want to call it that."

"Okay," Frankie said. "Time was when you wouldn't turn down a drink, but then you wasn't drinkin' beer then, either. Thanks for eatin' with me."

"My pleasure," Brown said, pushing his chair back.

"Bull," said Frankie. "You just like steak. G'wan, get outa here. I'll see you tomorrow."

Frankie watched as Brown went over and pinched Maria and then went out the door. He pulled a big white handkerchief from his rear trouser pocket, accompanying the action with a great deal of snorting. He replaced the handkerchief, struggled laboriously to his feet, and waddled back to the kitchen, to the glassed-in space he used for an office. Easing himself into an ancient wooden chair, he picked up the telephone and dialed. While the phone buzzed in his ear he reached out and shoved the door closed. The little room was stifling, and he pulled his handkerchief out again and wiped his face. "Hello," he said into the phone. "Yeah, it's me. Who the hell was you expectin'? An' where you been all goddamn day, I been tryin' to get . . . Yeah, well I ain't payin' you to shack up. You can shack up when the job's done." The telephone squawked indignantly. "All right, all right, how'd it go? . . . Fine. It ain't gonna make the papers, is it? . . . All right, you can come in tomorrow afternoon an' get the other half." Frankie hung the phone up gently and smiled contentedly. He reached out and opened the door to let in some air. He sniffed the odor of simmering seasoned tomatoes, smiled, folded his hands across his ample stomach, and closed his eyes. In a few minutes he was snoring softly and gently, in the sonorous tones of a man whose scores are settled and whose soul is at peace with God and the world.

Big Betsy rumbled into Lightnin' Ed's just as the Philadelphia pitcher tossed a perfect strike that would have entered the catcher's mitt with a solid, satisfying meaty thump had it not first encountered the bat of the Pittsburgh Pirates' lead-off man with a resounding, unforgiving crack and vanished from the big TV screen by way of the fence in the upper right-hand corner. "Shit," muttered Leo, "everybody knows they're gonna lose, but do they have to start in the first damn inning?" Big Betsy ignored both Leo and the TV—she hated baseball with a rare passion. It represented competition. Jowls joggling and her breasts bouncing, Big Betsy started down to the end of the bar to wait for Leo's hurried attentions, but on her way she passed what she at first took to be a lampshade and then realized was a man, sitting at the bar. Big Betsy ground to a halt and rotated her head for a more detailed inspection. It was definitely male, and that made it a prospective customer, but if it was a john, it was about the weirdest john Big Betsy had ever seen. His eyes fixed on the TV screen, the weird john licked the back of his hand, sprinkled salt on it, took hold of the shot glass in front of him, grasped a wedge of lemon, licked the salt, bit the lemon, and swallowed the entire contents of the glass. Big Betsy blinked and shook her head. She waited until the next batter did whatever the next batter did, and then she leaned over the bar. "Hey, Leo," whispered Big Betsy. Since Big Betsy's whisper could have competed successfully with a fog horn, Leo came rushing over. Big Betsy moved on until she reached the far end of the bar, with Leo in hot pursuit.

"What is it?" demanded Leo when he caught up with her. "I don't wanna miss none of the action."

"Me neither," said Big Betsy. "An' that's just what I wanna know—what is it?"

"What's what?"

"That," said Big Betsy, jerking her head.

"Oh," said Leo. "Damn if I know. It just walked in off the street."

"Lord!" exclaimed Big Betsy. "You mean they let it walk around loose?"

"Well," said Leo, "I guess maybe if it was uptown they'd lock it up, but down here, who cares? Now I gotta get back to the game. You want a drink?"

"Nah," said Big Betsy, shaking her head sadly, "it's that time a the month." Leo nodded understandingly and got her carton of milk out of the cooler. Big Betsy sighed. "I sure hope that check comes through a little early, 'cause I sure am sick a this white cow piss."

"It's good for your ulcer," said Leo, pouring the milk.

Big Betsy grunted and looked down at the weird john. "He sure does like baseball," she observed. The weird john was sitting tensely on his stool, eyes firmly on the screen, hands clasped as if he were praying.

"Oh yeah," said Leo. "He's a real nut. He give me his own damn pregame show, quoted me battin' averages an' ERAs like they was gospel."

"Goddamn, Leo," said Big Betsy, "what the hell is an ERA?"

"Ask him. He knows everythin'. I betcha he could tell you what color Richie Allen shits."

"All I wanna know," grumbled Big Betsy, "is when ma goddamn welfare check is comin' in so's I can quit ruinin' ma insides with this . . . this . . ." Big Betsy waved both hands at the glass of milk in a gesture of total disgust.

But Leo wasn't listening. He had eased himself into a position from which he could see the TV. Big Betsy watched for a while, frowning constantly and superimposing a grimace each time she took a sip of her milk. The half inning ended, and Leo turned to wait on the dozen or so customers who were crowded into the section of the bar directly in front of the TV set. Big Betsy glowered in frustration. Twelve men in the room and she couldn't even promote a short Coke because they were all too busy watching some dumbass toss a ball of horseshit at another dumbass while another dumbass tried to hit it with a stick. Big Betsy watched, cursing. She was put out by the inattention of all of them, but she was particularly put out by the inattention of the weird john, who, according to Big Betsy's indisputably professional opinion, should have been particularly susceptible to her charms, since he had never before been exposed to them. Forty-five years of experience had taught Big Betsy to respect the seductive powers of unfamiliarity, but this particular individual seemed immune. Big Betsy thought he might be a faggot, but Big Betsy had heard somewhere that faggots did not like sports. In fact, that's how you could tell which little boys were going to grow up bent. Big Betsy glumly decided that she could not write off the weird john's lack of interest to homosexual tendencies. Anger rose within her, increasing with every sip of milk she took. She thought hard. A light came into her eye

"Haw, haw, haw," laughed Big Betsy the whore, throwing her head back as far as it would go and straightening her back to accentuate her bosom. She peered around through partly closed eyes as the sound of her braying laughter echoed in the confined space of Lightnin' Ed's. But nobody came over to ask her what was so funny. Nobody looked interested. Nobody even looked mildly distracted, except Leo, who gave her an angry, silencing glare and then turned his attention back to the TV set. Big Betsy brought her head forward once again and allowed her back to slip into a relaxing slump. She sipped her milk, made a face, sighed. For long minutes she sat motionless, but then a light glimmered in her eye once again. She climbed off her bar stool and marched down to the knot of men before the TV. She eased in between them, making room for herself with dainty heaves of bosom and buttocks, until she was directly behind the weird john. She pressed her breasts firmly against his back. She felt him stiffen slightly. Smiling to herself, she increased the pressure and rocked gently from side to side. The weird john slowly raised his hands to the level of his shoulders and clenched his fists. Big Betsy grinned broadly and tried to choke the weird john from behind with pure mama pressure.

"GO!" screamed the weird john. Big Betsy beamed. She felt the warm glow of fulfillment burst like a small explosion somewhere in her belly, below the layers of girdle-encased fat. And then she suddenly realized that all the other men were shouting too. She looked at the weird john, discovered that his eyes had never left the TV screen, and glanced up in time to see the instant replay of a Philadelphia player climbing to his feet and dusting off his pants after sliding into third base with a triple. Big Betsy backed away in embarrassment, retreated hastily to the far end of the bar, mounted her stool, stared despondently at the wall. One fat tear of rage and frustration escaped from her eye and trailed down the side of her nose before vanishing into a gaping pore at the base of her left nostril. She sighed.

It was the first time in forty-five years that Big Betsy had confused an erection with a three-two pitch.

Willie T. was having a hate affair with everyone in the city named Brown, which, so Willie T. had discovered, was a considerable number of people to try to hate. That was precisely the reason that Willie T. hated them. There were so many Browns that Willie T. had no way of knowing which one of all the Browns he had discovered was the Brown he was looking for. He wasn't even sure that while he was busy finding all the Browns he wasn't looking for he had found the Brown he was looking for. Willie T. didn't know if he had been totally unsuccessful or far too successful, but they both amounted to the same thing: he couldn't give Leroy the Brown Leroy wanted, and Leroy was going to be unhappy, and when Leroy was unhappy everybody was unhappy, and when Leroy was unhappy with somebody in particular, that particular somebody became particularly unhappy. In the past such somebodies had been known to become so particularly unhappy that they had broken their own arms. Willie T. started getting unhappy.

He picked up the phone book, snorted, cursed, put the book down, picked up the phone, snorted, cursed, put the phone down, snorted, cursed, paced the length of the room, snorted, cursed, opened the door, went out to the bar and appropriated a full bottle of whiskey, snorted, cursed, returned to the office, bottle in one hand, shot glass in the other. He poured a shot, made a face, swallowed the whiskey, snorted, cursed and was reaching for the bottle again when somebody threw a bucketful of hot tar against the inside of his stomach. Willie T. gasped and sank down on the edge of the pool table. He felt marginally less unhappy. He regarded the bottle with a look of great respect.

Thirty minutes later, when Leroy made his entrance and sat down behind his desk, the bottle was one-third empty, and Willie T. was perched on the edge of the pool table, swaying gently and feeling far from unhappy. Leroy watched calmly as Willie T., no longer bothering with the glass, raised the bottle to the light, examined it, put it to his lips, took two large swallows, lowered the bottle, and wiped his mouth with the back of his hand. "Well?" said Leroy.

Willie T. jiggled and joggled and managed to turn without falling. "Fine, thank you. And yourself?"

Leroy smiled a shark smile. "Now don't you be playin' Chinese tag with ma ass, nigger," he said sweetly. The smile left his face and his lower lip protruded. "Didja find him?"

"Find who?" said Willie T. Leroy turned slightly darker. "Oh, yeah, I 'member now. Nah, man, I checked everywheres but there wasn't no sign of the ecgheckt," said Willie T. as Leroy reached across the desk, grasped him firmly by the throat, and elevated him two feet off the edge of the pool table.

"Don't you sit on your ass while you tellin' me what a muthafuckin' jackass you is; you stand up an' tell me."

"Ecgheckt," said Willie T. Leroy dropped him onto the pool table. Willie T. bounced quickly to his feet. "Jesus, boss . . ."

"Say it!" thundered Leroy. "Tell me what a muthafuckin' jackass you is. An' an idiot. I almost forgot the idiot."

"Just because I can't find one goddamn nigger in a whole goddamn city full a niggers don't make me a goddamn idiot," said Willie T. in a fit of drunken defiance. Willie T. was unaccustomed to neat whiskey.

Leroy smiled. "I done give up tryin' to figure out what does make you an idiot." He resumed his seat. "Well, maybe I didn't give you enough time. You got till tomorrow."

The whiskey had a dangerous effect on several portions of Willie T.'s anatomy. It had caused his brain to soften, his mouth to loosen, and his backbone to stiffen. "You can give till next Juvember," he snapped. "There ain't noplace left to look."

"You looked in the bars?"

"That, fool, was the first place I looked."

Leroy stared at him. "Whad you say?"

"I said the bars was the first place I looked."

"That's what I thought you said. Where else?"

"Where else? *Everywhere* else. I checked the hospitals, the phone company, the 'lectric company, the gas company, the welfare board, the Post Office, the churches, the runners, the pushers, the hookers, the pawnshops, *and* the goddamn po-lice, not to mention the Democratic party and the N double Ass CP. Honest to Jesus, Leroy, this nigger ain't human. He don't call nobody, he don't get no mail, he don't cook nothin', he don't pray for nothin'. He don't buy nothin', sell nothin', play nothin', snort nothin', shoot nothin', smoke nothin', fuck nothin' . . . I mean he don't do *nothin'*."

"He bothers me," snapped Leroy, "an' when I finds him I'm gonna kick shit outa him. An' if you don't find him pretty damn quick you gonna start botherin' me. An' I knows where you are to start with."

Willie T. felt the warm embers the whiskey had left glowing in his gullet turn, one by one, into ashes. He started to sink down on the edge of the pool table, caught himself, and began to ease away from Leroy. "Get me some dinner," Leroy commanded.

"Sure, boss, sure," stammered Willie T., trying to remember how to walk, "uh, what brand?"

"The usual," Leroy growled.

Willie T. nodded spastically and stumbled toward the door. Just as he got there it·swung inward and caught him on the forehead. "Ugpumph," said Willie T., rebounding into the center of the room, where he fetched up against the pool table and then collapsed onto the floor. Cotton, his inertia undiminished by the resistance of Willie T.'s mass, continued through the door. He closed it softly behind him.

"Hope I ain't interruptin' nothin'," Cotton said.

"Nope," Leroy replied, "nothin' 'cept Willie T. fetchin' me a drink. Willie, you black-assed fuck-up, get up an' get me a goddamn drink. *If* you can find the bar. Then you get your tail on outa here. I want every bar on the street checked seven times tonight."

"Umph," said Willie T., twitching slightly.

"What for?" said Cotton. He walked casually over to the pool table, stepping carefully over the prostrate Willie T., and started to rack the balls.

" 'Cause I said so," snapped Leroy. "Who the hell's givin' orders around here?"

"I was just wonderin'," Cotton said soothingly, with a shrug of his massive shoulders. He finished racking the balls, selected a cue, picked up the chalk. "You ah, lookin' for somethin' special, Willie, or you just throwin' your little shit around?"

"Ahumpaha," said Willie T.

"He's lookin' for somethin' special," said Leroy impatiently. "What is this?"

"Just a little curiosity," said Cotton, smiling innocently and chalking his cue. He inspected the tip with a critical eye, added a touch of chalk, blew away the excess.

Willie T. rose to his knees, shaking his head groggily. Leroy glared at him. "He's still lookin' for Brown."

Cotton bent over the pool table, adjusted the cue ball with exaggerated care, using only the tip of the cue. "Oh," he drawled. "Course, this fool here couldn't find a pile a shit in a perfume plant." He straightened up and beamed benevolently on Willie T., then bent back to the table.

"Fuck you," mumbled Willie T. "I'ma find him. You just gotta be givin' me a little space. It ain't gonna take moren a minute." Cotton snorted without looking up. "You couldn't find him," Willie T said. "You can't look through no phone book, 'cause you can't read. Hell, you can't hardly talk good, even."

Cotton smiled and made a minute adjustment to the position of the cue ball. "You does enough talkin' for everybody. An' as for readin', readin' ain't everythin'." He made a minor change in the position of his feet and took a few experimental pokes with the cue.

Willie T. struggled to his feet. "Yeah, fatso? Then *you* find him."

Cotton looked at Willie T. and grinned. He turned his head back to the table and, without appearing to take aim, sent the cue ball rolling down the velvet to strike the massed balls at the far end of the table with a solid crack. "Already did," Cotton said, his eyes on the balls as they rolled here and there, striking each other with tiny clicks, bouncing off cushions, veering toward pockets, and dropping out of sight; first the fifteen, then the one, and finally the eight. Cotton looked up into Willie T.'s stricken face and chuckled. "Yes, sir. I done found the nigger." Leroy stood in silence while Cotton circumnavigated the pool table, deciding on his next shot. He settled on the five ball and bent his head in concentration, but just as he began the stroke Leroy's hand shot out and grasped the cue. The tip of it struck the cue ball a glancing blow and the ball spun madly for a few seconds without moving an inch. When it had stopped completely, Cotton allowed his eyes to travel back along the cue until his glance reached Leroy's hand, then on up his arm to look finally into Leroy's congested face. "I wish you wouldn't do things like that," Cotton said mildly.

"You play durin' recess," Leroy snarled, "an' I say when recess is. Right now school's in. Where is this muthafucka?"

Cotton smiled easily and looked pointedly at Leroy's hand. Leroy gritted his teeth but released the cue. Cotton smiled again and began to line up his shot. "Well," he said, bending over the table, "he *was* right outside."

"On the street?" demanded Leroy. "Muthafucka's got his nerve walkin' ma street again."

"He wasn't on the street," Cotton said.

"Humph," Leroy said. "Better not be."

"He was in the bar."

"In the *bar?*" said Willie T. "The Elysium bar?"

"Shut up, Willie," said Cotton.

"Boss, can he tell me to shut up?"

"No," said Leroy. "I'm the only one can tell you to shut up. Now shut up. Cotton, you mean to tell me he was settin' right out there an' you left him get away?"

"Sure," Cotton said. He sent the cue ball bouncing off the cushion to cut the five ball into the side pocket. "He was gettin' a six to go. I figured by the time I called you he'd be gone, so I followed him instead."

There was a long heavy silence while Cotton lined up a bank shot on the eleven. "Well, I don't believe it," said Willie T. suddenly. "I don't believe a single goddamn word. Cotton, how long did you follow this cat? An hour? Two?"

"I followed him home. Figured that was far enough."

"You mean to tell me you followed this cat all the way home. . . ."

"Easy as apple pie," Cotton said.

"Yeah. Too damn easy," said Willie T. "You know what I think?"

"I'm still tryin' to figure out *if* you think," Cotton said.

"I think it's a setup," said Willie T. "How come this big bad dude who's supposed to be movin' in an' takin' over don't even know if he's tailed?"

Cotton sighed and shot the four ball. "Well, Willie, I guess maybe he just didn't notice me."

"Guess not," snapped Willie T. "Guess I wouldn't notice neither if a fuckin' hippopotamus was to follow me home."

Cotton looked up, his broad features crowding themselves into a much smaller space. "If I was you, Willie, I'd watch that little shit, 'fore I put ma foot right through your contraption."

"Damn," said Leroy, low and dirty in the back of his throat. Cotton and Willie T. stared at the clenched fists, the scowl of hate on Leroy's face. "Damn. Cat goes walkin' in ma streets in the broad daylight. Cat goes prowlin' in ma space an' don't even take the time to look around. Cat goes prancin' into ma bars tellin' folks what to do. Cat goes an' does all that, I say the cat goes. Period."

"But what if he does work for Gino?" said Willie T. softly.

"I don't care if the nigger's on the board a directors in hell. Cotton, where—"

"Upstairs from Rayburn Wallace," Cotton said. He raised his eyes and looked directly at Leroy. "An' upstairs from Mrs. Wallace, too, a course."

Leroy's expression of hate was tempered by bewilderment. "Jesus, he's after ma women, too." He spun on his heels and charged out of the room. Cotton chuckled softly, snorted, and turned back to the pool table.

"Phew," said Willie T. "I sure hope that cat don't work for Gino."

"What if he does," said Cotton.

"What if he does?" screamed Willie T. "When Leroy pounds him Gino pounds us, that's what if he does." Willie T. began to gibber.

"Shut the shit up," said Cotton. He put the pool cue down, walked over and slapped Willie T. Willie T. fell to the floor. Cotton hauled him back to his feet, dusted him off. "Take it easy now, Willie," Cotton said. "Leroy ain't gonna pound that dude. Leroy ain't gonna pound nobody. Leroy's turnin' into the biggest, softest piece a chicken dirt since the Little Red Hen had a shit fit. Hell, he keeps you around just so he don't have to go too far to find somebody he don't have to be scared of." Cotton grinned and slapped Willie T. on the back. Laughing uproariously, he sauntered out. A stunned Willie T. started to sink to the edge of the pool table but checked himself, out of habit, and peered over his shoulder at the door.

Brown was on his hands and knees, using a screwdriver to chisel away at the hardened accumulation of dirt, mucus, and chewing gum adhering to the underside of the rickety wooden table. With each thrust the table gave an outraged squeak and rocked back and forth on uneven legs. The room, a kitchen, was clean but bare, containing only an ancient gas stove, a dilapidated refrigerator, a stained porcelain sink, a few sagging cabinets, two chairs, the table, and Brown, who smiled in grim contentment as he chipped away at the rocklike mass. Brown had, with some difficulty, levered the window open, and a breeze blew through it bringing a teasing eddy of relative coolness into the room's humid oppression, and, along with it, the sounds of traffic and a crying baby and the too-sweet smell of garbage rotting unprotestingly in the alley.

Brown paused and leaned back against the wall and sighed. He wiped his brow with the back of his hand, leaving a long streak of dirt which turned instantly to mud as it encountered the sweat on his forehead. Brown examined the back of his hand, shrugged, and wiped it on his once-white shirt, picked up the screwdriver, and again attacked the residue beneath the table. He worked away for a few minutes, grunting and grimacing from the effort, stopping suddenly when he heard someone coming up the stairs.

Brown got quickly to his feet, moved silently toward the door. It rattled slightly as someone touched the knob. Brown flattened himself against the wall, grasped the screwdriver tightly. There was a soft, hesitant knock on the door. Brown relaxed slightly. "Come in," he said. Nothing happened. Brown swallowed and worked his fingers on the handle of the screwdriver. He held his breath, reached out and grasped the door handle, and jerked the door open, springing back against the wall as it swung.

"Adlai?"

Brown relaxed completely, moved away from the wall, and faced the still-empty doorway. "Do come in," he said.

She stepped gingerly across the threshold, stopped just inside the door, glanced at the peeling walls, then looked at Brown. "Hello, Adlai," she said.

"Hi," Brown said.

Her glance traveled around the room, lingering on each example of unsavory deterioration, settling finally on the chairs. "May I sit down?"

"Huh? Oh, yeah, sure, sit down. Over here." Brown held the rickety chair as she slid onto it, crossing her legs with a light screech of nylon. "Do you want something to drink? I've got instant coffee and some iced-tea mix. There's nothing else except tap water and beer and the water's awful and I know you hate beer."

"I'll have a beer," she said precisely.

"A beer," Brown said. "Right." He took a can of beer from the refrigerator, pulled off the tab, and poured the contents into an empty jelly jar. "I don't have any real glasses yet," Brown said apologetically.

She looked at him, took a sip, made a face, took three or four deep swallows, and lowered the jar. "Now," she said, "will you please tell me why you're hiding from me or running from me or whatever it is you think you're doing?"

Brown got another beer out of the refrigerator, taking his time about it. "Do you expect me to answer that?" he said finally. "If you do you'll have to rephrase the question."

She raised the jar and took a few more swallows. Brown watched her move and realized that she hadn't started drinking with the beer. It made him feel a little stronger. She placed the jar on the table with a jerky movement of arm and hand. The liquid sloshed against the glass, fizzed angrily, subsided. "Are you coming back?" she asked.

Brown took a deep breath, closed his eyes, opened them, looked at the peeling wall. "I don't think so," he said. He hesitated a moment, then looked full into her face. She slumped slightly and began to cry. "Oh Jesus," Brown said, "please, Alicia, don't cry." He reached over to place a hand on her shoulder.

She jerked away from him. "Shut up, Adlai," she said. There were no tears in her voice. "I mean, God, Adlai, after all this time you stand there and tell me you don't think you're coming back, and I'm supposed to smile and say, yes dear, thank you dear?"

Brown took his hand away. "You're right. I'm sorry. Go ahead and cry."

"Thanks. Thank you very much." She wiped her eyes with the back of her hand, reached for her purse. Brown pulled out his handkerchief and handed it to her. She looked at it, accepted it, blew her nose. She sniffed once or twice. "What is it, Adlai? Do you think there's something wrong with me? Do you? Please tell me if you do, because you know what? I think there's something wrong with you. Definitely."

Brown pulled the other chair out from under the table, twisting it around so that the back of it formed a barrier between them when he settled down astraddle it. "There's something wrong with me," he said. "I can't stand being a gigolo."

"What?"

"Gigolo. Kept man."

"You're a poet."

"I'm a pet," Brown snapped. "Example. Earl's party. There I am in the corner. Dialogue: 'Oh, Doris, who's that? *That*, darling, is Adlai Stevenson Brown, the distinguished poet. Really? I've never heard of him. Of *course* you haven't, darling. He's *obscure!* Isn't that *divine?* You must *meet* him. He's just like obscure poets are supposed to be—he uses dirty words and he has three names. Yes but—who's that? Oh, that's Miss Hadley. They're together. She has the money. But nothing lasts forever. Come meet him.'" Brown smiled wryly.

"That's the way you felt?" she said softly.

Brown looked at her. "No, baby, that's not the way I felt, that's the way it *was*. If I ever need money I'll get Earl to be my pimp."

"And it was all my fault."

Exasperation danced in the corners of Brown's eyes. "It doesn't matter whose fault it was. What matters is what I have to do about it."

"And my happiness doesn't count for anything?"

"Sure," Brown said. "But not as much as my survival. I was dyin' up there, Alicia. Sooner or later I was maybe gonna let myself go all the way and really die. Can't you see, I had to do something."

"What? Live in a dump? You know what I think, Adlai? I think that's a lot of crap, that's what I think. Crap. Just like all the other crap you fed me, about how you were going to be one of the world's great artists. Only you didn't tell me the world's great artist wanted to—to—eat like a hog and drink like a fish and—and—screw like a billy goat so he wouldn't ever have time to produce any of that great art. Maybe that's just as well. Maybe that art wouldn't be so great. All you've done for the last year is send out old poems and line wastepaper cans. When you weren't too drunk to find the wastepaper can."

Brown grunted. "Well. You can always hide the bottles and have me fixed. That'll take care of the fish and the billy goat. I don't know about the pig, but I'm sure you'll think of something."

"I couldn't have your balls cut off, Adlai. You don't have them any more."

Brown sighed and leaned forward, propping his chin on the back of the chair.

"I'm sorry," she said. "I didn't mean that."

Brown looked at her.

"I'm sorry. I said I was sorry."

"A white mother complex," Brown said musingly. "That's what you've got. 'Don't use language like that, Adlai. Don't drink so much, Adlai. Sex is dirty, Adlai, so don't get a hardon. Don't put your feet on the table, don't pick your nose, don't play with your shit—'"

"Can't you say three words without—"

"See!" Brown shouted.

"Oh, God, now he's screaming. Just like a five year old. Look at him gritting his teeth. Ooooh, aren't we fierce?"

"Shut up," Brown mumbled.

"Rough, too. He gives orders. I wonder if he can dress himself?"

"Shut up," Brown said.

"But he *does* tend to repeat himself. I think I liked him better drunk. At least then he'd go to sleep."

"Will you please shut up?" Brown said.

"Please? He said 'please.' Maybe he'll put his paws up and beg."

Brown's hand shot across the chair back and grabbed her wrist. The jelly jar upset and beer ran in a foaming wave across the table. Brown hauled her to her feet, kicking over the chair between them, and squeezed her wrist until a little yelp of pain escaped her throat. Then he let her go, suddenly, and bent over to retrieve his chair. He sat down in it, breathing heavily. She stood looking at him for a while, then took a step toward him, her foot making a soft splashing sound in the beer that had dripped from the table to form an amber pool on the floor. "Adlai?"

"I remember," Brown said, not looking up at her, "when I would have done my best to kill anyone who touched you like that." He got up and went to the sink, took the rag that hung over the gooseneck in the rusty drain pipe, wet it. The plumbing gave an agonized screech as he turned the faucet. He went back and knelt by the table near Alicia's legs and began to wipe up the spilled beer, listening with insane intensity to the slapping sounds made by the wet rag, the small noises of her clothing, and the creak of the chair as she sat down again.

"Adlai?"

"What?"

"I don't see why you have to do whatever it is you have to do right *here*. It's so ugly. Why couldn't we find you some place—"

"No," Brown said. "I have to do it here. Because . . ." Brown stopped and looked around at the peeling walls. "I don't know. There's something here. It explains something to me."

She looked at him, nodding her head. "So *that's* it. A research project. An anthropological study of the natives in their native habitat. Or maybe it's political science or whatever they're calling Marx now. You know, a quest for reality in the capital-H heart of the capital-G ghetto with the capital-P people. You can be the capital-PP proletarian poet, only in blackface. Reality and truth and virtue all add up to poverty. That is so *stupid.* . . ."

"No," Brown said. "It's not a research project. And the middle of the ghetto isn't real. You don't cut with the side of a knife. Only the edge is real. And this is the edge. One block away is Lombard Street, and the houses cost sixty thousand, and they worry about brownouts cutting down on their air-conditioning. Here it doesn't even matter what the houses cost because they're all condemned anyway, and you don't think about air-conditioning, you half expect they're gonna cut off the air."

"But *you* don't have to be here. *You* don't have to live here."

"We *all* live here," Brown said. "And all the carpets and college degrees in the world won't do anything but help you forget."

Alicia looked away. "I don't think you *want* to forget."

Brown smiled. "No," he said, "no, I'd love to forget. Only we don't get to forget. That's the one big difference between white folks and black folks: black folks never get to forget. Not for very long, anyway." Brown looked at her, then turned his gaze back to the wall. They sat in silence.

"Do you still go over to Franklin Field to run?" she said finally.

"What?"

"Franklin Field. Do you go over there to run?"

"Oh," Brown said. "No. I run on the street. Franklin Field's too crowded."

"Even in the summer?"

"Yeah," Brown said.

"Oh. Well. I guess . . ." She stood up abruptly. "Thank you for the beer."

"I spilled most of it." Brown rose too and went to the sink to wring out the rag.

"I don't like beer much anyway."

Brown hung the rag back on the gooseneck and wiped his hands on his tee shirt. He walked to the door and stood awkwardly beside her, rubbing his hands across his chest long after they were dry.

"Adlai?" She reached out, lightly touched his bare arm. He pulled her to him, held her tightly against him, kissed her.

"It wouldn't do any good," Brown said.

"You want me."

"It doesn't matter if I want you. It wouldn't do any good."

"If you want me to beg, I'm begging."

"All right," Brown said.

"I'll let you come right back. I promise I won't try and make you stay."

Brown looked at her, smiling faintly. "I have a bed here."

"You want to—here?"

Brown smiled sadly. "I told you it wouldn't do any good." He stepped away from her.

Her lips tightened. "You'll never make it, Adlai. You don't belong down here. No matter how hard you try, you don't belong down here and you never will." She spun away, moving toward the door.

"I don't belong with you and the cocktail parties and the duplex Cadillacs," Brown said. "I don't need all that."

"You'll be back," she said. She pulled the door open and stepped out into the hall.

❧

Leo reached up with his hammy hand and clicked off the TV set, making that mundane action and gesture of total disgust. "Shit," Leo said. "I'ma open me a bar in Pittsburgh, where leastways they can win some damn ball games." The row of disgruntled faces which, until the final out, had been crowded in front of the TV set, nodded in agreement. Leo's strange customer bobbed his head emphatically. Leo poured him another shot of tequila and took payment from the change reposing on the bar. Leo watched in the mirror as the weird customer solemnly sprinkled salt on a wedge of lemon, bit it, and swallowed the tequila. Leo shook his head and rang up the sale.

"You know, Leo," said the strange customer, "I still have a ticket to the nineteen sixty-four world series."

"Yeah," said Leo. "What was they? Eight games in front with ten games to go? An' then they blow it. Ain't that a bitch?"

"I've been in this town for almost ten years and we haven't won a thing in all that time."

"We got pitchin' problems," said Leo.

"Yeah. And hitting problems. And fielding problems. And base-running problems. And it's not just baseball. There isn't a team in town that wins."

"Yeah," said Leo, "things is so bad the only thing they give even odds on is the school-board elections."

"Even odds?"

"Yeah," said Leo. "You know. Odds."

"Oh yes. Of course. Odds."

"My God," muttered Leo, moving away in response to a lifted eyebrow. 'My God."

Big Betsy had been sitting in dejection at the far end of the bar, musing on the ravages of time, the inequities of age, and the unendurable perversity of a world in which a man would rather watch a bad ball game than buy drinks for a lady. After one round against the baseball game Big Betsy had failed to answer the bell, and had stayed in her corner contemplating the human condition and nursing her skim milk. But the sudden death of all the frustrated moans that had been roiling around Lightnin' Ed's cinderblock walls caused Big Betsy to emerge from her brown study and once again respond to her surroundings. She noticed that Leo was filling orders without annoyance and that the men were no longer crowded in front of the TV set but were ranged out along the bar, and those who had come with women were paying attention to their companions once again. The TV speaker was silent, the screen dark. Big Betsy took in all these data and concluded that the baseball game was over. Clutching her handbag, Big Betsy vacated her stool and marched to the door marked, in block letters, BROADS.

Locked in what she preferred to call the ladies' powder room—a sour-smelling cubicle containing a commode, a dirty washbasin, a roll of toilet paper suspended by a twist of coat-hanger wire from a spike driven partway into the wall, a paper-towel dispenser (empty), a sanitary-napkin dispenser (full), and a wastepaper basket (overflowing), and the inevitable cracked mirror—Big Betsy prepared to fill the power vacuum created by the expiration of the baseball game. While she had conceded the battle she had not given up the war. Behind the door marked BROADS Big Betsy prepared her counterattack. Opening her purse, she took out the tools of her trade and laid them out on the flat top of the toilet tank. She meticulously cleaned the sink and set to work with eye make-up, and Murine for her reddened eyes, lipstick—two shades, one darker to de-emphasize the dimension of her dangling underlip—for her mouth, blusher for her sagging jowls. She removed her dentures and scrubbed them vigorously. She checked her fingernail polish and adjusted the black wig that covered the gray wool that topped her head. She examined herself in the mirror and pronounced herself passable. She packed her equipment back into her purse, hiked up her skirt, pulled down her white linen drawers, and sat down on the toilet seat, which strained at its mountings, and micturated with a sound like the firing of a battery of Gatling guns.

Big Betsy emerged into the barroom and advanced on the weird john with a glint of steely determination in her eye. Seeing that the stool next to him was unoccupied, she cut her engines, put her rudder hard over, and dropped anchor. "Hi there," said Big Betsy. She smiled, tilting her face around to make sure he got a good look at the fake beauty mark that adorned her left cheek.

"Uh, hello," said the weird john. His Adam's apple bobbed. "Can I do something for you?"

Big Betsy stared at him. She had never liked it when they gave up without a struggle, and she wasn't used to it either—nobody had given up to Big Betsy without a struggle in at least fifteen years. At least nobody who was both sober and sighted. Big Betsy wasn't even sure he had given up; it had sounded more like he was propositioning her. Big Betsy's mind was about to reject that idea as being totally impossible, but her ego rescued it and sent it back for further consideration.

"Huh?" said Big Betsy. The weird john smiled at her. He reached out and picked up the saltshaker, licked the back of his hand, sprinkled on some salt. "Uh, I don't know," said Big Betsy, recovering a trace of composure which vanished as soon as the weird john calmly squeezed some lemon over the salt on the back of his hand, licked the mixture off, and downed the contents of a shot glass in one gulp. "Well, you could buy me a drink," Big Betsy said.

"I," announced the weird john, "am drinking . . ." He paused and looked surprised. "Leo," he called, "what am I drinking?"

Leo turned away from the cash register and peered at him. "Tequila," Leo told him. "You want another one?"

"Please. Two."

"Two?"

The weird john nodded toward Big Betsy. "Oh, no," said Big Betsy, who was quite flattered at what she took as a subtle attempt to erode her defenses, "I'll have me somethin' else."

"You want the usual, Betsy?" Leo inquired, pouring out a fresh slug of tequila.

"Naw," said Big Betsy, "I'll have me some gin. I'ma need it." Leo wordlessly reached for the gin bottle and poured Big Betsy a double shot.

Big Betsy took a large swallow to fortify herself before she turned back to business. She was just in time to watch the weird john pour a little tequila over the salt-and-lemon mixture in the palm of his hand and lick it off. "Are you sure you sposed to do it that way?" said Big Betsy. "I don't think you sposed to do it that way."

"I was experimenting," said the weird john.

"You're just like the dude was in here the other night," said Big Betsy. "You both talks funny."

"How so?" said the weird john.

"My God," said Big Betsy, grabbing for the gin.

"Mine as well," said the weird john. He looked at Big Betsy, his gaze piercing. "To be honest, I was not experimenting at all. I just forgot the correct way to do it."

"That I can believe," said Big Betsy. "I bet you forgot how you sposed to drink that there whatever it is, too."

The weird john looked confused. Big Betsy smiled to herself, feeling that once again she was steering the conversation into businesslike channels. She leaned forward, allowing her left mammary to press insistently against the weird john's arm. The weird john seemed to get the message; he leaned toward her. "You want to know something?" said the weird john.

"Baby, I know it already," said Big Betsy, "but I'd love to hear you say it."

The weird john looked around, leaned closer. "I'm on a secret undercover assignment."

Big Betsy straightened up. "Aw shit! Don't tell me you're one a them goddamn cunts from the goddamn vice squad! Well you listen here, you honky-rented asshole, if you think you gonna be haulin' Betsy off to the pokey you got another think comin', 'cause I ain't goin' nowhere, an' it's gonna take a damn sight more than a skinny little shit like you to move me. Now you wanna try an' haul me in, you go right ahead." Big Betsy glared at the weird john for a minute, then climbed indignantly off the stool, gathered up her purse.

"Huh?" said the weird john.

"You heard me," snapped Big Betsy. She shot him a final glare and waddled away, muttering dire threats and swearing to drink skim milk until her welfare check came through.

6 Friday

Brother Fletcher sat by the window in his lumpy overstuffed chair, letting the golden morning sunlight warm his throbbing head, holding his Bible in his hands. He was not reading—but it gave him comfort to hold it. The morning air belched over him, already hot and sticky and charged with exhaust fumes. At his elbow was a glass of iced tea, lemoned and sugared, all but stirred by Mrs. Fletcher, who, guessing Brother Fletcher's mood (if not his condition), had withdrawn, leaving him to his meditations.

Brother Fletcher wished that she had stayed.

He opened the Bible, his hands moving absently over the thin rice-paper pages that rustled softly in the breeze. His eyes picked out a word here and there, and from the glimpses of words whole verses took shape in his mind. But the verses did not blossom, as they usually did, into larger and grander understanding; something cackling in his mind made the verses sound irrelevant.

Brother Fletcher wondered if he were not irrelevant.

There had been a time, years—not that many, but enough—before, when Brother Fletcher had been committed to saving the world and convinced that he would eventually succeed. After he had realized that he wasn't going to do that at all, there had been a time when he had still wished that he could. And then there had been a later time when, reconciled to his impotence in greater matters, Brother Fletcher had wanted only to save the people who clearly needed it, those he saw and pitied. But then he had realized with a shock that some people felt *he* needed help, that some people, often the same people whom he pitied, felt sorry for him. So Brother Fletcher had gone back to wanting to save the world, but with the certain disturbing knowledge that most of it did not want to be saved. He did not try to force salvation. He wanted only to save the people that he loved. Sometimes he wanted only to save himself, and in those guilty moments he wondered if Carleton T. Fletcher was capable of saving anybody from anything. But while Brother Fletcher had often doubted himself, he had never before lost faith in the power of his belief. The fault had, to Brother Fletcher's mind, lain with men, men who sinned, or who forgot, or who failed in their purpose. But now, sitting before the window with the hot breath of the city blowing heresies in his ear, Brother Fletcher wondered if what he had thought was salvation was anything at all, if life on earth were really just a prelude to glory, if Mumbo Jumbo, God of the Congo, were not to be preferred to invisible Jehovah and his enigmatic Son. Brother Fletcher had ventured out into the Land of Nod and found, much to his surprise, that he liked it better than the Garden. He had entered the den of lions and discovered that, while there were perhaps no lambs, the lions themselves were capable of a lamblike innocence. He had emerged, paradoxically drunken and sobered, recognizing for the first time that there was a difference between lambs and sheep. Sitting before the window, the white lace curtain slapping gently in his face, the black-backed Bible in his dark brown hand, Brother Fletcher felt himself slipping into doubt. Perhaps the Reverend Mr. Sloan had the right idea after all: all you needed to do was to give them a little music, a lot of wine, and a manufactured miracle or two. It kept them happy, which was more than you could say for the Gospel according to Matthew. It convinced them they were safe and saved and right and good in a world where safe meant dead and right often meant dead, too. It assured them that God heard their prayers for a color TV or a hit on the number. It let them think it was always summer because it kept their backs to the wind. It let them consider the lilies when the alternative in too many cases was to consider the poppies. Part of Brother Fletcher realized all that, recognized the right of people to hide, and even shared the desire, but another part of him longed to grasp the great Christian congregation by the throat and shake it until it wanted what it *should* want. As if, Brother Fletcher thought, smiling to himself, he knew.

Brother Fletcher sighed and picked up his glass of iced tea. He thought about his wife, the things he could have bought for her, the time he could have spent with her had he not had such passion for his faith. He could have given her a house in the country instead of an apartment in a smog-ridden city. He could have given her a husband who came home at night instead of one who was always attending an endless succession of committee meetings, services, teas, luncheons, and fried-chicken dinners. He should have stayed with the denomination instead of staying with The Word of Life; in time he would have been assigned to a decent church somewhere in the south, in the country, where life was easier and more pleasant. But he had chosen to stay with The Word of Life. Brother Fletcher would have felt a lot less guilty if Mrs. Fletcher had questioned and complained a little, but she never had. She deserved everything that Brother Fletcher knew she didn't want. He had thought that what he was doing was worth the price, but now he didn't know. He felt certain there was no salvation in The Word of Life; it was a three-ring circus complete with funny costumes, colored lights. Brother Fletcher felt dirty and stupid every time he looked down from the stage at the fat stupid sweaty faces, and he felt guilty thinking of them that way, but that was what they looked like. They loved the prancing, and they took the praying like children eating their spinach so that they could have ice cream later on. They flocked and paid through the nose and clapped and shouted and Brother Carleton T. Fletcher, assistant magician, second-degree mesmerizer, deputy dispenser of pabulum and pureed prunes, was sick unto death and wanted out. And yet he could not be sure it was meaningless. He could not be sure he wasn't helping somebody. Maybe he did not know what meaning was: God moves in mysterious ways and who was Carleton T. Fletcher to say that The Word of Life wasn't one of them? Perhaps all he could do in true humble Christianity was to give them what they asked for, let them sing and shout and feel themselves washed in the blood of the Lamb, and then sit in front of the window inhaling the halitosis of the city, Bible in hand, and try to cleanse his own soul, to try to find the peace for himself that The Word of Life seemed to give to others. In Lightnin' Ed's he had had a glimpse of it, but to bring himself to accept that fact would be to upset all his years of belief.

Brother Fletcher stared out the window, over South Street's softening tar, watching the winos line up in front of the barred windows behind which the state dispensed oblivion. Brother Fletcher felt suddenly helpless. He took a sip of iced tea, frowned because he had forgotten to stir it. Then he opened the Bible and tried to read.

Rayburn signed his name on the back of the check and joined one of the lines of people waiting for the attentions of a teller. Rayburn chose the line which seemed the longest and waited comfortably, glancing around at the well-dressed women and business-suited men in the other lines, smiling to himself as they noticed the rapid advancement of Rayburn's line and compared it with the snail's pace of their own. Rayburn's line included several members of the bank's nighttime cleaning staff, cashing their weekly paychecks. Rayburn nodded to one or two of them, but his eyes were on the teller. The teller's name was Victoria Bender, and she was the fastest bank teller in the world. She stood proudly at her window, her pen making quick neat strokes, the crisp bills snapping off her fingers. Occasionally Victoria would take a dislike to a customer, and if she didn't like someone Victoria would go by the book, which meant checking identification and signatures and everything else under the sun, but usually she sped people through so quickly that she was worth two tellers. Rayburn got into Victoria's line even when he wasn't in a hurry because he loved to watch her work and because he suspected Victoria had a special liking for him.

The line advanced smoothly and in almost no time at all Rayburn was next. He glanced around disdainfully at the people in the other lines, pulled his beret lower on his head, sniffed, and stepped up to the window.

"How doin', honey, did you come fo' some money?" said Victoria. She giggled tightly and wiggled slightly. Rayburn smiled.

"Right," he said in a clipped, businesslike tone of voice. "Cash for all but ten. That"—he produced a savings passbook and a deposit ticket— "goes in here." Victoria grinned at him, accepted the paycheck, deposit slip, and passbook, made a few notations. She tapped a few times on her adding machine, tore off the tape, then turned to the rank of auditing machines on the counter behind her. She inserted the passbook in one of them, typed a few digits, punched a button. The machine clattered for a moment as if deciding what to do, then emitted a grunt and a clank and spat the passbook out into Victoria's waiting fingers. Victoria looked at it, nodded approval, stepped back to the window. She counted out cash, placed the cash in the passbook and the passbook in an envelope, and gave the envelope to Rayburn. "Thanks," Rayburn said, slipping the envelope into his pocket without looking inside.

"Hurry it up," said the customer behind Rayburn.

Victoria looked at him. He was a beefy, red-faced white man in a baggy blue suit, and Victoria took an instant dislike to him. She turned back to Rayburn and batted her eyes. "Baby, baby, what you gonna do with all that gravy?"

"Ain't tha' much," mumbled Rayburn, feeling his face grow a little warm. He looked at Victoria and observed, not for the first time, that she was a very attractive woman, except for her front teeth, which slanted out a bit too far and which had a bit too much gold in them.

"Sure it is," said Victoria. "That's a nice piece a change. What you gonna do, buy yourself a Cadillac?"

"Nah," said Rayburn, "what am I gonna be wantin' with a car like that—eats gas an' takes up more room than a damn elephant? Nah, I been lookin' for someplace to invest it."

The man behind Rayburn snorted. Rayburn felt his neck grow warm. Victoria's dislike for the man grew, and she decided that when she did get around to him she would go by the book. "You hang onto that money, sweetheart, and don't go lettin' no woman get her hands on it."

The beefy man inched forward. His stomach pressed against Rayburn. Rayburn planted his feet and refused to budge. "Come on," said the beefy man.

"Wait you turn," snapped Victoria.

"I've been waiting—"

"So keep on," said Rayburn. "Pretty soon you'll get so good at it you can join the Urban League." He turned and smiled at the beefy man. "An' get offa ma ass."

"Well," sighed Victoria, "I suppose I'd better wait on the, uh, gentleman."

"Sure, baby," said Rayburn, "only I guess I oughta count this here money before I leave." He winked at Victoria. Victoria winked back. Rayburn began to count laboriously.

"Come *on*," growled the beefy man.

Rayburn raised his head. "I done tole you to stay offa ma ass. Now you done made me lose count." He sighed and began to count from the beginning.

"I don't think he *can* count," muttered the beefy man.

Rayburn sighed and started counting all over again. The beefy man remained silent. Rayburn folded the bills and slid them into his pocket. "See you, honey," Rayburn said. He stepped away from the window. "Come on now, honey," the beefy man said to Victoria. "Let's see if you can figure out how to read this before next Christmas."

Victoria smiled at him sweetly. "I ain't your honey," she said. "Now, do you have some form of identification?"

Rayburn stood on the corner outside the bank and considered the disposition of his wealth. There was no food at home. The rent was due. And the gas bill. The electric bill, thank God, had not yet arrived. A little drinking money for Les. A little for him. That would leave just enough to buy her a little present with. Not much, not enough to make her happy, but perhaps enough to keep her quiet. Rayburn walked over to Chestnut Street and turned downtown, walked along, peering in shop windows. The department stores were farther down, and these were small, expensive shops. He moved on. Maybe he ought to just take the money, go somewheres. Canada. Got to be different in Canada. Goddamn right. Canadian whiskey. Dog sleds, penguins, eskimos, polar bears.

Rayburn began to walk with a purpose. He quickly covered three blocks, found the establishment he wanted, pushed open the door. A bell tinkled, and the girl behind the counter said, "May I help you?" without taking her eyes away from the magazine she was reading. Without replying Rayburn took the two steps necessary to bring him to the counter. The girl looked up, saw Rayburn standing a foot away from her, and the smile attached to her face slipped. "Yes?" she said, backing up a step.

"I wants to go to Canada," Rayburn said.

The girl peered at him. "Canada?"

"That's right—Canada," Rayburn said. "Ain't you ever heard of it?"

"Yes, yes, of course," said the girl, pressing her thin lips together.

"Well, all right then, I wants to go. How much?"

The girl stared openly at Rayburn's sweat-stained shirt. She pursed her lips, brushed a strand of dirty-brown hair back behind her ear. "Well," she said, "what sort of vacation did you have in mind?"

"Honey, I ain't plannin' no vacation. I wants to go to Canada, that's all, an' all I want for you to do is to tell me how to get there an' how much it costs. Now can't you do that?"

"Yes, yes, of course. Which, ah, part of Canada did you want to visit?"

"This here's supposed to be a travel agency," Rayburn said, resting his hands on the counter, "so why don't you tell me?"

"Well, I mean, ah, don't you know what Canada is *like?*"

"What's wrong with it?" demanded Rayburn.

"Nothing's *wrong* with it. B-b-but don't you think you ought to know what to expect when you—"

"If I knowed what to expect what the hell would I be wantin' to go for? Wouldn't be much point to it, now would there?"

The girl sighed. "Well, for a start, maybe you should go to Western Canada. It's, ah, slightly more economical." She looked pointedly at his clothes.

"Cheap, too?" asked Rayburn.

The girl looked quickly up at his face to see if he were laughing at her. His face was expressionless. She ignored the question. "I don't think you'd like Quebec."

"Quebec?" said Rayburn. "Isn't that the place where they parley-voo the France?" The girl nodded. "That," said Rayburn, "has *got* to be different. How much?"

"You speak French?"

Rayburn shrugged expansively. "I dunno, honey, I ain't never tried. Didn't talk Japanese, either, when I got there, but I had a good time in Tokyo." He smiled at her, turned, and leaned his back against the counter, hooking his elbows over the edge.

"Tokyo?" the girl said in a small voice.

"Yeah," said Rayburn. "Tokyo. It's in Japan."

"I know that," she snapped. She looked at him suspiciously. "What were you doing in Tokyo?"

Rayburn stared out at the street for a minute as if deciding whether or not to answer. "Guvment sent me," he said finally.

"*You* work for the government?"

"Not no more. Useta."

"Doing what?" she demanded.

Rayburn turned and stared at her. She blushed. "I was with the de-fense department. You got any matches?" He reached into his pocket and pulled out a crumpled cigarette.

The girl reached below the counter and pulled up a packet of matches. Rayburn leaned back. She held the matches out in a slightly trembling hand. Rayburn closed his eyes. Fumbling, she pulled out a match, struck it, and held the flame to his cigarette. Rayburn took the first drag, held the smoke in for a minute, then let it stream out his mouth and nose, acting as if someone always lit his cigarettes for him. The girl laid the matches down, leaned forward, and propped her minuscule chin on her hands. "What's it like in Japan?"

"Not bad," said Rayburn. He took another drag on his cigarette. "You know, baby, like mountains an' rivers an' trees an' a couple waterfalls an' the same damn shitty cities an' dirty air. Ain't no big thing."

"But it *has* to be!" she exclaimed. "It's Japan."

Rayburn looked at her. She was an incredibly homely girl—not ugly, just terribly plain and slightly overweight. "Japan's just like anyplace else," he said.

"Oh," said the girl. Her fingers toyed with the book of matches. Suddenly she looked up. "If you've been to Japan, how come you've never been to Canada?"

"They didn't send me to Canada," Rayburn said. He waved his cigarette around, searching for an ash tray.

"Oh," she said. She turned and bent over, showing a pastel flash of panties, found an ash tray, and placed it on the counter.

Rayburn trimmed his cigarette. "Don't matter anyways," he said. "Canada ain't gonna be no different neither."

"Don't you want to go any more?"

"Nah. What for? So they speaks French. Big deal." He straightened up and stubbed out his half-finished cigarette. "It's the same everywhere."

"I just can't believe that," she said. Her gray eyes looked out the window at the passing traffic. "I just can't believe that. There's got to be more than that to Japan, more than just trees and mountains and rivers. . . ." Her voice trailed off. Rayburn looked down at her pinched, chinless face, which rested on her plump, pale hands. "Was it *really* just the same as here?" she said pleadingly, raising her face, searching his eyes with hers. Rayburn felt anger and hatred rising within him. He wanted to kill her. He opened his mouth, closed it, opened it again.

"Nah, honey," he said, "I was kiddin'. Japan was real cool. All them folks was runnin' around in funny clothes, all them gals was all painted up an' walkin' around like their feet was tied together. It was somethin' else."

"What color was it?" she demanded excitedly.

"Color?" said Rayburn. "What you mean, color?"

"You know. Countries have colors, like Ireland is green and Holland is yellow and Greece is golden brown . . . oh, maybe it's silly, and I've never been there, I just sell the tickets, but it seems like places have to be colored something."

"Yeah, yeah, yeah," said Rayburn. "Well, I'll tell you. It was all different colors. Lots of blue an' lots of orange, but all kinds a colors."

"Oh I *knew* it," she said happily.

"Yeah," said Rayburn, smiling too. Then he caught himself, pulled his beret down, made his features stern. "Well, I done wasted enough time around here." He stepped to the door, opened it, paused to look back at her. Her eyes were staring at a poster on the wall that said JAPAN in blue block letters beneath an orange pagoda. The tinkling of the bell brought her attention back to Rayburn.

"Oh. Are you sure you don't want to go to Canada?"

Rayburn smiled at her. "Yeah," he said, "yeah, I'm sure." He gave her a dirty leer, and she smiled back at him. He stepped out onto Chestnut Street just as a bus went by, blasting the sidewalk with black diesel exhaust. "Blue and orange," Rayburn mumbled to himself as he turned toward South

Street. "Blue and orange. Shit." But as he walked he smiled and whistled tunelessly.

Jake leaned against a crumbling wall, staring through the heavy screening and soot-smeared plate glass at the rows of bottles on display in the State Store. The pain in his stomach gnawed at him. Jake sucked in a few wincing breaths, his eyes never leaving the bottles. The pain gradually subsided to a dull ache. He rubbed his belly with one hand while the other searched through the pockets of his pants, shirt, coat, and sweater in search of some money. The search proved fruitless as it had several times in the two hours Jake had been standing there.

The cars and trucks trickling off the Expressway onto South Street cast fleeting glints and shadows across Jake's form, the sun, reflected from windshields glinting at him like a winking eye. Occasionally a patron went past Jake and entered the store, and Jake's eyes would hungrily watch the shadows moving inside until the customer emerged carrying a brown paper bag. Somewhere a siren wailed, and Jake automatically turned his head away from the store window. The source of the siren was invisible, but Jake caught sight of a gangling figure moving down the other side of the street. Jake pushed himself away from the wall and shuffled out to the curb. Traffic prevented him from crossing immediately, so he turned and shambled along, keeping an eye on the far sidewalk. When there was a break in traffic Jake crossed and pursued his quarry, gaining slowly but steadily.

The tug on his sleeve caused Brother Fletcher to stop and turn, and the sight of Jake's stubble-encrusted face made him take a step backward. "Reverend?" Jake said.

"Yes," said Brother Fletcher, his hand beginning the inevitable journey toward his pocket. Brother Fletcher's wife maintained that he was the softest touch on South Street, and he was. He gave money that he didn't have to almost anybody who asked, drawing the line only at the gang of heroin-addicted devil-worshipers who hung around the occult-supplies store on Twelfth Street, and feeling guilty about that. Jake was so obviously a charity case that he didn't even need to ask. Brother Fletcher pulled out some change and extended his hand. Jake looked down at the coins.

"What's that for?" Jake said.

"Why, wine," said Brother Fletcher.

"I don't take no handouts," Jake snapped.

"What?" said Brother Fletcher. Jake looked at him scornfully. Brother Fletcher put his hand back in his pocket. "Then what—"

"I wanted to thank you for puttin' me up the other night."

"What are you talking about?" said Brother Fletcher.

"Ain't you the preacher up there to The Word a Life?"

"Well, one of them, yes."

"Well, all right then. You let me sleep in there the other night when I wasn't feelin' too good."

"Oh," said Brother Fletcher, "yes. Now I remember."

"Yeah, well I just wanted to say thanks."

"Well," said Brother Fletcher a trifle uncomfortably, "you're quite welcome. But it isn't necessary to thank me."

"Why not?" Jake demanded.

"Why, well, because any servant of God would have done the same."

"So? An' I wouldn't be too sure a that. How 'bout that muthafucka— oops, 'scuse ma French, how 'bout that Sloan?"

"Uh, yes, I'm sure Reverend Sloan would—"

"C'mon now," Jake said.

Brother Fletcher grinned sheepishly.

"That's better," Jake said approvingly. "Y'know, for a preacher you're damn near human."

Brother Fletcher felt his neck grow warm with a flush of pleasure, a reaction that he found embarrassing. "Thank you," he mumbled.

"Say what?" Jake said.

"I said, 'Thank you.' "

"Oh. I'm gettin' so I don't hear too good all the time. I guess I'm gettin' a little old."

Brother Fletcher regarded Jake's dilapidated features. "No," he said, "I don't think it could be that. You don't look that old."

"Well I ain't *that* old," Jake snapped. "All the same, I'm gettin' on up there. I don't move as fast as I used to, an' ma stomach's no damn good no more. Hurts all the damn time."

"Have you seen a doctor?" Brother Fletcher asked.

"What for? There ain't but one cure for old age, an' I ain't ready for dyin' yet."

"No, no, of course not."

"I got a lot a good years left."

"I can see that," said Brother Fletcher.

They stood facing each other in a slightly uncomfortable silence. "You know," Jake said finally, "I generally get along pretty good with you fellas. Onliest thing wrong with you is all that religion makes your brains a little soft."

Brother Fletcher opened his mouth and closed it again with a sharp clacking sound.

"Whad you say?"

"Nothing," said Brother Fletcher, "nothing at all."

"You know," Jake said, "I don't even mind talkin' to you. Some a you fellas don't know how to keep their traps shut. They're all the time preachin' some shit, uh, 'scuse ma French, an' tryin' to make folks feel 'shamed a theyselves for tryin' to have a good time an' get along in the world. But you ain't said moren ten words. You must be the shortest-winded preacher this side a Hell."

"Thank you," said Brother Fletcher, "I think."

"Tell you what. Seein' as how you're such a good fella, maybe we oughta have lunch together some time." Jake peered at Brother Fletcher from beneath his grizzled brows.

Brother Fletcher pulled at his nose to conceal a smile. "Why that's a fine idea. Are you free today?"

"I ain't never free," Jake said, "but I can be reasonable."

Brother Fletcher laughed appreciatively. "Fine. Where—"

"Leo's got the best sandwiches on the street," Jake said quickly. "Only maybe you wouldn't feel right goin' there, seein' as it's a bar. You know what a bar is. Don't you?"

"Oh yes," said Brother Fletcher.

"Well don't you be jumpin' to no conclusions. I mean, all bars ain't the same. Lightnin' Ed's ain't like some places I could mention."

"Did you say Lightnin' Ed's?"

"Yeah," Jake said. "You been there?"

"No!" said Brother Fletcher. "But I've—heard about it."

"Yeah?" Jake said. "I didn't know you fellas kept up on that kind a thing."

"It's a minister's responsibility to be aware of the pitfalls awaiting the unwary," said Brother Fletcher loftily.

"Yeah, well," Jake said. "I bet y'all have one hell of a good time checkin' out them pitfalls. C'mon." Jake started off down South Street, leaving Brother Fletcher standing on the sidewalk, gasping indignantly. After a minute he grinned ruefully and followed along.

Leo had just finished constructing another leakproof sandwich of radical design. He had used a hard roll carefully mashed down on the inside so that the crust formed a reservoir that Leo felt certain would sufficiently contain floods of mayonnaise, ketchup, and pickle juice. Leo had used an abundance of these materials, desiring to submit his theoretically perfect design to the most rigid of practical trials. With quivers of anticipation jiggling inside his belly Leo grasped the sandwich firmly in both hands, opened his mouth, inserted the sandwich, and was about to subject his construction to the pressure test when Jake came through the door followed by a tall bony man wearing a clerical collar. At the sight of the collar Leo's hands went lax and the sandwich fell, smearing mayonnaise, ketchup, and pickle juice all over Leo's white-aproned front. "Shit," said Leo. "I mean, g-g-g-good afternoon, Reverend. Lord, I mean God, I mean, ah, what a mess." Leo flapped his hands helplessly. The remains of the sandwich slipped from his apron onto the top of the bar. Leo grabbed for a damp side towel but couldn't decide whether to clean himself or the bar with it. Finally he pulled off his apron and used it to wipe the bar. Jake sat on a stool, cackling at the performance, while Brother Fletcher stood, shifting his weight from one foot to the other, embarrassed by Leo's embarrassment.

"Aw, take it easy, Leo," Jake said. "He don't bite."

"He's a preacher," Leo said defensively. "You hadn't oughta bring a preacher in here without warnin' me."

"This one's okay. He don't even give a damn if you says damn, long as you don't put God in front of it. Right, Rev?"

"I ain't never had no preacher in ma bar before," Leo said.

"You prejudiced against preachers, Leo?" Jake asked innocently.

"Hell, no!" roared Leo. "I ain't prejudiced against nobody. But shit—ah, 'scuse me, Reverend. I mean, I ain't got nothin' against preachers. . . ."

"Well then, what's all the noise about?" Jake demanded.

"Well, what about ma other customers?"

"Please," said Brother Fletcher, raising a hand. "I understand perfectly." He moved toward the door.

"Wait a minute," Leo said. "I wasn't meanin' for you to leave or nothin'."

"I thought you were," said Brother Fletcher, a bit stiffly.

"God, no. I mean, 'scuse me, no. It's just—well, ah, don't you guys wear undershirts or nothin' under there?"

"You want me to remove my collar?"

"I'm sorry," Leo said, "but this here's a bar an' if some a ma customers caught sight of a preacher's collar, why, it'd be almost like seein' a cop car parked outside."

"No need to explain," Brother Fletcher said briskly. He quickly removed his collar and shirt and stood in his undershirt. "How's that?"

"Thanks, Rev," Leo said. "Now you can have one on me. You do drink?" Leo peered at Brother Fletcher. Brother Fletcher felt his face grow warm. " 'Scuse me, Rev," Leo said slowly, "but ain't I seen you in here before?"

Brother Fletcher swallowed. "I—"

"Nah," said Leo. "Couldn't be. Now I got Coke an' stuff like that, if you don't want a beer or nothin'."

Brother Fletcher breathed a sigh of relief. "I guess one beer wouldn't keep me out of heaven," he said.

"Hell, no," Jake said. "You know what they say. One drink an' you might get in, two drinks an' you gotta get in, three drinks an' you can't get up that high." Jake laughed uproariously, Leo grinned, and Brother Fletcher gave a hearty, uncomprehending horselaugh.

"Yeah," Leo said, "an' four drinks an' you can't get out." Jake and Leo smiled at each other.

Brother Fletcher was suddenly aware that something was expected of him. He felt horribly inadequate, but then inspiration struck him like a bolt of lightning. "Yes," he said, "but no matter how many you have, once you're in you never want to leave." He laughed happily and raised his beer.

It was a hot afternoon. The sun burned in a sky so blue it seemed that the color had been pounded into it with a sledgehammer. Waves of heat hung shimmering above the roofs of parked cars, reflected off the windshields of moving ones in quick, sharp glints. The rolling tires made kissing sounds as they pulled away from the insistent grasp of heat-softened asphalt. The bellowing exhaust from the number forty bus was a slightly warmer, dirtier current in the sea of hot, filthy air. In the transom space over the door of Bad Boy Bob's Bar-B-Q an exhaust fan labored, sending the aroma of sweet-sour sauce dancing out onto the street to the beat of one bent blade that banged against part of the housing. Bad Boy Bob switched the fan to high, and the beat quickened while everything else in sight slowed down. The winos congregating near a burned-out boarded-up bashed-in storefront sank back against the grimy wall and basked like black snakes in the sun's heat. Fast Freddy fingered his slips and waited for the Man; business had been brisk but Fast Freddy had the uncomfortable feeling that somebody was going to hit him big. Harry the Hype, swathed in sweaters, hung onto a parking meter, waiting for his connection. Despite the heat Harry the Hype was shivering—a junkie has no summer. Upstairs in the Elysium, Cotton climbed out of his bed, lumbered down the hall to the men's room, entered a stall, and emitted clouds of flatulence, two blobs of feces, and grunts of orgasmic satisfaction. Mrs. Fletcher pushed her shopping cart along the burning sidewalk, the perspiration on her skin making her clothes wet and heavy. Rayburn Wallace sat before his living-room window, staring out at the silver sparkle of a jet as it lined out for the other side of the world. Leslie, draped across the broken-down sofa, dressed only in her panties, flipped through the pages of *Black Stars* magazine and nibbled on a Hershey bar. In the cool dark interior of Lightnin' Ed's the afternoon crowd watched the Phillies losing another game to the Pittsburgh Pirates. Brother Fletcher, his conscience sleeping through the hot afternoon, clutched a frosty mug of Schmidt's beer and groaned along with everyone else as the Phillies slid into undisputed possession of the National League cellar. The Reverend Mr. J. Peter Sloan rolled down the Delaware River Expressway into the city, the air-conditioner of his Lincoln Continental going full blast, his stereo tape player pounding out James Brown's latest, which bore a striking resemblance to James Brown's previous. In her twenty-third floor apartment Alicia Hadley, Ph.D., tried to concentrate on the paper she was preparing for possible publication in the journal of the Modern Language Association, entitled "Reflections of the Nonviolent Civil Rights Movement in Contemporary Black Poetry." Leroy Briggs lay on his king-size mattress, his tiger-striped sheets twisting around his ankles as his pumping legs fought to carry him clear of the dangers lurking in his dreams. Adlai Stevenson Brown, occupation bartender, stood in the air-conditioned coolness of Frankie's Place, scribbling fragments of poetry on paper napkins. Patrolman Mario Arbruzzi completed the grisly process of hauling one corpse, property of the late Louis P. DiGeorgio, retired bartender, out of the Delaware River. Big Betsy considered a problem of fluidics—how to get both her body and sufficient water with which to wash it into a bathtub at the same time. Willie T. cruised down South Street in Leroy's Cadillac, checking the action and searching for any signs of invasion by Gino's Italian Army. The city panted through hot August Friday. The rivers oozed downstream, fighting sluggishly against the awesome pressure of the incoming tide. At desks and tables and benches and counters and consoles workers paused and sighed and thanked God it was Friday. In Center City Friday was the end day, and the buildings, the streets, the sidewalks would rest through Saturday and Sunday and come to choking life on Monday morning. On South Street Friday was the beginning and the asphalt panted in preparation.

The sun scorched its way down the western half of the sky, trailing red haze across a wino's vision, imprinting afterimages on the eyes of the no longer suffering Harry the Hype, who, connection made, eased northward to wait for the avalanche of evening pleasure-seekers with their snatchable purses loaded with cash if he were lucky, with credit cards if he were not. Alicia Hadley stepped from her shower and began half-heartedly to prepare for an evening out with a caramel-skinned stockbroker named Wendell Isaac Whyte. A sheepish and slightly inebriated Brother Fletcher hurried home, his clerical collar somewhat bent out of shape. A soaked and scrubbed but still odoriferous Big Betsy armored her face for the evening's campaign. Cotton considered the remains of a sixteen-ounce steak done hardly at all, sighed, and ordered another. Rayburn Wallace slipped a sandwich and an apple into a brown paper bag, kissed his sleeping wife on her sweating forehead, and left for work. Willie T., wincing, paid for refilling the cavernous gas tank of Leroy's car. The Reverend Mr. J. Peter Sloan, sipping brandy on the rocks, listened to a recording of the previous month's Love Feast, savoring the sound of his own cultured voice reproduced in stereophonic sound. Leslie woke from her afternoon nap, called Rayburn's name, smiled when there was no answer. Mrs. Fletcher stared as her husband rushed into the apartment and went directly to the bathroom without stopping to say hello. Fast Freddy sat contentedly in a corner of the Elysium's lounge, sipping beer and thanking God that no stupid nigger had managed to hit the number. Adlai Stevenson Brown hung up his apron, accepted his pay in cash from Frankie, and said good-bye. He shoved the money into his shoe, stuffed a mass of paper napkins into his pocket, and stepped out onto the street.

The hot afternoon air struck Brown like a foam-rubber-covered fist. Sweat sprang out on his brow and ran from beneath his arms. He crossed Walnut Street into Rittenhouse Square, dodging a well-dressed woman walking a carefully clipped poodle, and continued on across the Square on the diagonal, coming out on Eighteenth Street. By that time the heat had begun to feel good to him.

Brown moved along through the ranks of redbrick townhouses and then, quite suddenly, entered the half block of dilapidation that preceded South Street. Each day, walking home, Brown had marveled at the speed of the change from prosperity to poverty, from neat to ramshackle, from white to black. It was not at all like the transition from day to night: there was no modulation like dusk, or dawn. It was more like the snapping of a switch, the crossing of a threshold. It was the sharply illustrated difference between inside and outside, and it was the sharpness of it that bothered Brown more than the change. And the change bothered him a great deal. It bothered him that there was a change at all, and it bothered him that he changed as he crossed: spoke differently, smiled differently, cursed differently, perhaps even thought differently and felt differently. It was as if, crossing the visible border, Brown left something like a piece of luggage in a coin locker, and on the other side he picked up the piece of luggage he had deposited there at his last crossing. Brown turned left onto South Street and headed toward the apartment he had rented. On his way he passed the Elysium Hotel and recalled that he was out of beer. He retreated into a sheltering doorway and, concealed from the eyes of the ungodly, worked his pay envelope out of his shoe. He transferred a ten to his pants pocket, shoved the envelope back, and crossed the street. He entered the Elysium, ordered a six to go, and walked out again. The event did not go unnoticed. Willie T. saw him.

Willie T. was consumed by zeal and was impressed with the need for quick and definitive action. He put down his glass of Coca-Cola on the rocks and let his mouth drop open. "Did you see that nigger?" Willie T. demanded.

"Who?" said Charlene, who was engaged in a subtle seduction, rubbing her left thigh against Willie T.'s leg and pressing her left breast against Willie T.'s arm. "What you talkin' 'bout, honey?"

"That was that sonofabitch Brown," said Willie T.

"He the one that's got you boys on the rag?" Charlene inquired.

Willie T. spun around and laid his open hand against Charlene's temple. Charlene's eyes rolled dazedly for a few moments. "Don't talk dirty," snapped Willie T. "That's all you silly cunts are good for, drinkin' an' smokin' an' fuckin' an' talkin' dirty. You cut it out, now, you hear?"

"You hurt me," protested Charlene.

"Did not," denied Willie T. "If there's one place I can hit you without worryin' 'bout doin' no harm it's upside the head."

"Damn," said Charlene. "You act as if I was the one runnin' you off the Street."

"Why you . . ." Willie T. raised his hand again.

"I was just kiddin', Willie baby, honest I was!" Charlene squealed.

Willie T. lowered his hand, giving the rest of the barroom a disdainful look. "Don't kid," Willie T. said. Charlene nodded humbly.

"Well, Willie, I see you're followin' in Leroy's tracks like always, an' beatin' on women."

Willie T. turned at the sound of Vanessa's voice. "I guess you wishin' you did have somebody to beat you," Willie T. said.

"You volunteerin'?"

"No," said Charlene emphatically.

"Maybe," said Willie T.

"Sorry," said Vanessa, "you ain't hardly big enough. Why you just stick to kissin' Leroy's behind?"

"Why don't you go to hell?" said Willie T.

"Why don't I shit on a plate so you can have a hot meal?" suggested Vanessa.

Willie T. choked on his Coca-Cola. "See what I mean? You can't do nothin' but screw an' drink an' talk dirty. An' *you*"—he glared at Vanessa—"can't even screw right."

Vanessa swallowed and her jaw tightened. "You shut your mouth, nigger, or I'll—"

"Sure, baby, sure. I got to be goin' to see Leroy 'bout that Brown now." He grinned at Vanessa triumphantly.

"You do whatever you want," Vanessa said tightly, "only get outa ma sight."

"What you think Leroy gonna do, baby?" Charlene said.

"Oh, now, I don't know," said Willie T. He leaned back against the bar. "We got him kinda calmed down, but Leroy ain't gonna like that joker just walkin' on in here an' gettin' a six-pack."

"Shit," said Vanessa. "You mean to tell me Leory's done started a local chapter of the AA?"

"With regards to Mr. Jokerass Brown," said Willie T., "it's more likely Leroy's gonna be buyin' him a life membership in Fraternal Order a Crippleass Niggers. Leroy ain't fond a the joker, an' when Leroy ain't fond a somebody, that just ain't too cool for somebody. As you"—Willie T. paused to favor Vanessa with a bright smile—"well know."

"Leroy's still fond a me," Vanessa said. "He just forgets sometimes."

"Yeah," Willie T. agreed. "Leroy told me you was one a the most forgettable moments in his life."

"Tut, tut, tut. Sad, ain't it? Leroy done forgot about what you ain't never gonna get a whiff of."

"Ain't hard to get a whiff," Willie T. said. "All you gots to do is stand downwind."

"That ain't me you smellin'," Vanessa told him. "That's the shit on your nose from where Leroy stopped a little sudden."

Willie T. gritted his teeth. "Maybe after me an' Leroy takes care a this Brown fool, maybe we'll just keep on goin' an' take care a you."

"Humph. That's some combination," said Vanessa. "Leroy an' you. Sounds like Sampson an' his ass's jawbone."

"Oh, they need a good combination," Charlene said. "Brown's the dude that's got Leroy runnin' scared."

"Leroy ain't runnin' noways, I done told you that," snapped Willie T.

"What did you say?" demanded Vanessa.

"I said Leroy ain't runnin'—"

"Not you, fool. Whad you say, Charl?"

"I just said Brown was the dude"—Charlene hesitated and looked uneasily at Willie T.—"uh, that Brown's the one Willie T.'s gonna run right into the river."

"Um hum," said Willie T. in satisfaction. "Gonna run him clean to Camden. With," he added modestly, "a little hep from ma friends."

"He's here now?" said Vanessa excitedly. "Where?"

"Nah," Willie T. said, "the cat done split. Took one look at me an' ran like a preacher after a plate a fried chicken."

"Damn," said Vanessa, "I wish I'd a seen him."

"He wasn't nothin' to see," Charlene said. "Scrawny-lookin' dude, didn't look like he could scare piss outa a baby. Wonder what he done to scare Leroy?"

"Goddammit, woman, how many times do I have to tell you, Leroy ain't scared. He's just bidin' his time. One a these nights we gonna trot on up there an' wring this fool's neck like he was a Christmas turkey. . . ."

"On up where?"

"Why, up to your sister's place," said Willie T. "I got it all figured out. See, Leroy goes up the front steps an' I climbs up the—"

"Hey, 'Nessa!" shouted Charlene.

"Humph," said Willie T. "Wonder where that silly bitch is off to?"

"I'd say she was off to visit her sister," Charlene said.

"Damn sister better get her ass around here," said Willie T., glancing at his Timex. "Leroy gonna be wantin' her." He settled himself on the bar stool, pressing against Charlene. "Hey," he said, straightening suddenly, "you don't think she's gonna tip Brown off or nothin', do you?"

Charlene leaned over and blew into Willie T.'s ear. "How come we always got to be talkin' 'bout these other folks, sweetie? Let's talk about you an' me."

"All right, mama," said Willie T. obligingly. "I don't mind if we does." Willie T. smiled seductively and pressed closer to Charlene.

Love Feast night at The Word of Life. The Reverend Mr. J. Peter Sloan felt a deep flush of affection for himself as he watched the congregation fill the theater. Mr. Sloan motioned to his acolytes and stepped into his air-conditioned dressing room. He removed his baby-blue bell-bottom trousers and handed them to an acolyte. He slipped off his gold Bradley-collared orlon shirt and handed that to a second acolyte. He sat down and raised his feet and allowed a third acolyte to remove his authentic Mohawk moccasins. From still another acolyte he accepted a rich purple robe of spun cotton and rayon and shrugged into it. He sat down again and allowed the boy to place a pair of high sandals on his feet and lace them up, and then Mr. Sloan rose again and took from the hands of still another acolyte a ' silver chalice filled with chilled red wine. The Reverend Mr. Sloan tipped his head back and drank deeply. As the boy carried the cup away Mr. Sloan reached out and patted him benevolently on the rump.

His wig framing his face like a wooly halo, the Reverend Mr. Sloan flung open the door of his dressing room and stepped out into the wings. Sister Fundidia Larson, who had been conferring with the organist, saw him emerge and crossed to him, her face glowing. Mr. Sloan met her with a chilly, wry smile, enfolded her with his left arm, his fingers trailing down across her left breast.

"Sister Larson," said Mr. Sloan, "I have matters to discuss with you. I was hoping you would join me for dinner some evening soon."

Sister Fundidia's features were transformed by a wave of pious joy. "Oh, Reverend . . ."

"Tut, tut, tut," said the Reverend Mr. Sloan. "Really, I think we can dispense with some of these formalities. You needn't call me 'Reverend' when there's just the two of us."

"Oh, ah, what should I call you?" asked Sister Fundidia.

"Oh, 'sir' or 'm'lord' will do nicely," replied Mr. Sloan.

"Yes, m'lord," said Sister Fundidia.

Deep in the bowels of The Word of Life, in his cubbyhole office next to the boiler room, twisted in the unfamiliar throes of a post-hangover depression, sat Brother Fletcher. Brother Fletcher was not at all fond of his office—it was too tiny, too square, too isolated, too hard, altogether far too reminiscent of a cell in some ancient monastery—but fond of it or not, Brother Fletcher could not help thinking that it was a very appropriate place in which to have a crisis of faith. Far higher than it was wide or deep, the room seemed like the barrel of a giant microscope and Brother Fletcher was a bug on a slide. From far above, personified by the single round fluorescent fixture, the eye of God peered down upon him. He had been drunk. Brother Fletcher was aware of the elaborate rationalizations that had permitted him to enter Lightnin' Ed's Bar, and that awareness didn't bother him half as much as the inescapable fact that he had enjoyed himself. Sitting before Leo's big color TV he had experienced a fellowship that he had never found within the walls of any church. It had been a long time since Brother Fletcher had watched a ball game with people who groaned and cheered and complained as loudly as he did. He knew that sooner or later he would once again shed his collar and enter Lightnin' Ed's.

He doubted that he would go to Hell for it. His faith had been shaken by the simple, frightening realization that all his days in the church had been directed toward leading and working for the salvation of others, and while it had made him feel useful and occasionally important, it had never brought him the happiness and contentment he had found watching a baseball game in a beer garden. To Brother Fletcher that seemed like heresy.

In the well-equipped kitchen of The Word of Life Sister Cozie Bacon put the final touches on the trays of communion elements, checking the crispness of the wafers, tasting the grape juice to make sure the grain alcohol lacing was sufficient. Sister Cozie Bacon smiled and tasted the wine one more time. "Amen," she pronounced solemnly.

His sermon completed, the Reverend Mr. Sloan left the stage. He never remained to celebrate the Love Feast with the congregation; the Reverend Mr. Sloan preferred his own, more intimate feast. He gave one anticipating look at Sister Fundidia's robed form, then entered his dressing room to prepare himself for the ride back to Trenton.

Brother Fletcher stood alone on the stage. Brother Fletcher wore a plain brown robe of coarse heavy material. His feet were bare. He stood before the congregation, sweating not solely from the heat, seeing the sea of celebrants approach and recede at the curving edge of the stage. Brother Fletcher's toes curled and wriggled as if trying to dig into the floor. He pronounced the words of the ritual; the crowd roared responses that they knew by heart. Volume increased as anticipation grew. Brother Fletcher signaled the choirmaster, and the organ began a slow gospel throb. The sea waved toward Brother Fletcher, waved and clapped its hands. "Amen," intoned Brother Fletcher.

"AMEN!"

Suddenly Brother Fletcher wished that it were real, or that he could once again believe it was real, not just engineered sham. "Amen," said Brother Fletcher. "Let the church say amen."

"AMEN!"

"We've come this far by faith," said Brother Fletcher. He said it quite gently, but the microphones caught his voice, the amplifiers puffed it up, the speakers cast it out, a deep basso rumble that shook the walls.

"HALLELUJAH!"

"Jesus saves," whispered Brother Fletcher. The sound system took it and boomed it out like the Voice of God announcing Armageddon.

"JESUS SAVES!"

A signal from Brother Fletcher and the band raised their instruments and began to honk slow, jazzy gospel. Sister Fundidia rose and began to croon softly. The stage manager turned a knob on his console, and the reproduced version of Sister Fundidia's croon altered slightly in timbre.

Mrs. Fletcher sat in the front row watching the glistening sweat roll down Brother Fletcher's face. She thought to herself that he moved oddly, like a man going through motions. She knew that Brother Fletcher's heart was not in it. But he was good. God, was he good! He spoke to the crowd with his hands; soundlessly, he spoke to them. A fat woman in the second row leaned over, stretching straining fingers toward the stage, her armored breasts banging the back of Mrs. Fletcher's head. Mrs. Fletcher took no notice. On the stage, Brother Fletcher moved with the music. Arms outstretched, hands cupped, he dipped into the ocean before him. His fingers found hidden strings. He pulled, drew them out, felt the tension increase. Face slack, eyes screwed shut, as if he were searching by touch alone for a particular cord in the invisible net of emotion and frenzy, he stood before them. He nodded his head and, as if by miracle, the communion elements appeared throughout the sanctuary. Hands formed whirlpools about the laden trays as they reached for bread, wine, the body, the blood. Organ and horns were joined by thudding bass drum, and Sister Fundidia's croon became a wail of pain and ecstasy. Suddenly Sister Lavernia Thompson rose from her seat in the fourteenth row and began to sing in a high screeching nasal voice. The people around her looked at her. Ushers moved to restrain her so that the established order of worship might proceed. Brother Fletcher waved them off.

Brother Fletcher moved to the extreme brink of the stage, his features set and intense, his eyes hard and tender. Sister Lavernia's cries echoed throughout the church. The band stopped in confusion. The organ stopped. Brother Fletcher impatiently waved Sister Fundidia into dumbness. He stood silent and still and straight while Sister Lavernia wailed on alone, her voice like a cat's screeching in a darkened alleyway. Flecks of foam appeared at the corners of her slack mouth, and she began to babble in some unrecognizable tongue. The ushers stirred uneasily.

Brother Fletcher moved out still farther, hung on the edge of the stage almost beyond the point of balance, his toes curling over the wood in search of purchase. He stretched out his hand, palm up, fingers spread. Sister Lavernia foamed and ranted. Brother Fletcher raised his hand slowly, deliberately, and Sister Lavernia seemed to shrink into herself for a moment, gathering herself, before exploding into renewed wailings. The loose sleeve of the robe slipped down, exposing Brother Fletcher's arm, shining with sweat, the muscles standing out in sharp relief as he raised his hand slowly, higher, and higher, and higher. Brother Fletcher's head began to nod and the drummer picked up the rhythm with gentle bass beats that were felt more than heard. Brother Fletcher stood with his body turned sideways, his arm outstretched toward Sister Lavernia. Sister Lavernia wailed on, her eyes focused on him, eyes that were startlingly calm in the contorted face. As his hand reached the limits of its upward journey Brother Fletcher twisted his wrist so that his palm faced downward. Sister Lavernia jerked in tight little spasms. Brother Fletcher began to lower his hand, and as he lowered it Sister Lavernia began to subside. Her fingers, which had been grasping desperately at the seat in front of her, began to loosen. Her body sagged. Her face lost its tension. She became, by slow degrees, a woman possessed by nothing more than old age. Brother Fletcher stood firm as she dropped to her seat, his hand hanging limp and dead at his side. His fingers twisted slightly, then tightened into a fist. Brother Fletcher abandoned the ritual and stepped into the wings. The faithful murmured, but the organ swelled and the horns took up their jazzy blare, so the shoulders shrugged and the hands reached, the mouths opened up and gobbled their wafers and gulped their wine. Mrs. Fletcher stood up and wormed her way back through the crowd, back fourteen rows to the shrunken shape of Sister Lavernia. She placed a hand on the old woman's shoulder, but Sister Lavernia did not notice—she remained a quiet huddle of old black dress, smelling of weariness and age, of greasy cooking, of camphor balls. Her eyes were open, staring at nothing, but they were filled with a strange light.

He left the bank early, because it was Friday and the work week was over, because it was payday and he had money in his pockets, because he worked alone, and he could not stand to be alone any longer. In the heat of the afternoon he had gone home, opening the door and closing it behind him, finding Leslie draped over the faded material of the overstuffed chair he had long ago liberated from a rubbish heap, one leg propped on each armrest, wearing one of his work shirts and a pair of torn black underpants, mouth working on a wad of gum that made a bulge along her jaw, reading a back number of *Vogue*. "Whadyoubringme?" she had said without looking up, reaching out a hand toward the lipstick-smeared Winston that lay in the cracked saucer she was using as an ash tray.

The sharp corners of the box of scented soap he had bought for her poked into his thigh. He looked at her, at the litter on the floor, and felt something inside him break. "Why the hell don't you ever clean up in here?"

"What?" she said incredulously.

"I said, 'Why don't you ever clean up in here?' "

"What you think I am, the fuckin' upstairs maid?"

Rayburn opened his mouth, closed it. "Never mind," he said. Leslie had sniffed and returned to looking at pictures. Rayburn went out into the kitchen and began to empty groceries out of the paper bag he carried.

"You get paid?"

"No. I run into Santy Claus out there in the goddamn street, an' he give me this here sack. Said to hold onto it till Christmas."

"What the hell's got into you today?" Rayburn heard a rustle of paper and a flat slap as she threw the magazine down, turned to see her standing in the doorway, her bare feet spread apart, hands on hips, shirt hanging down, the shirttails swinging and brushing gently against her taut thighs.

"Maybe I'm tired all the sudden a lookin' at this goddamn *mess* every goddamn time I come home." Rayburn waved a hand toward the tower of greasy plates rearing up out of the sink, the coating of blackened grease on the stove.

"Well maybe that's just too goddamn bad. You so fussy, why don't you clean it?"

"I do clean it, an' you dirties it, an' maybe I'm just gettin' sick a all that. Maybe I'm thinkin' I oughta get the hell out an' leave you right here with it." He turned his back on her, fixed his eyes on a brownish stain above the sink where a hapless cockroach had long before met his end. "There's plenty a women in this city. Plenty."

"Then why don't you go get you one? Huh, baby? Why don't you go on an' get you one?"

"I don't know," Rayburn mumbled. "I'll be damned if I know."

"You know. You know all right."

" 'Cause I'm a damn fool, that's why."

"That ain't why," she said, and he had felt her move closer to him, place her hands, cool, against his neck, had felt his blood begin to pound. He fought her. He had moved away, pressed himself tight against the edge of the sink until the hard edge of the white porcelain had cut into his belly. "That ain't why," she repeated, pursuing him, insinuating her body against him, pushing, pressing. Rayburn had felt her breasts against the back of his sweat-soggy shirt, feeling, or imagining he felt, the hardening of her nipples. He had tried to keep himself cold, thinking of mountain streams and ice, but he felt her cheek against his shoulder and her hands, one slipping between the buttons of his shirt, the other fumbling at his belt buckle and, finding the edge of the sink a barrier, moving around and down. "That ain't why." Rayburn had gritted his teeth, stiffened his spine, had tried to push away, but the hands, slow-moving, gentle hands, had stayed. In spite of himself he moved away from the cover of the sink, and her other hand, swift as a snake, captured his belt, slipped inside his pants, and began to fondle him, squeezing him tightly, too tightly. Slowly, hating himself, he had turned and gathered her to him. She undid his fly, guided him. Rayburn clutched the back of her thighs, raised her, brought her savagely downward, feeling her panties rip and part before him. She moaned and wriggled like a speared fish, hurting him, but he had felt the molten juices flow, near to boiling, near to eruption, and he had held on looking down into the glowing hot darkness, and then he did boil, and burst, and subside, lowering her, gasping. Her feet found the floor. He felt warm peace roll over him while her head lay against his chest, while his eyes gazed unfocused at the water-stained ceiling, while he knew that this time, by God, there was no smile on her face. The sound of honking horns had reached his ears. He felt himself slick from her juices and his own, felt her warmth and weight against him, felt a little bit triumphant, a little smug. And then he had felt the movement, tiny, like a scurrying bug, and had looked down to see her jaws working on the wad of gum. Rayburn put his tools away and left the bank.

The night was getting cooler. The furnace breath of noon was now a baby's sneeze, feeling almost cool as it brushed across his sweat-damp skin. He moved quickly, straight down Seventeenth Street and along South, climbing the stairs, turning the key. Leslie was not there. He shucked his clothes, stepped beneath the shower, washing himself roughly, forcing the soap to lather in the cold water. His body felt slimy and weak; he scrubbed it.

He dried himself with an almost-clean towel that he found only after a considerable search. He dressed in clean underwear, slacks, a brand-new white shirt that someone had given him for Christmas years before. He stepped out on the street.

He could not bring himself to enter any of his favorite bars; Lightnin' Ed's, Dick Bell's, The Reynold's Rap, all were full of familiar people who knew him, knew his story. He turned north, toward Center City, moved away from the dim lights and the jukeboxed soul, his footfalls echoing in the redbricked, treelined respectability of Pine Street. He wandered back to the Square, dodged the hippies, dodged the traffic on Walnut Street as he crossed against the light. A taxi driver honked his horn; Rayburn indolently gave him the finger and walked on. In the next side street, nestled between an underground theater and an expensive boutique, he found what he had been looking for.

Rayburn stepped into the bar. His eyes, adjusting slowly to the darkness, saw forms and faces arrayed along an oval bar, seated at small tables beyond a wall of greenery. The forms were indistinct. The faces were white, every single one of them, and Rayburn felt a beautiful feeling of alienness steal over him, filling him with a sudden sense of power. He swaggered over to the bar and took a stool, pleased at the slightly increased volume in the hum of conversation that he imagined had followed his entrance. The bartender, short, swarthy, came over and asked Rayburn what he wanted, betraying a reluctance that made Rayburn feel even stronger. They didn't want him here, and that made him feel comfortable. They were a little afraid of him, and that made him feel powerful. They didn't know his name or his face or his friends or his life, and they never would. He was alone and free.

"Scotch," Rayburn said. "On the rocks."

"What brand?" said the bartender.

Rayburn shrugged expansively. The bartender gave him a professional smile and poured him a generous slug of the cheap stuff. Rayburn laid a dollar bill on the bar. The bartender took it away. Rayburn waited for his change, then he looked up and saw the $1.00 showing in the window of the cash register. He forced himself to shrug, sip the drink, look around. A flat-faced man at the bar looked at him with an expression of disgust and indignation on his face. He got up and moved. Rayburn sniffed and finished his scotch. He laid a five on the bar and waited patiently until the bartender filled his glass again. Four ones replaced the five. Looking at the bills lying ungathered on the bar, Rayburn began to feel rich and important. He leaned back in the padded bar chair and surveyed the place as if he owned it.

In the dining area on the other side of the jungly divider, a plump, dark-haired waitress scurried back and forth. The side of her face was heavily made-up, almost, but not quite, enough to conceal a set of dark bruises. Rayburn wondered what they could be from. He thought of Leslie. He drained his drink. The bartender refilled his glass and took a bill away. A paunchy man with thinning black hair greased and sticking to the top of his head emerged from the dining room and came toward Rayburn. Rayburn watched him, his eyes small and tight.

"Howya doin'?"

"Just fine," said Rayburn.

"Ain't seen you in here before."

"Ain't never been here before," Rayburn said.

"Hey, that's fine. You come back. Glad ta see ya." He patted Rayburn on the arm. "I always like to get to know my customers. I'm Frankie."

"Rayburn," Rayburn said.

"Okay, Rayburn. Everything okay?"

"Sure is," Rayburn said. "An' gettin' better." 'Better' was three miniskirted girls. Frankie smiled mirthlessly and faded away. Rayburn looked at the girls. One of them saw him, smiled. She looked old. Rayburn looked away.

The flat-faced man leaned over. "Crow bait," he said.

"No shit," said Rayburn. He drank in silence. There were two bills in front of him.

He drank too quickly. He put up another five, watched it explode to four ones before shrinking—four, three, two. Time dragged, and Rayburn floated, wafted back and forth by the sound of voices with white overtones, laved by the alien rhythms of Sinatra and Bacharach and Martin that flowed from the jukebox. He realized that he was drunk, smiled, and drank on, pausing only for brief guttural comments to the flat-faced man and sojourns in the men's room that became longer and longer. People came and went, drifting through his sight in a parade of pale ghost-faces. All his feeling lodged in his arm and his lips and his throat and his bladder; the rest of him was numb and paralyzed. And then one face floating by stopped and held, rose out of the fog toward him, but not all the way; Rayburn dropped lower, to meet it in the middle ground of murkiness.

"Hi," she said. White face. Tight curls, blond, from a bottle. Body plump, breasts huge, tight red pants on surprisingly thin hips. Buttocks sagging from lack of muscle tone. "Can I buy you a drink?" Rayburn nodded drunkenly, raised his glass.

He stood before the jukebox, staring down at the titles glowing in the darkness. His eyes did not want to focus. No James Brown. No Smokey. No Mayfield. No Hayes. Al Martino and Dinah Shore. "Les dance," Rayburn mumbled, "les dance to goddamn muthafuckin' Dinah bitch Shore." She wouldn't dance—no one danced there—but she bought him another drink and told him he was beautiful. "Shit," Rayburn said, thinking what a fine piece of ass it was. Then he looked at her, in a moment of relative clarity, realized it was not a fine piece of ass. Not at all. But it would do. He raised his glass. She smiled and drank imported beer, watching him with flat gray eyes. Rayburn rose and stumbled to the men's room, inserted a quarter in the vending machine, chuckling to himself. He slipped the prophylactic into his pocket. In a flash of confidence he bought two more. It was his last quarter. When he got back she took his arm and led him gently out the door.

They stepped into a darkened alley that whispered of ancient sin. He clung to the side of a building, and she held him—looking up, she drew his head down, pressed his thick lips against the red lines of lipstick penciled on her face. Rayburn thrust his tongue between her teeth, felt her mouth open and her tongue strike swiftly at him like a frozen needle. He ground his hands into her soft, low-slung breasts.

Her car was powerful, big, air-conditioned, wired for sound, and she wove it expertly through the sparse traffic: up Walnut Street and across the river, into an underground lot beneath a tall apartment house. She got out. Rayburn got out too and stood beside the car, his back pressed tight against the metal. She stood in front of him, coyly smiling. Rayburn pulled her against him and held her, feeling her soft breasts flattening out against his chest, thinking how far from South Street she was, how far she made him. She giggled, took his hand, and pulled him after her toward an elevator. The machine lifted them upward into the sky. The doors opened. She led him down a carpeted hallway, opened a locked door, pulled him in. She slammed the door, set the night latch, hooked the chain, leaned back against the door, and began to tug unceremoniously at his clothing.

"My husband is away," she said. "On business."

Brother Fletcher could not sleep. He tossed and turned. He twisted. He kicked the sheet off, and then he forced himself to lie quietly and breathe slowly and evenly, and to listen to Mrs. Fletcher's hearty, untroubled snores. He closed his eyes and numbered the sheep that, in his mind's eye, leaped over a section of rail fence. Brother Fletcher wondered why all sheep followed along and jumped over the fence when it would have been far easier to walk around it. Brother Fletcher's mind drifted off into speculation concerning the psychology of sheep; predictably, he lost count, and one unfortunate sheep vanished in mid-air above the fence as Brother Fletcher gave up and opened his eyes. Sleep was beyond him, he decided, and rather than disturb Mrs. Fletcher with his gyrations he would get out of bed. Slowly and carefully, so as not to make the mattress creak, he swung his feet to the floor. He slipped his robe over his bony shoulders and tiptoed quietly to the door. He grasped the doorknob firmly, clenching his teeth in expectation of the squeak that was sure to come no matter how careful he was. The door slipped open noiselessly. Brother Fletcher took a deep breath, gritted his teeth, and stepped soundlessly through. Beyond the door he relaxed, letting the air out of his lungs. All he had to do now was to avoid the squeaky board halfway down the hall. He congratulated himself on his previously unsuspected capacity for stealth and prepared himself for the running of the final gauntlet.

He took a deep, careful, silent breath.

"Fletch, what are you doin' up?"

"The Devil," muttered Brother Fletcher. "Nothing."

He heard the mattress creak, and an instant later Mrs. Fletcher appeared in the doorway. "What is it?"

"Nothing, I told you," snapped Brother Fletcher.

"All right," said Mrs. Fletcher. "You been awake an' tossin' all night long 'count a nothin', an' now you're sneakin' around in the middle of the night 'count a nothin'. Fine with me. Only you tiptoe like an elephant."

Brother Fletcher sighed. "All right. Something *is* wrong. But I don't know what it is."

"I do," said Mrs. Fletcher. "You want some coffee?"

"It'll keep me awake," Brother Fletcher said automatically. Mrs. Fletcher shot him an amused look, and he dropped his eyes and grinned sheepishly. Mrs. Fletcher finished putting on her bathrobe, and Brother Fletcher followed her into the kitchen, sinking down onto a chair and watching while she prepared the coffeepot. "All right," he said. "What is it?"

"It's that Sloan," said Mrs. Fletcher promptly, making it sound like the name of one of Satan's chief lieutenants.

"Oh, Harriette, he's not that bad."

"He's bad enough to keep you up at night." Mrs. Fletcher placed the coffeepot on the stove and sat down across from him. "I know what I think of him. And I know what you think of him. Do you?"

"All right," he said, "but that's been bothering me for a long time. Whv is it so—bad right now?"

"Maybe it's time you left."

"And go where? Do what?"

"It doesn't matter."

"Yes it does," he said. "I'm a preacher. I can't preach without a church. And I can't do anything else besides preach. So if I leave The Word of Life, we starve."

"We've starved before," said Mrs. Fletcher shortly.

Brother Fletcher's jaw tightened. "Well we're not going to starve any more. We're not starving now."

"You ain't sleepin' now either," Mrs. Fletcher observed. She got up and took down two cups and poured coffee into them. She added cream and sugar to one cup, skimmed milk to the other, and gave the first cup to Brother Fletcher. He sipped at it.

"OW!"

"It's hot," said Mrs. Fletcher.

"Thanks," said Brother Fletcher drily.

"Fletch?"

"Umhum?" said Brother Fletcher, sucking at his scalded tongue.

"You ever think maybe you oughta start your own church?" Brother Fletcher was silent. "Fletch?"

"I was just thinking," Brother Fletcher said slowly. "Yes, I had . . . no. No, I never thought about it really. I couldn't have, because I just started thinking about what a church really *is*. Do you know what I mean?" He looked at Mrs. Fletcher, who nodded wisely, although she didn't have the slightest idea of what Brother Fletcher was getting at. "I mean," Brother Fletcher went on, "I always thought about a church as a place where people went and prayed and sang. . . ."

"Isn't it?"

"Well, yes. But is that all?"

"You want some more coffee?" said Mrs. Fletcher.

"For God's sake! Don't you understand what—no, of course you don't. I haven't told you."

"Told me what?"

Brother Fletcher took a deep breath. "Suppose I told you about a place where people could go and just sit and talk to other people, and where everyone was welcome. They didn't pray and they didn't preach, and nobody tried to tell anybody else who God was and what He looked like and what He wanted. They just went there and . . . were there. Suppose I told you about a place like that? Wouldn't you call that a church?"

"Either that or a . . ." Mrs. Fletcher began, but then she caught the seriousness of Brother Fletcher's expression, stopped, and sighed. "I don't know nothin' 'bout what a church is supposed to be, or what it's supposed to do. But I do know about that Sloan, an' if he's workin' for the Lord I'ma pay the trashman to haul *my* soul away. An' if you want to sit in an alley and call it a church, go ahead. It won't make no difference, because good's good an' bad is bad, an' that Sloan is bad."

"I never had any problems with good and bad," Brother Fletcher said. "It was right and wrong I never quite figured out."

Mrs. Fletcher looked at him closely, decided he was joking. She got up and took the cups over to the stove and poured more coffee. She stirred slowly, then stood still for a few moments. "Fletch?" she said suddenly, "what about the . . ." She stopped.

"What about what?"

Mrs. Fletcher hesitated. "Well . . . just sometimes I think maybe you should push that Sloan around a little. I mean, tonight, nobody was interested in his foolishness, they—"

"They were interested in a circus," snapped Brother Fletcher.

"I'm not talkin' about folks like that simple-minded Fundidia—"

"Tut, tut, tut," said Brother Fletcher.

"Tut, tut, tut, yourself," snapped Mrs. Fletcher. "Fundidia ain't got the brains she was born with. I'm talkin' about people like Lavernia Thompson. That old lady ain't got nothin' in the world but that church, an' that Sloan is fixin' to run it right out from under her."

"But what can I do?" mused Brother Fletcher, half to himself.

"I know what I'd do," said Mrs. Fletcher. "I'd hit him upside the head with a fryin' pan."

"The meek shall inherit the earth," said Brother Fletcher.

"If there's anything left," countered Mrs. Fletcher.

"Maybe," said Brother Fletcher. "But I guess I can't do anything without feeling I'm doing it for someone besides myself. Suppose I could do something about Sloan. If I did it just because of something *I* wanted, I'd be just the same as Sloan." Brother Fletcher shook his head. "No, if God wants The Word of Life to change, he'll have to give me a better reason than my suspicions."

"Do it for Lavernia."

"One old lady."

"How many old ladies do you want?" Mrs. Fletcher demanded hotly. Brother Fletcher looked up in surprise. "You didn't see her," said Mrs. Fletcher. "You went on back behind there an' I know you was thinkin' how it didn't mean anything, but I *saw* that old lady. . . ." She stopped suddenly and turned to face him, and he saw tears in her eyes. "How many old ladies do you want? How many are there?" Her voice broke and the tears escaped her eyes and rolled down her cheeks. She lowered her head. "Fletcher, I'm gonna be an old lady someday." She raised her head and looked at him, then went quickly down the hall.

7 Saturday

In the morning, while the garbage trucks scuttled like fat roaches over the streets west of the Schuylkill, Rayburn Wallace had stepped from a carpeted elevator, walked across a carpeted lobby, emerged into the nearly fresh air. The sun was a bloody ball in the eastern sky, losing color as it climbed, and he had walked into it along Spruce Street. His brain was dull from fatigue and the aftereffects of alcohol and his stomach was uncomfortably full of the strawberries and cream she had fed him, calling it a hero's breakfast. He had devoured the fruit and then carried her back to the bedroom, where he had fallen upon her as if to drive her back through the sheet. "Am I all white women to you?" she had murmured throatily.

"Jesus," Rayburn had muttered, stopping in mid-thrust, "ain't one enough?"

Later, he had showered long and hard in a big tiled shower stall, with hot water. She had dried him, enfolding him in a big, fluffy white towel, and then had watched hungrily while he had dressed. Rayburn, walking into the sunrise, clapped his hands and giggled. Rayburn Wallace, fucking in a fancy apartment building with elevators and a doorman, fucking in a bed with silk sheets, fucking some rich white man's rich white wife! He thought about Leslie and his smile widened. This would show her. He thought of what he would tell her—nothing, he decided, not a blessed damn thing. He'd just walk in an' get in bed an' go to sleep. Rayburn giggled, addressed the row of traffic meters stretching east. "Only she ain't gonna let me go to sleep. She'll wake up for sure an' say, 'Where the hell was you all night,' an' I'll say 'Out,' an' roll on over. And she'll keep on pesterin' me, wantin' to know where I been. But I ain't gonna tell her. It's 'bout time she had some a her own damn medicine." Rayburn walked stiffly on. She'd say, Rayburn, you been cheatin' on me, an' he'd just laugh her into silence. She'd say he better tell her right now, an' he'd give in an' say, All right, an' he'd tell her. He'd say, Honey, it was like this. I come home an' you wasn't here so I went on out to have me a drink, an' I didn't feel like messin' with the same old niggers 'round here, so I went on uptown, an' I goes in this one place. There ain't nothin' in there but a bunch a white folks all dressed up, but the drinks is cheap, so I started drinkin' with them white folks, an' all the sudden there's this white woman an' she's buyin' me drinks an' tellin' me I'm beautiful, an' then we went on over to her place an' I'm a little tired on account of I didn't get a whole lot a sleep, you know what I mean? He'd smile and chuckle. An' she'd say, Gone, nigger, with that shit, where was you? An' he'd say, All right if you can't deal with the truth. He'd make like he was goin' to sleep but she'd come crawlin' all over him, lickin' at him an' kissin' at him, but he'd just shove her off an' say, Gone, woman, lemme get some rest. I done give all that away, since you wasn't here to get it.

Rayburn had grinned as he walked across the bridge, savoring his story, rehearsing, editing. South Street rolled over in its sleep, snorted, slumbered on. The first trucks rumbled out of the beer distributor's garage on Twenty-fourth, and a fleet of yellow taxis rolled out of the lot on Grays Ferry. A forty bus had come roaring across the bridge and passed him. Rayburn had climbed the stairs slowly, dragging out the moments of anticipation. Stopping on the landing outside his door he had straightened his clothes, brushed the dust from his shoes. Then, thinking better of it, he had unbuttoned his shirt and turned up his collar on one side. He had opened the door, slipped inside. This, by God, would show her. He stepped into the living room, bent carefully to slip off his shoes. Holding them in one hand, he had stepped defiantly toward the bedroom. And then he had dropped the shoes on the floor and stared, with slowly dawning comprehension, at the unperturbed covers of the empty bed.

Now he rolled in the growing coolness of evening. The film of stale perspiration that coated his body was turning cold. He woke up. His mouth did not taste like the bottom of a bear pit. His head did not throb. He felt surprisingly well. He lay staring up at the peeling ceiling, at the tentacles of paint that hung down toward him. He had slept the day away, hoping she would come back. Now he was awake. There was a pressure in his belly. He rolled out of bed, went into the bathroom, stood before the toilet, but then he realized that that wasn't it, so he turned around, backed up, sat down, rose immediately, lowered the toilet seat, and sat down again. He felt the pressure twist into pain and grunted as the gas escaped noisily. He got up, used the toilet paper, shoved the flush handle home, but the wad of paper stubbornly refused to enter the whirlpool and become a contribution to the city sewer system. Rayburn felt a wave of malevolence as he watched it. He stalked into the kitchen, found a glass, filled it with water, returned to the bathroom, and poured the water onto the paper. The paper seemed to try to slip away, but Rayburn adjusted his aim and pursued relentlessly, finally catching the paper squarely. It sank immediately. Rayburn sniffed, set the glass on the sink, pulled the handle again, and marched back into the bedroom. It was not until he saw the bed that he remembered she was not there, and then he felt bad, worse than he had ever felt before. His head ached and his bowels twisted. He sank onto the rumpled sheet, stretched out, stared up at the ceiling once again. The mottled plaster swirled in his vision, forming faces—her face, the faces of faceless men, young, virile, strong, rich. Rayburn lay, legs extended, arms stretched out, fingers grasping the edge of the mattress as if to keep him from falling off, watching as the paint tentacles elongated, dripping toward him. Rayburn opened his mouth in a silent scream, his face contorting, drawing the skin tightly across his skull. He managed to turn his eyes away. His breathing gradually slowed. When he opened his eyes, the ceiling was once again the ceiling.

"Monday," he said suddenly. "I'ma do it Monday." He'd go to the bank on Monday an' tell 'em what they could do with their goddamn buckets and fucking brooms. And he'd tell that Victoria Bender to give him his money. She'd count it out for him, lickin' her lips, an' when she got finished an' gave him the money she'd say, You leavin' right now, honey? Right this minute? An' he'd just nod at her. An' she'd want to know where was he goin', an' he'd say he didn't know, someplace foreign, Spain, maybe, an' ask her did she know Spain was all red and green. She'd want to know was he takin' his wife an' he'd say no, his wife couldn't keep up with him no more, he needed him a new woman. She'd say how she always thought maybe her an' Rayburn oughta get together, an' he'd just stand there for a while, like he was thinkin' about it, but then he'd shake his head an' say, nah, he was travelin' light, an' his feet was itchin' too bad to hang around. But he'd tell her not to worry, he'd be back that way some time.

![]

It was, at first glance, a normal Saturday night at the Elysium Hotel. The drinks contained the usual percentage of water. The jukebox swallowed the usual number of quarters. The Muslim desk clerk took time out from reading the latest copy of *Muhammed Speaks* and renting out rooms by the hour to take trips to the men's room, where he refilled the condom machine and emptied the coin box before some desperate junkie forgot that this was the stronghold of Leroy Briggs and tried to make off with the cash. The whores lounged in the bar, and the fairies flitted through the lobby. On the surface all was normal, but in a dim corner of the barroom Willie T. sat, looking sad and drinking neat whiskey. When Cotton strolled in after his usual dinner of steak, fries, and onion rings at the Delmonaco, Nemo, the bartender, sent one of the waitresses over to whisper to him and point him toward the corner. "Balls," said Cotton as he began to navigate the narrow channels between tables, chairs, legs, knees. When occasionally he missed a turn and bumped someone, he apologized politely but firmly, and moved on. Willie T. saw him approaching, smiled with unusual warmth, and downed another shot. Cotton coasted to a stop. "Your mother know you're drinkin' that stuff?"

Willie T. peered up at him. "Ma mother was a wash woman an' she went to church every damn Sunday. She worked her fingers to the bone, I mean to the *bone*, so's I'd have a chance to make somethin' of maself. I swore I wasn't never gonna do nothin' wrong, I was gonna be one a them rich powerful folks, an' she wasn't gonna have to be givin' up nothin' no more. I ain't hardly never touched a hard drink before in ma whole damn life, Cotton, you know that?"

"Ain't hard to guess," Cotton said. "I'm sorry I brought your mother—"

"Ma *mother*," Willie T. said. Tears began to flow from his eyes. "She always said to me, 'Willie, you don't start that drinkin' an' runnin' around, you get in with the folks what runs things in this world.' An' I done it, too. You an' me an' Leroy, Cotton, we had this here street right here." Willie T. raised his fist and shook it in Cotton's face. Cotton backed off a step. Willie T. let his fist fall. "Right here. An' we let that Brown sonofabitch just walk right in, an' Leroy don't even want to do nothin'."

"Now, Willie," Cotton said soothingly, "you got yourself all bent outa shape over nothin'. I ain't seen this here Brown doin' all that much—"

"Oh yes," Willie T. said emphatically. "Oh yes he is. He come waltzin' in here, big as fuckin' life, an' bought him a six-pack to go. He done it two nights straight. Now you know, Cotton, one time could be an accident, but two times ain't."

"Now, Willie, maybe he just likes beer."

"Oh yeah? Well lemme tell you, I watched that dude's place all damn day, an' he didn't come out but one time. An' you know what he done? He come out wearin' a goddamn track suit an' he went runnin' up an' down the street like some kinda fool for half a goddamn hour, an' then he went back inside an' didn't come out again all goddamn day. Then tonight he comes in here. Don't you tell me not to worry. That nigger's up to somethin'." Willie T. wiped tears from his eyes, poured himself another shot of whiskey and downed it.

"Well—" Cotton began.

"Well, hell," snapped Willie T. "An' when I went to tell Leroy that this cat was doin' all this shit right in the middle a the street, you know what? Leroy says I'm busy. Damn right he was busy. That bitch was settin' up in Leroy's chair an' Leroy was on his knees kissin' her goddamn feet. Somebody's stealin' the damn street right out from under us, an' Leroy's suckin' some bitch's toe."

"Are you serious?" Cotton took a seat.

"He skipped dinner, too," Willie T. said.

"Nah!"

"Where you think I got this here bottle? I took it in to him, but he said he was busy."

"Doin' what? He wasn't still—"

"Worse," said Willie T. "He was teachin' her to play pool. She had her ass parked right up on the corner a the table, an' he was tryin' to tell her how to hold the cue, an' she kept pokin' him in the gut with it, an' he was smilin'. *Smilin'!*" Willie T. shook his head and downed another shot.

Cotton got up and maneuvered his bulk over to the bar. "Nemo, how come you give him a bottle? You know Willie don't drink."

"Wasn't me," said the bartender. "That there's Leroy's six o'clock bottle. Willie went in with it an' he come back out with it."

Cotton jerked his head toward the office. "Leroy in there?"

"Yeah. But he says he's busy."

Cotton snorted and set sail. He stepped into the office a second after his knock and discovered Leroy and Leslie locked in an embrace, far too occupied to notice his entrance. He closed the door and waited patiently for them to come up for air, but when he detected a subtle motion of Leslie's hand toward the buckle of Leroy's belt, Cotton cleared his throat. The pair continued to couple, and Leslie's hand continued its motion. They turned slowly, like a statue on a rotating pedestal, until Cotton had a perfect view of Leroy's back and Leslie's face. Leroy gasped loudly. Leslie smiled. "Gotcha," she said. Cotton made one effort to look away then gave up and stared. Leroy gasped again. "Um," said Leslie, and her face sank out of sight behind Leroy's shoulder. Cotton watched as the arm she had around Leroy sank down until it surrounded his knees. Cotton swallowed heavily, and his eyes bulged slightly. He felt around behind him for the doorknob. Slurping sounds reached Cotton's ears, and Leroy moaned. Cotton backed hastily through the door. Just as he closed it Leslie's hard pixie face appeared beside Leroy's hip and she gave Cotton a lewd wink. Cotton slammed the door and tottered back to the dim corner where Willie T. sat, drinking neat whiskey.

"They been at it all damn day," said Willie T., "kissin' an' toe-suckin' an' now they're playin' pool. You wanna drink?"

Cotton nodded and, ignoring the proffered glass, raised the bottle and took a long healthy gulp.

"He still tryin' to teach her how to hold the cue?" asked Willie T.

"Willie," said Cotton, "honest to Jesus, I think she already knows."

"He ain't done nothin' useful all damn day," Willie T. said. "He ain't got no energy. We gotta do somethin' or that bitch is gonna suck the life outa him."

"Amen," Cotton said, reaching for the bottle.

She had waited in the darkness for a long time, leaning back against a door, the splinters of wood digging into her bare back, flecks of paint sticking to her sweaty skin when she adjusted her position. She held her bag along one slim leg, her hip thrust outward in a stance of blatant suggestiveness. Once it had been a pose. Now it was the way she stood. It was also the way many others stood, and so the rollers and runners who saw her standing that way chuckled to themselves and passed the word: 'Nessa was turned out again. She stood watching a doorway on the other side of the street, making no motion or sound of invitation, but the rollers and runners ignored that; she was turned out again. They came and went, chuckling. It was Friday, and the street was alive with them. It was Friday, and if it wasn't quite Saturday, it was the next best thing. Saturday was tomorrow, and tomorrow was a promise, and, like most promises on South Street, had at least a 50 per cent chance of remaining unkept.

She had waited patiently, watching the sun go down, watching the street come to life, watching the traffic smother the pavement. The neon cross above The Word of Life had presided over a doorway that swallowed ticket-bearing throngs. Vanessa knew all about the Love Feasts at The Word of Life—she had attended as a special paid guest of the Reverend Mr. J. Peter Sloan. But now she was interested in another doorway, beside a burned-out store. She had watched as her sister Leslie emerged from it carrying a suitcase and headed for the Elysium. She had watched as Rayburn went in and came out again. Then she had glanced at her watch, bitten her lip, and turned away. Now it was Saturday; the promise nad come true. She walked up South Street, passing the open bar doors, and the eager lips of Those Who Knew whispered into the anxious ears of Those Who Wonder that 'Nessa was out again, walking the street. Hands came out of shadows, fingers clutched like spiderwebs, and even after they fell away something clung, something a little stale, a little moldy, something not quite clean. She only bothered to brush away the hands that moved too far or clung too long.

It was shaping up as a slow night for Saturday at Lightnin' Ed's. Leo was half hoping for a pleasant surprise to liven the evening, but Vanessa did not fall into that category. Vanessa was trouble as far as Leo was concerned, so when he looked up and saw her bow her head to get through the low door of Lightnin' Ed's, he motioned her to a vacant stool and made her a Singapore Sling. "On the house," he said, setting it in front of her. "It's been nice seein' you. Good evenin'."

"I think I'd rather pay for it," Vanessa said.

"Suit your own self," Leo said easily. "Good-bye. Drop in again the next time you get up to this end a the street. But make it a social call. I don't like it when you're travelin' on business."

"I'm waitin' for somebody," Vanessa said.

"He just left," Leo informed her, "an' he took his wallet along with him."

"I see," Vanessa said. "Since you gave me a drink, Leo, ι guess'you won't mind if I drink it."

"Course not," Leo said, "but I wouldn't want to hold you. I know people in your line a work got to keep movin'. I'll put it in a paper cup an' you can carry it out." He reached for the glass.

Vanessa picked it up and raised it to her lips. "Shit, Leo," she said, "are you really gonna make me go outa here with a paper cup? God, the word'll get around I'm on ma way to the clinic. That kinda talk is hell on business."

Leo grinned for an instant, then cut it off. "C'mon, 'Nessa, you know what happens every time I let you work in here. . . ."

Vanessa set the glass down, hard. "I ain't," she snapped.

"Ain't what?"

"Ain't hustlin'."

Leo sighed. "Look honey, I wasn't born yesterday. I know Leroy done give you the air, an' that means you're back on the street."

Vanessa looked at him, smiled, took a sip of her drink. "Leo, sposin' I was to explain to you exactly why I ain't hustlin', will you quit actin' like a goddamn nanny goat?"

"Honey," said Leo, "if you can prove to me you ain't nustlin', I'll be happy to reserve a stool for you from now until next doomsday. Right next to Betsy."

"Umph," said Vanessa. "That's what I love about you, Leo, you're a prince among old maids. I ain't hustlin' because Leroy pays me not to hustle."

"Uh huh," Leo said, "an' in the off-season he pays you to take care a his baseball cards. You *really* expect me to believe that Leroy pays you not to hustle? Whad I ever do to make you think ma head was stuck on with Scotch tape?"

"Now listen, Leo, you know Leroy. Nothin' but the best for Leroy. He don't have no truck with whores. So even if he don't want me, he don't want nobody sayin' Leroy's ex is out there walkin' the street. So he pays me."

"I'll be damned," Leo said.

Vanessa grinned. "I get ma stool reserved?"

"That's the damnedest piece a shit I ever heard," Leo said. "Leroy *pays* you . . . I'll be damned. I swear, I thought I'd heard everything but . . . why, damn, 'Nessa, have a drink."

"I got one, Leo," Vanessa said.

"Oh," said Leo. "Yeah." He grinned broadly. "Leroy pays. . . ." He chuckled.

"Tell me one thing," Vanessa said.

"Sure," said Leo.

" 'Member when I said I was waitin' for somebody? Well I am, only he don't know it. I just heard from this dude that I could find this other dude in here, you know? Well this dude I'm lookin' for, I don't know him too good, truth is I ain't never seen him before, but it ain't like you're thinkin', Leo. Anyway, I ain't never seen him, so when he comes in you gotta tell me." She took a gasp of breath.

"An' you ain't hustlin'?" Leo demanded.

Vanessa shook her head. "Leroy'd turn purple."

Leo looked up at the ceiling. "I'm crazy," he said. "All right, who you lookin' for?"

"Name's Brown," Vanessa said.

"Oh," Leo said. "Brown."

"You know him, don't you?"

"Yeah," said Leo. "Oh yeah, I know him. I know him all right. Brown. He's that crazy fool was in here last week, an' I ain't seen him since, an' I hope to Jesus I never *do* see him again, because that is one crazy nigger."

"Betsy said he hung around here."

"Betsy says lots a things. Betsy files a tax return so the guvment'll think she's still trickin'.''

"Great," said Vanessa. Just then Big Betsy waddled into Lightnin' Ed's. She caught sight of Vanessa and tried to put it into reverse, but her momentum carried her six feet inside the bar. "Anybody ever tell you you was a fat-cunted liar?" Vanessa inquired.

"Leo," said Big Betsy, "ain't you gonna tell this bitch to watch her mouth?"

"Nope," Leo said. "An' don't worry 'bout gettin' blood on the floor 'cause Jake'll be in tonight to clean up."

Big Betsy turned to Vanessa. "Don't you talk to me that way. I'm oldern you an' you oughta treat me with some kinda respect." Glaring, Big Betsy lowered herself onto a stool.

"I oughta lay a bottle upside your head," Vanessa told her. "You told me Brown hung out in here an' now Leo says he ain't been in but that one time."

"He'll be back," Big Betsy said. "They may go far, but they always come back to their sweet mama."

"Uh, huh," said Vanessa. "That, ah, sweet mama, that'd be you?"

"Who else?"

"Jesus," Vanessa said. "I hope he forgets all about you, 'cause if he don't he won't never be back here till they start sendin' niggers to the moon."

"Course he'll be back," snapped Big Betsy. "He needs somebody like me." Leo pulled his handkerchief from his hip pocket and held it over his face. Big Betsy looked at him in annoyance. "He does," she insisted. Sounds halfway between chokes and sobs issued from behind Leo's handkerchief. "You sick or somethin', Leo?" Big Betsy demanded.

Leo took the handkerchief away from his face. "No," he said, wiping his eyes. "I ain't sick."

"Well, you sound sick," Big Betsy informed him acidly, "an' you looks sick, an' you must be catchin', 'cause you're makin' me sick."

"That's too bad," Vanessa said. "Brown's gonna come in here with the hots for Betsy, only she's gonna have to tell him she's sick."

"You'll see," vowed Big Betsy. "That Brown, he's a real man. He knows what he wants. He ain't out after some little semipro piece, he wants a woman that can understand him, somebody knows their way around."

"Right," Vanessa said, "an' that's why he wants to get in bed with you."

Big Betsy regarded her haughtily. "The trouble with you, 'Nessa, is you got a one-rut mind. Me an' Brown, we ain't into that stuff. We got us a more mature thing. We talk 'bout life an' . . . well, you know, that kinda stuff. Brown, he's an educated dude, you know. Our thing—"

"Shit," said Leo, "the dude wasn't in here but one night."

Big Betsy shook her head sagely. "Leo, there's some men you never know, an' then there's some you can talk to for three minutes an' it's like you knowed 'em all your life."

"You mean two minutes, don't you?" Vanessa said.

Leo was staring at Big Betsy. "Oh my God," he said, an expression of disgust on his face, "now I *am* sick. I useta have me a nice bar. Now I got whores that wants to be preachers an' preachers that wants to be winos an' next thing you know Jake'll be in here tellin' me he's decided to take up hustlin'."

"You got a hard life, Leo," Vanessa said.

"An' I ain't even mentioned the nuts tryin' to be gangsters an' the pensioned-off hookers."

"That's what you get for openin' a bar," Big Betsy told him. "You shoulda stuck to bein' the Goodyear blimp."

"Nah," Leo said, "there was too many ups an' downs, an' if you fart once you'd crash."

"You're full a hot air anyways," Big Betsy said.

"An' you're full a shit," Vanessa told her.

"An' you're full a nothin'," said Big Betsy. "You're just one big hole."

"If you wasn't so old an' fat an' ugly, you might bother me," Vanessa said.

"Sure I'm old an' fat an' ugly. You can't do nothin' about gettin' old an' ugly, so you might as well eat. Least I ain't useless. I talk to folks. I spread joy an' womanly understandin'."

"You couldn't spread a dose a clap," Vanessa said. "Who told you all that bullshit?"

"Ain't bullshit," declared Big Betsy. "It was *him.* That's what he said. Said I was full a ancient wisdom an' womanly understandin'. Nicest thing anybody ever said to me."

"That I can believe," Leo said. "When'd he say all this, before or after he tried to commit suicide?"

"What?"

"Leroy."

"Oh," said Big Betsy. "After."

"That explains it," Leo said. "Anybody who's been that close to death is bound to say some pretty weird things."

"You leave him be," said Big Betsy. She got up and went down to the far end of the bar. "An' leave me be. An' if he comes in, don't you try to steal him, 'Nessa."

"My God," Leo said, "I think she's jealous "

"Am not," snarled Big Betsy.

Vanessa sighed. "Gimme another drink, huh, Leo?"

"Okay," Leo said. "But I don't figure he's gonna show up."

"I know," Vanessa said. She looked out the doorway at the darkening street. "I just want to sit someplace. Someplace quiet." She turned her head to look at him. "That's all right, ain't it, Leo? To stay here, I mean?"

Leo set her drink up on the bar. "Sure," he said. "That's just fine."

"Haw, haw, haw," laughed Big Betsy the whore. Leo watched the TV with calm impassivity, his jaws making circular motions as he devoured his after-dinner snack. Vanessa did not look up from her drink. Big Betsy laughed again.

"Shup," said Leo, without turning away from the TV. He reached out and grasped a large mug of beer, raised it to his mouth. His lips poked out as if he were getting ready to kiss someone, and he drew off the head in quick, audible slurps.

"Say what?" demanded Big Betsy.

"Said shup," said Leo. "I wants to listen at ma ball game."

"That's all you do all goddamn day is listen at the goddamn TV. It's goddamn sinful, that's what it is."

Leo took a bite of his sandwich.

"Leo, you black bastard, are you listenin' to me?"

Leo sighed and finished chewing, swallowing slowly and carefully. He paused a moment, nodded to himself, raised the beer, took a pull, lowered the glass, swished the beer around inside his mouth, swallowed, nodded again, looked up at the ceiling, burped, and nodded a third time. Finally he turned his head to regard Big Betsy. "If I was to listen to everythin' you says, I wouldn't never have time to piss, let alone eat, sleep, shit, or make any money." He took another bite of sandwich.

Big Betsy's eyes, nestled deeply inside mascara and wrinkles, smoldered. "Leo," she said, "sometimes you go too far."

"Betsy," said Leo, "you never go quite far enough." He rose ponderously and went to turn up the volume, then returned to his stool.

Big Betsy opened her mouth, then shut it with a clacking of dentures. She rooted around in her handbag and found a quarter, went over and dropped it into the jukebox. She punched buttons at random, her finger falling savagely. Her jaws were clenched. The strains of "When Irish Eyes Are Smiling," sung by Perry Como, echoed in Lightnin' Ed's, and the walls, used to the Motown sound, shuddered. Big Betsy returned to her stool, a smile of triumph on her face. Leo looked at her mildly, reached up and connected his earplug to the TV. Big Betsy stared at the "flesh-colored" earplug shining in Leo's dark ear, her face reflecting utter frustration. She got up and walked around to the other ear and began singing along with Perry Como. Leo looked at her, shrugged, rose, and disconnected the earplug. Big Betsy smiled triumphantly until Leo turned the volume of the TV all the way down and returned to his seat. He cheered softly as he munched his sandwich and slurped his beer. Big Betsy stared at the screen. Names, batting averages, counts of balls and strikes were being flashed in white letters. Periodic shots of the scoreboard gave all the information needed. Big Betsy sagged in defeat just as her money ran out and Perry Como escaped from South Street. The only sound was the crunch of Leo's jaw and his periodic cheers. Big Betsy flounced off to the ladies' room. Leo grinned and got up to turn up the sound, but before he reached the TV set the door opened. Leo stared. "Jesus! What happened to you?"

Rayburn Wallace stood in the doorway. His clothes, dirty and torn, were soaked with perspiration. Sweat ran down his face and neck, came welling out of his hair like water out of a sponge. His eyes were wild. "She's gone," Rayburn said. "I been everywhere, lookin'."

"Oh," said Leo. He stepped toward Rayburn, but Rayburn was already in motion, doing a jerky-robot walk toward the nearest bar stool, stopping, when he reached it, with a wobbly jiggle, as if in response to some electrical command delivered through an invisible wire. He dropped onto the stool. His head sank and hung on his neck like a pendulum weight. "What you need," Leo said, "is a good stiff drink." Rayburn did not reply, but his head seemed to swing slightly. Leo poured a highball glass half full of gin, and filled a mug with beer. "Here you go." Rayburn's right eyelid blinked slowly, showing the eye behind it dim and red, like that of an ill-tempered dragon roused from a deep sleep. Rayburn gazed at Leo for a moment with the single red eye, then reached out and took hold of the gin glass. He stuck out his lips, opened his mouth, and belted the whole thing in one gulp. He slammed the glass back onto the bar, sniffed, looked at Leo with his one eye, sniffed again, then grabbed wildly for the beer and poured it down his throat. He gasped. Leo smiled.

Big Betsy waddled out of the ladies' room, hitching her girdle up around where her hips had once been. "Damn," she muttered, "these things is sposed to be livin', but this one's close to death."

"No wonder," Leo said under his breath.

Big Betsy sat down at the bar and looked at Rayburn, who, having extinguished with beer the fire the gin had kindled, sat swaying back and forth. "Leo, man," said Rayburn, "be a pal an' get this po' nigger a drink."

"What the hell happened to him?" said Big Betsy.

"Wife left him," said Leo, pouring out a more conventional slug of gin.

"When'd it happen?"

"He just got here, Betsy," said Leo patiently.

"I was just astin', Leo."

Leo looked up at the TV. Rayburn downed his gin. "Shit," said Big Betsy, "there ain't gonna be no business tonight. Too much competition." She shot an angry glance down the bar at Vanessa, who was paying no attention. Big Betsy turned a sour eye on Rayburn. "Serves the bastard right," said Big Betsy. "He shoulda knowed that light-skinned gal wasn't nothin' but a gutter whore." She said it loud enough for the world to hear, and Vanessa looked up for a minute, then looked away. Rayburn sat stoically, not batting an eyelash. Leo stared at her.

"I'll be goddamned, if that ain't the spic callin' the wop a greaseball."

"Is not," said Big Betsy. "I ain't never tricked no good man into marryin' me."

"That," Leo told her, "would take the best damn witch doctor in the world. There's dumb men, but there ain't *any* that dumb."

"I had ma share a offers," snarled Big Betsy.

Leo snorted. "Goddamn. He struck out. Three on, one out, an' the fucker strikes out. I don't know why the hell I don't move someplace where they got a team that can at least hit a goddamn fly ball."

"You better believe I had offers," Big Betsy said.

Leo looked at Rayburn. "How you doin', Rayburn?"

"Ain't doin' shit," said Rayburn. Both his eyes were open now. "How 'bout another drink?" Leo looked at him doubtfully. "Goddamn you black Jew!" Rayburn snarled. He pulled money out of his pocket, bills, all ones. "I can pay, by Jesus!"

"I know you can pay," Leo said easily. "I just ain't sure—"

"Goddamn you!" shouted Rayburn. He half rose from the stool, his body shaking. His face was twisted into a mask of anger, but tears leaked from his eyes. He sat down again. "Please, Leo, man. Ma woman lef' me. If ma bartender won't gimme a drink, what I'ma do?"

"Try soberin' up," suggested Big Betsy.

"You try shuttin' up," said Leo.

Rayburn slowly turned his head until his eyes were trained on Big Betsy. He looked at her steadily, unblinking. Big Betsy met his gaze for a moment, then looked away, her eyes jerking around as if the walls, the floor, the ceiling, everything in the room were too hot to look at; then she looked back at Rayburn, meeting his eyes for one defiant instant before she spun on the bar stool with surprising quickness, like a basketball on the nose of a seal, and looked toward the other end of the bar. Rayburn's gaze remained fixed on the hump of fat behind Big Betsy's shoulders. She wiggled uneasily, as if feeling his eyes on her. Leo, moving slowly and silently, poured a slug of gin and a glass of beer and held them ready on the inner rail of the bar. Rayburn stared at Big Betsy's back, and as if in response to the heat and pressure of his eyes she began to move again, slowly this time, in a ponderous half-revolution clockwise, until her face was once again visible. Her eyes met Rayburn's and she looked away, but her body continued its slow turning. She looked at his face again.

"Ma wife done run off," Rayburn said.

"You want some scotch an' milk?" asked Leo.

Big Betsy shook her head. "This here's talkin' business." Her jowls sagged dejectedly, but her eyes were soft and serene. She looked at Rayburn. "Gimme gin."

Leo wordlessly poured her gin and set it in front of her. He moved away, retrieving his earplug and attaching it to the TV set. He started to sit down but stopped, shrugged, and went down to the end of the bar. Rayburn and Betsy were sunk in shadow. Betsy patted Rayburn's arm. Rayburn grabbed her hand. Leo placed a full bottle of gin on the bar. Big Betsy looked up at Leo, then at the bottle, then glanced at the pile of money in front of Rayburn. Leo shook his head, waved a hand, and went back to his ball game.

It was near to closing time, and Leo stood leaning against the bar, thinking how depressing it got, six days a week watching glasses being lifted to mouths, a Saturday night with few customers, all of them unhappy. Leo drew himself a short beer and looked around the room at the handful of dark shapes. At the far end of the bar, merged into a lumpy blob of shadow, were Big Betsy and Rayburn, swaying slowly out of time with the juke. All night long Rayburn had been feeding the machine quarters, and Leo had sworn he was going to use his shotgun on the thing if he had to listen to "I Heard It Through the Grapevine" one more time. Around the bar, tucked back in the corner where the wood met the cinderblock wall, half obscured by smoke and dimness, sat Vanessa. She had been sitting there all night long, sipping Singapore Slings and watching the door. She had consumed ten drinks, and Leo speculated as to whether she had not moved because she didn't want to or because she couldn't. Leo didn't see Jake until he heard the wino's voice at his elbow. Leo turned his head slowly, he was too tired to move fast. Jake shoveled a handful of coins onto the bar, and Leo poured him a glass of wine. Jake raised it. "Seen him again," Jake said.

"Huh?" said Leo.

"I seen him. Walkin' around like—what you call them things that walks around? I seen one in a movie one time." ·

"Zombies?"

"Yeah, that's it. He was walkin' around like one a them there. Talkin' to hisself."

"How come you can hear what folks is sayin' to theyselves bettern you can hear what they says to you?" Leo said.

Jake grinned. "Now, Leo, you know half a bein' hard a hearin' is bein' hard a listenin'. 'Sides, I didn't say I heard what he was sayin', I just heard he was sayin' it. Ain't he been in here?"

Leo sighed. "Ain't *nobody* been in here. 'Sides, I wouldn't know him if I saw him."

Jake looked up in surprise. "What you mean, you wouldn't know him?"

"Well, I might," Leo said, "if you was to tell me who the hell you're talkin' about."

"Why, Brown. Who else?"

"Oh, shit," Leo groaned. "Not him again. I don't want to hear that damn name ever again. No, he ain't been in here, an' I can prove it, because the place is still standin' an' *she*"—he jerked his head toward Vanessa—"is still settin'."

Jake peered through the gloom. "Who's she? Say, ain't that—"

"Sure is," said Leo.

"But wasn't she—"

"Sure was," said Leo.

"An' then he—"

"Sure did," said Leo.

"An' 'fore that wasn't she—"

"Sure was," said Leo.

"An' now she's—"

"All night," said Leo.

"Damn," said Jake. "An' you let her stay?"

"Yeah," Leo said tiredly. "She wasn't botherin' nobody. Says she ain't trickin' no more."

"Yeah," Jake said. "I hear Leroy pays her to stay outa circulation so folks won't say he screws whores."

Leo looked at him in amazement. "Goddamn, Jake, is there anything on this street you don't know about?"

"Yeah," Jake said. "I don't know how come ma wine glass is always empty, an' I don't know why that Brown keeps walkin' around like a—whad you say you called them things?"

"Zombies," Leo supplied.

"Yeah." Leo refilled the wine glass and removed a dime from the pile of change on the counter. "Leo," Jake said in a philosophical tone of voice, "by the time a man gets to be my age he finds out it's a good idea to keep his eyes open, 'specially if he don't hear too good. Now in the case a Brown, it wasn't ma eyes, it was ma legs."

"Your legs," Leo said.

"That's right, ma legs. I was coppin' a few Zs in that alley down the other side a the Delmonaco, an' here comes that Brown fallin' over me, wanderin' around like one a them zomblies."

"Zombies," Leo corrected.

"Yeah."

"Well, so long as he don't come in here pickin' fights, he can wander clear to Hell," Leo said.

"You'd a thought you was in Hell if him an' Leroy'd both come in while she was here."

Leo shrugged. "An' then there's Rayburn."

"His wife left him," Jake said. "She's shackin' up with Leroy."

"What? You kiddin'?"

"Nope," Jake said. "I wish I was. It's gonna ruin Rayburn." He looked down the bar, then looked back at his wine.

"Maybe we'll get lucky an' it'll ruin Leroy," said Leo. "Rayburn used to be pretty good with that razor."

"Humph," Jake said. "Like the old man said to the hooker, I ain't payin' two bucks for what used to be. 'Sides, Rayburn'd have to carve away for half an hour on Leroy 'fore he got to anythin' important. Leroy ain't got no heart, an' he ain't got no guts; he's just an' oversize stomach an' a king-size gall bladder, an' the rest of him's full a shit."

Leo snorted and shook his head. "I wish I understood women."

"Women is easy to understand," Jake said. "They're just like men, more or less, almost, an' sometimes."

"Well, I sure don't understand that one. I never saw a man as crazy about a woman as Rayburn was 'bout that one. So now—"

"How 'bout a refill," Jake said.

"Sure," Leo said, pouring it. "Jake, how come—"

"How come all these questions," Jake said. "Maybe you oughta ask your pet preacher."

"*My* pet preacher! Who hauled him in here?"

"Who let him stay?"

"We're all crazy," Leo said.

"Yeah," Jake said. "Probly all end up like Brown, wanderin' around like zomblies."

"Zombies," Leo said.

"I know how to say it," Jake snapped.

Rayburn rose unsteadily and staggered toward the door. He stopped in front of Leo, focusing his eyes with difficulty. "Night, Leo," he said with exaggerated dignity.

"You gonna be all right gettin' home?" Leo said.

Rayburn thought about it. "Home?"

Leo looked at Jake. Jake eyed the rafters. "Home," Leo told Rayburn, "is where you're goin', because it's closin' time. Now, can you make it that far?"

Rayburn thought about it a little too hard and nearly lost his balance. Jake reached out to steady him. Rayburn shrugged his hand away. "Certainly," he said. "Certainly I can make it that far. How far is it?"

"How far—it's seven blocks, Rayburn. Seven goddamn blocks."

"Better tell him which direction, Leo," Jake advised.

"Seven blocks," said Rayburn. "That's a long way."

"You shoulda figured that out before," Leo said. "Ain't nobody here to hold your hand."

"I ain't astin' nobody to hold ma hand," Rayburn said. "I'm fine." He turned on his heel and collided heavily with the wall.

Leo sighed. "Siddown, Rayburn. I'll see you get home."

"I can make it," Rayburn said, pushing himself away from the wall. He rocked back and forth on his heels.

"Better point him towards the door, Leo, 'fore he hurts hisself," Jake said.

Leo glared at him. "Just siddown, Rayburn."

"I don't need no help," Rayburn said.

"Yeah, sure," said Leo. "Now siddown right there."

"I can make it," Rayburn insisted. He sat down heavily.

Leo sighed. "Okay, everybody, closin' time."

"Thank God it's Saturday," Jake said. "I ain't been feelin' too good lately. I think sleepin' in alleys upsets ma stomach." He swallowed the rest of his wine and waited for a refill.

"Rotgut upsets your stomach," Leo told him.

"Nah," said Jake, "wine's good for you. Ma old man useta tell me how wine helped him with his constipation, kept him healthy. Course he died when he wasn't nothin' but sixty-seven. . . ."

"G'night, Leo," said Big Betsy. She paused to look at Rayburn. He gazed at her glassily.

"Whad you tell him, Betsy?" asked Leo.

"Told him his wife was a low-down rotten cunt that didn't know a man when she saw one."

"Whad he say?"

"Same thing he's sayin' now." Big Betsy turned away from Rayburn, snorting in disgust. "What the hell's the matter with him, Leo? That girl's been screwin' around since the day he married her, an' everybody on the damn street knows it but Rayburn. You know, the fool sat there cryin' an' sayin' it was all his fault. Leo, I'm tellin' you, the fool is a fool. Ain't you, Rayburn?" Rayburn smiled glassily. Big Betsy punched him on the shoulder. Rayburn swayed gently. "Ain't you a fool, Rayburn?" said Big Betsy. She punched him again. Rayburn swayed. Big Betsy hit him again. Her jowls jiggled. "Ain't you, Rayburn?" Rayburn swayed.

"Leave him be," Vanessa said. She came up behind Big Betsy.

Big Betsy glanced at her, sneered, punched Rayburn again. "Ain't you a fool?" said Big Betsy.

Leo started to reach across the bar. "Lay off, Betsy."

"A fool," said Big Betsy, and she made to hit Rayburn again. Vanessa caught her arm and held her.

"Let him be," Vanessa said.

Big Betsy abandoned Rayburn and turned on Vanessa. "Well, well, if it ain't our local vendin'-machine cunt. Anybody got a quarter?"

Vanessa's nostrils flared but she said nothing. She stepped around Big Betsy and hauled Rayburn to his feet. "I'm takin' him home," she announced.

"Merry Christmas," Leo said.

"You like 'em drunk, 'Nessa?" said Big Betsy.

Vanessa got Rayburn into low gear and steered him toward the door. "Shut up, Betsy. I'm just helpin' him home 'fore you beats him to death."

"He's already beat to death," Big Betsy said. "Can't nobody help him."

"Don't need no help," said Rayburn. Vanessa pushed him out the door.

"Go to hell," Big Betsy shouted after them. "Way I hear it, 'Nessa, the onliest way you *can* please a man is if he's too drunk to do nothin'."

"G'night, Betsy," Jake said. "You could lick your weight in police dogs, you're such a bitch."

"Jake, you're a goddamn wino," Big Betsy said. "You're a goddamn wino an' I'm a goddamn whore an' Leo's a goddamn bartender with olives for balls an' a pickle for a prick."

"We're all goddamn somethin' or others," Jake said.

"Yeah," said Leo. "Sounds like I'm a goddamn salad."

Big Betsy waddled unsteadily toward the door, stopped, and stared out at the street. Leo extinguished the lights. Big Betsy turned ponderously, facing the darkness. "Goddamn, Jake," Big Betsy said, "I can remember when you was fuckin' handsome." She turned again and waddled out.

"Happy Saturday, Leo," Jake said, draining his glass.

Black sky hanging above him, black water flowing below, Brown sat in darkness on the South Street Bridge, armed with three six-packs of sixteen-ounce cans. He sat near one of the little bastions inserted in the bridge's design by some romantic architect in an age when lovers strolled and paused to look down at a shining river. Brown was no strolling lover, and the Schuylkill was no lover's inspiration. Or a poet's, either. Brown had come looking for inspiration; now he sat working through the sixes, crushing the thin cans in his hand as he emptied them, tossing them outward over the railing. He could not hear them slap the water; that sound was hidden in the background of other sounds—tiny ones nearby, loud ones far away—that merged into a single low moan. Brown listened through the persistent hum for the noise of crushed aluminum can hitting chemical river, heard nothing but the city's moanings, and opened another can.

It was Saturday, late, almost Sunday, and the other westbound bridges were laden with traffic. South Street's bridge knew only the infrequent passing of the forty bus, an occasional cab, an occasional car.

It was after one when Brown finished the last beer, crushed the can, tossed it over the railing. He rose, stretching, groaning like an old man. The lights of the refineries swam before his eyes for a moment, then subsided into a steady pulsation in rhythm with Brown's heartbeat. Brown's mind floated somewhere above him, giving precise instructions to a body that refused to respond precisely. Brown turned himself with great care, put his feet in low gear, and steered himself down off the bridge. In the shadows he paused to relieve the awesome pressure building up in his bladder. The stream of urine wandered; Brown, overcorrecting, had to do some fancy footwork to keep his shoes dry. He nearly fell, stumbled back, and the errant stream baptized a Volkswagen from bumper to bumper. Brown regained his balance and his composure, completed his mission, headed home.

South Street was restless, as if reluctant to admit that Saturday was over, that Sunday was here, that Monday was sure to follow. Brown walked downtown at what he thought was a good rate of speed, stumbling along like an elderly turtle paralyzed on one side, catching himself against buildings to keep from falling. The three-way intersection of Grays Ferry, Twenty-third, and South presented a difficult problem: there were no walls to fall against for the immense distance of thirty yards. Brown leaned against a car, after checking carefully to make certain it was parked, and considered. It was a question, Brown decided, of inertia and geometry. He had detected a tendency of his feet to steer to the right, and he would therefore have to point himself far enough out into the middle of the street so that when he had traversed the width of the intersection, he would be on the sidewalk on the far side with a wall handy to collapse against. Brown was pleased with his undiminished capacity for logical thinking. He reviewed his reasoning, checking for possible flaws, overlooked elements. Finding none, he stumbled out into the middle of South Street just as a large automobile came roaring down off the bridge. The driver hit the horn and the brakes at the same time. Brown heard the horn, felt the headlights coming toward him, and played a remarkable game of chicken, not flinching or changing course in the slightest as the heavy car swerved past him. "Watch where you're goin'!" the driver shouted.

"Eat shit," Brown retorted amiably, just before a relay closed in his brain and he realized what had almost happened to him. Brown staggered weakly over to the cracked watering trough and vomited into the mass of dead leaves and paper scraps that clogged it. When he straightened up, he was sober enough to realize how drunk he was. Brown considered the extent of his inebriation and was duly awed.

He stumbled out of the intersection and along South Street until he reached the alley beside Lightnin' Ed's Bar and Grill. Brown entered the alley and sat down on a garbage can to collect his thoughts. From the deeper recesses of the darkness came a sudden sharp squalling sound made by quarreling cats, a scratching of claws on cobbles, then quiet. Brown spoke to himself, trying to draw his scattered thoughts together. He peered at himself from outside, saw himself being drawn and quartered to the four corners of the earth, tried to pull it all back to one spot, a garbage-choked alley in a smog-smothered city. He closed his eyes, and something twisted in his mind. He got up and staggered against a wall, pushed the wall away and tumbled into a garbage can. Rotting refuse accepted him, garbage aroma rose and enfolded him, bacon grease and banana peels clung to him. He shoved himself out of the garbage, left the alley in a desperate, shambling run, banging back and forth between the buildings on either side. He burst out onto South Street, turned left, ran toward the bridge. His steps were short, choppy, and he forgot to breathe for the first block, so that as he pounded up the ramp onto the bridge he was gasping. He ran across the bridge, not stopping until he reached the traffic light at Thirty-third Street. The light was red. Brown tried to stop, stumbled, and fell into the gutter.

He lay there for a few moments, then pushed himself up and sat on the curb. Something smelled terrible and he realized that it was him. He grunted in disgust, got to his feet, looked around him. He sighed, gritted his teeth, and headed back across the bridge, walking carefully, like an eighty-year-old man aware of his brittle bones. He was nearly sober as he walked down the ramp onto South Street. He moved along close to the walls, clinging to the shadows, skulking like a robber. He sniffed and increased his pace, trying to outrun the smell of himself. He reached the door beside the gaping storefront, opened it, stepped into the darkness. The smell already in the stairway mingled with the offensive odor of Brown, and he held his breath as he started up the stairs. From above him came a noise like the scrabbling of nails on wood. Brown stopped, flattened himself against the wall, his heart pounding. There was a tingling on the patch of skin just below his breastbone as he anticipated the rusty blade of some turkey-crazed junkie sliding home. Brown forced himself to breathe quietly, wasting no time cursing himself for drunkenness, lack of caution. The scrabbling sound came again: short, harsh, fingernails on wood. Rats. Brown relaxed, took a step. "Who's that?" demanded a voice out of the darkness. Brown slammed himself back against the wall, listening. It had been a woman's voice. Brown eased down along the wall into a crouch, leaned forward onto the balls of his feet, turned his face into the darkness. He waited for his eyes to adjust. He calmed himself. He listened. "Who's that?" the woman said again. She was on the right side of the stairs, Brown decided. He eased over against the left wall. "Who is that down there?" The woman's voice was a little ragged now; the silence was getting to her. Brown took a deep breath, preparing for a low charge. "Who *is* that?"

"Who's that?" Brown whispered. Silence from the darkness. A car hissed by on the street.

"Who's *that?*" the woman's voice demanded.

"Yeah," said a third voice, male. "Who dat who say who dat when she say who dat?" The third voice broke into a heavy, drunken laugh which turned into an anguished croak as Brown, his nerves gone, came rumbling up the stairs, aiming for the solar plexus of the third voice. Brown's aim was perfect, and his head sank into a soft belly. A retching sound, a sudden wetness, an increased stench combined to inform Brown that the third voice was attached to a stomach that had just spewed all over his back. Brown heard somebody gasping for breath. Brown did not gasp for breath; he tried to avoid breathing altogether. Light flared, and Brown looked up into the flame from a cigarette lighter. He blinked. As his eyes adjusted he noticed that the lighter was an expensive one, held by a slim, dark manicured hand. The light moved toward him, and Brown leaped a few steps up above the landing. "Who the hell *is* that?" Brown shouted.

"We been through that, ain't we?"

Brown cursed, grabbed the lighter, burning his hand in the process. He wrestled it away, then snapped it on again. "Yeah, we been through it before, an' we gonna keep on goin' through it. Now who the fuck are you?" He shoved the lighter toward her face, stared at her. She looked back at him calmly. The vomit soaking through the back of Brown's shirt made him slightly impatient; he shot out his other hand and grasped her above the elbow. "What the hell are you doin' here?"

She looked down at his hand, smiled slightly. "Ma name's Vanessa. An' I was tryin' to haul this piece a drunk meat on home, until the goddamn marines landed. Or is it Captain Midnight?" She raised her eyes and glared at him. Brown let go of her arm. "Ain't none a your damn business anyways."

"You his wife?"

"Him?" Rayburn moaned, clutched his stomach, tried to sit up.

"Yeah," Brown said. "Him."

"What would I want with a piece a cat shit like that?"

"Yeah, well," Brown said sourly. "All right, let's get him inside."

"I ain't got no key. I was lookin' through his pockets when the fuckin' cavalry charged."

"Did you find the key?" Brown snapped.

"Nope."

"Well," Brown said, "if he ain't got no key, maybe there ain't no key." He stepped down onto the landing, tried the door. It swung open.

"You pretty smart, Stonewall," Vanessa said.

Brown glared at her. She smiled innocently. Brown bent over Rayburn. "Hey, man. Can you walk?"

"Walk?" muttered Rayburn. "Hell yeah, I can walk. I can fuckin' fly. I was in the fuckin' air force. Ask anybody. I'ma fly me right outa here, soon as I gets maself together."

"Lemme give you a hand," Brown said. He thrust his hands beneath Rayburn's armpits and lifted, sliding his back up along the wall.

"Whee!" Rayburn said, "I'm flyin'."

"Yeah," Brown grunted. "Now let's see can you walk."

"Sure I can walk. Man can fly, he sure can walk," Rayburn said. He took two unsteady steps, then collapsed on the landing in a loose, sour-smelling heap. "Tole you I could walk."

Vanessa snorted. Brown glared at her, looked at Rayburn, sighed.

"Okay, baby. You gonna get that airlift." He grunted, hauled Rayburn to his feet, pulled him onto his shoulder, straightened.

"My, ain't we strong!" said Vanessa.

"Shut up," Brown said. He carried Rayburn through the door. Vanessa trailed along behind. "Which way's the bedroom?" Brown said.

"How the hell would I know?" Vanessa snapped. "You think I'd go to bed with that?"

"I don't care if you screw squirrels, this sucker's heavy, an' I can't be standin' around here all night." Brown turned carefully so that Rayburn's dangling arms and legs and head wouldn't hit anything too hard. He spotted the dim outline of a doorway, headed for it. Vanessa started to follow him through but stopped at the sound of crashing pots and pans and shattering crockery.

"Oww," roared Rayburn.

"Shit," said Brown.

"That mattress must be a killer," Vanessa called. Rayburn's legs reappeared as Brown backed out. "Oh," said Vanessa, "ain't that the bedroom?"

"No, it ain't the fuckin' bedroom," Brown snarled. "Why don't you pretend you're useful an' find the goddamn light?"

Vanessa moved away. "I done crashed," Rayburn said.

The lights came on, illuminating the littered living-room floor, the greasy furniture, the peeling walls. "God," muttered Vanessa.

Brown headed into the bedroom and deposited Rayburn on the bed. He held his breath while he pulled off Rayburn's clothes, not being too careful about buttons. He dropped the clothes on the floor, pulled the sheet over Rayburn, who snored his appreciation, rolled over, and farted his thanks. Brown backed away. "He do stink, don't he?" said Vanessa from the doorway.

"He do this often?" Brown said.

"Only on George Wallace's birthday an' when his wife leaves him," Vanessa said. Brown sniffed, moved past her. Vanessa looked at Rayburn. "He's just a sad old muthafucka. Ain't got no harm in him. Ain't got no room for harm, he's too full a shit. He stinks." She whirled and looked at Brown. "You stink too."

Brown ignored that. "You gonna stay here with him?"

"What for?" Vanessa snapped.

Brown looked her up and down. "There's some folks ain't above friskin' dead men," Brown said.

"I see. Meanin' there's some people who likes to roll drunks."

Brown shrugged, turned away, headed for the door. Vanessa came after him, stumbling through the littered living room as Brown turned off the light and stepped out onto the landing. In the darkness she ran into the back of him. "Yuk!"

"Watch where you're goin'," Brown said, starting up the darkened staircase.

"Hey," said Vanessa. "Where you goin'?"

"Home," Brown said.

"You live up there?"

"No, I'm climbin' the steps for exercise. Good night." At the top of the steps a door slammed, leaving Vanessa in darkness.

South Street slumbered in the night, black and quiet, heat-softened tar firming in the growing cool as the nighttime darkness flowed on toward dawn. Yellow streetlamps dripped gold light that pooled at the bases of rotting poles, buildings lounged against the sky, gap-tooth rows like an old man's mouth—ceramic fillings and shocking breath. South Street slept in a thousand snores that rumbled out of open windows, tiptoed from behind closed doors, lurked around the alley mouths, in the sleepy sounds of pleasure and pain, banging bedsprings, glugging drains. In the dim recesses of Lightnin' Ed's, Jake snored and snorted and clutched his gut, twisting on the rotten canvas of Leo's army-surplus cot. Leroy Briggs, the muscle man, sweated his substance into the night, forcing one more heroic spasm out of aching lungs and emptied loins to satisfy his ladylove, who tugged and clutched and screamed for more. South Street tied the city's rivers like an iron bracelet or a wedding band, uniting the waters, sewer to sewer, before they met at the city's edge. In their apartment near the Schuylkill, Brother and Mrs. Fletcher slept, holding hands beneath the sheet. South Street, once a youthful strumpet, now old and ugly, beyond the days when lonely men would buy her body, accepted Big Betsy's rancid sweat, while blocks away, on the other side of the river that somehow drew a line, a woman stood on a balcony, looking out at the sleeping city—streets, rivers, bridges—and traced the row of yellow lights amidst the white of the vapor lamps. That was South Street. The hippest street in town. She thought of Brown. Rayburn Wallace turned and moaned, flopped on his back on the grimy sheet, threw out an arm, called a name. No one answered. South Street slept.

Brown stood under the cold shower until he felt like he was capable of imitating someone who was completely sober. He stepped out, shivering, pulled his robe around him, draped a towel over his head and rubbed his hair briskly as he went through the bedroom to the kitchen. He raised the towel and reached out to turn on the gas beneath the coffeepot, but discovered that the burner was already on. "I figured you'd want some," Vanessa said from behind him. Brown jumped two feet, twisting around in mid-air like a cat. "Jumpy?" Vanessa inquired sweetly.

"Don't do that any more," Brown said. He took a mug from the cupboard, poured himself a cup of coffee, added milk and four sugars.

"You gonna *drink* that?" Brown looked up at her, then at her cup, which held black coffee.

"Nope," Brown said. "I'm going to shove it up your nose unless you get the hell outa here."

Vanessa smiled. "Can't I finish ma coffee?"

Brown stared at her. "What the fuck do you want anyway?"

Vanessa raised her cup, sipped daintily, put it down. She smiled at Brown, rose gracefully, moved around the table. Brown moved quickly to keep the table between them. Vanessa stopped, put her hand on her hip. "God, you sure is jumpy!"

"Just somethin' I picked up playin' with frogs," Brown said.

"What do you play with now?" Brown glared at her. "Careful, darlin'. Your kids'll be idiots, an' you could go blind."

"All right," Brown said. "Now will you please get outa here and let me get some sleep?"

"I could use some sleep maself," Vanessa said.

"So get it," Brown said.

Vanessa looked at the door to the bedroom.

"No," Brown said. "Thank you."

Vanessa looked at him. "You queer or somethin'? I ain't never known nobody to turn it down that wasn't queer."

"Yeah," Brown said, "I'm queer."

"Well, don't worry 'bout that, sugah. I know all the tricks."

Brown looked at her. "Yeah," he said drily, "I can just believe it."

Vanessa smiled. She kicked her shoes off and moved around the table, pressed herself against him. Brown's hands stayed motionless at his sides. She pressed her cheek against his chest, leaving dark smears of make-up on his robe. Her hand moved toward the belt. "You're wasting your time," Brown said. "I don't have any money."

Vanessa jerked away from him, slammed a fist into his stomach. Brown grunted. "You sonofabitch," Vanessa said. She backed toward the door. "You think I got to be standin' here beggin' some square-ass half-queer muthafucka for some a his little shit? I'm sorry Mistuh Mother, I didn't know I was talkin' to Jesus Christ." She glared at him for a solid minute before she burst into tears.

Brown sighed. "I'm sorry, okay. I didn't mean—"

"You think you're sorry now, you wait ten minutes. You gonna be wantin' to change your mind but it'll be too damn late. Christmas don't come but once a year, an' reindeer ain't got no reverse." She wiped her eyes on the back of her sleeve.

"Look," Brown said, "you want another cup of coffee?" He grabbed her cup, poured it full again. Vanessa stayed where she was. "Come on," Brown urged.

Vanessa looked at him sourly, came over and sat down. Brown handed her the cup. She raised it, her dark eyes showing over the rim. Brown sat down across from her, rocked back on the rear legs of his chair. He looked at her musingly. Vanessa slammed her cup down on the table. "Why you keep starin' at me like that?"

"I was just wondering why you—"

"Just lucky I guess," Vanessa said sarcastically.

"Good answer," Brown said. "Wrong question. I was trying to figure out why you made me a cup of coffee."

"Oh," Vanessa said. She peered at him. "You talk funny, you know? Like you was a schoolteacher or a professor or somethin'."

Brown looked at her steadily.

"Well, are you?"

"Am I what?"

"Some kinda schoolteacher or somethin'?"

"Yeah," Brown said. "Or somethin'. You hungry?"

"Huh?"

"Hungry," Brown said. "Food. Eaty-eaty. Big nigguh buck gonna make-make wid da cook-cook. You wantum eat?"

Vanessa stared at him for a minute, then broke into a fit of laughter, throwing her head back and bringing her hands up beside her face and grabbing the top of her head as if she were trying to keep it from coming off. The laughter went on for too long, took on a harsh, rasping undertone. Brown moved uneasily. Vanessa stopped laughing suddenly, as if someone had thrown a switch. "I'm all right."

"Sure," Brown said. "You want somethin' to eat?"

"Like what?"

"Eggs," Brown said firmly.

"I don't like eggs."

Brown shrugged philosophically. "Me neither." He grunted and rose from the chair, went to root around inside the refrigerator.

"Hey," Vanessa said, "you better get a longer bathrobe or paint your ass blue to match."

"It's a normal ass," Brown said. "You may turn your head, regard it in quiet reverence, or kiss it. Take your pick."

"Yeah," Vanessa said, "I heard all about how you likes folks to kiss your ass."

Brown had been backing away from the refrigerator, his arms loaded with eggs, bacon, cheese, and bread. He stopped dead. "Where'd you hear anything about me?"

"It's all over the street that some cat named Brown made Leroy Briggs eat shit."

"Oh," Brown said, "that."

Vanessa looked at him. " 'That' *could* get you killed."

"I'm worried," Brown said. He began breaking eggs into a bowl one-handed, moving in an easy rhythm, box to bowl to garbage bag. Vanessa watched him with interest. Brown took the fourth egg from the carton, cracked it on the counter, allowed the contents to fall into the garbage, and dropped the shell into the bowl. He looked down, shook his head. "Shit." He began fishing out the pieces of shell.

Vanessa giggled. "You know what that reminds me of? That cartoon, you know, with the horse, an' he's shootin' this gun an' then he blows the smoke away an' shoots it again only one time he blows when he should be blowin' an' shoots when he should be blowin', you know, an' he blows his head clean off." She grinned at Brown, but the grin faded. "You don't remember that?"

"Not exactly," Brown said.

"I guess you never watched much TV. I useta watch it all the time, 'fore they came an' took it back."

"Well," Brown said drily, "it's just as well they took it back. It woulda kept you off the streets."

"Damn," said Vanessa. "What kinda cheap shit is that?"

"Brown cheap shit," Brown said. "Sorry. I got a weird sense of humor." He opened a cabinet and began taking down spices and sauces. Vanessa's mouth dropped open as he started dumping things into the bowl with the eggs.

"What the *hell* are you puttin' in there?"

"A shot a salt, a pinch a pepper," Brown said. "Plus oregano, paprika, garlic, Worcestershire sauce, ketchup, A-1, mustard, grated cheese, parsley—"

"An' you're gonna *eat* that?"

"God, no," Brown said. "I'm gonna turn it into a steak first." He waved a fork above the bowl, mumbled a few words, started to whip the mixture up, using strong sharp flicks of his wrist. He started to whistle, stopped in surprise, and chuckled at himself. He looked at Vanessa and shook his head in wonder, then turned back to the stove.

"You ain't nothin' like I figured you'd be," Vanessa said. "I figured you'd be like Leroy. Big, tough, mean."

Brown sighed. "At least I'm mean. Now if it's not against your religion, would you mind explainin' why you spend so much time worryin' about me?"

"It was either you or some other gorilla," Vanessa said. "An' it costs thirty cents to get to the zoo."

"Uh, huh," Brown said. "Interested in primates, are you?" He poured bacon grease into a skillet.

"Yeah," said Vanessa. "See, I been tryin' to finish ma education so I can get a good job, maybe be a go-go dancer or a secretary. Only I don't know if I can stand the cut in pay."

Brown poured the mixture into the snapping grease, stirred it around with a fork. "You sure you don't want no food?"

"I told you, I don't like eggs."

"Ain't eggs," Brown said. "Didn't you see me turnin' it into steak?"

"Hell," Vanessa said, "I ain't fallen for that kinda shit since this old man told me he could change ma pussy into silver. He did, too. Took me back in the alley and stuck his finger up me for half an hour an' then he give me a quarter."

Brown said nothing. He watched the bubbling eggs, stirred the mixture with a wooden spoon.

"That turn you on?" Vanessa said.

"I ain't no pinball machine," Brown said.

"Oh, I am," Vanessa said. " 'Slot-machine 'Nessa. Five balls for a dime.' That's what they used to call me, 'fore I got smart an' stopped givin' change, just like the subway. How 'bout that?"

Brown flipped the omelet over.

"See," Vanessa said, "I got your ass figured out, professor. You one a them social-workin' muthafuckas come down here to see what's happenin' with the fuckin' natives. Doin' some kinda bullshit study for the guvment so they can figure out some kinda poison that'll kill off all the rats an' roaches an' the dirty-assed niggers without hurtin' y'all knee-grows. I got your bag figured."

Brown slid the omelet onto a plate, carried it over to the table, and sat down. "Good. You got me figured. Now you can get up off me for a while."

"Aw, professor," said Vanessa, "don't you want to hear no more stories 'bout what it was like growin' up in the ghetto? You can make a whole book outa it. Call it *Slot-Machine 'Nessa*. Don't you wanna hear how I first got turned out?"

"Not while I'm eating," Brown said.

Vanessa settled back into her chair. Brown forked food into his mouth, chewed diligently. He stared out the window. "Shit," Vanessa said. "I thought you was somethin' special. I figured you had to be, frontin' off Leroy an' gettin' the whole damn street runnin' around tryin' to find out who you are."

"I sent my Superman suit to the cleaners," Brown said.

"Yeah, well, I guess you can't do me no good then, can you? I guess you're just doin' your silly little thing like every other simple fool."

"Probably," Brown said. He put the last forkful of egg into his mouth, stood up, put the plate in the sink. The fork slid off and clattered loudly against the stained porcelain. When he turned away from the sink, she was looking at him, or he thought she was until he realized that her eyes were staring right through him. He sat down in the chair and looked at her. "I'm a bartender," Brown said.

Vanessa sighed.

Brown nodded. "Yeah. An' how the hell did it get to be any a your damn business what I am, or what I do?"

"I better go home," she said, rising. Brown got up too, stepped behind her as she went to the door. She opened it and turned, brushing against him. She looked up and Brown saw tears in her eyes. He stood woodenly, staring, while the tears spilled over and ran down her face, eroding deep gullies in her make-up. Brown patted her arm awkwardly, and she let herself sag against him. Brown felt an unmistakable warming in his body, and it amused him and disgusted him and made him feel foolish. She slipped her arms around him. Her face, muddy with make-up, rubbed his chest. Brown shifted his weight, trying to avoid the friction and warmth, but she followed him, rubbing against him like a cat, purring softly. He sighed and stroked her back. "You want me," she said softly. There was a note of wonder in her voice. She pulled her face away from him, ran her fingers lightly over his arm, his chest. She raised her hand and pulled his head down.

Brown kissed her dutifully, allowing her probing tongue to force his lips apart. Somewhere in the moist darkness her tongue met his and a darting battle began, his tongue forcing hers back, pursuing it hotly into the cavern of her mouth. Brown felt her hands on him. He tried one last time, tried the trick of sliding out and looking down from above and laughing at himself, but he found himself chained by her tears and warmth and darting hands. She stepped away. "I'm a whore," she said. "I'm a whore an' I don't want to do it—like a whore. Don't come in for a minute, okay?" She looked at him pleadingly. Brown nodded, watched as she went to turn out the light, then made her way through the darkness to the bedroom and closed the door.

Brown shook his head, went over and sat on the windowsill. He looked out over the alley, trying to straighten out the feelings of desire and disgust and amusement and sympathy that whirled inside him. He wished that he smoked so that he could light up and hold something in his hands for a few minutes and then flip the butt and watch it go glowing down into the darkness below. He heard the bed creak. He heard her call.

The bedroom smelled unfamiliarly of perfume. He stumbled over something going through the door. The bed protested the added weight as he climbed into it. Her voice was a voice in darkness; she eluded him on the far corners of the sheet. "Sometimes," she said hoarsely, "sometimes it don't work too good. I'm just tellin' you so you know. It's like—like I can't tell when I'm not workin', you know?" She came to him, pressed against him. Brown ran his hand up and down her back. "It's gonna be all right this time," she said. "It's gotta be."

8 Monday

Early morning fought through the smog and fell exhausted through the open window, glinting redgold in the hair on the back of Brown's hand. The hand moved slowly, casting a shadow as it traced out letter shapes, word shapes, with a cheap ball-point pen. Brown wrote on a paper bag—he had run out of lined legal pads—and struggled to keep the words in nice neat rows, but they insisted on wandering downward as they stretched out toward the right margin. The hand moved hesitantly, spasmodically, like a hand on a Ouija board, writing a word, crossing one out, writing another, crossing out two more. His grasp on the pen was tight; the normal pinkness under his nails was tinted by pressure a bizarre greenish-white. Beneath the skin of his forearm, muscles moved visibly, and drops of perspiration glistened in the hair. Brown, hunched over the table, face close to the paper, did not look up when the bedroom door swung open and Vanessa stumbled sleepily into the kitchen, rubbing her eyes with balled fists. She lowered her hands and stared at Brown, shifted her weight, causing a board to creak; Brown did not notice. She cleared her throat once, then again, more loudly. Brown made a period with his pen, put it down, and looked up. "Good morning," he said brightly.

Vanessa looked at him and groaned. "You always get up this early?"

"Gettin' up's easy," Brown said. "It's stayin' up that's the problem. You want some coffee?" Vanessa groaned again and went to pour herself a cup. "Actually," Brown said, "I only get up this early on holidays."

Vanessa sat down and scowled at him over her coffee. "What damn holiday is this?"

"On this day in history, in sixteen-nineteen," Brown told her, "Black Amos became the first American slave to plot armed resistance against his master."

"Humph," said Vanessa. "I bet he didn't do it at no six in the mornin'."

"So go back to bed."

"I ain't tired," Vanessa said, and yawned. "What you doin' out here anyways?"

"Nothing," Brown said. He slipped the paper bag and the pen into the drawer beneath the table. Vanessa shot out her hand and grabbed the bag out of the drawer.

"Pomes?" she said incredulously. "You some kinda poet or somethin'?"

"I told you," Brown said. "I'm a bartender."

Vanessa looked at him, glanced at the paper. "This must be good. It's got lots an' lots of big words."

Brown reached over and took it away from her. "It's not finished," he said.

"Well, I'm toooo sorry, Mistuh Brown, suh. I didn't *know* you was so damn touchy about your fuckin' hen tracks."

"There's nothing to be sorry about," Brown said. "I just don't like people looking at things when they aren't finished."

"Oh," Vanessa said. "I thought maybe it just you got pissed off 'cause some undereducated whore had the nerve to say it was good."

Brown sucked air through his teeth, eyed her speculatively. "You sleep naked, or you leave the chip on?"

"That depends on who I'm sleepin' with," Vanessa snapped.

"I thought you couldn't tell the difference."

"I warned you," Vanessa said. "Don't say you wasn't warned."

"It takes a little time," Brown said gently.

"Two *days?*"

Brown put a hand on her shoulder. "Sometimes it takes a long time. Sooner or later—"

"Shit," Vanessa said, shrugging his hand away. "What makes you think I'm gonna hang around with you waitin' for your damn prick to turn green? An' what are you, some kinda expert on fuckin'?"

"Me? No," Brown said. "I'm an amateur. But I'm enthusiastic." He put the paper bag back in the drawer, closed it, got up, and went over to the refrigerator. He took out a can of beer, snapped the top open, took a long swig. Vanessa watched him, a look of distaste on her face. Brown flipped his chair around with one hand, straddled it. He gulped more beer and belched.

Vanessa shook her head in disgust. "Just ma luck. I'm lookin' for a man an' I get a goddamn poet."

Brown looked at her, finished the beer, and sent the can arching across the room into the garbage bag. The bag was full; the can bounced out again. Brown grunted, rose, went over and stuffed the can into the bag, leaned out the window, and let the bag drop into the alley. It split open, exposing beer containers and wet coffee grounds. Brown remained leaning out the window, staring down at the alley, at the garbage, at the dark shape of a wino sleeping deeper in the shadows.

"I'm scared," Vanessa said.

Brown pulled himself back inside, twisted around. "What?"

"I said I was scared."

"What of?"

"I . . . I ain't never been with nobody like this before. It's like bein' a virgin. I guess—I don't remember much about bein' a virgin. But it's the first time it mattered if it was any good. For me, I mean. Ain't nobody much cared if it was any good for me, 'cept maybe Leroy, an' he wouldn't a cared except it bothered him he couldn't make me come. But it was just like I was somethin' that didn't work right, like his car wouldn't start or somethin'. So he traded me in on a newer model." She smiled a little. "You know, I ain't never done like we done yesterday, settin' around doin' nothin', readin' the Sunday paper, goin' for a walk. A goddamn walk! On South Street. Jesus, if I ain't walked on South Street enough by now. An' wakin' up in the mornin' an' havin' a cup a coffee. Like we was on TV or somethin'." She shifted her eyes to look out the window where the sunlight bounced off the building across the narrow alley. Brown shifted uneasily.

"I just ain't never cared about me before," Vanessa said. "Some old drunk fool jams hisself up inside you, he don't care what happens, so long as he gets his money's worth. He ain't payin' for you to have a good time. There ain't nobody thinkin' about you but you, an' it's hard to keep thinkin' about yourself all by yourself." She looked at Brown for a minute, then down at her coffee. "Well, hell, what do you want? I'm a damn whore."

"My great-granddaddy was a slave," Brown said. "One of 'em. One a the others probably owned him. So what?"

"It matters," Vanessa said. "It has to matter." She looked up at him.

"What do you think about when you look at me?" Brown opened his mouth, closed it again. Vanessa looked at him, smiled bitterly. "Never mind."

"Shut up," Brown said. He pushed himself off the windowsill, pulled the drawer open, grabbed out the paper bag and shoved it at her. "Read it," Brown said. "Don't just look at the words. Read it."

Vanessa stared at him, accepted the paper, read. Brown stood absolutely still. It took her a long time. Finally she looked up. "This ain't got nothin' to do with me," she said. "It's about South Street. Who the hell wants to read about South Street?"

"You wanted to know what I thought about when I looked at you," Brown said. "There it is."

"Yeah. Garbage. Rats. Roaches. Drunks. Jesus, Brown, if that's what I make you think about, excuse me while I kill maself."

Brown reached over and took the poem away from her, looked at it. "You ever hear the story about the frog that got turned into a prince?"

"What? Oh, Jesus! 'Sides, you got it backwards."

"No, I don't," Brown said. "You listen. See, once upon a time there was this frog. Lived in the lily pond. Well one day this princess, she come tippin' down to the lily pond. The frog, he looked at her an' he says to hisself, 'Hey there, ain't that a fine-lookin' piece a somethin'! An' rich, too.' So this simple jiveass goes hoppin' up on the bank an' says hello. Now the princess, she ain't never seen a frog that could talk as pretty as this frog, just like he was a reglar poet or somethin', an' he runs his jive on her an' pretty soon she's just hummin' away. She even started takin' off her clothes, only all the sudden she stops an' says, 'Hey, how're we gonna make love if I'm a princess an' you're a frog?' Now the frog, he figured that as soon as he started to put it to her she wasn't gonna much care *what* he was, so he says 'Damn, why soon as you kiss me one time I'ma turn right into the handsomest damn prince in the whole damn world, an' what's the matter with you, bitch, don't you watch Walt Disney?' But she wasn't havin' any. She put her panties back on an' took him on up to the castle an' introduced him to her daddy, the king, whose name just happened to be Martin Luther, an' fixed him up with a fancy room an' a horse an' air-conditionin' an' dressed him up in fancy clothes an' kept him readin' books, taught him how to do all kinds a bullshit. They'd only make it in the nighttime, 'cause the princess, she didn't want anybody to know she was makin' it with a frog. Well bit by bit, that old frog got brainwashed to the point where he thought he *was* a goddamn prince. They even had the emperor come around an' check him out, an' when the emperor said, 'Boy, run down to the cleaners an' fetch ma white suit,' the frog took off an' come back with an' empty hanger. An' they lived happy ever after, except that frog kept hoppin' back to the lily pond, an' that just drove the princess crazy, that an' the fact he kept wantin' to screw in the daytime. . . ." Brown's voice trailed off. He looked out the window.

"Is that all?" Vanessa said.

"I don't know," Brown said.

Vanessa got up and walked to the window, looked out. "That alley's full a shit," she said. "There's a wino sleepin' in it. Looks like Jake. He's been sleepin' in that alley for years. In the same damn shit." Brown grunted. Vanessa turned to look at him. "I said there's a wino out there sleepin' in his own shit. He stinks. Anybody could smell him clear up here, unless they was a fool like you with Chanel Number Five smeared all over his upper lip." Brown looked at her, then looked away. She moved around to stand in front of him. "An' I'm a whore, an' I probly stink a little, too. Don't I? Lily pond, shit. A goddamn toilet bowl is more like it. An' there ain't no frogs swimmin' around in no toilet bowls, just turds waitin' around for somebody to flush 'em away. How you like bein' a turd, Mr. Frog?"

Brown went and stood behind her and put his hands on her shoulder. She shrugged them away. He put them back. She shrugged them away again, twisting in the same motion, so that her back was to the light, her face a dark shadow. Brown raised his hands. "Don't touch me." Brown dropped his hands and stepped away. "They better?" she said dully, her voice coming out of shadow.

"What?" Brown said.

"In bed. Are they better?"

"Who?"

"White women. Who else?"

"What the hell are you talkin' about?" Brown said.

"What you was talkin' about, princesses an' shit. I ain't stupid. I knew what you was gettin' at. I guess I ain't no big deal for you, now am I, after you done had all that, a black whore."

Brown smiled and shook his head. "Princesses come in all colors." He stepped close to her, and she looked up at him, placed her hands against his chest but did not push him away.

"Whad you have to come down here for, Brown? You ain't doin' nothin' but mess people up with your shit."

Brown looked at her. She stared at him, then dropped her eyes. Brown reached out and lifted her face, and she stared at him past flared nostrils. "Go away," she said. Brown took her by the arms. She pushed against his chest, and Brown felt the muscles in her arms tighten beneath his fingers. He pulled her to him, and her long fingernails dug into the skin above his nipples. Brown squeezed her arms. Her muscles relaxed. Her knees sagged. She let him pull her against him. Her fingers left his chest, wandered over him. "I'm gonna be as good as them," she said. "I'ma be just as good."

The day had begun with a rude awakening, when a bag of garbage had burst on the cobblestones ten feet away, but in light of later developments, Jake had to admit that it was beautiful. While wandering along outside the Elysium he had discovered a wallet containing fifteen dollars. With luck and careful husbanding, fifteen dollars would keep him in decent wine for three solid days. Jake had deposited all but two dollars in his left shoe—the one with the fewer holes—and the wallet in a mailbox. The problem then became waiting out the two hours until the liquor stores opened. Jake turned away from the mailbox and considered his options thoroughly, and that in itself wasted a good bit of time. There were the traditional wino time-wasters, like loitering in the lower lobby of the Reading Railroad Terminal or in the Penn Center bowling alley, and there were other doors that were open to him because of his newly acquired wealth; he could go to one of the twenty-four hour movie houses on the other side of City Hall and watch reruns of *Major Dundee*. He rejected the traditional out of a distaste for routine. He rejected the cinema because he considered spending money on anything besides wine and—occasionally—food an unnatural act if not a mortal sin. But there were other, more imaginative alternatives. Since it was summer, the fountain in Kennedy Plaza would be going. Jake was fond of the fountain, but Kennedy Plaza was also the location of the tourist information center, and the police took a very dim view of winos enjoying the fountain and disgusting the tourists, which was useful if you wanted to spend a little time in a nice comfortable cell, but, having just come into money, Jake valued his freedom. There were the porno houses along Market Street and north toward Chinatown, where he would be safe from the police, but Jake considered himself far too sophisticated for porno houses. Besides, every time he entered one, they laughed. Of course, he could always join the inevitable line-up in front of the liquor stores, which would offer an opportunity to greet old friends, but Jake did not feel like standing in line; his stomach hurt, not sharply but insistently. Having wasted the better part of fifteen minutes considering his options, Jake turned north and headed, as he had known he would from the beginning, for the Post Office.

Jake was something of a snob. He went out of his way to pass the winos idly ranked in front of the State Store like the bottles displayed inside, behind the wire screening and the heavy plate glass. Jake sniffed and shuffled on by, secure in the knowledge that he was of a higher caste, that his territory was not limited to South Street, that his horizons were not delineated by the Delaware and the Schuylkill. He was known at dozens of bars, in North Philly, in Mantua, in Woodland Village. He was known as a proud man who always paid, and if it was not full price, that was only right, since he had consumed enough to be classed as a wholesale buyer; his discount was not charity but a small courtesy shown by appreciative bartenders to a faithful client. While he never slept anywhere but South Street, he ranged far and wide, pursuing his trade, which was shining shoes at the Pennsylvania Station, and his hobby, which was rumormongering. Jake made it his business to know everything that it was none of his business to know. He gathered information constantly, and one of his favorite sources were the FBI's "Wanted" posters in the Post Office. He would spend hours flipping through the posters, which were clamped into a heavy notebook bracketed to a bulletin board on the Post Office wall.

Jake was not interested in what he called chickenshit crime—burglary or embezzlement—and he looked with disgust upon kidnapers, counterfeiters, rapists, and extorters. Jake's imagination was fired only by the clever and the violent, by bunko artists and confidence men, by armed robbers and murderers. He felt profound respect for anyone whose crimes smacked of the political, but he was not yet sure how he felt about airplane hijackers. He was down on deserters and draft dodgers, but rather ambivalent about income-tax evaders; having essentially no income, Jake was ambivalent about income tax.

He shuffled north along Nineteenth Street, heading for the Mid-City Branch office on Chestnut, which was conveniently located one short block from a State Store. It was a beautiful morning, not yet too hot. The flood of office workers had been sponged up by the office buildings, leaving only a few people on the street. That suited Jake; he had no fondness for office workers, although he viewed them with profound compassion. There, but for the grace of God, went he. He turned west on Chestnut Street, shooting a brief glance at the State Store just past the corner, and momentarily considering speculating some of his wealth on a state lottery ticket, as the sign in the window advised. He might win fifty thousand dollars, and fifty thousand dollars represented an awful lot of wine. But Jake knew that he would never win the fifty thousand dollars. Nobody who needed it ever won the fifty thousand dollars, since if you were unlucky enough to be broke in the first place, it was unlikely you would be lucky enough to win fifty thousand dollars. Besides, there was no bank that would cash a check for fifty thousand dollars presented by a scruffy wino, and it was a little too much to expect the state to pay off in cash. All in all, Jake decided, the lottery was great for solid citizens, but for winos it was better to play the numbers. Unfortunately Leroy Briggs ran the numbers on South Street, and Jake refused to have anything to do with anything that had anything to do with Leroy Briggs. As he pushed open the stubborn wooden door of the Mid-City Branch of the United States Post Office, Jake decided that if he ever *did* win fifty thousand dollars, he would be willing to expend a large portion of it getting rid of Leroy Briggs and his other nemesis, the Reverend Mr. J. Peter Sloan.

Under the mistaken impression that his shuffle had become a nonchalant stroll, Jake moved across the Post Office lobby to the bulletin board. He made himself comfortable and began his preliminary inspection, greeting old friends among the gallery of felons—hollow-eyed, hollow-cheeked, hollow-chinned faces that stared glassily out at him or peered listlessly at the margin of the page. Jake noted a few absences—the famed FBI manhunt had cornered a few miscreants—and a few changes. Jake was pleased to note that one of his favorites, Willie Jack Bartrum, had committed two more murders in the course of a bank robbery in El Paso, Texas. Because of this successful exploit, Willie Jack's price had risen by five thousand dollars. Willie Jack Bartrum had been on the loose for nearly seven years, since his escape from Raiford Prison in Florida, in the course of which he had killed a white guard. The poster hadn't said that the guard was white, but Willie Jack was wanted hysterically by the FBI—he had the highest price in the book—and Jake was perfectly capable of putting two and two together. The deed assured Willie Jack Bartrum of a special post of affection in Jake's heart, and every time he saw a new escapade added to Willie Jack's catalog of extra-legal adventures, Jake felt a surge of racial pride and a warm feeling of brotherhood.

Jake turned away from Willie Jack and began to study the book, refreshing his memory and noting the changes. Jake did not bother to memorize the names and faces of white felons—he had noticed, over the years, that whites had an unfortunate tendency toward chickenshit crime. He turned the pages slowly: a bank robber, two extorters, jury-tampering, bunko, armed robbery, jailbreak, more bunko, a black man inciting to riot. Then something hit him. His eyes widened, and he flipped back through the book to one of the newly added bunko artists. He looked carefully at the picture, squinted, and looked again. He checked the listing of known aliases. He checked the date on the poster and cursed softly. He chuckled, looked at the face that stared up at him, ran his finger down the list of charges. Jailbreak in California. Embezzlement. Bunko. He whistled softly.

He glanced around, and, finding himself unobserved, he tore the sheet from the book and stuffed it into his pocket.

In the cool dark depths of Lightnin' Ed's, the soon-to-be-acting pastor of The Word of Life Church sat in confrontation with his conscience. Settled on a bar stool, hunched behind the slowly dissipating foam on a long cold beer, Brother Fletcher pondered the problem of his ascension. A church of his own again, but this time a big church, with big problems. It would have been a difficult task for a saint, an awesome responsibility for the most sanctified of mortals. For a sinful doubter, as Brother Fletcher believed himself to be, it was a dangerous attempt, almost hubristic. A man who had not only walked in the council of the ungodly, stood in the way of sinners, and sat in the seat of the scornful but who had, while sitting there, drunk spirits and watched a baseball game had, in Brother Fletcher's humble opinion, no business at all leading anybody anywhere, and what should have been a high point in his career was a millstone about his bony neck. Brother Fletcher sipped his beer and sighed.

Jake came shuffling through the door at the far end of the bar, blinking his eyes in the darkness. "Howdy, Reverend. Leo," Jake said.

"Afternoon," said Brother Fletcher, feeling guilty because he welcomed Jake as an interruption in his train of thought.

"Uh," grunted Leo, without turning his attention away from the TV set. In the afternoons, when there were few baseball games and even fewer customers in Lightnin' Ed's, Leo indulged his passion for soap operas. Leo had been watching the soap operas for fifteen years, and there was no bored housewife anywhere in America who was any more obsessed with them. Every afternoon, after serving the lunchtime crowd, Leo would switch on the set and adjust the brightness and the color controls to darken the actor's flesh tones so that they looked more like normal people and, drawing himself a beer, would settle back to watch the tragic antics as a *Search for Tomorrow* discovered that *As the World Turns* there is *Another World* across the river from *Somerset* which, due to a *Love of Life* and despite a *Secret Storm*, managed somehow to *Return to Peyton Place*. The soap operas had changed Leo's life, making him a far more thoughtful and aware individual. Leo had never given much consideration to issues such as abortion, divorce, mercy killing, probate, or contraception, but the soap operas were full of these things, and Leo's mind was duly expanded. Leo's spiritual awareness had been expanded as well; although he had never considered reincarnation, the actors and actresses kept dying off in one series and reappearing in another with only minor alterations in appearance, and Leo had thus become convinced that there was, although he did not know the actual term, transmigration of souls. Perhaps most important, Leo found the soap operas tremendously uplifting, for against the background of whores and winos and dead-end downers who frequented Lightnin' Ed's and inhabited the limbo between the Schuylkill and the Delaware, Leo's afternoon TV projected the images of doctors and nurses and lawyers and judges and businessmen and their neat, middle-class homes and families, who, while they had problems, also had the money to go with them; who, when rushing off to deathbeds, accident sites, and clandestine trysts, went in cars or cabs or airplanes. On South Street people rarely went far, and when they did go they flew Greyhound.

Jake was used to Leo's afternoon passion. He dropped a dime on the bar and waited patiently. Leo's eyes never left the screen while he reached out, grasped a glass in one hand and a bottle of muscatel in the other, and poured Jake a drink. Jake ran his fingers along the top of the bar where Leo had spilled a few drops. "What's happenin', Leo?" he inquired with a glint in his eye. He stuck his fingers in his mouth and sucked on them contentedly.

"Shup," Leo said.

Jake listened to the dialogue for a few minutes. "Shit," he commented, "that lyin' bastard ain't never gonna marry her. He's just after some nooky."

"Shup, y'old fool," Leo snapped. "Can't you see I'm tryin' to listen at somethin' here?"

Jake looked down at Brother Fletcher and winked. "Hey, Leo, did you hear? They're passin' a law says all bartenders got to weigh less than a hundred an' ninety."

"Um," said Leo, biting his thumb out of concern for the tense scene being portrayed in living color on the TV screen.

"Know what else? They gonna raise the liquor tax."

"Um," Leo said. "Dammit, girl, can't you see he's after the money? . . . Umph."

"What's more—"

"Will you shut the fuck up an' drink your goddamn wine?" Leo snarled. "You're more commotion than a flock a fuckin' pigeons."

"Male or female?" Jake demanded.

"Both, obviously," offered Brother Fletcher.

Jake gave him a look of startled approval. Brother Fletcher felt his face grow warm. "Maybe," Jake said, "they're queer pigeons."

"I'ma queer your damn pigeon," Leo threatened, "an' shove it right up your skinny ass if you don't drink your damn wine an' shut your damn mouth an' let me watch ma damn TV."

"Sorry, Leo," Jake said meekly.

"Humph," said Leo, and turned back to the set just to be told for the six thousandth time that Ivory Snow not only gets your baby's diapers softer, but whiter, too. "Shit," Leo said.

Jake chuckled. Leo glared. Jake picked up his wine and carried it down the bar. He perched on the stool beside Brother Fletcher. "How many souls you save today, Rev?"

Brother Fletcher smiled sourly. "I think I'm losing one."

"Well," Jake said, "don't worry. It's early yet."

"That's what worries me," Brother Fletcher said. "At the rate I'm going Satan will own South Street by midnight."

"Humph," Jake said. "Satan already owns South Street. It's you fellas supposed to be tryin' to get it back."

"I know," Brother Fletcher said with a sigh.

"Say, uh, Rev, I was just kiddin'. I didn't mean no harm. . . ." Brother Fletcher waved his hand in a gesture of dismissal. "Kiddin' makes things easier," Jake said. "But I guess you fellas don't have a whole lot a time for that stuff. I guess talkin' to God is pretty serious. Must be hard."

Brother Fletcher sighed. "I've never found it particularly difficult to talk to God. Talking to God is easy. It's about the easiest thing there is. It's getting an answer that's difficult."

Jake thought for a minute. "Yeah, I see what you mean. I guess it's like talkin' to Leo when he's watchin' them damn shows."

"Maybe," Brother Fletcher said. "Maybe that's what God's doing."

"Say, uh, Rev?" Jake said hesitantly.

"Yes?"

"Ah—sposin', just sposin' now, a fella had this problem. Like maybe there was this high-yaller sonofabitch an' this other fella had the goods on him an' could do the bastard right in, only he didn't know whether he ought to do it or not. Could he come an' talk to you about it?"

"Of course," Brother Fletcher said promptly.

"An' what would you tell him?"

"Well, ah, that would depend."

"Depend? What on?"

"Well, on what he wanted to do to this other man, and what the other man had done to him—"

"He's a high-yaller sonofabitch," Jake interjected.

"That doesn't tell me very much," Brother Fletcher said.

"Umph," Jake said, and sipped his wine in silence for a few minutes.

"Well, sposin' somebody did come to you like that, could you give him an answer right off or would you have to talk to God about it?"

Brother Fletcher sipped his beer thoughtfully. "Well," he said after a long pause, "if it was really difficult and special, I might want to pray about it before I said anything."

"Uh huh," Jake said, nodding. "An' how long does it take to get an answer?"

Brother Fletcher sighed and shook his head. "I don't know," he said sadly. "When I was younger I used to be able to get an answer"—he snapped his fingers—"just like that. Now, every year it seems to take longer and longer."

"Hum," Jake said. "Well, I guess it would. Things always takes longer when you gets older. Now when I was a young fella I could whip it out an' piss quickern you could say Jack Robinson. I useta piss out a quart a wine so fast they wanted me to join the fire department. Now it takes me longer to piss it out than it does to drink it down. Man, I just stand there and stand there and stand there, an' *nothin'* happens. I guess it's the same way with you an' your prayin'. You're gettin' on up there is all."

"I've been thinking," Brother Fletcher said, mouthing the heresy gingerly, "I've been thinking that maybe everything isn't as simple as it used to be and God doesn't have all the answers ready. Maybe He has to figure them out now, just like anybody else." Brother Fletcher felt his stomach muscles tighten and his heart beat faster as he waited in primitive fear for the Big Voice thundering or the Bolt of Lightning.

"Could be," Jake allowed. "Could be God's gettin' on up there too, an' them answers just don't come quick like they used to. How old you figure He's gettin' to be?"

"Huh?" said Brother Fletcher.

"God," Jake said. "How old you think He is?"

"Well," said Brother Fletcher, feeling confused. "I don't think . . . well, God doesn't have any age. I mean, He was always here. The beginning of everything."

"Damn!" Jake said, impressed. "That's pretty old." He looked around the empty bar as if expecting to be observed, then leaned close to Brother Fletcher. "You know, Rev, I guess I shouldn't tell you this, but I never went to church much. While they was havin' the service, I mean."

"I never would have guessed," said Brother Fletcher.

"Nah," Jake continued. "I never went in too much for this God business. I mean, I never knowed who was runnin' things, but you ain't got to be no personal friend a the engineer to know if the train is off the damn track. Way I see it, He's pretty lucky He don't have to get elected, 'cause—well, I don't know about noplace else, but around here the sucker couldn't get into a crap game, let alone win an election."

"Well," said Brother Fletcher slowly, "I don't think we can judge what God does, we just have to believe that He has His reasons and if we knew them we'd understand that—"

"Yeah, well, maybe," Jake said. "Now listen, gettin' back to ma fr'instance. Sposin' you was to talk to Him about it an' He didn't come up with an answer right away, but you needed one quick. What then?"

"Well, you could look in the Bible to see if—"

"You mean like somebody had the same problem before?"

"That's right," Brother Fletcher said.

"Well," Jake said, "you know of any cases where somebody had the shit on a real high-yaller sonofabitch?"

Brother Fletcher sucked thoughtfully at his lower lip. "Not exactly. But God said, 'Vengeance is mine,' and Jesus said, 'If a man smite thee on thy right cheek, turn unto him thy left cheek also.' "

"Humm," Jake said. "That vengeance business is easy to understand, only I ain't after no vengeance, I just wanna get rid a the bastard. What happens if that fella hits you on the left cheek?"

"Turn the other one," Brother Fletcher said automatically.

"He done already hit that one," Jake reminded him. Brother Fletcher sighed. "Well," Jake continued, "never mind, Rev. I guess you fellas never did have a whole hell of a lot a luck dealin' with real live sonsabitches. I got along all these years without astin' God what to do. Only I figured . . ." His voice trailed off.

"Figured what?"

"Well, nothin'. Only, well, a man's gettin' up there, he starts to thinkin', you know. Now I don't figure God's gonna be too upset about a little wine an' whatever I done way back when, but I figure what a man does toward the end, that must be pretty important." Jake looked at Brother Fletcher very earnestly. "I don't want to go to no Hell, Rev. I been livin' seventy-four years, an' I don't want to be endin' up in Hell."

"I don't think—" Brother Fletcher began. He stopped. "You've got a lot of time left," he said lamely.

"Oh yeah," Jake said, "I know that. I ain't in no hurry. Just the same, if a man's got somethin' important to do after he's gettin' up there, he wants to make sure it's right, you know what I mean? That's why I ast you."

"But I don't really know anything about—"

"You know what's right, don't you?" Jake said.

Brother Fletcher hung his head. "No," he said, "no, I don't really know what's right."

Jake stared at him in disbelief. "But *you* gotta know. You're a damn *preacher!*"

"I guess I'm not really much of a preacher," Brother Fletcher said sadly.

"Well, damn," Jake said. He drained his glass. Brother Fletcher looked intently at his beer. Jake regarded him sourly, picked up his glass, and shuffled up to Leo. A commercial was on, and Leo was temporarily among the living. He uncorked the wine bottle as Jake approached.

"Havin' a nice talk with the Reverend?" Leo inquired.

"Damn!" Jake said.

Leo nodded understandingly. "He's been there all day, just sittin' an' drinkin' beer an' starin' at the wall."

"Say what?"

"I said he's been there all day," Leo repeated.

"You don't have to shout," Jake snapped.

"I wouldn't if you ever cleaned your damn ears. I bet you got half a Lincoln's Gettysburg Address stuck in there."

"Screw your ass," Jake said, but the commercial had ended and Leo was plunged back into the midst of soap powder and domestic crisis. Jake watched Leo watching the TV for a while, then he turned away with a snort and went back down to Brother Fletcher. "That Leo," Jake said, "he ain't no good no more. That damn TV done turned his brain to oatmeal. I tell you, Rev, the worse thing they ever done was to invent color TV. Useta be when you looked at TV you knowed it was TV on account of it was black an' white. Now they got it all lookin' like for real, an' who the hell can tell the damn difference?" Jake sipped his wine and snorted in disgust.

"Jake," Brother Fletcher said suddenly, "you do believe in God, don't you?"

"Hell, yes, I ain't no communist. Only communists an' white folks don't believe in God, an' I sure as hell ain't white."

"But you drink wine."

"What the hell has that got to do with it? If you don't mind me sayin' so, Rev, you been actin' a little—"

"This," said Brother Fletcher, "is His blood, which was shed for you and for many for the remission of sins. As oft as you take it, do it in remembrance of His death and Passion, until His coming again, and may it preserve your soul unto everlasting life." Brother Fletcher raised his glass.

"Huh?" Jake said.

"Drink," ordered Brother Fletcher. Jake stared, shrugged, raised his glass, and drank. "Amen," Brother Fletcher said.

Jake nodded, sat mystified. "You okay now, Rev?"

"No," Brother Fletcher said. "I am not okay. My soul is sick. For one month I will be the minister of The Word of Life Church. I think I would rather serve communion in a bar."

"Yeah?" Jake said. "How come only for a month?"

"The Reverend Mr. Sloan is going off on a junket. He'll be back in a month."

"What if he was to stay away?" Jake asked. "You'd just keep on bein'—"

"Don't talk about it," said Brother Fletcher.

Jake stared at his wine for a while, then slowly raised his head. "Don't it say somethin' somewhere about helpin' your brother?"

"It says something everywhere about helping your brother," said Brother Fletcher listlessly.

"Well now," Jake said. "If you was to do somethin' wrong, only it was to help somebody else, even if it was still wrong, it wouldn't be as much wrong, would it?"

"No," said Brother Fletcher, "I guess not."

Jake grinned and punched him on the arm. "Don't worry, Rev. You still got a hotline to Jesus, an' I'm gonna buy you a drink. Leo!"

"Shup," Leo said.

Rayburn basked in the dying light that penetrated the boardroom's brown-tinted windows, his work shoes, the once-brown leather dulled and discolored by years of foot-sweat and disinfectant, propped audaciously on the polished tabletop, the rubber heels making dull marks on the wood. He leaned back in the big swivel chair. "Fellow board members," he said. His voice did not carry far or echo—the feeble vibrations were swallowed up by the ranks of leather chairs drawn up along the length of the table, by the heavy, rich curtains, by the thick pile of the carpet. Rayburn frowned at the deadness of the sound, leaned forward, cleared his throat. "Fellow board members," he said again, more loudly. The echoes still died, sucked up by the ponderous softness of chairs and curtains and carpet. Rayburn sighed, and allowed himself to sink back into the chair.

It was an evening of anniversary. Rayburn Wallace had been working at the bank for precisely fifteen years. Rayburn shrugged himself still deeper in the chair and reflected back on his long career in the towers of finance. His rise, while not exactly meteoric, had at least been steady. He had begun in the nether regions, wiping grease and oil from cement floors, and had risen through the spilled ink of central duplicating, the empty lipstick containers and discarded chewing-gum wrappers of the typing pool, through the reams of obsolete computer print-out in auditing, and finally, to the cigar ash and balled memoranda of the executive suite. He had been given his key to the executive washroom. High above the blaze of street lights, Rayburn had knelt, scrubbing, before the thrones of power. It took him half of his eight-hour shift to clean the rest rooms and the rugs. The rest of the time he spent in promoting himself through the offices of the vice-presidents to the office of the president and now, after fifteen years of faithful service, to the Chair.

"This meeting," Rayburn intoned, "will now come to order." The sound of his voice was still not right. It was lacking in the harmonics of authority, the subtle resonances of power. Rayburn frowned, shrugged; it was his first night as chairman; perfection could hardly be expected. The chairman turned in his leather chair and gazed out at the sunset bloodying the sky over West Philadelphia. The sun hurt his eyes, and he squinted. The door opened and Victoria Bender, his secretary who had been at his side throughout his steady rise to the utmost pinnacles of success entered, smiling deferentially. "Mr. Wallace?"

"Yes, Miss Bender."

"There's a man here. A Mr. Briggs. He doesn't have an appointment but I thought—"

"Miss Bender," Rayburn said sternly, "you should know that the attention of the chairman is not needed every time some silly-ass pimp wants a loan to buy a new Cadillac."

"Yes, sir," said Victoria, "but I thought maybe this might be special on account of there's a lady with him who says she's Mrs. Wallace."

"Hell," Rayburn roared, "that's no lady, that's ma slippery-ass wife. Throw the bitch out the window. Maybe fallin' twenty stories'll cool down her britches."

"Are you serious, Mr. Wallace?" Victoria, awed at his tough-mindedness, stared at him.

"Nah," Rayburn said languidly, "we'd get into trouble. There's a law against dumpin' garbage on the street." He chuckled and sighed. "Send 'em on in."

"We wants to see the man," Leroy Briggs protested, "not some damn janitor."

"That's Mr. Wallace," Victoria Bender said coldly. "Now, who are you?"

"I'm Leroy Briggs," said Leroy Briggs.

"Do you have any identification?"

"Rayburn, honey, I been missin' you," Leslie said.

"Ain't suprisin'," Rayburn said, buffing his manicured nails against his monogrammed shirt.

"Well, where you been, baby?"

"Oh I comes an' I goes. That's why you been missin' me—all you ever wanted to do was come."

"Ain't that enough?" snarled Leroy Briggs.

"What's the problem, Miss Bender?" Rayburn inquired.

"This gentleman cannot produce three pieces of identification."

"Why, Miss Bender!" Rayburn said in shocked tones. "Why, don't you know this here is Mr. Leroy Muthafuckin' Cocksuckin' Shiteatin' Asslickin' Briggs. Ain't that right, Leroy?"

Leroy Briggs glared at him impotently.

"You best say somethin'," Rayburn advised. "If you ain't who I think you is, we gonna have to get the po-lice up here to make sure you ain't up to nothin' suspicious."

"I'm Leroy Briggs."

"Miss Bender, get that man's name down on a form ninety-six. Could be a form sixty-nine," Rayburn explained to Leroy, "but you too damn fat for that."

"Name, please," said Victoria crisply, seating herself at the typewriter.

"Leroy Briggs."

"*Full* name," snapped Victoria.

"That's it."

"Ah, Mr. Wallace, this gentleman says his full name is Leroy Briggs."

"Don't forget your middle names, Leroy," Rayburn advised. "Victoria loves her rules."

Leroy gritted his teeth.

"Name, please?"

"Leroy . . ."

"*Name*, please?"

"Leroy Muthafuckin' Cocksuckin' Asslickin' Briggs."

"Well, you forgot Shiteatin', but then that's obvious," Rayburn said. "Now, what can I do for you?"

"You can't do shit for a mosquito," Leroy Briggs said. "I wants to see the president a this bank, an' that sure as hell ain't you."

"That's right," Rayburn said. "I'm the chairman of the board."

"I thought you was a janitor," Leslie wailed.

"Well, I was," Rayburn said. "But honesty and hard work will always be rewarded."

Victoria Bender smiled at Leslie. "I always knowed Mr. Wallace was gonna go far. Why, even when he wasn't nothin' but a night-shift janitor he saved his money an' he was dependable. I just knowed he was gonna go places. An' speakin' a goin' places, you better hurry or you'll miss your plane."

"Plane?" said Leslie.

"A little vacation," Rayburn said. "Mexico. Three months. An' Victoria?"

"Yes, Mr. Wallace?"

"Rayburn," Rayburn said.

"Rayburn," Victoria said reverently.

"If you knowed I was gonna be goin' far, you musta knowed I was gonna be takin' the one person in the whole damn world that stayed in ma corner all these years."

"You mean . . . me?"

"Well, I sho' as hell don't mean her. Now, right here I got the plane tickets for both a us."

"But I've got to pack," Victoria protested.

"Shit," Rayburn said. "You got me, baby, an' I got you. Anything else we get when we need it. All right, baby?"

"All right, darlin'," Victoria sighed, her eyes shining.

"But what about ma business?" Leroy Briggs said.

"Mind it," Victoria snapped.

"Now, now," Rayburn said gently. "Leroy, on account a your, ah, association with ma wife here, I'ma make sure you gets special treatment. Victoria, get me the president. George, I'ma send a man over to you, his name's Briggs. You find out exactly what he wants. Then you tell him to go fish. Thanks." Rayburn slammed the phone down. "George handles all ma light work," he explained. Rising, he offered Victoria his arm.

With a cry of rage Leroy Briggs grabbed Leslie and slung her off the top of the building. "I knowed he was gonna throw her over sooner or later," Victoria confided.

There was a short wail followed by a meaty thunk. "Damn!" said Leroy, peering over the edge. "The bitch landed right on ma car."

"You need a car loan, Leroy," Rayburn said, "you come right here. You just saved me the price of a divorce lawyer."

"What's it like in Mexico, baby?" Victoria said.

"It's all gold and silver, baby, all gold and silver."

Below, in the street, sirens wailed.

"A *what?*" roared Big Betsy the whore.

"You heard me," Leo said.

"Well, what the hell is a goddamn preacher doin' in a goddamn bar?"

"Most likely he's drinkin' a little beer an' watchin' the ball game an' not botherin' nobody with a lot a bullshit, which is a lot moren I can say for some folks."

"Drinkin' *beer?* Damn, Leo, everybody knows preachers don't drink beer."

"Now, how'd you find out so much about preachers? I'd say you been tryin' to whore your way into heaven, but even preachers don't got that much charity."

"I learned 'bout preachers the same way you learned 'bout women," Big Betsy informed him. "Somebody told me. Damn, Leo, you can't start havin' a bunch a preachers hangin' out in here. The place'll go to the damn dogs."

Leo regarded her sourly. "There's a rumor goin' round that I'm already runnin' a kennel, 'cause you spend so much time in here."

"Kiss ma ass," Big Betsy said. "You ain't got no respect for your old customers. You gonna have a bunch a preachers in here eatin' fried chicken an' scarin' the tricks away."

"Betsy," Leo told her, "you wouldn't have no more customers if they was to line up every damn preacher in South Philly an' blow his damfool head off. Only way you gonna get more business is if they make it illegal to screw a woman that ain't got a senior citizen's card."

Big Betsy's sagging jowls sagged further. "That, Leo, was cold."

"Well if you don't wanna get froze," Leo said, "then you get up offa ma case. The man is a preacher, just like I'm a bartender an' you're a whore. Everybody's got to get along the best they can doin' the best they knows how. Preacher's got a right to have a quiet drink if he wants one without everybody forkin' shit on him just 'cause he peddles Bibles instead a peddlin' his ass or somebody else's. He's a nice dude, an' he don't make no trouble, an' he don't bother nobody, an' he knows more about the Phillies than Dizzy Dean an' the damn TV computer put together, an' he don't try to tell me who I can have in ma bar an' who I can't, so you can just shut your goddamn mouth an' fuck off."

Big Betsy stared at Leo, her mouth open. "Damn, Leo. You queer for the dude or somethin'?"

Leo gave her a long, hard look, then he leaned over and whispered in her ear. "You cool it, fat stuff, or I'ma tell everybody 'bout the time you tried to make it with the beer bottle."

"That was a long time ago," Big Betsy protested.

"It had to be," Leo snapped, " 'cause even a beer bottle couldn't keep it up over you any more."

"Damn, Leo," said Big Betsy.

"You just let him be if he comes in. You hear?"

"I hear you talkin'," Big Betsy said.

"You best quit hearin' me talkin' an' commence to listenin' to what I'm sayin'."

"I am, I am," Big Betsy said. "You say he's okay, then he's okay. After all, it's your bar, Leo. You got a right to have anybody in it you wants. You wants a preacher, you gets a preacher. You wants a honky, you can get one a them, too."

"Ain't nobody said nothin' 'bout no honkies," Leo snapped.

"Well, it's the next step, Leo," Big Betsy said. "You get a couple preachers, the next step is to have a bunch a honky social workers. Next thing you know they done fixed the street, put in new sewers, built a new school, an' raised the taxes. There goes the damn neighborhood."

Leo uneasily examined her logic for a moment, then gave up and stuck to his guns. "All I got, an' all I'm gonna have, is one damn preacher. I ain't no preacher-lover, but he's a nice fella. There's gotta be some nice preachers somewheres."

"I ain't never met one," said Big Betsy.

"Well, you oughta meet this one."

"What the hell . . ." Big Betsy stopped suddenly and her face assumed an expression that screamed of calculation. "Well, now," she said slowly, "maybe I should. I mean, if the man drinks beer maybe he's up for a little action." Leo put down the glass he had been polishing and stared at her. "W'hell," said Big Betsy defensively, "maybe I'm just what he's been lookin' for."

"I doubt it," Leo said. "He sure musta seen you by now. You're too damn big t'overlook."

"Maybe he's shy," snapped Big Betsy. "We ain't been introduced. You gotta introduce us, Leo."

"Oh, God," Leo muttered. "Betsy, I got better things to do than play pimp to a preacher."

"Humph," said Big Betsy. "Trouble with you, Leo, is you don't change your Kotex real reglar."

"You remember what them things is for, do you?" Leo said. "You not only look like one, you got a mem'ry like one." He grinned at Big Betsy, who ignored him pointedly for a few moments, then sighed.

"All right, Leo. Like what?"

"A snaggle-toothed elephant," Leo said.

"Fuck off," said Big Betsy, and marched off toward the ladies' room. Leo grinned and went back to polishing glasses.

It was shaping up to be a quiet night, one of the nights when Leo loved his job, a night free from drawn knives, squabbling couples, sick drunks, maudlin whores, irate wives, henpecked husbands, and idiots who insisted on playing Russian roulette with Leroy Briggs. Such nights had been rare of late—the hot summer seemed to be drawing the sweat and blood and ornery out of everybody. Leo had felt the change in himself as the August heat had taken its toll. He had begun to notice the hard edges of things, instead of sensing the softer interiors: when he looked at Big Betsy he saw her bitchiness before he saw her loneliness, he saw Rayburn Wallace as weak rather than meek, as powerless more than as gentle. Leo realized suddenly that over the long hot weeks he had been withdrawing into himself, spending more time with the TV. Leo drew himself a long, cold beer and took a thoughtful swallow. Then he leaned over and unplugged the set. Tonight, Leo decided, the bar would get his full attention. He would dedicate the evening to breaking out of the crust that the summer had baked onto him. He stretched, expanding his beer-and-sweat-stained shirt past all reasonable expectation. He slurped his beer and trundled down to make amends with Big Betsy, who was now sitting and smoldering at the far end of the bar. Impulsively, Leo poured a shot glass full of gin and placed it before her. Big Betsy eyed it with suspicion.

"What the hell's that?" Big Betsy demanded.

"It's a slug a gin," Leo said. "Beefeater."

"I can see that, Leo," Big Betsy snarled. "What the hell's it doin' there?"

Leo regarded the shot glass appraisingly. "Not much," he admitted.

"Well what the hell's it *for*, Leo?" said Big Betsy with exaggerated patience.

"It's for you."

"For me?"

"That's right," Leo said. "That there gin is a peace offerin'."

Big Betsy stared at him for a moment, and then her face burst into a jack-o'-lantern grin. "Damn, Leo, I knowed you'd come around. You might almost be human." Big Betsy reached out and grasped the glass. She leered at Leo, but in an instant the leer turned into a scowl, and she flung the gin straight into Leo's face. "Only trouble with your thinkin'," she continued without noticeable rancor, "is that I ain't hardly desperate enough to be givin' no pieces away for one lousy slug a gin."

Leo stood with gin running out of his sparse hair and onto his face, dripping off his nose and onto his thick lips, off his chin and onto his broad chest. He made no motion. Leo appeared to be in shock.

"Haw, haw, haw," laughed Big Betsy. "You sure do look like a goddamn fool, Leo. Shame to waste good gin, but it's worth it. Haw, haw, haw." Leo remained catatonic. His tongue flicked out and, ever so gently, absorbed the liquid that had dripped down to within its range. His eyes blinked as a few drops of gin trickled into them, then closed. Big Betsy stopped laughing. "Leo?" said Big Betsy. Leo did not move. "Leo!" Leo remained motionless, like a lumpy carving in dark wood. "Omigod," said Big Betsy. "Omigod."

Brother Fletcher entered Lightnin' Ed's just as Big Betsy reached out a crooked forefinger and jabbed her long fingernail into Leo's protruding paunch. Leo rocked back on his heels, nearly toppling over backward before the counterweight of his pot belly swung him back into balance. Big Betsy emitted an anguished choke and tried to back away from Leo's rigid form while still perched on the bar stool. As a direct result, Betsy and bar stool became a tangled mass on the floor, which Brother Fletcher eyed with some astonishment. Big Betsy bounced up like an overinflated volleyball, while the stool, two of its legs snapped neatly by the sudden application of Big Betsy's full weight, remained on the floor. "Omigod," whispered Big Betsy, her eyes on motionless Leo.

"What's the matter?" asked Brother Fletcher.

Big Betsy pointed her finger at Leo, looked down at it, and quickly hid her hand behind her back. "Omigod," said Big Betsy. "I done made poor Leo bust a goddamn blood vessel. I done give poor Leo a stroke, or he's havin' a fuckin' fit, an' it's all ma fault. Omigod."

To Brother Fletcher it appeared that it was Big Betsy who was having the fit. She jabbed Leo in the solar plexus with her forefinger; breath escaped burbling through Leo's pursed lips, but his face remained immobile and his body rigid. "Omigod." She tore her eyes away from Leo and focused them on Brother Fletcher. "I threw a whole glass a Beefeater in his face, an' now he's havin' a fit. Poor Leo, I done done him in. I didn't mean it."

"Of course not," soothed Brother Fletcher. "But I really don't think a glass of gin . . ." Brother Fletcher stopped suddenly, realizing that he had not the slightest notion as to the possible effects of a glass of gin administered externally, or internally, for that matter.

"It wasn't the goddamn gin," Big Betsy wailed. "I shot Leo down. Shot him cold."

"You *what?*"

Big Betsy nodded. "In flames. I burned him clean. You see"—she turned her wistful gaze on Leo—"me an' Leo, we ain't exactly in *love* or nothin', but, well, we been together a long time, you know? An' I guess Leo just couldn't take it when he fin'ly got around to astin' for some an' I turned him down." She turned back to Brother Fletcher. "Some men's like that, you know. A girl says no, an' they got to be takin' it ʌll personal."

"I'm sure he'll . . . recover," Brother Fletcher said.

"I don't know," Big Betsy said doubtfully. "I shouldn'ta done like that t'old Leo." She wiped a tear from her eye. "I mean, I always figured me an' Leo'd, well, you know, sooner or later. Right now I got ma career, but . . ." Her voice trailed off. She regarded Leo sadly.

Brother Fletcher looked down at Big Betsy's plumb-bob breasts and congested face and repressed a shudder. He reached out and removed the side towel from Leo's lax fingers. "Here," he said, handing it to Big Betsy. "Why don't you go run some cold water on this?"

"What for?"

"We'll put it on his head."

"Oh." Big Betsy looked pityingly at Leo for a moment, then waddled off to the rest room. As soon as the door had closed behind her Leo stuffed both hands in his mouth and fell across the bar, his big body shaking.

"You all right?" asked Brother Fletcher.

"No, no," moaned Leo. "No, the damn bitch is killin' me. I'm dyin', Rev, I'm dyin'." Leo wiped tears from his eyes and tried to push himself off the bar, which was creaking ominously from his weight.

Big Betsy burst from the ladies' room holding a soggy side towel in both hands. The water ran down her fat arms and dripped off her elbows. She stopped and stared. "He ain't dead!"

"You keep breathin' in ma damn face an' I will be dead," growled Leo. He stopped laughing and managed to push himself off the bar.

"I thought you was gone, Leo," Big Betsy said.

Leo looked at her calmly, snorted, picked up a fresh side towel and started polishing glasses.

"I thought sure he was a gonner," Big Betsy said to Brother Fletcher. She laid the wet side towel down on the bar.

"I, ah, think you can stop worrying," Brother Fletcher said.

"Worrying?" snapped Big Betsy. "Me? 'Bout Leo? Why the hell would I wanta worry about Leo? He ain't good for nothin' 'cept pourin' gin. An' beer," Big Betsy added as Leo placed a frosty mug in front of Brother Fletcher. "An'," Big Betsy continued, "there's plenty bartenders can do that better. Leo can't even pour a lady a glass a gin without gettin' it all over his ugly face."

"But—" Brother Fletcher began.

"What lady?" Leo cut in. "I don't see no damn lady."

"He's blind, too," Big Betsy confided.

"But you—" began Brother Fletcher.

"If I wasn't," Leo said, "I sure as hell wouldn't be able to stay in the same damn room as you. Every time you goes to take a piss I gotta buy a new mirror."

"What . . ." began Brother Fletcher. Then he closed his eyes, shook his head, and took a long swallow of his beer.

"Don't you pay no attention to Leo, Cutie-pie," Big Betsy said, patting Brother Fletcher's arm. "Leo don't know if his mother was Lassie or Rin-Tin-Tin." She turned to Leo and glowered. "You know somethin', Leo? You think you're hot shit an' you go around puttin' down your old friends. But hot shit don't end up to be nothin' but cold turd, Leo. You remember that." She sneered at Leo and whirled on a mystified Brother Fletcher. "You know what Leo done?" she asked accusingly.

"No," said Brother Fletcher quickly.

"Well, I'll tell you," Big Betsy said. "You oughta hear it. You oughta know what kinda fool you been buyin' beer from. Leo's tryin' to turn this place into a fuckin' Sunday School. How you like that?"

"Uh, Betsy," Leo said quickly, "I do believe it's gettin' to be time you shut your mouth or your ass or whatever you been makin' noise with."

"You don't know shit, Leo," Big Betsy said. "You don't even know the difference between your mouth an' your asshole."

Leo looked up at the ceiling, his tongue jammed into his cheek. "Betsy, now, I know *ma* mouth from *ma* asshole, but in your case there just ain't that much difference. Now why don't you just close whichever—"

"This here conversation," Big Betsy said with frosty dignity, "is *strictly* between me an' Cutie-pie here. Now quit bein' jealous an' go piss."

"Yes, ma'am," said Leo obediently, his eyes still on the ceiling, "but I still think—"

"I doubt it," Big Betsy snapped. Leo shrugged, made a motion of washing his hands, and moved away, being careful to stay within earshot. "Don't you mind *him*, Cutie-pie," Big Betsy said, settling herself on the stool next to Brother Fletcher like a hen on a nest. "He just doesn't want nobody to know he's turnin' this place into a damn church social. You ain't gonna believe this, but he started lettin' *preachers* in here."

Brother Fletcher choked convulsively and half-swallowed beer sprayed across the bar top. His features under rigid control, Leo moved in with his side towel and mopped up the mess, wordlessly refilled Brother Fletcher's glass. Big Betsy was pounding Brother Fletcher on the back. Brother Fletcher clapped a hand over his mouth to hold his plate in. "You gonna be sick, Cutie-pie?" gasped Big Betsy between pounds. "Leo, see what you done with your damn foolishness? Cutie-pie's fixin' to heave."

"Maybe I made him sick," Leo said, "but you're the one beatin' him to death. Let up on him, for God's sake."

Big Betsy stopped pounding, permitting Brother Fletcher to reposition himself on the stool and his dentures in his mouth. "You all right, Cutie-pie?" Big Betsy asked urgently.

"F-f-f-fine," spluttered Brother Fletcher.

"See, Leo?" accused Big Betsy. "The thought a havin' preachers in here messes folks all up."

"Uh huh," said Leo.

Brother Fletcher reached out a shaking hand, picked up his beer glass, and drained it to the dregs.

"You oughta pay more attention to the way folks feels, Leo," Big Betsy said.

"Uh huh," Leo said. He drew Brother Fletcher another beer. Brother Fletcher looked at him gratefully.

"Preachers is all right," Big Betsy continued, "but only where they belongs. Same as everybody. Now a preacher ain't got no more business in a bar than I does in a damn monastery. Ain't that right, Cutie-pie?"

Brother Fletcher reached for his glass.

"It ain't like I got nothin' against preachers," Big Betsy went on. "I *like* preachers. I even know a few can hold their end up in bed. Matter a fact, I knowed quite a few. But they didn't hang around in no bars scarin' the johns away. Hell, no. They stayed home an' ate fried chicken an' fucked widders like preachers is supposed to."

Leo grinned wolfishly and set another beer in front of Brother Fletcher, who this time did not bother to look up.

"Course now," Big Betsy ruminated, "I did know a preacher one time that wasn't satisfied with fuckin' widders. He useta go over to this woman's house in the afternoon an' tear off a piece, an' then he'd go on downstairs an' eat up whatever was in the icebox 'fore her man come home. That sorry fool be comin' home 'bout six o'clock after bustin' his nuts all damn day an' he say, 'Hey, baby, what's for dinner?' an' she say, 'Well, we was gonna have fried chicken, but the preacher was over an' he done ate everythin'.' Well, after this fool went hungry for about a week in a row he decides to come home early an' see can he get in some greasin' 'fore the preacher ate everythin' up. Only when he comes in the kitchen door there ain't no preacher. Ain't no preacher in the dinin' room neither. So he tiptoes on upstairs an' there's the preacher with his head down there 'tween that woman's legs just chewin' away. Well the dude hauls off an' pulls the preacher outa there an' knocks him over in the corner an' says, 'Damn, Rev, ain't it bad enough you gotta be fuckin' up ma eatin', now you gotta be eatin' up ma fuckin', too?' Haw, haw, haw."

Leo hugged himself, a formidable task. Brother Fletcher made a grab for his glass and downed the contents like a shot. "Haw, haw, haw," roared Big Betsy. "Ain't that a blowjob? Ain't that a fuckin' blowjob?" She slapped Brother Fletcher soundly on the back. Brother Fletcher felt his upper body accelerate rapidly in the direction of the wall until it was arrested sharply by his spine. Brother Fletcher choked. Leo slapped another glass of beer into Brother Fletcher's feebly clutching fingers, and Brother Fletcher poured it down his throat. "Damn," said Big Betsy in admiration, "you sure can put it away. That must be five you had since you got here, an' that wasn't but a minute ago."

"Is that all?" moaned Brother Fletcher. "It felt longer."

"You got it backwards, Cutie-pie," Big Betsy informed him. "First you feel it, an' *then* it gets longer. Haw, haw, haw."

"Sweet Jesus," breathed Brother Fletcher. He hauled himself off the stool just in time to avoid the slap that Big Betsy had launched at his back, and tottered off to the men's room.

"Nice fella," Big Betsy commented. "He ain't no powerhouse, but he sure can soak up some suds."

"Uh huh," Leo said.

"I ain't seen him before. He's new, huh, Leo?"

"Uh huh," said Leo.

"Can't you say nothin' but 'uh huh'?" demanded Big Betsy. "You sound like a fuckin' cow."

"I sound like a fuckin' bull," Leo said. "A fuckin' bull goes 'uh huh.' A fuckin' cow just goes 'uh.' "

Big Betsy gave Leo a look of complete disgust. "That," she said, "is foul."

"Sorry," Leo said meekly.

Brother Fletcher returned from the men's room, his face a trifle ashy. He walked carefully, like a septuagenarian strolling over hot eggs, and slid gingerly onto his stool. "Do you think I could have another beer, Leo?" he said softly.

"Why sure, Re—ah, Cutie-pie," Leo said.

"Whatsa matter, Leo, can't you remember the man's name?" snapped Big Betsy. She turned and smiled seductively at Brother Fletcher. "Leo may look like a chocolate-covered elephant, but he's got the mem'ry of a two-year-old M and M." She turned her glare on Leo. "Only he ain't gonna be meltin' in ma mouth *or* in ma hand."

"Could I have another beer, Leo?" Brother Fletcher said.

"You got one," Leo said.

"Oh," said Brother Fletcher. He picked up the glass and emptied it. Leo refilled it wordlessly.

"Don't you pay no attention to Leo, Cutie-pie," Big Betsy said. "Leo just don't know what to do with hisself when there's a real man around. All Leo knows is to talk some dirty fuckin' shit an' the rest of the time he hangs around with preachers. Next thing you know it'll be choirboys, an' Leo gonna sprout ten pair a wings." Big Betsy grinned acidly and made flipping motions with her hands.

Leo grinned at her. "Now, Betsy, I do seem to recall you was talkin' about how you was gonna be slingin' some action the preacher's way soon as he showed up. Ain't that right?"

"That is true, baby," said Big Betsy soothingly, while shooting thirty-eight caliber glares at Leo. "I did say that, but that was 'fore *you* got here. I mean, 'fore you come in onliest thing in sight even comin' close to bein' a man was Leo, an' next to Leo any damn thing would look good. Small, but good. Even a preacher. But that don't make no difference now I got you."

"Leo," said Brother Fletcher, "another beer." Leo complied, grinning happily. Brother Fletcher downed the whole thing.

"Preachers ain't nothin' when you get right down to it," Big Betsy said. "I'd rather be with you, Cutie-pie, than with any damn preacher." Big Betsy reached out and stroked the back of Brother Fletcher's neck.

"Leo," croaked Brother Fletcher. Leo filled the glass. Brother Fletcher took a swallow, turned to Big Betsy. "I wish you wouldn't do that."

"Aw, now, Cutie-pie, don't be that way," whined Big Betsy. "I tell you, that preacher ain't nothin' to me. The last time I made it with a preacher he wasn't even no good. Couldn't get it up until I got him thinkin' I was a plate a fried chicken an' his pecker was a fork. An' then he wanted to use his fingers. So then I told him it was ham an' red-eye gravy, an' then he ate for *hours*. Haw, haw, haw."

Brother Fletcher looked distinctly uncomfortable, and even Leo turned slightly gray. "You want another beer?" Leo asked.

"You haven't got anything stronger?" Brother Fletcher asked weakly. Leo nodded and poured out two glasses of scotch. He gave one to Brother

Fletcher and lifted the other to his own lips. As he set the glass down Jake shuffled in.

"You an' me, Cutie-pie, we gonna have a time no preacher ain't even thought about," Big Betsy said.

"Evenin', Betsy. Evenin', Leo. Evenin', Reverend," Jake said.

"Evenin', Jake," Leo said.

"Whad you say?" asked Big Betsy.

"I said 'evenin',' " Leo said blandly.

"Not you. *You!*"

"I said evenin', too," Jake said. "What the hell?"

"You said, 'Evenin', Reverend,' " Big Betsy accused.

"That's right," Jake said. "That's what I said. Good evenin', Reverend."

"Good evening," said Brother Fletcher solemnly.

"Omigod," said Big Betsy.

"What the hell's goin' on?" demanded Jake.

"Oh, nothin'," said Leo. "We just been tryin' to figure out which is bigger, Betsy's foot or her mouth. Mouth won."

"Omigod," said Big Betsy. "Omigod. I didn't mean—lookahere, Cutie —I mean, Reverend, I'm sorry—"

"It's all right," Brother Fletcher said gently. "No one could take offense from a lady as lovely as you." He smiled. His eyes were a little glassy.

"Wahuh?" said Big Betsy.

Leo looked at Jake, held up eight fingers. Jake held up eight fingers with a questioning look on his face that quickly changed to an expression of disbelief. Leo nodded slowly. Jake shook his head. Leo shrugged. Brother Fletcher smiled happily and began to slide off the stool. Leo grabbed him by the collar, and Jake held him erect while Leo came around the bar. They deposited him gently in one of the booths along the wall. Brother Fletcher opened his eyes, smiled, said thank you, and went into a sound sleep. Big Betsy regarded him with a horrified look on her fat face. "Omigod," said Big Betsy. "Omigod."

"Snap," Leslie said, clicking her nails in Charlene's face. "I got him just like that."

"For real?" said Charlene, impressed. "I'da thought there was more to Leroy than that."

"Oh yeah," Leslie said, "but dig it; it's like ridin' a horse. When you wants the horse to turn, you don't got to turn the whole damn horse, you just got to turn his head."

"Oh yeah," Charlene giggled, "an' you mean you got this here horse by the ears?"

"Unh, unh," Leslie corrected, "I got this here jackass by the balls." She laughed merrily until Vanessa's voice cut through from behind her.

"What the shit you know about horses?"

Leslie twisted around. "You shouldn't sneak up like—"

"I know you got jackasses figured out, you married one, but where'd you find out about horses?"

"I watched you," Leslie snapped. "That way I knew all the mistakes."

"You best be careful the horse don't throw you."

"Horse don't throw you 'less he gets restless," Leslie said. "You got to keep him satisfied. Only time folks get thrown off is if they can't ride."

"Let's have a drink," Charlene suggested. Vanessa moved around from behind Leslie, forcing her to twist the other way.

"What you want, Big Sister?" Leslie said sweetly. "I guess I'm the hostess."

"Usual," Vanessa said.

"I'll get it," Charlene said. "Only I can't remember what you call them things."

"Flyin' Fucks," Leslie said.

"Singapore Slings," Vanessa said.

Charlene nodded, rose, went over to the bar. "Nemo, lemme have a Bud, a Seven-and-Seven, an' a Singapore Fuck."

"You ain't been around much lately, Big Sister," Leslie said.

"I been busy," Vanessa said.

"I heard you was turnin' into a regular ole hustler," Leslie chuckled, without smiling, "*again.*"

"Smart-ass muthafucka," Charlene grumbled as she slammed the drinks down on the table and glared over her shoulder at the grinning bartender. She flounced around the table and resumed her seat. "You know what that Nemo faggot-ass said to me?" She looked back and forth between Vanessa's dark angry eyes and Leslie's gray smiling ones.

"Don't you worry, Big Sister," Leslie said. "I told Leroy to keep you on the payroll."

"Said if I didn't get outa his face he'd give me a fast Philly fuck. Ain't that awful?"

"Your husband misses you," Vanessa said.

"Well," Leslie said with a sigh, "poor Rayburn's always been missin' a lot. You been messin' with ma Rayburn, Big Sister? You ought to go visit him. The two a you was just made for each other. See, he can't—*ride,* neither."

"I don't eat no leftovers," Vanessa snapped.

"Well, from the way I hear it—"

"Damn!" Charlene protested. "How come you two always got to be goin' at each other like a coupla dogs?"

"Dog an' a cat," Leslie said. "She's the bitch."

"That makes you the pussy," Vanessa said.

"Leastways I can do moren piss with it."

"Damn," Vanessa said. "I didn't know you knew you *could* piss with it."

"How come you always—"

"It's just our way of showin' how much we love each other," Vanessa said sourly.

They glared at each other across the table.

"You hear what that faggot-ass Nemo had the nerve to say to me?" Charlene said.

"Whad you come in here for?" demanded Leslie. "You ain't got no reason to come in here no more. He's mine now."

Vanessa shook her head. "You better not let Leroy hear you talkin' like that. He might not like it. He might smack you one or send you on back to Rayburn. He might get so mad, he'll give you to Willie T. for Valentine's."

"You just let ma Willie be," Charlene shouted. "Y'hear me? Y'all bitches just let ma Willie be."

"Leroy does exactly what I tell him," Leslie boasted.

Vanessa arched her brows, then shifted her eyes a fraction to stare at a spot just behind Leslie's head. Leslie spun around as if she had been pinched. Vanessa giggled merrily. Leslie turned back, her eyes cold. "Where is his lordshit, anyways?" Vanessa asked.

"Takin' care a business," Leslie said shortly.

"Why," said Vanessa in mock astonishment, "I thought you was all Leroy had on his small mind."

"He's gettin' ready to deal with somebody," Charlene said. "An' somebody better look out."

"Leroy better look out," Vanessa said. "Onliest way he could deal with a pile a shit is to run it down with his car. He's gotta do damn near everything with that pimpmobile. He's subject to get it confused with his cock. I 'member one time he woke up in the dead a the night an' went runnin' out screamin' 'bout how he'd done double-parked his prick."

"Why don't you shut up," Leslie said.

"I guess maybe they figured they was gonna tow it away," Vanessa went on. "Then there was the time he got his balls in reverse—"

"Shut up," said Leslie, half standing. "You're just jealous."

Vanessa sipped her drink. "Charlene, we got to go shoppin' sometime. We ain't been in a while." Leslie glared at her. "Siddown, honey, your ass'll get cold," Vanessa said.

The door to the office opened and Leroy emerged, escorted by Willie T. His big head twisted as he peered around the room. Willie T. nudged him; Leroy looked, nodded, and advanced on the three women.

"Sure, 'Nessa," Charlene said. "Soon as I get ma next check, we go. I'ma get me one a them—"

"Go where?" Leroy said, moving up behind Leslie and placing his dark hands on her bare saffron shoulders. Leslie rolled her head back and gave him an upside-down smile.

"Shoppin'," Vanessa said shortly.

" 'Nessa needs a new dildo, baby," Leslie said.

"Why hell, I give her a ball-point pen for Christmas. Won't that do?"

"Hot damn!" said Willie T. "That was a good one."

"Shup, Willie," Leroy said.

"You shouldn't be talkin' to Willie T. that way," Charlene protested.

"I talk to him any way I feel like," Leroy said.

"He don't mean nothin', baby," Willie T. said.

"Shup, Willie. How you been, 'Nessa?"

"Fine," Vanessa said. She raised her drink.

"I question that," Leroy said.

"How you likin' your new saddle, Leroy?" Vanessa said.

"Fuck you, 'Nessa," Leslie said.

"Saddle? What you talkin' about?"

"Oh, I guess it must be a surprise you ain't sposed to know about yet."

"I don't like surprises," Leroy said.

"Neither did your mother, but that didn't stop them Indians."

"I wouldn't let no bitch talk about ma mama," Willie T. said. "I'd kick the bitch right outa here if she was to start in talkin' about ma mama."

"Ain't nobody *got* to say about your mama," Vanessa told him. "You the spittin' image—bow legs, round heels, hair in your teeth, come on your tonsils, an' shit all over your nose."

"You gonna throw the bitch out, Leroy?" demanded Willie T.

"Shup, Willie. You wrong 'bout the tonsils, 'Nessa. He had 'em out when he was a kid."

"You was in the hospital last week, Willie? Sorry, I didn't know."

"Lay offa ma Willie," Charlene said ominously.

"Ain't nobody worried about layin' on him but you," Vanessa said.

"I pays you to stay off the damn street, bitch," Leroy said. There was a heavy silence. "I like to keep my eye on everything I own, an' I own you."

"Just 'cause you buy eggs don't mean you own the chicken farm," Vanessa said.

"I got a lease on the chickens," Leroy said. "An' they better not lay 'less I say so. If you ain't workin' for me, you ain't workin'. Now I heard you was out on the street."

"I was goin' someplace," Vanessa said sullenly.

"You was always *goin'* someplace," Leroy said. "Only you never could do nothin' when you got there. I heard you was in Lightnin' Ed's."

"Sure was," Vanessa said. She looked up at him defiantly. "I sure was. An' I'ma go back there right now. I gotta meet somebody." She pushed her chair back. "I just come down here to see how the field niggers was gettin' on."

"Who you got to meet?" Leroy demanded.

"What do you care?" said Leslie.

"A friend," Vanessa said. "Nobody you know. Or maybe you do. He buys beer in here sometimes, an' he stays in Lightnin' Ed's sometimes. On Saturday nights." She smiled at the shock on Leroy's face. "See y'all," she said, gathering up her purse. She wiggled her fingers in a coy wave and swept out.

Slack, slouching, too tired for artistry, Leo slapped a sandwich together without care or craftsmanship. The tobacco smoke in the air had reddened his eyes, the thumping jukebox had bruised his ears, the blended aromas of sour beer breath, stale smoke, ancient sin, and pure B.O. had driven his olfactory nerves into sulky retreat. He could still feel, however, and what he felt most was pressure: of bunion against shoe leather, of sole against floor, of belly against unsympathetic restraint of belt. His mouth tasted like he had rinsed it with water from the Schuylkill. Only a bartender, Leo reflected humorously as he forced the sandwich past his dentures, could get the hangover without having the pleasure of the drinking or the benefit of sleep. But all in all it had been an interesting night. It had amused Leo, and that made up in part for his aching feet and the small profit. There had been a few jokes, quite a few laughs. A beer night. Now it was quiet, near to closing, and muddy air oozed through the open door. The sounds in the bar were not the sounds of conversation but the sounds of four people's breathing: Brown, Jake, Rayburn Wallace, and Leo himself.

Jake was thoughtful. Leo had rarely seen Jake thoughtful—Jake had always claimed that thinking was an occupation for young folks, and that at his age he had figured out everything he needed to know, except how to die, which did not concern him. But all night Jake had sat nursing a few glasses of port, staring pensively across the bar. He had not paid for his last two drinks. Not that that bothered Leo, but it was unlike Jake to forget to pay his nickel. Jake clearly had something weighty on his mind. It had Leo worried. He was afraid that Jake's brain might rupture with the strain.

Rayburn had Leo worried, too. He had come trailing in after he finished work and he had ordered Jack Daniels. Leo disapproved of Jack Daniels. Leo disapproved of anything produced in or associated with the territory south of the Mason-Dixon line. Besides Jack Daniels whiskey, Leo disapproved of Southern Comfort, Budweiser beer, Washington D.C., the man-in-space program, Lyndon Baines Johnson, and chicken-gumbo soup. He refused to eat peanuts when he attended baseball games and cursed George Washington Carver. He had never forgiven Hank Aaron for continuing to play for the Braves after they moved to Atlanta. It was quite all right, in Leo's opinion, for Rayburn to drown his troubles in British gin or Scotch whisky, but not Jack Daniels. Rayburn, not sharing Leo's moral scruples, had done away with nearly half a bottle while mumbling vague curses in an inaudible monotone. Leo had served his drinks and shaken his head. Rayburn had poured the whiskey down.

Leo shook his head again as he shifted his glance and caught sight of the third solitary drinker—Brown. Jake worried Leo with his unusual pensiveness. Rayburn annoyed him with his sudden penchant for Confederate whiskey. Brown scared him because Leo knew that anybody who made Leroy Briggs the slightest bit uncomfortable should be put away for the protection of himself and innocent bystanders. Leo knew that Leroy Briggs was a coward and therefore deserved to be treated with the utmost respect—Leo had seen many cowards perform impressive feats of wanton violence to prove their bravery. Brown, on the other hand, was not a coward. He was a nut, possibly with mob connections. Leo was not afraid of Leroy Briggs any more than a snake trainer is afraid of a king cobra, but, like the snake trainer, Leo was very careful. Leo knew what bothered Leroy, what made him angry, and just how far he could strike. Brown was an unknown quantity, a rustling in the bushes. When Brown had entered the bar Leo had been quick with the shot glass and the scotch bottle, but Brown had shaken his head and had asked for a beer. When Leo had brought the beer Brown had paid for it even though Leo had had no intention whatsoever of requesting money. Then Brown had asked for a couple of napkins, had borrowed one of Leo's pencil stubs, and had begun scribbling away like a man possessed. Leo, having retreated to the sandwich board, observed Brown from behind half-closed eyes. Brown's scribbling was accompanied by much wall-staring, finger-snapping, foot-tapping, face-making, and other abnormal behavior. Leo had become a trifle upset. Now, with Brown still performing, Leo's unease had approached semi-gigantic proportions. He shoved his sandwich into his mouth with one hand while with the other he reassured himself of the convenient positioning of his billy club, his rubber truncheon, his sap, and the taped lead pipe he had, on occasion, bent around particularly thick or stubborn heads. Brown's skull did not appear to be exceptionally sturdy, which Leo found in keeping with his belief that Brown was soft in the head, so the sap or the truncheon should do it. Still, Brown looked tough, and his hair was long and springy enough to offer some protection. Leo decided that, if the time came, he would use the billy club and keep the pipe handy just in case.

Leo finished his sandwich and his war plan just as Brown gestured to him. Leo wiped his rubbery lips with a damp side towel and went over, one hand trailing along the underside of the bar, ready to snatch up a bottle to administer as an external tranquilizer should Brown become violent without warning. "What can I do for you, cap'n?" Leo said carefully.

"Could I have another beer?" Brown said, plopping the pencil stub down on the bar.

Leo hesitated, realizing it would take two hands to draw the beer. But failing to draw it might cause Brown to become violent. Leo sighed with the weight of the dilemma, shrugged finally, and drew the beer. Brown looked at the glass. Leo started to turn away. "Ah, could you wait a minute?" Brown said. Leo stopped abruptly, snapping to what, in a smaller man, would have been quivering attention. In Leo's case it was more of a slosh than a quiver. Brown stared at him. "Is somethin' wrong with you?"

"Wrong?" said Leo.

"Yeah," Brown said. "You know. Wrong."

"Oh," Leo said. "*Wrong.* Naw, suh, there ain't nothin' wrong."

"Then why are you standing like that?"

"Like what?" Leo said.

"With one foot on top a the other one."

Leo looked down. "Oh. Yeah." He untangled his legs.

"Can I buy you a beer?" Brown said.

Leo stared at him. "Huh?"

"I said, 'Can—' Fuck, what's wrong with you, can't you understand English?"

"Yes, suh," said Leo, "I can understand English." He stood, solemnly and obstinately uncooperative. Brown's mouth tightened and Leo, seeing the bunching of muscles along Brown's jawline, steeled himself for a psychopathic assault.

Brown's breath hissed from his nostrils. "Fuck it," he said. He looked down at the napkin in front of him, balled it up. "It's no good anyway."

Pride surged in Leo's thorax, overcoming caution. "What the hell you mean, ain't no good? It's the best damn beer on South Street. Most a these penny-ante pissant niggers don't even *have* draft beer. They shove that bottled shit, costs twice as much an' don't taste half as good. That's on account a they don't own their own bars. Some white muthafucka owns 'em. You think that white man cares if a black man gets to drink good beer? Hell no, he don't care. Give 'em shit, that's what he say. An' simple-ass niggers swallow it. Now I don't care if you *is* some kinda weirdo, you gotta know the difference 'tween good draft an' that bottled wino piss." Leo glared at Brown pugnaciously.

"I wasn't talkin' about the beer," Brown said.

"Well, I don't give a fanny fuck if you wasn't," Leo informed him. "Y'all youngbloods comes around thinkin' you knows so damn much 'bout drinkin', lemme tell you, fool, when I was your age we was mixin' wood alcohol with Moxie just to get a buzz on."

"I wasn't talkin' about the beer," Brown said.

"Well, I guess you damn well better not a been," Leo snapped. He looked at Brown. "You wasn't?"

"No," Brown said.

"Oh," said Leo. He swallowed. "Oh," he said again. Brown sucked in his cheeks to hide a smile. Leo sniffed. Brown grinned. Leo frowned sternly. Brown threw back his head and laughed. Leo stood his ground for a moment, then smiled sheepishly, then began to roar with laughter.

Jake looked up from his wine. "What's so damn funny?"

Leo recovered himself and his roar subsided to a chuckle. "It wasn't nothin'."

"Damn," Jake said. "Ain't nothin' happenin' in here all damn night, an' when somethin' does happen you gonna keep it to yourself."

"Leo thought I was tryin' to proposition him," Brown said. Leo snorted and grinned.

"You'd do better tryin' to make it with Betsy," Jake said.

"Shit," Leo said, "I'd rather sleep with me than sleep with Betsy."

"Least Betsy wouldn't let somethin' happen without tellin' me what it was," Jake said. "C'mon, Leo, you know I'm hard a hearin'."

"When it suits you," Leo said.

"Well, there ain't no use in bein' hard a hearin' when it don't suit you," Jake said, assuming the long-suffering air of a patient guru with a slow pupil. Leo looked at Brown, Brown looked at Leo. Brown opened his mouth and rolled his eyes back. Leo collapsed, laughing, across the bar. The bar almost collapsed, too. "Now dammit," Jake said, "are y'all just gonna keep on actin' like a bunch a hung-over hyenas or you gonna tell me what's so damn funny?"

"It ain't nice to call folks names," Leo said blandly.

"Ain't nice, shit," Jake said. "You gonna stand there beatin' off your belly, or you gonna pour me some more wine?" Leo sighed and lifted the bottle from below the bar. Brown drained his glass and handed it over for a refill. Jake accepted his glass, looked at it. "Now you gonna tell me?"

"Tell you what?" Leo said.

"Jesus fuckin'—" Jake exploded.

"Why don't y'all just shut them garbage cans you been usin' for mouths," snarled Rayburn, turning on his stool and staring at the three of them. "Bunch a fucked-up niggers, all you want to do is set around makin' noise an' talkin' a bunch a grade-B bullshit. Sometimes y'all make me sick."

"Uh, oh," Jake said.

"It must be that cracker whiskey he's been drinkin'," Leo said. "Shit's got him thinkin' he's a member in good standin' a the White Citizens' Council."

"I'm tired a you all," Rayburn said. He pushed himself away from the bar, tripped, sprawled onto the floor. Leo watched impassively as Jake backed away from Rayburn's prostrate form. Brown looked at the two of them, shrugged, and went over to help Rayburn up. "Get your goddamn black hands offa me," Rayburn snapped.

"Let me help you," Brown said, grasping Rayburn's arm. A quick flash in the darkness, the sounds of ripping cloth, a sharp intake of breath. Brown leaped away, stood staring uncomprehendingly down at the neat slice across the front of his shirt, the thin red line of blood welling out of the skin of his chest.

"I said, lemme be, muthafucka," Rayburn said. "You mess with me an' I'll make minute steak outa your black belly."

Brown stared silently. "An' I'ma make a shit-flavored milk shake outa your stupid head, Rayburn," Leo said. "He was only tryin' t'help you up."

"I don't need no help from no black-assed, sissy-lipped, poop-nosed—" Rayburn stopped abruptly as the side of Brown's foot connected solidly with the side of his head, groaned, and rolled against the bar. Brown kicked the razor out of Rayburn's reach, picked it up, examined it, then looked at the line of blood on his chest. "You got any iodine?" he said mildly. Leo wordlessly pulled the first-aid kit out and set it on the bar. Brown looked at it, impressed by the size. "I guess you get lots of, uh, accidents in here."

"Mostly when you're around," Leo said.

"Bastard damn near sliced ma throat," Brown said.

"He wanted your throat, he'da had it," Leo said.

"He just wanted you to leave him be," Jake said. He sat down next to Brown. "He told you he didn't want no help."

Brown looked at Jake. Leo poured out a shot of scotch, set it in front of Brown. On the floor, Rayburn stirred and groaned. Brown looked down at him, his face expressionless. Rayburn groaned again and sat up. "Some black sonofabitch is gonna be sorry," Rayburn said. He raised a hand and rubbed his head and looked around. Brown glanced at Leo. Leo stared straight ahead. Brown looked at Rayburn. "You black sonofabitch," Rayburn said.

Brown slid off the stool. "You can't go slicin' pieces offa people an' expect 'em to kiss your foot," Brown said.

Rayburn pushed himself to his feet, squinted, focusing on Brown. Brown moved away from the bar, stood with feet planted, arms swinging. Rayburn's hand moved slowly, then plunged into his pocket, fumbled for the razor. Brown held it out. Rayburn stopped fumbling, stared at the razor, then at Brown. Brown flipped the razor to him. Rayburn caught it clumsily, opened it, looked at the blade, glanced at the red slice on Brown's shirt. He closed the razor, sat down on a stool. Brown looked at Leo. Leo dropped his eyes. Brown stepped over to Rayburn. "I didn't mean nothin'," Brown said.

"What do you want?" Rayburn said dully.

"Nothing," Brown said. He went back and sat down.

9 Thursday

Leroy Briggs sat dazedly dozing in the deserted darkened barroom of the Elysium Hotel, grasping a bottle of Beefeater gin from which he took occasional swigs of heroic proportion. A very few feet above him, Leslie lay waiting for him to finish the business he had said he had to take care of. "Business" was the Beefeater, and when that bottle was gone there were a few more behind the bar. Leroy had told Leslie he would be up soon, which was a patent lie—Leroy knew he would not be up for quite a while, and therefore he had absolutely no intention of mounting the stairs at any time in the foreseeable future. The thought of Leslie, lying quivering and voracious, with her juices flowing and her nervous system in high gear, filled Leroy with complete, total, utter, absolute dread. He shivered, stroked the bottle lovingly, then lifted it to his lips. The hardness of the glass pressing against his lips, and the flow of gin across his tongue, down his gullet, and into his fear-knotted stomach filled him with false warmth and imagined strength. Leroy resolved to finish this bottle and then one more, and then go upstairs. He was pleased with this decision, the self-confidence it implied. He took another pull on the bottle.

Leslie was not Leroy's only problem, but she represented them all. Leroy felt himself slipping, felt the stranglehold he had for years maintained over the comings and goings of half of South Street's population slipping, and he knew that that was as good as saying he was finished, because Leroy had been ruthless with the competition, and there was no reason to suppose that the competition would be any less ruthless with him. It was very unfair, Leroy thought. He raised the bottle despondently, sucked at it, darting his tongue in and out of the opening to control the flow of the warming liquor. He relaxed and hummed softly to himself. Then he sat up suddenly as someone entered the dark bar. "Who zat?" Leroy demanded.

"King Kong, lookin' for a tree to hang his ass in." Cotton maneuvered himself skillfully through the darkness to a berth next to Leroy. "You havin' a private party, or can any fool come?"

Leroy sniffed. "Man, at ma damn parties *only* fools can come."

Cotton chuckled and accepted the proffered bottle. He raised it, lowered it, sighed appreciatively. "I 'spected you'd be upstairs takin' your ease," Cotton said.

Leroy slowly turned his head to glare at Cotton, but Cotton looked straight ahead. "I'ma take ma ease down here if that's all right with you," Leroy said.

"Fine with me," Cotton said. "I always did swear a man could sleep better in a chair with a bottle than in a bed with a buzz saw." He raised the bottle, looked at it, drank, handed it back to Leroy, who accepted it somewhat ungraciously and drank in silence. "Sometime—" Cotton began.

"You shut your goddamn mouth," Leroy said. "I ain't no goddamn Willie T. that you got to be shittin' into ma ears."

"Well, it's for sure somebody's been shittin' in your ears, or in your eyes, up your damn nose, or someplace, 'cause lately head's sure be full of it an' it sure has been comin' outa your mouth."

"Shut up," Leroy said dully.

"Lately there's been so much shit comin' outa your damn mouth, it's hard to tell which is your hind end. I don't know if you use a napkin when you eat, or toilet paper."

"Didn't I tell you to shut up?"

"You losin' your mem'ry along with everythin' else?"

Leroy growled briefly, then sighed and took another drink.

"Time was you'd a killed me least three times by now," Cotton said.

"Time ain't no more," Leroy said softly.

"What?"

"Nothin'," Leroy said. "Just some bullshit somebody tried to sell me one time."

"You buy it?" Cotton asked.

"I don't know," Leroy said. He took another swig and handed the bottle over. "Didja ever think—?" he began, then stopped.

"Oh," Cotton said, "occasionally. Wouldn't do to do it too often. Willie T. might find out what a fool he is."

"Willie T.," Leroy said, and snorted.

"Yeah, Willie T.," Cotton said.

"You drinkin' that or parkin' it?" Leroy said. Cotton took a quick drink and handed the bottle back. Leroy took it, looked at it, shrugged, upended it above his open mouth. The remaining gin trickled out. Leroy tossed the bottle aimlessly across the barroom. It landed without breaking, bounced away in the dimness. "Willie T.," Leroy said with a derisive snort.

"Yeah," Cotton said. "Willie T." He gave a short chuckle.

"Willie T.," Leroy said, laughing.

"Willie T. says everybody on the street's sayin' you done lost it," Cotton said.

Leroy stopped laughing. "So what? Willie T. don't know his prick from his pinky."

"Ain't much difference," Cotton said.

"Yeah," Leroy said, laughing again. "There's another bottle—"

"I know," Cotton said. He levered his bulky body out of his chair, went behind the bar, fumbled briefly in the darkness, returned with another bottle of Beefeater. He twisted the cap off. "Leroy?"

"What?" said Leroy, reaching for the bottle.

"I been hearin' it, too."

Leroy's hand stopped in mid-motion. He drew it back slowly and deliberately. "An' what you sayin', Cotton? You think I'm losin' it?"

"Ain't ma—" Cotton began, then stopped.

"I ast you a question, nigger."

Cotton sighed. "I think you done already lost it, Leroy. Question in ma mind is, you gonna get it back?"

Leroy sat very still for a minute. "Cotton, why don't you just say that again. I think I heard you the first time, but I'd hate like hell to kill you by mistake."

Cotton shoved the bottle toward him. "Will you cut that shit, Leroy, you been watchin' too much fuckin' *Gunsmoke*. Man, that shit ain't hardly necessary. You ast me a goddamn question an' then you get an attitude about the damn answer. Damn, Leroy, you so full a shit." Cotton hauled the bottle back and took a swig.

"What you mean by sayin' I lost it?" Leroy demanded.

"I mean you lost it. Niggers backin' you down in bars, niggers rippin' your ass off in every damn deal, whores you sposed to be ownin' runnin' up one side a the damn street an' down the other, an' now some silly bitch has got you so fucked up you scared to sleep in your own damn bed. You know you lost somethin', baby. I hate to tell you."

Leroy took the bottle back. "Siddown, Cotton." Cotton sat down. "I'm that bad, huh?"

"You been lookin' that bad," Cotton said, "an' that's the truth."

"Maybe I'm gettin' old."

"You started that the day you was born," Cotton said disgustedly.

"Have a drink," Leroy said.

"No thanks."

"Then I will."

"Help yourself."

Leroy took a long pull. "Maybe I'll retire," Leroy said. Cotton stared at him in disbelief. "Yeah," Leroy said. "That's 'zactly what I'ma do. Retire. Gone down to Florida."

"Yeah," Cotton said. "Eat shit with the alligators."

"Go fishin' every day. I ain't never been fishin' much." He took the bottle back and sipped at it.

"You better fish for catfish," Cotton said sourly. "Old men don't get no closern that to pussy."

"I'm tired a pussy," Leroy said. He raised the bottle, missed his mouth, and hit himself on the nose. "Ow."

"Just as well," Cotton said. "Old men don't get none anyway. They can't get it up but once a year, an' they so damn excited when they do, they comes in their long johns."

Leroy snorted and managed to get the bottle aimed right. "Ain't always got to be gettin' it up. You can always eat it."

"Only old men ain't got no teeth."

"I'll gum it then," Leroy said.

"If you can stand the smell."

"They don't all smell," Leroy said.

"All the old ones do. You don't think no young girl gonna be foolin' around with no senior citizen don't do nothin' but catch fish?"

"Ain't never thought about it," Leroy admitted. He raised the bottle up beside his ear, grunted, lowered it, managed to get it pointed right.

"Well, you had enough anyways," Cotton said.

"That's right."

"Ain't interested no more."

"Nope," Leroy said. He raised the bottle, paused, lowered it. "It don't matter how old y'are, they still go down for a Cadillac."

"That's true," Cotton admitted. Leroy grunted in satisfaction, raised

the bottle, and began to drink. "*New* ones," Cotton said. "If you be retirin'
like an old man, you got to be drivin' an old car. Ain't no money for nothin'
else." Leroy choked and spewed halfway across the barroom. "Course,"
Cotton continued, "you'll be savin' money on booze."

"On booze?" Leroy said. He looked at the bottle. "Howma be savin'
money on booze?"

"Old man can't drink no booze," Cotton said. "Old man, he be drinkin'
wine, or maybe beer, or maybe a little milk."

"Wine!" Leroy exploded. "Wine, shit, wine's for winos."

"Yeah," Cotton agreed. "You ever see a teen-age wino?"

"An' damn, beer, beer ain't nothin'. There's sposed to be a preacher
goes into Lightnin' Ed's to drink *beer*."

"Uh huh," Cotton said.

"Well, hell, I can't be drinkin' no damn beer if even a damn preacher
drinks it."

"Uh huh," Cotton said.

"An' milk, damn, milk is for babies."

"Uh huh," Cotton said. "An' whores."

"That's right," Leroy said. "I forgot whores. Umph. I sho' ain't no
who'." He took another drink, lowered the bottle, stared at Cotton. "You
been tryin' to con me, muthafucka, ain't you?"

"Who, me?"

"Yeah, you. All this shit about old men an' shit. Only I'm too smart. I
know ain't every muthafucka gets retired gotta be drinkin' wine an' beer an'
goddamn milk."

"Oh yeah?" Cotton said. "Who you know that done retired?"

"Well, there's—humph," Leroy said. He took a few more drinks while
he thought about it. "There's Jim Brown. He retired."

"Yeah," Cotton said. "He retired all right. He quit gettin' his brains
beat out every damn Sunday so he could stand naked upside a Raquel
Welch. Brother, if that's what you call retirement, show me the way."

Leroy nodded thoughtfully. "I guess that might be just as hard as gettin'
your brains beat out. Well, how 'bout Joe Louis?"

"How 'bout him?"

"He retired."

"That's right," Cotton said flatly. "He retired."

Leroy sat in silence. "How 'bout that congressman?" he said, finally.

"Powell? He died."

"That's right," Leroy said thoughtfully. "He did die."

"He wasn't that old, neither," Cotton said.

"Now, you look," Leroy said. "I know ain't *everybody* retired ends up a wino or a whore drinkin' milk or somethin'. How 'bout Lyndon Johnson? How 'bout Harry Truman?"

"What about 'em?" Cotton asked. "You plannin' on gettin' elected President 'fore you retire, or you figure bein' white's gonna be enough?" Leroy stared at him. "Leroy," Cotton said softly. "Leroy, niggers just don't *get* to retire. They gets to get shot, or they gets to starve, or they gets to drink theyself to death, an' if they lucky they gets to stop doin' what they been doin' an' start doin' somethin' else, but we sure as hell don't get to go to no Florida an' lay around all day on some damn beach. Hell, you already got a suntan. All right, I spose there is some silly-ass sonofabitch somewhere, some damn janitor or car mechanic or some such shit, some fool that puts his money in the damn bank an' pays his social security so when he gets to be sixty-five he can collect his sixty-five dollars an' sixty-five cent on the sixty-fifth a the month, but Jesus Christ, Leroy, you ain't gonna be happy with that. You want that kinda bullshit?"

"No," Leroy said.

"Well, all right," Cotton said. "You better get your ass back together."

"I got ma ass together," Leroy said. He raised the bottle, drank the rest of the gin down, tossed it away into the darkness. "Tomorrow mornin' we gonna go outa here an' whip these simple niggers into line. Retire, shit. I ain't no fool. I don't know what got into you, simple ass, come around here tryin' to tell me I got to retire."

"Sorry, Leroy," Cotton said.

"You come around peddlin' that kinda shit again an' you'll be inventin' a new kind of sorry." He pushed himself out of the chair, stumbled against the bar, stayed upright by half lying across it.

"You think you can make it to bed?" Cotton asked.

"Sure," Leroy said.

"You don't need no help?"

"Hell, no."

"What 'bout Leslie?"

"What about her?"

"She's up there waitin' for you."

"So?"

"She's gonna want to fuck all night."

"With who?"

"With you."

"I ain't in the mood."

"Maybe you better sleep in ma room, then."

"Now what the hell kinda talk is that? You think I'ma get outa ma own damn bed just on account a some horny bitch? She can't keep quiet an' let me sleep, she can damn well sleep someplace else." He sniffed, took a deep breath, and went staggering toward the doorway, banging into chairs and tables as he went. Cotton rose and moved easily to the bar, went behind it, got himself a beer, and opened it. He listened as Leroy's fumbling footsteps faded on the stairs, then sounded on the floor above. Cotton moved out into the Elysium's lobby, still listening. He heard the two thuds and clank as Leroy's shoes and belt buckle hit the floor. He heard the creak of bedsprings, dull murmurings of voices. Suddenly there was a yowl, as if someone had stepped on a cat, followed by a boom as something heavy hit the floor. Grinning, Cotton finished his beer, belched, and began to mount the stairs.

Jake hurried across the South Street Bridge, his baggy pockets ajangle with the loose change he had earned panhandling outside Thirtieth Street Station. Jake preferred to earn his money shining shoes, but it had been an exceptionally bad day and the only remedy for his personal liquidity crisis had been a vast infusion of nickels and dimes and, occasionally, quarters, extracted from the somewhat guilty-looking commuters rushing to catch the Paoli Local. Panhandling hurt Jake's pride, his feet and, lately, his belly, but it was better to make small sacrifices than to go without wine, or to tap the emergency reserve bottle he kept hidden deep in a dark cranny of his favorite alley. With Jake it was a point of pride that he had always kept something put aside for a rainy day; it assured him that he was a cut above the average wino, who, Jake believed, never was successful because he never looked far enough ahead.

But as Jake hurried across the bridge he cursed himself for lacking foresight in another area; it had been a long day, and there was a frightening chance that he would not reach Lightnin' Ed's before closing time. He was so occupied with thinking about his destination that he failed to pay sufficient attention to where he was going; he stumbled over something and sprawled full length on the concrete. Hands reached down and helped him up. "Why don't you watch where the hell you goin'?" Jake snapped, peering at the man in front of him. It was too dark to see much.

"*You* were going. I was just sitting here."

Jake recognized the accent. "What you doin' here, Brown?"

"Settin'," Brown said.

"Humph," Jake said, and started to move on. Then he stopped. His nose twitched like a rabbit's. "You been drinkin' a little beer, huh?"

"No," Brown said. "I have been drinkin' a whole hell of a lot of beer. I have already drunk almost two six-packs."

"Uh huh," Jake said encouragingly.

"I might just drink a couple more 'fore I gets through."

"Uh huh," Jake said skeptically. "You best hurry on then, or all the bars be closed."

"I ain't sweatin' none," Brown said. "I always come prepared. Cuts down on unwanted pregnancy."

Jake peered at him. "Beer?"

"That's right," Brown said.

"You got this beer up here?" Jake said.

"What you think, I goes someplace else to drink it? Course it's here."

"Uh huh," Jake said.

"You wanna hear the poem I just wrote?" Brown asked.

"I don't hear too good sometimes," Jake said.

"You want a beer?" Brown said in a whisper.

"Don't mind if I do," Jake said.

"I'm glad you're so fond of poetry," Brown said.

"All right, I'll listen to your goddamn pome."

"I appreciate that," Brown said. "Why don't you have a beer?" He reached down and pulled up a frosty can, popped the top, and handed it over.

Jake lowered himself onto the concrete walkway with a contented sigh. He sipped the beer. "Hey, damn, this here's still cold."

"Naturally," Brown said. "I don't like warm beer. Nobody does except Englishmen, and they are clearly insane."

"How you keep it cold?" Jake said, sipping with great interest.

"I drink it," Brown said, "as rapidly as is humanly possible." He pulled out a can, popped the top, and poured half the contents down his throat.

"You gonna get sick that way," Jake said.

"Never," Brown said. "Now, for the poem." Grasping his beer firmly, he climbed up and perched on the bridge railing. Jake stared up at him, mildly amazed. "This poem," Brown announced, "is called 'To a Sin-City.' " Brown pumped his arm for balance. "Whoops."

"After you kill your ass, can I keep the rest of the beer?" Jake asked.

"Only if you shut up an' listen to ma damn poem. I set here half the fuckin' night makin' up the muthafucka." Brown cleared his throat. "*In the sheer-walled canyons, beneath the glassy eyes of ten thousand windows, the City sings its lies. Hymns of patriotism, dirges of brotherly love, rounds of—*" Brown broke off. "Goddamn, I forgot it." He lowered himself and straddled the rail.

"You sit like that an' you subject to forget all about rememberin'," Jake said, helping himself to another beer.

"Hell," Brown said. "Well, anyway, here's another one: *A single smokestack, choking out its black despair on the rising sun.*" Brown stopped, looked expectantly at Jake. "Well? What you think?"

"Not bad. What is it?"

"Japanese haiku," Brown said.

"Imported, huh?" Jake said. "An' here I thought it was Schmidt's."

Brown looked at him, shook his head, dropped back to the walkway. He gulped the rest of his beer and tossed the can out over the railing.

"You hadn't oughta do that," Jake said.

"That river's so damn dirty already it don't make no difference."

"That's what the last guy threw a beer can in said."

Brown nodded. "You're right."

"At ma age," Jake said, "y'ain't got no time to waste bein' wrong."

"I read you, brother."

Jake looked at him. "You sure do talk funny."

Brown sighed, leaned back against the bridge railing, took out another can, opened it, and dropped the tab back into the bag, where it rattled against the full cans. "That's a nice sound," Jake said.

"I thought you didn't hear good," Brown snapped. "What you mean I talk funny?"

"Well, I don't know," Jake said. "Just sometimes you sound like everybody else, an' sometimes you sound like you pass the time readin' dictionaries." Brown snorted. "An' sometimes . . ." Jake stopped and looked at Brown.

"Sometimes what?"

"Nothin'."

"What?"

"All right. Sometimes you sound like you was speakin' Eyetalian or somethin'. You know, kinda like you was diggin' around for the right word." He looked at Brown anxiously. Brown nodded slowly. "It ain' 'zactly like you was makin' nothin' up or nothin'," Jake went on. "More like you was tryin' to remember somethin'."

Brown stared at him. "Where'd you come up with all this?"

Jake shrugged. "Only way you live to be ma age is by keepin' your eyes wide open an' both ears on the ground. I hear pretty good when I hear," Jake said modestly. He placed his empty beer can on the sidewalk beside his first one. Brown hospitably extracted another can and popped the top. "Put the tab inside," Jake said. "It improves the flavor." Brown shrugged, complied, and handed the can over. "Thank you," Jake said. He peered at the label. "Damn. It *is* Schmidt's. Thought you said it was some kinda Japanese typhoon or somethin'?"

"That," Brown said icily, "was the poem."

"Oh," Jake said. " 'Scuse ma ass. I don't know nothin' 'bout pomes. Or Japanese, neither. Rayburn's your man for that. Went there in the Koreen war. Said he drank socks an' ate octopuses an' fucked gushy girls."

"Do tell," Brown said shortly.

"I speaks a little French an' some Spanish an' a touch a Portuguese."

"Uh huh," Brown said.

"Bet you're wonderin' where I learned all that, ain'tcha?"

"Readin' the State Store price list," Brown said.

"Smart ass," Jake said. "I speaks Latin, too."

"Every damn nigger in the world speaks Latin," Brown said.

"Ooyay antkay," Jake said.

"Ukfay offnay," Brown replied.

Jake grunted and reached for another beer. "You can't do pomes worth shit," Jake said.

Brown set his beer down and glared.

"Them pomes sounded like a damn white man. You wanna hear a pome, now *I* got a—"

"Yeah," Brown said sarcastically, "let's hear a poem from the wino."

"Beero at the moment," Jake said easily, "an' you, youngblood, are miles ahead a me. I was young once too, you know."

"So what?"

"They don't call you a wino until you gets old an' smells bad an' sleeps in alleys. If you live in some room someplace, then you're just a common drunk, an' if you're young an' lives in an apartment, why then you're a heavy drinker." He paused and looked at Brown. Brown said nothing. "An'," Jake went on, "if you're white, you gets to be an alcoholic, an' if you're white an' rich an' you live in someplace like Bryn Mawr, then you ain't an alcoholic, you're a national problem." Jake sucked on his beer. "Bein' a wino ain't easy, you know. You gots to give up a lot to be a wino."

"Like what?" Brown said.

"Damn near everything, one time or another. You gots to work harder to be a wino than you does to be President. You got to give up—bein' reglar. Can't be worryin' 'bout no clothes. Can't be worryin' 'bout no car. Can't get uptight 'bout no house, or no job. Can't be too worried 'bout food. An' women—no women. I tell you, Brown, women's been the downfall a many a good wino. That's why it's hard for a young man to make the grade. Young man like you, you give him a choice 'tween gettin' drunk an' gettin' fucked, thirteen an' a half times outa fourteen he gonna get laid. It's a big temptation. But you take an old man like me, he don't get too much pussy tossed at him to begin with, an' when he does, ninety-two times outa a hundred an' four he'd rather drink. Eleven times outa them other twelve it's some fat old cunt been around so long it's like a cross between a sewer pipe an' a pickled egg, an' that one last time that he does get interested an' the woman's still warm an' got two legs an' don't look like a damn buffalo, he's either gonna come in his pants or hang there like a dead squirrel."

"Uh huh," Brown said. "That the way it is with you?"

"Hell, no, you silly-ass muthafucka!" Jake roared. "I ain't got no problems like that. I got women hangin' over me all the damn time. I just ain't after it no more. Women's too damn much trouble. I'll take me a bottle a red wine any time. It keeps you warmer, it don't keep on after you if you don't want no more, it don't wake y'up in the middle a the goddamn night an' it don't never complain if you roll over an' goes to sleep soon as you're done with it."

Brown laughed shortly and reached for another beer.

"Yessir, youngblood," Jake said. "All the time folks be tellin' you what's good for you. Guvment says you can't smoke without you catch cancer. Drinkin' does somethin' else to you, messes up your guts or somethin'. Shit. I tell you, youngblood, there's more niggers died climbin' onto some damn woman than ever died just sippin' a little wine. An' there's ten times as many died chasin' pussy as ever caught up to any. An' if you don't die chasin' it an' you don't die fuckin' it, then you get a goddamn ulcer worryin' 'bout who been gettin' into it when you ain't around."

"Don't worry me," Brown said.

"It will," Jake said. "You keep on chasin' pussy, specially the pussy you been chasin', an' it will."

Brown looked at him. "What—"

"I know what I know. You keep on chasin' pussy, an' sooner or later you end up dead. You so hot on poetry, I'ma give you a pome."

"All right," Brown said.

"First give me a beer." Brown handed it over. Jake cleared his throat. "You think I oughta stand up?"

"Why sure," Brown said. "You can't lay down heavy shit while you sittin' on your ass."

"Mostly I do lay down shit while I'm settin' on ma ass. But I guess this here's different."

"Definitely," Brown confirmed.

Jake nodded, rose carefully, pausing to rub his stomach. He swayed in the nonexistent breeze. "Damn, I'ma fall in the river." He took a swallow of beer. "You ready?"

"Lemme get another beer here."

"I'm the poet now, dammit," Jake snapped.

"All right, sorry," Brown said. He set his empty can down and rooted around in the bag.

"Ain't all gone, is it?" Jake said anxiously.

"Unh, unh," Brown said. "Can't be." He pulled out a full can, began to put the lined-up empties into the bag.

"Hell," Jake said impatiently. He staggered over and place-kicked the empties into the river. He spun around and glared at Brown. "You don't know shit about pomes, you know that? Why hell, that piss you was squirtin' a while ago didn't even half rhyme."

"Wasn't sposed to," Brown said.

"Well what damn kind a pome don't rhyme?" Jake demanded. "Now here's a pome for you. It rhymes. An' it's got, what you call it? A message. Yeah. See, too much pussy-chasin' turns a man into a fool. It turns his brain to oatmeal an' it makes him tend to drool, 'cause his mouth is gettin' mushy. An' he has a runny stool. An' he pisses out his money while he wears away his tool. See, when a nigger wants some nooky he's got to go through shit. Gots to give up all his gamblin' for a little squeeze a tit. He's gotta quit his cussin' just to pat a little ass, an' to get down to real fuckin' he puts water in his glass. But he goes ahead an' does it, 'cause he's hungry for a feast. He opens up his zipper an' he limbers up his piece an' he gets into that pussy, yeah, he proceeds to bang away. His joint is full a juju an' his ass is full a play an' he's snortin' an' he's gruntin' like a constipated hog while the stupid bitch is layin' there just like a half-dead log. Well he can bang away till midnight, fuck on to the risin' sun, but when he's damn near killed hisself she say, 'Baby? Are you done?' Oh he jumped on like a fuckin' lion, but he crawls off like a lamb, an' deep inside his gut he knows it wasn't worth a damn. Bet you thought I didn't know no pomes. Gimme a beer." Jake took a final swallow and tossed his can away with a Byronic flourish.

Brown took a deep breath, swallowed heavily. His expression was that of someone who bit into an apple pie and got a mouthful of black pepper. "No," Brown said weakly, "no, I figured you knew some poems." He handed Jake a beer.

"That there was a hell of a pome, wasn't it?"

"Oh yeah," Brown said quickly. "That's just exactly what it was."

"You oughta be makin' up pomes like that, 'stead a messin' around with them Japanese hootchikoos."

Brown raised his beer and took several deep swallows. Jake sniffed and, relaxing from his pose of recitation, leaned back against the heavy concrete barrier that sealed the sidewalk off from the street. Two feet away, through the cement, cars moved by, dropping off the crown of the bridge and into the depths of South Street. Jake sipped his beer. "This here's a damn fine spot for drinkin'. Can't nobody see what you're doin'. You could put a whole damn quart in one end an' piss it right out the other, all without movin' a step."

"Jake?" Brown said suddenly. "Is it like that all the time? A lot, I mean?"

"Like what?"

"The woman layin' there, not doin' nothin'."

"You a virgin or somethin'?" Jake asked.

"Or somethin'," Brown said.

"Whores a little outa your reglar line, huh? Now, now, I know what I know."

"Well, does it have to be that way?"

"How the hell would I know that? I don't know nothin' 'bout that kinda shit. You the young man, you sposed to think you know all about 'em. Well, lemme tell you one thing, there ain't nobody that knows nothin' 'bout women. Not even women. *'Specially* not women. *They* think they make sense. Believe me, ain't nobody knows nothin' 'bout women. Ain't nobody never did. Ain't nobody never gonna. Best thing's to get drunk whenever you around 'em. An' since there's always some woman poppin' up somewhere, the best thing to do is stay drunk. Pass an old man another beer."

Brown took Jake's empty can and put it into the bag. He handed Jake a fresh one. Jake popped the top, slurped at the foam that welled from the keyhole-shaped opening. "Drink faster, youngblood. This stuff's gettin' warm."

Brown raised his can half-heartedly but lowered it immediately. "Well, dammit, you gotta know somethin'."

"Have another beer," Jake said easily.

"I drink too much damn beer," Brown said.

"Hell," Jake said. He peered at Brown over the top of the can. "Some woman been on your ass 'bout drinkin'?"

"*I'm* on ma ass about drinkin'."

"If there's some woman ridin' your ass that hard, you best just leave her go. An' if you ridin' your own ass that hard, somethin's the matter with your brain. Probly too much—"

"Pussy," Brown finished for him. He swallowed the rest of his beer, reached into the bag and fumbled around. "Damn."

"Ain't no more?"

"Nope," Brown said. "We done killed it."

Jake dropped his eyes to the can he held in his hand. His fingers tightened slightly, then he shrugged. "You want some a this here?" He raised his eyes and looked at Brown.

Brown smiled slightly. "You go on," he said. "I had plenty."

Jake swallowed, hesitated. "You sure?"

"Yeah," Brown said. "You go ahead."

"All right," Jake said. He raised the can, drained it quickly, lowered it, belched. Brown reached out and took the can, added it to the collection in the bag, and then rose to his feet. The lights of the city twisted, the afterimage hanging on his eyes like splashed oil. Points of light moved, becoming multicolored streaks, and moving lights, on cars, an airplane, became thin sheets. Brown sank down again, closed his eyes. "Had a little much?" Jake inquired politely.

"Let's see you stand up an' walk a tightrope," Brown said sourly.

Jake sniffed and pushed to his feet. "See here, youngblood, I was—" He stopped, grabbed at his stomach.

"Jake?" Brown said. He got up quickly.

"Ain't nothin'," Jake said. "Just ma goddamn guts actin' funny on account a all that beer. Ain't used to it." He straightened up, grunting. "I gotta piss." He reached for his fly.

"Here?" Brown said. "What if the cops go by?"

"Why then we wouldn't hafta piss on the bridge, we could piss on them." Jake stepped to the railing and opened his pants. He looked at Brown. "Ain't you got to go too?" Brown nodded, swallowed, stepped to the railing. A single stream of urine arched out into the darkness. "Ah," Jake said enviously. "Onliest bad thing about bein' old is it takes you half the night to get a piss goin'." He grunted with effort.

By the time Jake turned away from the railing, clumsily zipping his pants, Brown was leaning uncomfortably against the concrete barrier, looking around uneasily. Jake smiled a smile that suddenly became a grimace of pain. He turned, pushed past Brown, and started to shuffle down off the bridge, clutching at himself. Brown stared at him, caught up the bag of empties, and hurried after. Jake staggered against the railing, recovered, plowed on, and Brown could hear him breathing in short, adenoidal gasps. "Hey," Brown panted. Jake staggered on, his pace increasing as the bridge sloped off into the gentle curve that led to the street. Brown broke into a run and caught up to him, but the narrow space between barrier and railing kept him from pulling even, so Brown moved along behind in an awkward combination of run, stagger, and ballet as he tried to keep from tripping over Jake's run-over heels. "Will you slow down, you silly-ass bastard?" Brown shouted. Jake obeyed immediately—his legs folded under him and he collapsed to the cement. Brown tried to stop, couldn't, tried to jump over him, misjudged the curve of the bridge and, while in mid-air, slammed his hip against the outer railing. Visions of falling over into the river crossed his mind just before his knees made contact with the sidewalk. His vision went red from shock and pain—the cement was like warm sandpaper. He pushed himself up on his hands. A few feet away Jake lay across the metal plate that linked the bridge walkway with South Street's sidewalk, looking like a heap of old clothes rejected by the Salvation Army. Brown crawled toward him. Beer cans lay strewn all around like the twisted metal plane crash. Brown brushed them aside. The heap of clothes moaned softly, twitched, and clutched at its middle.

"Hey," Brown said. "Jake." Jake moaned. Brown got to his feet and stood staring down, rubbing his hands against his pants and swallowing. Jake belched, and the heady aroma of his breath—fresh beer, sour wine—rose like a visible cloud. Brown's nostrils twitched. "Jake?" he said again. Jake made no response. Brown sniffed uneasily, dropped to one knee, wincing at the pain, as the abraded skin came in contact with the sidewalk. "Wake up," Brown commanded desperately. Jake moaned his insubordination. Brown set his jaw, swallowed, reached out and grasped Jake's arm. He was shocked at the greasy feel of Jake's sweater but fought the urge to jerk his hand away; instead, he worked it through the layers of clothing until he found Jake's shoulder, thin and harshly bony. Brown squeezed and shook gently. "Hey." Jake moaned.

Brown looked around at the empty street. Beyond the barrier a car swept past. Brown swallowed, took a deep breath, reached out his other hand, and began to unpile the rags that contained Jake. He pulled the pipe-cleaner-thin legs out straight, lowered the cuff of a trouser leg that had ridden up exposing an indecent ashy band of skin above a dirty sock. He tried to spread out the limp arms but even in unconsciousness Jake hugged his belly tightly, as if trying to hold his guts in. Brown gave up on the arms. He loosened the ties of Jake's shoes, peering close to make out the complicated collage of knots that served as strings, gagging at the smell that escaped the holey leather. Then he undid Jake's greasy purple necktie and unbuttoned the collar of Jake's grimy flannel shirt. "Damn," Jake wheezed weakly. "Let a man fall down one time an' right away somebody's either tryin' to rob him or give him a blowjob." Brown gasped and leaped back, caught his heel, and sprawled on his rear end.

"Y'old bastard!" Brown muttered, getting up. "All that play-actin'—"

He stopped as the light from a passing car showed him the pain on Jake's face. "What's the matter with you?"

"Nothin'," Jake said. "It's just ma goddamn guts. I ain't gonna be dyin' or nothin', so don't get your damn hopes up."

"I ain't," Brown said. "I don't give a damn if you live forever. That's why I'ma take you to a hospital. Layin' where you are, you're a goddamn traffic hazard."

"Well, you just hazard your ass on outa here, nigger, 'cause I ain't goin' to no damn hospital."

"You need one," Brown said. "And I'm going to take you there if I have to carry you."

Jake looked up at him. "Think you could stand to touch a smelly old wino that long?" Brown's eyes dropped. "Damn," Jake went on, "who the hell made you Jesus Christ anyways? You want to get me somethin' that'll make me feel better, you go . . ." He stopped, looked at Brown suspiciously.

"Go where?" Brown said.

"Go to hell," Jake said.

"Huh?"

"Gone, get outa here an' leave me be." Jake pushed himself, groaning and gasping, to his feet. "I know what I need, an' I know where to get it, an' you just keep the hell away from me, 'cause I know what you're after." Brown looked mystified. Grumbling, Jake turned and shuffled off up the street, clutching his middle and, from time to time, looking back over his shoulder to make sure Brown was not following.

Before he finally made it to the bedroom Rayburn had vomited on the stairs, vomited on the landing, vomited in his living room and in the kitchen sink, had dry-heaved above the unflushed toilet bowl. When his stomach at last ceased its twistings and jerkings, Rayburn waved his hand vaguely at the flush lever, catching it with his fingertips just as he lost his balance. He used what little coordination he retained to pull his face back away from the bowl; his falling dragged his hand across the lever and flushed the mess away. An unpleasant odor wafted gently from the toilet—Rayburn, on the floor, his cheek against the cold cracked linoleum, his lips against unyielding porcelain, retched again before dragging himself into the bedroom. He threw one arm over the edge of the bed and managed to raise his torso a few inches before the aged bedsprings creaked and dumped him back on the floor.

He lay quietly then, in the midst of a cliché: a neon light outside the window sending red light across the rumpled sheets of an unmade bed, blinking on and off, on and off, like an electric pulse. Rayburn's own blood pounded in his temples, his lungs sucked in the heavy hot air, forcing out vomit-soured breath which made the dust devils hiding beneath the bed, tinted pink by the blinking light, dance drunkenly across the floor. The sign went on and off. Rayburn breathed and pulsed and fought the urge to defecate in his pants. Inside his head, beneath the dull gray sheath of alcohol, a portion of his brain looked around at him and his surroundings and chuckled derisively. "Shup," Rayburn mumbled, moving dry lips across dusty floor. The laughter sounded again—bright, hard, not-quite-musical, like the whine of an overloaded motor. "Shup," Rayburn said. He opened his eyes. The flickering light stabbed back behind his eyeballs—on and off. Rayburn's eyes blinked closed and open, exactly out of phase, and all he saw was red-tinged darkness, and all he heard was the scratching sound as his eyelash brushed the floor.

But gradually other sounds came through the darkness. The light outside hummed almost inaudibly and made a small sound like a tiny bell ringing in cotton each time it went on and off. His stomach sloshed its juices, and his pulse beat bass. From above him, through the ceiling, came the sounds of light footsteps, then a groaning as the floor accepted a shift in weight from feet to bed. Some woman, Rayburn thought, some woman up there. He listened for more sounds from above him, slowing his own breathing, fighting to control the hollow gurglings and empty rumblings in his stomach, cursing the cottoned-bell ting and electric hum of the neon light, trying to hear if there were other feet up there moving around, or in the bed, wiggling toes pointed toward the ceiling beside the woman's toes, or down, above the woman's curling toes. Rayburn listened carefully and decided that the woman was up there by herself, her body lying in the night's heavy heat, covered only by a sheet thrown carelessly across her legs. The sweat would be gathered in the hollows of her body—in the armpits, under the flare of the nose, in the warm folds of elbow and knee, beneath the breasts, behind the ears, between the toes, in the tender creases where pudendum met thigh, in the navel. Now, just now, Rayburn knew, the sweat would be gathering, conjured by heat, preserved by humidity. It would be, Rayburn knew, not quite fresh, but not stale; it would be sliding along the thin edge between ripe and rotten, pungent and putrid. She would be lying half-awake, her body swollen with sleep, her legs heavy, her thighs parting at the slightest pressure, her mind unable either to accept or reject. Now was the time to come to her, when she was alone and unaware.

He levered himself off the floor and sat in the blinking darkness for a moment, his head throbbing, the wide-awake part of him jumbled, confused. Above him, she was waiting. He felt his body stiffen, knew the need to hurry before all the firm ripeness became overripe—too soft, too sweet. He stretched out a hand to the wall, the other to the bed, forced himself to his feet, staggered into the living room. He stood at the door, leaning against it, thinking about her up there waiting, conscious of him as he was of her, waiting and wondering why he did not come, what was taking him so long. He fumbled with the doorknob, dropping to his knees as he tripped in his spoor of vomit, and hit his head against the wall. He paused to let his brain steady, and clutching at himself with his hands he thought about her lying there, heaving, humping the air, thighs parted, love juices mingling with sweat, fingers writhing over mouth, breasts, belly, plunging into the juicy cleft, pumping wildly for an instant before flying up to cover the mouth that called his name. His hand found the doorknob, twisted the wrong way, twisted back. He pulled on the door, realized he was leaning on it, moved back and stopped suddenly. He heard the street door open. Footsteps, heavy, mounted the stairs. A voice cursed as the footsteps paused on the landing outside Rayburn's door. Rayburn trembled. There was the sound of a shoe sole scraping on wood accompanied by more cursing, then the footsteps continued to climb, reaching the hallway above. Rayburn heard a door open.

Wide-eyed, wide-mouthed, Rayburn stumbled along beneath the footsteps, following them into the bedroom again. Shoes hit the floor, a belt buckle. Rayburn stood in the flickering light staring upward at the ceiling, holding his breath. He heard the creak of depressing bedsprings, the light murmur of voices. He groaned and half staggered to his own empty, sour-smelling bed, fell onto it and lay, spread-eagle, staring up at the pink ceiling that flickered into being every second or so to hang there for a second or so. Rayburn listened to the mocking voices above him, the filtered alto and bass, and hated them. Then the voices faded, stopped, and he hated them even more. Above him the bedsprings creaked once and then were silent. Rayburn rolled onto his side, Rayburn's bedsprings, too, groaned. But then, above him, the springs creaked again, not once but many times, in the slow cadence of love. Rayburn turned and lay staring once again, the rhythm from above him descending slowly, heavily, out of time with the quick electric flickerings of the neon light. Rayburn thought of the motions above. He closed his eyes, shut out the teasing light. Slowly, in time with the rocking rhythm, he unzipped his fly, unbuttoned his pants, unbuckled his belt, sought inside his underwear with cold dry hands. He caressed his body gently to the slow cadence of the bedsprings, thinking of the woman—her flesh, which had been quietly perspiring into the heat and solitude, now sleek with moisture, salty like the sea, every pore a fountain, every hollow a pool, her mouth twisting, her fingers caressing him, stroking him. Rayburn felt himself harden and grow, thinking of her, feeling her hands upon him. And then he opened his eyes. The pink ceiling materialized above him and Leslie's face smiled down at him. He felt shame, knowing his hands were on his body, but he kept on, fighting, forcing his mind to the woman above. But it was no use. His hands abraded. His body softened.

Above him the bedsprings creaked creaked and squealed in frenzy for a few moments, then resumed to another rhythm slower still, deeper, before subsiding into silence. Rayburn rolled onto his stomach, then back, lay in the intermittent light, one hand hanging to the floor, the other balled loosely over his groin. The ceiling appeared, disappeared, reappeared above his head. He closed his eyes, but the light came through, dim and mocking. He rolled and lay facing the wall. The light blinked on and off. Mesmerized by that rhythm, he slept.

The window was open, sucking in great syrupy draughts of dirty air, sounds, smells, South Street. Vanessa lay on the sagging mattress, her body covered by a single sheet and a layer of sweat scented with powder, flavored with salt. Her mind flowed out into the darkness, searching for Brown.

She had climbed uneasily up the stairs, knocked hesitantly on the door. There had been no answer. She had thought to go away. She had knocked again. Then she had gone in.

In his absence, Brown's rooms did not reek of him. She had wandered through them—kitchen, bedroom, bath—trying to find something that would tell her that Brown and no one else lived there. Brown was not spectacularly neat. The garbage bag in the kitchen was full to overflowing with quart beer bottles and odds and ends of paper. She got a feeling of Brown from that. But the trappings of the room could have belonged to anyone—a greasy skillet in the sink, a fork, a cloudy glass, a coffeepot. The bedroom was much the same—a pair of cheap black shoes set close together but at an odd angle, as if they were being worn by an invisible cripple, a pair of blue jeans, two pairs of black pants. In the drawers a few badly folded white handkerchiefs, white tee shirts, black socks, a half-dozen new nylon shirts. Drip dry. Permanent press. The bathroom: shorts, a jockstrap over the tub edge. A Gillette razor. Wilkinson blades. Lifebuoy soap. Prell shampoo. Right Guard deodorant. In the medicine cabinet Bayer aspirin and Alka-Seltzer   .

In the kitchen she sat in one of Brown's hard chairs, took a deep breath, and opened the drawer beneath the table. She had to pull hard—the drawer stuck, as if it were trying to resist her—she forced it, then stared uneasily at the sheaf of poems inside. She longed to rip the poems up, to dump them out the window into the alley below. She poked around in the drawer, found something she had missed. It was another poem, not on the yellow lined sheets like the others, but on the panel of a paper bag. She remembered seeing it before, but it was different now—Brown had been over it, changed it somehow. It was about South Street. She didn't understand why anyone would want to write a poem about South Street—South Street was someplace you tried to forget. But she read the poem, trying to understand not it, but Brown, tried to imagine him coming off the bridge, moving—not walking or riding, just moving, running maybe—down South Street. She read the poem with that picture in her mind. He would move quickly at first, his feet hardly touching the ground, but then he would slow, float like the shadow cast by a cloud as it drifted across the sun. It didn't sound like Brown thought South Street was pretty, but it did sound as if he thought it was beautiful. And it sounded as though he hated it, in his own way, as much as she did.

She had been startled by the sound of the lower door opening, footfalls on the stairway. Brown. She froze for an instant, then began to put the papers quickly back into the drawer. He would hate her for touching them. She pushed at the drawer but it stuck again. She panicked, shoved it. It wouldn't go. She felt tears of frustration in her eyes, but then she realized that the steps had halted. Below, a door opened, closed with a bang. The sound echoed, faded. Vanessa pushed at the drawer. It slid obediently shut.

She sat there for a few minutes, wondering why Brown frightened her when Leroy did not, when all the drunks and junkies lined up from one end of South Street to the other did not. She had risen from the table and turned out the lights, drifting in darkness back into the bedroom. She took off her clothes, hanging them neatly in the closet. She had turned down the sheet, climbed onto the bed, and lay, listening, breathing.

South Street stole through the open window, a sour-sweet stench in the soggy air, covered her body with a layer of moisture. Vanessa lay in the heavy heat searching the darkness with her eyes, trying to find what Brown found in it, in half-dead winos and garbage piles, trying to understand what was so inspiring about elephantine cockroaches and rats the size of cannon shells. It made no sense to her. She was tired of picking up magazines and reading articles about the ghetto. All they talked about was rats and roaches. Brown was crazy. She didn't give a damn. Among the trash cans and garbage in the alley below, a hungry animal—cat, dog, wino—foraged. She wondered what was down there, what it was looking for.

She had drifted off to sleep when Brown came in. He smelled her heavy perfume. He smiled to himself, closed the door, slipped off his shoes, and padded into the bedroom. He stood above the bed, looking down at her. The sweat had soaked into the sheet, and as his eyes adjusted to the dark Brown could see the wrinkled whiteness clinging to her dark, smooth curves, her skin altering the sheet's color, adding a bluish cast. Brown set his shoes down carefully, slipped quietly out of the rest of his clothing, or tried to—the beer had affected his coordination—eased onto the bed, lay congratulating himself on his quietness.

"You mad?" Vanessa said.

Brown jumped. "Goddamn! Can't spooks say nothin' 'cept boo all the damn time?"

"Sorry," Vanessa said. "I forgot you was so damn jumpy."

"I ain't," Brown said. "I just got hair-trigger reflexes."

Vanessa snorted. "Well, are you?"

"Am I what?"

"Mad."

"No," Brown said. "I am drunk. If I acted the way I act when I'm drunk when I was sober instead of acting the way I act when I'm sober, then maybe I'd be mad. But since I only act the way I act when I'm drunk when I'm drunk, I am usually not considered mad. It is the measure of our sick society that a man is not considered insane so long as he only acts that way when he is drunk, and acts sober when he is sober. But not too sober. True sober behavior is threatening."

"Anybody ever tell you you talk a whole lot an' don't never make no damn sense?"

"How can you expect me to make sense when I'm drunk? I make perfect sense when I'm sober."

"I ain't never *seen* you sober," Vanessa said.

"And with the luck of Ananse, you never will."

"Who the hell is Nancy?"

Brown laughed. "Never mind."

"I knocked," Vanessa said defensively.

"What?"

"I knocked. You wasn't here, so I just thought I'd come in an' wait—"

"An' then you got sleepy an' crawled into bed. That's fine. I like that. Only don't bust ma chair an' eat up ma goddamn porridge."

Vanessa giggled. "How 'bout if I turn into a pumpkin?"

"It's a little late for that," Brown said.

"A warm pumpkin."

"How warm?"

"Warm."

Brown rolled onto his side, shifted closer to her, and laid his hand on her belly. She sighed, rolled, backed up against him. Brown stroked her hip, his exhalation tickling her neck. "Brown?" she said.

"Um hum?"

"You goin' to sleep?"

"Course," Brown said. "What the hell else do drunks do?"

"Oh."

"Why you ask?"

"Well, I just didn't want you to think you had to—you know. I mean, I just come up here to be—"

"Anybody ever tell you you talk a whole lot an' don't make no damn sense?"

"But I—"

"Shup."

She waited tensely for him to begin, for the hand that fondled her hip to move on, for his other hand to make the inevitable journey to limp nipples, but Brown's hands stayed where they were, only the one hand softly stroking. She felt all the tension concentrate on that one hand, sensing the slightest variation in the stroke. The tension coiled inside her and she thought she couldn't stand it. She squirmed, made impatient sounds, tried to twist and force his hand down. "Shhh," Brown said. She quieted, tried to relax. She felt as if she were going to sleep. She felt faintly bored. She wondered if she preferred boredom to frustration. She felt Brown's body pressed against her back, his legs against her legs, his knees in the hollows of her knees, his chin cradled between her shoulder blades. She felt a small urge to scratch somewhere, but she lacked the energy. She felt a slight desire to go to the bathroom, but she did not want to move. She imagined she was paralyzed, that her legs and arms would not work. Then she felt a wetness spring up between her thighs, a slow excitement. She felt Brown, as if suddenly sensing her arousal, come erect and press gently against her buttocks. She tried to roll over but Brown held her where she was, continued with his strokings. She breathed shortly as if she had a pain in her chest. Brown slid lower, insinuated himself between her thighs. She felt him enter her, waited for the usual barrier to come down over her body. It did not. She stared into the darkness, feeling him moving in her, knowing who it was, but seeing no one before her, above her. She felt a sudden lightness, demanding release. The bed rocked. She felt herself softening, felt her body dissolve, tried to hold herself and let go at the same time. She felt a shiver in her belly and her eyes closed, the eyeballs tried to push through the lids. And then the barrier did come down. She hardened. She waited, her body still lubricated, pumping mechanically, until Brown gasped, thrust, subsided. She was glad he was behind her.

"That was good," she said, making her voice furry.

"Don't lie," Brown said. "You don't need to lie."

"It almost worked."

"Sooner or later," Brown said.

"It's easy for you to say that, dammit!"

"Yep," Brown said. "It's easy for me to say that."

"It almost worked." She stared into the night. "Hey," she said after a while. "You asleep?"

"Yeah," Brown said.

10 Friday

Leroy Briggs descended the stairs at the unprecedented hour of 10:00 a.m., causing a minor stir in the nearly unoccupied lobby of the Elysium Hotel; the desk clerk stared and stopped eating his breakfast—a bean pie purchased from his friendly *Muhammed Speaks* man—and Willie T. looked up from his copy of the *Wall Street Journal.* "Mornin', men," said Leroy in a John Wayne voice.

The desk clerk nodded respectfully.

"Mornin'," said Willie T. "Somethin' wrong?"

"Like what?"

"You're up pretty early."

"It's gonna be a long day. We got work to do. Come on, Willie, I'ma take you out an' buy us some breakfast." Leroy grinned toothily.

"But, but, but," stuttered Willie T., "it ain't but ten o'clock. The bars ain't open yet."

"I know that, fool. That's how come I always stay in bed till noon. But today I want me some *real* breakfast."

"You mean," Willie T. gasped, *"food?"*

"Well, Willie, you can eat whatever pleases you, s'long as it ain't attached to me. But, yeah, I want me some food. I want me some ham, an' some eggs, an' some grits—"

"Grits? What the hell's grits?" said Willie T.

Leroy looked at him and shook his head sadly. Willie T. gulped and clumsily folded his paper. "What you read that shit for anyways?" Leroy demanded. "*Wall Street Journal*, shit. Ain't no nigger never made no million dollars in the damn stock market. 'Sides, everybody knows how to get rich: buy low, sell high, pay your protection, an' kill any muthafucka that gets in the way. Now come on, Willie, quit fuckin' with that honky paper an' let's get it on." Leroy sniffed disdainfully and stepped out into the mid-morning sunlight. "Damn," he said, and blinking, pulled on his sunglasses. "These things don't work worth shit. Somebody been fuckin' with ma shades. I ain't seen the sun this strong in weeks."

"You ain't been outside in the daytime in weeks," Willie T. said.

"What you mean by that shit?" Leroy asked mildly.

"Ain't nobody never made no million dollars playin' no numbers, either," Willie T. said.

Leroy turned to look at him. "Now, Willie," Leroy said patiently. "I realize that maybe I ain't been as *active* as I mighta been lately. I know I been lettin' things slide a little, not taken care a business the way I shoulda been. I heard about them stories been goin' around 'bout how I done lost it. But, Willie, those folks been talkin' like that just don't know me that well, an' I'ma have to spend the day gettin' better acquainted. But you," Leroy smiled broadly and Willie T. felt his spine turn to jello, "you sposed to be knowin' me, Willie." Leroy's smile faded to be replaced by a look of profound sorrow, a look that was matched by the regret in Leroy's voice. "You ain't sposed to be listenin' to no tales. You ain't sposed to be thinkin' ole Leroy done turned into a chocolate marshmallow. You sposed to know that ain't hardly the case. You do know, don't you, Willie?" There was a note of pleading in Leroy's voice.

"Sure," said Willie T., almost curtly.

"Sure what?"

"Sure, I know," Willie T. said patiently. "Umpghfk," he added, as Leroy's left fist made violent contact with his unprotected face. "I, uglumfhgth," he went on, as Leroy planted a kick in his belly with sufficient force to score a field goal from seventy yards out.

"Sure, boss," Leroy coached gently.

"Ahh," said Willie T. from his position on the sidewalk. Blood trickled slowly from his mangled nose.

Leroy toed him. "That ain't quite right," Leroy said.

"Sure, boss," Willie T. gasped.

"That's fine, Willie," Leroy said, beaming. " 'Yes, sir' might be a small improvement, but we wouldn't want to get too formal, do we?"

"No, sir," groaned Willie T.

Leroy grinned. "I just *hate* kickin' ass on an empty stomach. That's why we gone go have us some breakfast. Your teeth okay?" Willie T. looked up at him resentfully. "I'm sorry I had to do that to you now, Willie, I really am. But you was gettin' *so* damn uppity. Now you go wash your face an' we go grease." Willie T. picked himself up and started back into the Elysium. "Don't be all day now," Leroy said. "There's lots more assholes gotta be reacquainted with Leroy Briggs." Willie T.'s pace increased perceptibly. "Hold it," Leroy barked. Willie T. stopped dead in his tracks. "Never mind washin' your face. We'll use you as a sample."

Willie T. turned to face him, wiped blood out of his eye. "Shall I get the car, boss?"

Leroy shook his head. "Naw. We gonna walk."

"Walk?"

"Uh huh." Leroy grinned wolfishly and set off in the direction of the North Carolina Bar-B-Q. Willie T. trailed lamely. "Yes, sir," Leroy said, squinting ahead of him at the shimmering concrete, "we gonna get with the times. We gonna have us a damn teach-in. We gonna give everybody a little elementary education, then we gonna pick out a few a them loud-mouthed cunt-lickers an' send 'em to high school. If they don't get the message, we may have to get 'em a scholarship to college. An' then, I'ma find that fuckin' Brown an' graduate his ass clean to hell."

Willie T., scurrying along beside him, stared. "We goin' after Brown, boss, for real?"

"Unh unh, Willie. *We* ain't goin' after Brown. *I* am goin' after Brown. He's all mine."

"But what if he works for Gino like he said?"

"He don't work for no Gino."

"How do you know?" Willie T. demanded.

Leroy stopped and turned. "Your nose stopped bleedin' yet? Must have, 'cause, nigger, you startin' to forget already. I say the nigger gets spent. An' I say I'ma be the one that spends him. An' I say he don't work for no damn Gino. An' if I say it's so, it's so."

Willie T. cautiously took a step backward before he said, "You say the sky's purple, that don't make it purple."

Leroy sniffed and considered the argument. "Willie, look at the sky." Willie T. looked up at the sky. "What color is it?"

"Blue," Willie T. reported.

"Right," Leroy agreed. "But in a minute now, you keep lookin', it's gonna change color. It's gonna be purple." Leroy reached out and grasped Willie T.'s crotch, firmly, but without squeezing. "What color is it now?" Leroy asked mildly.

"Purple," Willie T. said promptly.

Smiling, Leroy released him and headed off to the Delmonaco to prepare for a busy day.

The Elysium's barroom buzzed into Friday night—buzzed with the news of Leroy's miraculous rejuvenation. Leroy, everyone agreed, casting thoughtful glances at a morose and black-eyed Willie T., who sat in a corner drinking Coke and pondering Leroy's novel approach to higher education, had made a dramatic recovery. By actual count he had bashed fourteen noses, bloodied seven heads, blackened eleven eyes, broken two arms, sprained one ankle, kicked innumerable posteriors, and inflicted multitudinous lacerations, contusions, and abrasions in his campaign to reassure South Street of the degree of his control. Willie T. had watched the entire demonstration, trembling every time Leroy raised his shoe over the writhing and bloody form of a thoroughly convinced lackey, preparatory to tramping out his message with a terrible swift kick in the groin. Willie T. was not particularly bothered by the carnage, but he shuddered to consider what the rewards for his own insolence might have been. Injuries, serious and superficial, had at first been left behind Leroy like the trail of a tornado, but as the day had worn on and the word had spread that Leroy was on the rampage, various individuals had begun to do themselves bodily harm in desperate attempts to get out of the way. Leroy's day on the warpath had provided the emergency rooms of three different hospitals with quite a few lively moments. Apart from the mundane injuries, there was the crushed pelvis sustained by Harry the Hype as, in an effort to escape an advancing Leroy, he had tripped over the putrefying carcass of a deceased cat and fallen into the path of the only garbage truck that had been seen on South Street in some two and one-half months. That case had gone to Graduate Hospital. The interns at Philadelphia General had been confounded by the condition of Fast Freddy Fennel, whom Leroy had surprised while he was enjoying the professional courtesies of a lady of the evening. Leroy had grasped Fast Freddy firmly by neck and scrotum and had held his face tightly against the prostitute's somewhat pungent pudendum. Fast Freddy had passed out. Leroy had waited patiently for him to revive, passing the time by discussing the weather and the problems of the small-business person with the lady. Each time Fast Freddy had come to, Leroy had shoved him under again. Following the fourth submersion, Fast Freddy had suffered a mild fit. Leroy had personally summoned an ambulance, and Fast Freddy had been rushed off to intensive care. Leroy had politely finished off what Fast Freddy had begun, had complimented the young lady on her competence, and had paused for a slug of gin for lunch before setting off in search of one Twinkletoes Johnson, a homosexual booster, whom he had discovered in a deli at Fourth and Bainbridge, in intimate conversation with an Italian queen. Enraged by the incipient miscegenation, Leroy had thrown Twinkletoes belly-down over a table and had slit his pants up the back with a meat cleaver. Some minutes later the emergency-room staff at the Pennsylvania Hospital, though used to extracting odd items such as shot glasses, light bulbs, and six-ounce coffee jars from the anuses of the neighborhood's gay denizens, were somewhat shocked when, with much farting and groaning on the part of the patient and much tugging and swearing on the part of the attendants, Twinkletoes' bowels had disgorged three and a quarter pounds of knockwurst.

Leroy's program had been an unqualified success. South Street trembled where Leroy walked. Satisfied, he had returned to the Elysium around four in the afternoon, just as black clouds began to drift in over the city from the east. He had mounted the stairs to his chambers, where he had mounted Leslie and, after spurring onward for some time, he knocked her out onto the floor, consumed half a bottle of Beefeater, and went to sleep.

Some time later Leslie had descended the stairs, clad in a pair of sprayed-on pants that showed the curl of her pubic hair and a halter so brief it exhibited every bruise that Leroy had lavished upon her. She sat at her usual table and looked across the barroom at the morose Willie T., envying him his twin shiners. She had, with artful use of eyeshadow, managed to suggest yellow-green bruises around her own eyes, but the skin was not puffy and the color was not quite right, and close inspection would have convinced anyone that Leroy had failed to actually hit her—he had merely kicked her out of bed. Being kicked out of bed was, Leslie felt, all right, but it fell short of the true and total commitment in her relationship with Leroy that would have been symbolized by a pair of black eyes. Still, she did have a very ugly bruise on her back—no one could find anything phony about that—and she was more or less content. She reached across the table for one of Charlene's cigarettes, wincing pleasurably at the tenderness of her muscles.

"Damn if I'd let any man do that to me," Charlene said.

"Ain't any man," Leslie said. "It's Leroy."

"I don't care who it is," Charlene said. "Any nigger lays a hand on me, he's gonna be drawin' back a nub."

"Humph," Leslie said.

"I mean to hit me," Charlene clarified.

"An' if it wasn't a nigger, you wouldn't mind?'

"Shit," Charlene said, "you know I ain't gonna be messin' with no slimy honkies. They send me ma check every month, an' I don't got to be screwin' nobody for it. Mister Charlie sign his John Henry on the bottom line, an' that'll be as close to his ass as I'ma be comin'. An' I still ain't gonna be lettin' no nigger be bangin' me around."

Leslie looked at her and raised her eyebrows.

"You know what I mean," Charlene said.

Leslie smiled. "It's just Leroy's way," she said.

"Leroy's way gonna get him knifed in the back."

"By who? They all scared."

"Ain't nobody scared a nobody's back in the dark," Charlene said. "If I was you I'd go on back to Rayburn. He's your husband."

"Uh huh," Leslie agreed. "An' Leroy's ma *man*. Leroy walks up an' down, Rayburn sorta shuffles, like he's sorry to dirty the street. Leroy wants somethin', he takes it. Rayburn wants somethin'—lemme tell you. I 'member one time Rayburn wanted a radio, you know, one a them little transistor things, fit in your pocket? So the fool sees one he likes in the store window. Twenty-three dollars. Fool starts savin'. Two dollars an' thirty cent a week. Ten weeks later he goes down to the store with his twenty-three dollars in his hot little fist. Only he done forgot the sales tax. Five per cent. Dollar fifteen. So he waits another week. Goes on down. Twenty-four fifteen. Only they done raised the damn price. Twenty-eight ninety-nine. He comes on back, keeps on savin'. Two weeks later I hear they gonna raise the sales tax. I says to maself, Jesus, I can't stand no more a this. So I went on down an' stole me one a them radios. Gave it to him. Won't work. Needs batteries. Don't you know the crazy fool went back to the *same* store wantin' to know didn't the batteries come with it or did he have to buy 'em separate. Called the cops, but they couldn't believe *anybody'd* be that damn dumb, so they let him go. Cops kept the radio."

"That's sad," Charlene said.

"That's Rayburn," Leslie snorted. "He'd starve in a supermarket. Ain't 'cause he's honest, it's 'cause he's so dumb he can't even do nothin' wrong right."

"Well, maybe he ain't much, but at least he didn't beat you."

"Sure he did. I made him. Only he couldn't do that right, neither. Lemme tell you—"

"Oh yeah. Tell us."

Charlene looked up. Leslie resisted the urge to spin around. " 'Nessa, some day somebody's gonna kill you, you keep on sneakin' around like that."

Vanessa walked around and slid onto a chair. "I ain't sneakin', I just naturally move quiet." She smiled and signaled to the bartender. "Leroy been usin' your back to park his Cadillac on?"

"He's been parkin' her on her back," Charlene said disgustedly, "on the floor."

"From what I hear that's Les's most usual position—on her back on the bed, on the floor, on the table, on the street—"

"Shup," Leslie said.

"—over garbage cans, on a pool table—"

"I said, shut up."

"Why sure, honey, only don't you want me to tell Charlene 'bout the time I seen you ticklin' your pussy with a rat?"

"I don't want you to tell me about it," Charlene said.

"Oh, it wasn't *weird* or nothin'," Vanessa assured her. "I mean the rat was dead."

Charlene, looking a little ill, went off to the ladies' room. "You'd think she'd be used to me by now," Vanessa said mildly. She paid for her drink, plucked the pineapple off the top, and ate it.

"Leroy's been on the rampage," Leslie said.

"So I hear."

"I don't think he'll bother you, long as you keep outa his way."

"Little sister, Leroy ain't gonna do nothin' to me. An' you better do like I told you: find out where some bodies is buried 'fore them lovetaps he's been givin' you get a little harder. Leroy can get kinda strange."

Leslie swallowed heavily. "This afternoon he come in, you know, after he done beat up half the world? He had this big gun. Looked like a cannon."

"Leroy don't carry no gun," Vanessa said. "If he can't scare the piss outa it or beat the shit outa it or run it down with his car, he calls it Jesus an' tries to forget about it."

"He's got a gun now," Leslie said. She finished her drink in one gulp and called for another. She waited silently until it was set before her. "When he came in," she said, staring down at the glass, "he grabbed me an' ripped ma dress right off." She looked up at Vanessa. "Ain't nobody had to bother rapin' me in *years*, you know?" Vanessa nodded silently. "Well. After he got done, he pulled out the gun an' tries to stick it up inside me. I wouldn't let him, so he gave me the gun an' made me do it maself. He said it was all right, the safety was on an' 'sides it wasn't loaded. He made me. Then he takes the gun back an' sits there an' loads the damn thing, an' then he makes me do it again. He said it was okay, the safety was on. Then he takes the gun back and clicks the safety off. An' then he come for me again." Leslie shuddered and dropped her eyes.

"You didn't like it?" Vanessa said innocently.

"Not with the safety off. 'Nessa, you think maybe Leroy might be goin' a little bit crazy?"

Vanessa stared at her for a half a minute, then burst out laughing. "What's so funny?" Charlene demanded, depositing herself on her chair.

"Nothin'," Leslie mumbled.

"Honey," Vanessa chuckled, "honey, where in Jesus have you been? Everybody on the whole damn street knows Leroy's crazy. Been crazy. For years. Ain't that right, Charlene?"

Charlene's eyes were fixed on a point somewhere above and behind Vanessa's head. "Oh, I don't know. He seems fine to me."

"Well he don't seem fine to nobody got no sense. You ask him, Les. Ask him how come he don't never get offa the Street. All he does is get in that damn Cadillac an' drive down to the river, then roll on over to Bainbridge an' come right back up. He don't never go north a Naudain Street. He don't never go west a Twenty-fourth. Ask him how come. Ask him how come he shits every time he sees a white man."

"Why don't you ask him, 'Nessa?" Charlene said carefully.

"Yeah," Leroy boomed, "why don't you ask me?"

Vanessa turned around slowly. "Evenin', Leroy. I don't have to ask, I already know."

"I don't leave South Street 'cause there ain't no other place to go that's worth the trouble a gettin' there. An' I shit every time I see a white man from holdin' maself back from tearin' the pasty muthafucka's head off. That's why."

"Uh huh?" said Vanessa.

"Uh huh," confirmed Leroy.

"Wouldn't have nothin' to do with pizza pie, would it?"

"No," Leroy said.

"Ma mistake," Vanessa said.

"Yeah, bitch," Leroy said, "an' you been makin' quite a few a them lately. Now I ain't gonna be makin' no gang bang outa one little blowjob. An' I'ma forgive you. I'm even gonna keep you on the payroll. Leroy gonna take good care a you."

"Somebody else is takin' good care of me," Vanessa snapped.

"At the moment."

"What are you gettin' at, Leroy?" Vanessa said tiredly.

"Oh, nothin'. I just wouldn't be plannin' no long love affairs."

"You touch him, I'll kill you," Vanessa said flatly.

"Touch him? I ain't gonna touch him. I ain't even gonna get close to him. Les," he said, without takin' his eyes off Vanessa, "did you tell your sister here 'bout the bang-up time we had this afternoon?" Leslie said nothing, just dropped her eyes. Leroy didn't bother to look at her. "Uh huh, I figured you would." He smiled at Vanessa and turned away.

"Leroy," Vanessa said, "how do you say 'sir' in Italian?"

Leroy grinned amiably and disappeared through the door to the office.

"He's bluffin'," Vanessa said softly, mostly to herself.

"I don't think—" Charlene began.

"That's for sure," Vanessa snapped. She picked up her purse and rose. "Les."

"What?" said Leslie.

"You find out where some a them bodies is buried, an' you put some money away that he don't know about, an' you do it *now*." Leslie nodded. "You need help, you let me know."

"Okay," Leslie said. "But what about—"

"He's bluffin'," Vanessa said, without conviction. "You watch yourself." She turned and stepped toward the door. Just as she reached it Leroy emerged from the office and intercepted her.

"Off to kiss your boyfriend good-bye?" Leroy said, and grinned.

"You try—"

"You be nice to me now," Leroy advised. "I might not kill him. I might just run him off."

"I'll go with him," Vanessa said.

"Well, now," Leroy said. "Maybe he ain't gonna be wantin' no half-dead whore can't even fuck right. Course, maybe you don't fuck. I hear he's an educated fool. Been to college. Maybe he talks philosophy to you like he does with that fat old cunt down to Lightnin' Ed's. You get off on that jazz, 'Nessa?"

"We don't talk no philosophy," Vanessa said.

"No? Then what's a man like that gonna be doin' with a bitch like you?"

"Love me, maybe."

"After I run him off, maybe you just better forget about him. He ain't gonna be wantin' you."

"I'll go anyway," Vanessa said.

Leroy smiled coldly. "You just killed him," he said, and turned away.

In the dark comfort of Lightnin' Ed's, Brown sat sipping beer. It had been a hard day for him behind the bar at Frankie's—too many bright-eyed secretaries and young stockbrokers in sharkskin suits. Brown had begun to hate drinkers of mixed drinks. Straight whiskeys with water or ice or even soda were all right, but gin and tonics, vodka martinis, gin and bitter lemons he had no use for. He despised Manhattans. He sneered at whiskey sours. Seven-and-Sevens made him retch, and Brandy Alexanders were anathema. His feelings had quickly carried over from the drinks to the white-faced drinkers thereof, and now he rejoiced to sit on the customers' side of the bar, rubbing elbows with imbibers of beer and consumers of wine whose idea of vintage was a bottle of Thunderbird that had been sitting around for a week.

Behind the bar Leo rambled up and down, one eye on the needs of his customers, the other cemented to the TV screen. The Phillies were beating the Atlanta Braves by a score of seven to one, which pleased Leo no end. He had viewed each of the seven runs as a sword piercing into the vitals of the knights of the Ku Klux Klan. He was in an expansive mood, and he could even find it in his heart to forgive Hank Aaron for hitting a bases-empty home run. But Leo could not forgive the storm clouds which by their ominous gathering threatened to erase the Phillies' efforts. A rain-out in this situation would, Leo felt, be incontrovertible proof that God was a cracker.

"Damn," Leo said, as an Atlanta Brave, batting in the top of the third, stepped out of the box. "Can't that ump see what the fucker's tryin' to do? Make 'em play ball!" The batter stepped back in, fouled off a pitch, and stepped out again. "Shit," said Leo. "What they oughta do is to get some niggers in there for umpowerin', that's what they oughta do." He turned to Brown. "Ain't that right?"

Brown shook his head. "Can't have no black umpires."

"Why the hell not? Call balls an' strikes just as good as that Augie Whatshisname."

"Yeah, but he couldn't call folks *out*," Brown said.

Leo glared at him. "What kinda shit you talkin', fool?"

"Ain't shit," Brown said. "Can't have no nigger callin' folks out. Oh, I guess it might be all right if he was only callin' Aaron, or Willie Mays, or Clemente out. But sposin' he was to call that Staub fella out?"

"Well, what if he did?"

Brown sighed. "Leo," Brown said patiently, "baseball's the national game, right?"

"Right."

"Right. Now what that means is that what happens on the field is sorta like what happens all over, right?"

Leo nodded slowly.

Brown leaned forward, gesturing to emphasize his point. "Now you tell me, Leo, where'd you ever see a nigger callin' a white man out an' gettin' away with it?"

Leo swallowed and thought about it. "All right, but that's changin'. I mean, you're right, but I can remember when they wouldn't even let a colored man on the field."

"Sure," Brown said. "An' the first one they did let on damn near ran down every honky they had."

"Right. An' they loved him. Wasn't no damn prejudice; everybody loved Jackie Robinson."

"Sure they loved him. You know why?"

" 'Cause he was good."

"There was lotsa good niggers around, Leo, an' they never let 'em play. You know why they loved Jackie Robinson? 'Cause he stole bases. Now everybody *knows* niggers steal, so all they did was send Jackie out there an' let him do what they figured come natural. Now, Satch Paige, he wasn't lucky. Satch was a pitcher, an' there wasn't nobody could get a hit offa him. Couldn't let him play, he'd a made Ted Williams look like a 'lectric fan. An' the worst part of all was they say the pitcher wins the game, or loses it, don't make no difference. Point is they couldn't let no niggers be that important. When they finally do let a nigger pitch, it's some dude with a name like Alvin O'Neal McBean or fuckin' Mudcat Grant, an' they make him pitch in Pittsburgh, or in goddamn Minneapolis."

"That," said Leo, "is a lot a jive." The TV set roared. Leo spun around, but it was just another long foul ball. The storm clouds were thicker. "Damn," Leo said, "we can't win nothin'."

"Like I said," Brown told him. "It's that national game. Everybody plays. You gotta play to win. Only you never get to win."

Leo stared at him. "You scare me, you know that?" Leo said. Brown grinned. "No, I mean it," Leo said. "You really scare me. Half the time you seem like you as normal as anybody. Rest a the time . . ." Leo's voice trailed off.

"Rest a the time I act like I was crazy. You know what the difference between normal folks an' crazy folks is?"

Leo sighed.

"Normal folks acts half-crazy all the time. Crazy folks acts all crazy half the time an' all sane the rest a the time. In other words, they ain't never normal." Leo stared at him. Brown grinned.

"Haw, haw, haw," laughed Big Betsy the whore, who had been following the conversation with much interest and little comprehension. "He got you there, Leo."

Leo checked the progress of the ball game, which was not progressing noticeably at all, then turned to Big Betsy. "What I wants to know is, how come you acts crazy all the time?"

"I don't never act crazy," Big Betsy snapped. " 'Cept," she added coyly, "at that time a the month."

Leo snorted. "Which time is that, when they send out the welfare checks, or when there's a full moon?"

"You know what I mean," Big Betsy snapped.

"Betsy, the last time you had to worry 'bout gettin' knocked up was durin' the postwar baby boom. That's the Civil War, now."

Big Betsy's eyes narrowed. "Leo, it's a good thing you wasn't born a cat, or they'd a drowned you."

"I hear they tried to drown you, an' that's where all this water pollution come from."

Big Betsy made a noise like a loaded semitrailer grinding up Pikes Peak.

"See what I mean?" Brown said, grinning impishly.

Leo glared at him, turned back to the TV. The teams were changing. "Couple more innin's," Leo said, "an' it's in the books."

"Speakin' a craziness," said Big Betsy, "don't you think it's 'bout time you quit watchin' that *game?* Man your age oughta know there's things more important than *games.*"

"I know it," Leroy said. "There's money. There's politics. There's women." Big Betsy smiled. "They may be more important," Leo went on, "but they sure as hell ain't no more fun."

"Fun," snorted Big Betsy. "That's all y'all men think about. All ma damn life I had some man climbin' on top a me for *fun.*"

"I never went in for mountain climbin', did you, Brown?" Leo said. Brown covered his face with both hands.

"What you laughin' at, you simple-ass nigger?" Big Betsy demanded.

"Nothin'," Brown said quickly.

"You can say that again," Leo said. "Damn!" The image on the TV screen underwent violent convulsions and the rumble of thunder rolled in through the door of Lightnin' Ed's. "Shit! Seven to one an' it's gonna rain." As if in answer the Philadelphia batter connected solidly with the next pitch, sending the ball far over the wall in left field. "Not now, you asshole!" Leo roared. "Save it, save it." As the batter rounded third base the plate umpire waved the groundskeepers out to cover the infield. "Goddamn," Leo said, "if this kinda shit keeps up, we gonna be havin' George Wallace for President. You wait an' see."

꒰

The storm rolled in from the east—heavy black clouds, their soft underbellies tinted pink by the setting sun, banging in off the Delaware. From the window Brother Fletcher watched them advancing in confusion, tumbling over themselves, occasionally dropping so low they seemed to rip their guts out on the spires of Center City, but rolling on, wounds miraculously closing. The meek evening sky fell back, unprotesting. The rain came after the clouds—Brother Fletcher could detect its advance by the closing of windows, the sudden darkening of the sidewalk, the sudden shininess of the street. The white-lace curtain billowed in the gritty breeze, slapped at his face. Raindrops darkened it. Brother Fletcher closed the window.

"You're not going to watch the ball game?" asked Mrs. Fletcher.

Brother Fletcher shook his head. "It'll be rained out."

"Isn't there something about if they've already started—"

"It has to go four and a half innings. It's too soon."

"Sometimes games go fast."

Brother Fletcher turned to look at her. "Only if we're losing. If we're winning, it'll be rained out." The rain struck the window like machine-gun fire. The thunder boomed.

"I guess you were winning," Mrs. Fletcher said.

"God's an Atlanta fan," Brother Fletcher said.

Mrs. Fletcher looked up at him sharply. "You never used to talk about God like that," she said.

"No, I suppose I didn't. But I don't think He'll mind."

"I don't think it's right for a minister to talk about God like that. It's like you thought He was human."

"Oh no," Brother Fletcher said. "God's not human. If He were human He'd let us win once in a while." He smiled sadly, crossed the room and sat down. "Do you think I'm changing?"

"What?"

"Changing," Brother Fletcher said. "Do you think I'm changing?"

"Of course not," said Mrs. Fletcher. "What are you going to change to at your age, a frog?"

"I don't know," Brother Fletcher said. He sat silently for a few minutes, watching Mrs. Fletcher's fingers move over her sewing. "I used to raise puppies," Brother Fletcher said suddenly.

"What?"

"Puppies," said Brother Fletcher. "Baby dogs. What the hell are you, deaf?" Mrs. Fletcher's face registered total shock. Brother Fletcher realized what he had said, and he felt his face grow warm. " 'Scuse me," he said lamely.

"My God," Mrs. Fletcher said. "My God, it's true. It's all true. You been stolen by the Devil. What's her name? I'll scratch her eyes out!"

"Huh?" said Brother Fletcher.

Mrs. Fletcher slammed her sewing down. "I knew it. But I couldn't bring maself to believe it! Oh, Fletcher, how could you?"

"All I said was 'hell,'" protested Brother Fletcher. "I must say hell ten times every Sunday. I have to; nobody around here knows anything about heaven."

"This isn't Sunday. Hell is only the name of a place on Sunday. The rest of the week it's a bad word. Where did you learn words like that, Fletcher? Where do you g—no, don't tell me. I don't want to know. If I know, I'll kill her."

"Her who?"

"You know who. Whoever she is, that's who. And at your age. Think you'd be over that by now." Mrs. Fletcher shook her head sadly, glared at Brother Fletcher angrily, then suddenly burst into tears. Brother Fletcher jumped up and put his arms around her. "Get your sinful hands off me," Mrs. Fletcher sobbed, wrapping her arms tightly around Brother Fletcher's head and twisting it back and forth. "Leave me be. If I ain't enough for you after all these years—"

"What are you *talkin'* about, woman," Brother Fletcher demanded, trying to extract his head from the hammerlock.

"I tried ma best," Mrs. Fletcher wailed.

Brother Fletcher gave up the thought of escape and concentrated instead on squeezing her harder than she was squeezing him. Mrs. Fletcher, failing to get the message, tightened her grasp around his head. "I loved you as good as I was able," Mrs. Fletcher cried, "an' maybe it wasn't all that fancy, an' maybe I am gettin' old, but the Lord knows I tried."

"Umphgh," said Brother Fletcher, who now, in addition to being strangled, was being smothered as Mrs. Fletcher pulled his face against her bosom. "Umph."

"Yes, the Lord knows," Mrs. Fletcher said, looking down fondly on Brother Fletcher's head. Suddenly her features hardened and she thrust him away. "So where you think you get off, cheatin' on me for some old fried chicken?"

Brother Fletcher shook his head and gasped for air. "But—I don't *like* fried chicken," he protested weakly. Then he stared at her. "You mean—you thought—my Lord! Was I acting that strange?"

Mrs. Fletcher smiled tearfully. "You kept going out. And you did act strange. But I should have known it was just the beer."

Brother Fletcher gaped. "You know about the beer?"

"Let's just say I knew you weren't satisfied with the iced tea. And for a while I thought maybe you weren't satisfied with me, either." Brother Fletcher hung his head. "Fletch?" said Mrs. Fletcher.

"I'm sorry I let you think it. I'm ashamed I let you think it."

"How are you supposed to know what I'm thinking?"

"I should have told you everything." He sighed, sank down on the couch. "I guess I was afraid."

"Afraid? Fletch, I ain't crazy enough to get upset about a little beer."

Brother Fletcher's eyes twinkled. "Fried chicken, beer, what's the difference?" Mrs. Fletcher glared at him, then smiled. "But I wasn't talking about beer. I was talking about God."

"What?"

"God," Brother Fletcher said. "Remember Him? He plays for Atlanta. As if Aaron wasn't enough."

"What about God?" Mrs. Fletcher demanded. "Fletcher, what are you talking about?"

"It's called a crisis of faith," Brother Fletcher explained grimly. "It's a childhood disease, like mumps and measles, which can be very dangerous if you get them late in life. It's common in young men between the ages of fifteen and twenty-seven. Preachers are supposed to be immune." He looked at Mrs. Fletcher and smiled tightly. "I forgot to take my booster shots."

"You stopped believing in *God?*" Mrs. Fletcher said incredulously.

"No, no," said Brother Fletcher, "I'm too old to stop believing in God. But I realized I didn't know what it was I believed in. I realized if I met God on the street I wouldn't know Him from—Adam."

Mrs. Fletcher looked at him and shook her head. "But God isn't going to come walking down the street."

"No?" said Brother Fletcher. "Are you sure? How's He going to come?"

"Well, I don't know," snapped Mrs. Fletcher in exasperation.

"See?" said Brother Fletcher.

"See *what?*"

"You wouldn't know God if He came walking down the street. Because you don't expect Him to come walking down the street. All we know about God is what we wouldn't expect Him to do. We don't expect Him to do anything normal. You don't expect Him to just walk down the street. You wouldn't expect Him to wear sneakers, or drink beer, or like baseball games, or go to the bathroom, or wear false teeth. Or—"

264 ([*South Street*

"I sure wouldn't expect to see Him on South Street," said Mrs. Fletcher. "I wouldn't expect Him to do *anything* on South Street."

"No," Brother Fletcher agreed. "And you wouldn't expect Him to be wearing a diaper, either." Mrs. Fletcher nodded slowly. "I went into a bar," Brother Fletcher continued, his voice a musing rumble, "I drank some beer, and I watched a baseball game. . . ." He stopped and looked at Mrs. Fletcher. "You don't like The Word of Life, do you?"

"Well . . ."

"No. You don't. You go because I need you to go, and because when people hire a minister they think they've hired a family. But I wish you didn't have to go. Because The Word of Life isn't . . ." Brother Fletcher paused and took a deep breath. "If I had someplace I wanted to share with you, someplace I cared whether or not you enjoyed, it would be Lightnin' Ed's. Not The Word of Life. And if I wanted to change one place and make it more like the other, I'd want to change The Word of Life." Brother Fletcher stood up and walked to the window, looked out over the darkly glistening street. "If Leo wanted to come to The Word of Life . . ." His voice trailed off. He looked at the street. "They made me take off my collar. It was bad for business. Not me. The collar. It was a sign. And it was a relief not to be a minister. No. I take that back. It was a relief to have being a minister be just like being anything else, like being a janitor, or a bartender, or a whore." He gave the street one last glance, then turned back to Mrs. Fletcher. "If Christ comes back singing "Onward Christian Soldiers" and wearing a clerical collar, we'd all be better off in Hell. I prefer Leo's company to the Reverend Mr. Sloan's."

"Who's Leo?"

"The bartender."

"Oh." Mrs. Fletcher sat down, thought for a minute. Brother Fletcher started to turn back to the window. "So preachers are sinners and bartenders are saints, and if God came back he'd be a bartender."

Brother Fletcher smiled. "I don't think it's that simple. God probably wouldn't be a bartender. But whatever he was . . ." He stopped. "An innkeeper was just about like a bartender."

"The one who said there was no room?"

"No," said Brother Fletcher. "The one who let them sleep in the stable." Brother Fletcher turned back to the window.

"Are you going—out?" asked Mrs. Fletcher.

"No," Brother Fletcher said. "Not tonight. Is there any iced tea?"

"Plenty," said Mrs. Fletcher, jumping up to go make some. Brother Fletcher turned away from the window, settled down in his chair, and sighed in contentment.

Leo leaned on the bar, waiting for the evening to drain away like the rainwater running down South Street's litter-clogged storm drains. The rain had made for a slow night—bad for business, good for the soul—and Leo watched the evening end with feelings of relief mingled with a flush of contentment. He drew himself a beer and sipped it slowly.

"Rain's stopped," Brown said.

Leo nodded. "Never lasts long this time a year. Gonna be cold out there, though."

"It'll be misty," Brown said, "and the street will shine. It'll be beautiful."

Leo looked at him. "What's so damn pretty about a wet street?"

Brown's eyes focused on Leo. "What? Oh, I don't know."

"Is he talkin' that philosophy shit again, Leo?" Big Betsy demanded.

"I wouldn't know, Betsy," Leo said. "I wouldn't know if a cow was to crap in here. I can't tell the difference 'tween that an' your damn bad breath."

"Yeah, an' every time you blow your nose the snot comes out brown," Big Betsy responded. "You don't get a stuffed-up nose, you get constipation of the head."

"Yeah, an' you got diarrhea of the mouth," Leo said, grinning at Brown.

Brown laughed and shook his head. Big Betsy climbed off her stool and trundled up. "What the hell you laughin' at, Brown?"

Brown regarded her. "I would say nothin', but it appears to be quite a bit."

Big Betsy drew back and glared at him. Then a slow grin spread across her face. "Wasn't so long ago, nigger, you was callin' me a lady."

Brown shrugged. "You are a lady. A fat, big-mouthed lady."

"You forgot 'old,' " Big Betsy said.

"A fat, big-mouthed, *old* lady," Brown corrected.

"Amen," Leo said.

"Shup, Leo. I ain't too old, you know, Brown." Big Betsy batted her eyes coquettishly.

Brown repressed a shudder. "No," he said, "but I am."

"Haw, haw, haw," bellowed Big Betsy. "Didja hear that, Leo?"

Leo clapped his hands over his ears. "Yeah, I heard it, but you cut loose like that one more time an' I may never hear another thing. Damn, Betsy, you gotta be givin' a man some warnin'."

"Ma mama told me never to be given' no man no warnin'."

"You best lose some weight, then, 'cause now they can see you comin' from six miles away."

"Haw, haw . . ." Big Betsy stopped as Leo clapped his hands over his ears again. "Quick, Brown, now's our chance to talk about what an ugly muthafucka Leo is."

"You know . . ." Leo began, but he stopped abruptly and lowered his hands as the door opened and Rayburn slouched in. "Evenin', Rayburn," Leo said.

Rayburn looked at him, wordlessly took a stool. He stared straight ahead. Leo shrugged. "What'll it be?" Rayburn turned his head slowly, looked at Leo, then turned his head back. "Well, damn," Leo said, "I can't read your mind."

"He ain't got no mind," Big Betsy said. "Ain' that the truth, Rayburn?" Rayburn ignored her. Leo looked at Brown and shrugged. Brown was keeping a close watch on Rayburn out of the corner of his eye. "Smell him," Big Betsy said. "Stinks like a cross between a brewery an' a goddamn perfume factory. Where you been, Rayburn? You find that community-cunt wife a yours?" Rayburn stared straight ahead. "No, I guess you didn't—"

"Shut up, Betsy," Leo said.

"I guess not," Big Betsy continued doggedly. "If you had a found that half-breed bitch you'd be smellin' like a kennel instead a like perfume." Big Betsy moved up behind Rayburn and ran one fat finger down his neck. Rayburn held absolutely still. "Um hum," Big Betsy said. "Rayburn's been hangin' 'round some *expensive* women, from the smell of it. Only I don't smell no lovin' on him. Whatsa matter, Rayburn, couldn't you get over?"

"Shit, Betsy," Leo said, "if your nose was that good you'd pass out every time you took off your girdle. Now shut up an' let Rayburn be."

" 'Let Rayburn be,' " mocked Big Betsy. "Well I might—"

"Be quiet," Brown said softly. Big Betsy swung on him, her mouth open. "I said be quiet," Brown said. "He's got trouble enough."

"Humph," Big Betsy said. "What the hell you know 'bout trouble?"

"That sometimes you want to be alone with it," Brown said.

"He wants to be alone, how come he didn't stay out on the street?"

"If he had a knowed you was gonna be here he most likely would have," Leo said.

Big Betsy glared at him. "Another country heard from. 'Scuse me, I mean continent. Leo, you're a goddamn limp dick just like Rayburn."

"Sometimes I wonder how anybody could ever be anything else with you around," Leo snapped.

"Well, damn," said Big Betsy. She caught up her handbag and waddled toward the door, her stern swinging angrily.

"Don't forget to write," Leo called.

Big Betsy halted and rotated. "Have a picture postcard," she said. She raised her right hand, scribbled on the air. "To Mr. Leo Pissant Cocksucker. South Street. Havin' a wonderful time, the water's fine, an' I wish to God you was here, 'cause we ain't got nobody big enough to play tackle. Signed, Mopey Dick. Good night." Big Betsy spun around so quickly her momentum made her stumble slightly as she rumbled out the door.

"Damn," Leo chuckled. "That was pretty good."

"That smelly old bitch gone?" Rayburn said.

Leo regarded him mildly. "You mean Betsy?"

"I mean that smelly old cunt was just standin' there fartin' with her mouth."

"Well," said Leo, "I wouldn't be knowin' about the way her cunt smells. I haven't had ma nose in it."

"Smells like dead ol' pussy," Rayburn snapped. He glared angrily. "This whole place smells like dead ol' pussy."

"Quite an expert on the subject," Brown said sourly. "Necrophilia and bestiality."

Rayburn shifted his gaze. "Who asted you? You probly like that dead-cunt smell."

"All right, now," Leo said. "Betsy's gone. You wanna have a quiet drink an' keep your mouth shut?"

"Didn't come in here to keep ma mouth shut," Rayburn said. "I come in here to see some niggers." He looked around the empty bar. "I come in here to see me some niggers!" Brown looked at Leo. Leo shrugged. "Niggers!" Rayburn shouted. He looked accusingly at Leo. "Whad you do with 'em, Leo? Where'd they go?"

"They heard about Lincoln an' went to kiss his ring," Brown said.

"Where'd they go, Leo?" Rayburn begged. "Tell me."

"They went home to bed like normal people."

"Oh no, Leo," Rayburn said, "no, they can't be doin' that. Not niggers Not like—like they was normal people. 'Cause they ain't."

"Some ain't, an' that's for true," Leo said.

"See, Leo," Rayburn began, stopping as Leo frowned impatiently. Rayburn turned to Brown. "See," he said. Brown turned away. "Listen to me," Rayburn said. He said it softly without a hint of a shout, but there was something in his voice that made Brown turn back to look at him. "See," Rayburn said again, "niggers is uncommon. There's somethin' *different* about 'em."

"They don't use suntan oil," Leo said sourly. "You want a beer to wash down your bullshit with?"

"Ain't got no money," Rayburn said. Leo snorted, drew a beer and set it on the bar. He refilled Brown's glass, then drew one for himself. "Y'all want to hear a funny story?" Rayburn said.

"I hears 'em every day," Leo said shortly. Brown looked at him accusingly. Leo sighed. "I guess one more ain't gonna kill me."

"Thank you, Leo," Rayburn said. "I knew niggers would listen. White folks don't listen. I been up there tryin' to make 'em, an' all they does is laugh. So I come to find me some niggers. Niggers'll always listen."

"Maybe that's 'cause they ain't got nothin' better to do," Leo said.

Rayburn lifted his beer and sat swaying on his stool.

"You gonna listen to ma story or not?" he demanded.

"Yes, Rayburn, yes," Leo said. "Get on with it, for Jesus' sake."

"All right," Rayburn said. He raised his beer, sipped it, set it down again. Foam clung to his lips, hung white against his chin. He wiped it away with the back of his hand. "This here's a funny story, you know?" He paused to look at Leo. Leo nodded. "It's about this janitor," Rayburn said. "One time he run into this gal. Pretty gal. Hustlin'. Hustlin' everything: food, money, drinks, reefer, anything she could get her hands on an' her legs wrapped around. You couldn't blame her. It was the only way she could see to get along, you know? We all the same, just tryin' to get along." He looked at Brown. Brown nodded slowly. Rayburn nodded too, and for a moment their heads bobbed up and down, Rayburn's descending as Brown's rose. Rayburn stopped to sip his beer. The floor groaned as he shifted his weight. "Anyways, I—I mean, this janitor, he married her. He didn't have to or nothin'. Sure didn't need to. Five dollars was all he needed. I guess . . ."

"Guess what?" Brown said gently.

"I guess maybe he was just tryin' to get along, too. Anyways, they told him. They told him she was gonna bust his balls, said she was gonna run soon as she saw a crack a daylight. Sure. They was right." He swung his eyes to Leo. Leo lowered his head. "I knowed they was right. I didn't need nobody tellin' me that shit. It was like tellin' me the sun comes up in the mornin' or white folks hates niggers. I *knew* all that. I didn't care." He turned back to Brown. "See, didn't none of 'em understand me. They all thought I didn't know what she was doin'. Course I knew. Man'd have to be damn near dead not to know if other men, lots of 'em, was havin' his woman. But you see, I had her sometimes. She always come back to me. Havin' her that way was bettern not havin' her at all. She was the prettiest thing I ever saw, an' sometimes I had her. It was worth it, right?"

"I don't know." Brown said.

"No," Rayburn said, "you don't. You ain't never touched her. If you had, you'd know." He shrugged. "Or maybe it'd be different. Anyways, it don't matter, 'cause she did run. An' the funny part was, she didn't run on account a one a them others, she run on account a somethin' I done. She run 'cause *I* messed on *her!*" Rayburn chuckled drunkenly. Brown opened his mouth, glanced at Leo. Leo shook his head. Rayburn stopped laughing abruptly, the chuckle vanishing like a wire stretched almost to breaking, then suddenly cut. "You know what I done?" Rayburn demanded. He looked back and forth from Brown to Leo and back to Brown. "I laid me a white woman. You ever had a white woman?" Brown slowly opened his mouth. "Now, I don't mean no whore, now," Rayburn said quickly. "I mean a real white woman, kind wears expensive clothes an' twenty-dollar perfume. I had me one a them. You ever had one a them? Kind that drinks martinis an' drives a big car? I never had me one before. She was wearin' a diamond ring an' a pearl necklace, an' she was married to some fuckin' lawyer or somethin'. An' *she* came to *me*. *She* bought *me* drinks. *She* asted *me* to go home with her. An' you know, the only reason I done it was 'cause she made me mad. Both of 'em made me mad. Les made me mad, an' I was thinkin', All right, bitch, now it's ma turn. An' this white woman, she made me mad, too. They all make me mad. You see them white women walkin' down the street, oldern piss an' ugliern shit, an' they all so damn sure there ain't a nigger in the world would just *love* to fuck 'em, old an' ugly as they are, just 'cause they white. That's what kills me—they so damn *certain.* You watch 'em. Old woman in an elevator, a brother gets on an' right away she's uptight. Sit down next to her in the only empty seat in a goddamn bus an' she's gonna stand right up, if she don't get clean off. But all the time they be walkin' around wavin' it at you. All the goddamn time. An' you walk around lookin' at 'em wavin' it, an' soon as they catch you lookin' they start actin' like it was gold an' you was tryin' to steal it. They go walkin' past you, an' they're so damn *certain* you're just dyin' for a piece, an' maybe you was thinkin' about somethin' else all the time, but that don't make no difference. They're sure. You couldn't convince 'em you wasn't interested, an' if you could they'd just wiggle it a little to get your attention. So sooner or later time comes when you reach out an' take it. They offer it to you, you take it. 'Cause you got to know, you know? They shakin' it like it was made outa gold, an' you get to thinkin'. Maybe it *is* made outa gold. Maybe their pussies smell like perfume, an' maybe their tits are cherries, an' maybe their damn assholes drip butterscotch. I mean who the hell knows? Maybe there *is* somethin' special about it. Only there ain't. It's just another piece a tail that stinks in the mornin'." Rayburn sighed, raised his glass, drained it. Leo shifted uneasily. "It didn't mean nothin'," Rayburn said. "Not a damn thing. Not to me. Only when I come home in the mornin' Les was gone. Just on account a one piece a fat white pussy. Ain't that funny? Leo? Ain't it?"

"Yeah," Leo said thickly.

"Yeah," Rayburn said. He stood up, stood swaying. "I'ma leave this fuckin' city. Tomorrow. No. Banks is closed. I'ma leave Monday. Leo, if that bitch comes lookin' for ma ass, you tell her I done gone."

"Sure," Leo said.

"Tell her I done gone."

Leo nodded.

Rayburn nodded drunkenly, slapped Brown on the back. "S'long."

"So long," Brown said. Rayburn turned and staggered out. Brown looked at Leo, climbed off his stool, shook his head. "I don't know," he said.

"I do," Leo said bitterly. "I know all about it. I gotta know all about it 'cause I'm a goddamn bartender an' bartenders is supposed to know all about it."

"She gonna come lookin' for him?"

"Shit," Leo said. Brown shook his head, turned toward the door. "Leroy Briggs been kickin' ass," Leo said. "You be careful."

"Sure," Brown said shortly. He caught the note in Leo's voice, turned and smiled. "Don't worry."

"I ain't gonna be worryin'. I ain't got time to sweat over every damn fool buys a beer in here," Leo said. He sniffed, shifted his weight. Brown turned back to the door. "You need any help . . ." Leo's voice trailed off. Brown smiled over his shoulder, nodded, waved, and stepped out into the night.

The rain ran down over the windshield, distorting his view of South Street's lights, which glimmered dimly against the dark and troubled sky. Inside the car the lights glowed undistorted: the red lights for OIL and TEMP, the single green bulb on the tape player that blinked conspiratorially each time the channel switched. Loud music rocked through the padded interior, was soaked up by the deep pile carpet, the heavy leather seats. The Isley Brothers. Leroy tapped time on the leather-sheathed steering wheel with the silencer on the end of his Colt .45.

The rain banged and rattled on the roof, making him feel cold. He considered starting the engine to warm the car but discarded the notion—the sight of a big pink Caddy standing across the street with the engine running might excite the interest of someone in Lightnin' Ed's. It might tip Brown off. Leroy pushed the button to recline the seat, turned up the music, and resigned himself to the hardships of a stakeout. Absorbed in the music, he almost missed the opening of the door across the street. Almost, but not quite. He reacted swiftly, stabbing at the button that brought the seat to its fully erect position and at the same time punching the button that opened the window on the passenger's side. The unmistakable form of Big Betsy the whore squeezed through the door of Lightnin' Ed's and out onto the sidewalk. Leroy relaxed. Big Betsy extracted a wad of newspaper from beneath the folds of her raincoat, opened it out, and held it over her head. She peered across the street. "Y'all quit that hosin' over there," Big Betsy bellowed. "Haw, haw, haw." Leroy shoved the button, and the seat lowered him out of sight. "I can't see you, but I know what you're doin'," yelled Big Betsy. "You drinkin' an' listenin' to that there music an' *hosin'*, that's what." The seat reached its lowest position. Leroy tried to push himself further. "You best close that window, or your goddamn prick'll freeze solid, an' her cunt's gonna be drippin' icicles." Leroy pushed a button and closed the window, cutting off Big Betsy's cackle. She turned and waddled away down the street, splashing through the puddles like a raincoated duck. Leroy switched tracks on the tape player and tried to forget it. He watched the few cars that moved past him, noting the license numbers of the ones that splashed water on his car. He wrote the numbers down in a small red book. There were a lot of names in Leroy's little red book, and he had crossed off quite a few of them. The next one on the list, in bold letters, was BROWN. Leroy said the name softly, caressing the single complex syllable with his thick lips. He regretted not being a better shot, not being able to shoot Brown in the kneecap or in the testicles to make him suffer a while before he bled to death. Still, Leroy's plan, though lacking in artistic perfection, had a certain amount of elegance. It was, Leroy thought, worthy of him. He would follow Brown to his apartment, shoot him from the car window, leave him lying in the hallway, where Vanessa would have to step over him. Leroy considered the minor details of his plan, regretted the restrictions of time and space. But it would be enough—shooting the heavy gun in complete silence, then rolling away into the darkness, not speeding, moving slowly and steadily, the window powering quietly closed, the tape deck playing, while Brown lay twitching in a whirlpool of red. Leroy smiled.

The rain had subsided to mist and drizzle, and looking out at it, Leroy shivered. It was better cold, for if by some mistake Brown had time to cry out, he would shout into sound-deadening mist, to doors barred against the wetness, windows locked against the chill. The street would be empty; Brown would die alone. Across the street a rectangle of dim light showed and Leroy brought the seat up, switched off the tape player. A man's figure emerged from Lightnin' Ed's. Leroy lowered the window for a better view, waited tensely. The figure staggered heavily against a wall, and Leroy cursed. He did not want Brown to be so drunk he would not know what was happening, just mildly high so that it might take him a minute to realize he was dying. Just high enough that, for a second, he might get off on the sight of his own blood. Leroy sighed, but then he saw that the drunken man across the street was not Brown, but Rayburn Wallace. Leroy grinned, changed the tape to The Temptations doing "Love Is a Hurtin' Thing" while he watched Rayburn stagger down South Street, bouncing off the walls like a piece of driftwood in a flooded river.

The chill was getting to him. He reached down beneath the seat and pulled out a bottle, took a swig. He hoped Brown would not die before he had had a taste of the cold. He replaced the bottle just as the door of Lightnin' Ed's opened for a third time.

The night was quiet, cold, lonely, wet. Brown stepped out onto the street, shocked and shivering from the sudden chill. Strange weather, Brown thought, Philadelphia weather—heat for Christmas, snow in July. He peered guiltily down the shining asphalt corridor, but there was no sign of Rayburn and his load of troubles. There was no sign of anyone. There was only the mist-shrouded shape of a long car, dark and dead, parked across the street, the hum and blink of changing traffic lights, and Brown. He shivered, buttoned his collar to the top, and started home, moving quickly, in short tight steps, peering into the shadows, listening to the dripping of water, the congested gurgle of clogged sewers. Behind him a powerful engine ground and caught, settling into a restrained hum. Brown walked on, crossing streets quickly, noticing the spaces between the streets not as distance but as time, time left in the swelling drizzle, time before he could sink into bed. He paused at the last corner while the light cycled, then a car rolled past him, stopped across the street from his door. Brown, head down, half-asleep, paid no attention. Yawning, he moved along the sidewalk, stepped down onto the cobblestones of the alley beside the deserted store. He stumbled on the slick surface, cursed, and stopped. From the dark depths of the alley came a low moan.

Brown came wide awake. He stopped, shivering. Leo's warning echoed in his mind. He had a sudden vision of Rayburn's razor slicing through the darkness, too quick to be seen. Brown turned away from the alley and stepped toward his own door. The moaning sounded again. Brown stopped, hesitated, cursed, and plunged into the darkness. Ten or fifteen feet into the alley he stumbled over a garbage can and sprawled on the cold cobblestones, fell against something warm, stinking, wet. Brown recoiled, gagging. The something moaned. Brown held his breath, brought his face close.

"Jake?"

Jake gurgled as if his throat had been cut, writhed, coughed, spewed phlegmy blood. Brown stared down in shocked disbelief at the sudden darkness against his white shirt. Jake gurgled again. Brown stepped back. "Don't worry, Jake, I'ma get help. You stay right there." Brown backed a few more paces, fighting for his footing. Then he whirled and charged out of the alley, slipping and sliding on the cobblestones. As he emerged he spotted the car parked across the street, silver exhaust streaming from the tail pipe. "Hey!" Brown shouted, charging across the street straight toward the car's open window. "Help!" With a heavy clunk of engaging gears the car shot away from the curb, fishtailing on the wet pavement. Brown stood in the middle of South Street staring after it. "Paranoid bastard," Brown muttered. He looked around. The street was empty. Brown went back into the alley. He bent over Jake, wrapped his arms around Jake's body, lifted him, carried him out to the street. He looked around again, for a phone, a cop, a passing car. There were no phones. There were no cops. There were no cars. Brown felt his mind waver like the ghosty mist that surrounded him. In his arms the wino moaned. Brown turned east and started walking. For two blocks he hurried, but then his feet slipped into a slower rhythm in time with the dripping drizzle, the changing traffic lights, the rasp of Jake's breathing.

Brown walked on toward the eastern river, his wet shoes squeaking a weird lament, holding Jake's body tight against him, smelling Jake's odor, breathing his breath. Cross streets passed in the shining mist and Brown's teeth chattered with the cold, the effort, the stench of wine and soured blood. Brown, unthinking, ignored the phone booths that stood a block north on each cross street like shining sentinels. He reached Eighth Street, turned north, realizing, when he got to Pine Street, that he had gone too far. He struggled west again, past the manicured lawns sequestered behind iron fences, past the historical marker that said that the Pennsylvania Hospital had been founded in 1751 by Benjamin Franklin. He rounded a corner, saw a red sign that said EMERGENCY. He entered an alleyway, found a covered walk. Automatic doors opened inward, slamming back against his arm as he maneuvered Jake inside. Brown cursed. A nurse in a starched white uniform looked up, picked up a phone, and spoke into it before coming out from behind her desk. She pulled a long wheeled cart, draped in white, away from the wall. "Put him here." Brown lowered Jake onto the cart. An annunciator whispered softly. White-coated attendants materialized and whisked Jake away into the hospital's gleaming bowels. Brown stood, wet, bloody, confused. "Are you the next of kin?" asked the nurse.

"What?" Brown said.

"Are you the next of kin?" The nurse stood in front of him holding a clipboard.

Brown looked at her. "Yes," he said.

"What's your relationship to the patient?"

"We drink beer together."

The nurse sighed. "Where—"

"In an alley. He spit blood." Brown looked down at his clothes. "He spit blood."

"His name?"

"Jake," Brown said.

"Jake what?"

"That's all I know," Brown said.

The nurse sighed. "Does he have an address?"

"Is there a doctor in there?"

"The doctors are doing everything they can. Now, do you know your friend's address?"

"South Street," Brown said.

"Where on South Street?"

Brown shook his head as if trying to clear it, looked at the nurse as if he had never seen one before. "What?"

"Where does your friend live on South Street?" the nurse said with professional patience.

"He lives in an alley. Beside a garbage can." Brown's eyes were hard and angry. The nurse looked at him uneasily. Brown smiled sadly. "The alley is between Fifteenth and Sixteenth."

"Is it closer to Fifteenth or Sixteenth?"

"It's closer to Fifteenth," Brown said.

"Then," the nurse said precisely, "he lives at Fifteenth and South." She wrote it down.

"Fine," Brown said. "That's fine."

"You can have a seat in the waiting room," the nurse said.

"Is there someplace I can clean up?" Brown said, looking down at his chest.

"Down the hall," the nurse said briskly. "Would you like a towel?"

"Yes," Brown said, "I would like a towel." The nurse smiled nervously, took a towel from a shelf, and handed it to him. "Thank you," Brown said. He went down the hall.

The men's room was a hard, intense, shiny white, smelling of disinfectant. Brown stared at himself in the mirror above the spotless bowl. Drops of moisture in his hair sparkled like diamonds. Ruby flecks dusted his forehead. His shirtfront was a soggy crimson mass. Brown walked calmly into a toilet stall, knelt before the bowl like a penitent at an altar, and vomited his stomach dry. He stood up and flushed the toilet, went back and bent over the sink, placed his mouth around the spigot, and gulped cold water until he thought he would burst. Then he went back to kneel at the toilet. This time the vomit was almost as clear as water. Brown stood up, opened his pants, and urinated. He waited until the waves raised by the stream of urine had banged themselves to death against the white porcelain before he pulled the flush lever. He stepped back to the sink, stripped off his shirt, washed himself, dried, draped the towel around his shoulders, and went out.

The nurse was waiting for him, clipboard loaded, ball-point leveled. "I forgot to get your name."

"Brown. Adlai Stevenson Brown."

"How do you spell that?"

"B, R, O, W, N," Brown said.

"I know how to spell Brown," the nurse snapped.

"Don't be so sure," Brown told her. "Some folks spells it with an E on the end. Just like some spells fuck P, H, U, Q, U, E, an' just like—"

"There's no need to be vulgar," the nurse said.

"Just like some people," Brown continued grimly, "insist on dotting the *i* and crossing the *t* in shit."

"I meant your first name," the nurse said coldly. Brown ignored her and stared toward the gleaming doors through which Jake had been wheeled. "We'll let you know when there's any news," the nurse said.

"J, O, H, N," Brown said.

"What?"

"That's how you spell my first name."

"But you said your name was Adlai."

"I just changed it. I don't know how to spell Adlai. It was my old man's idea, not mine. He felt guilty because he voted for Eisenhower." The nurse, clutching her ball-point at port arms, began to edge away from him. "Eisenhower was a prick," Brown said. The nurse turned ashy. Brown turned and stepped toward the doors marked NO ADMITTANCE.

"You can't go in there," the nurse said.

Brown smiled at her. "Then you don't have anything to worry about." He stepped through the white doors into a long corridor, walked down it, peering through the doorways over the tops of flimsy gates that looked like they came from the saloons in TV westerns. Inside the third door he saw Jake stretched out on a table, connected by tubes to bottles of blood, surrounded by white-clad doctors and nurses.

"Perforated?" one of the doctors said.

"Perforated, hell. This one's guts must look like Swiss cheese."

A nurse giggled.

From a speaker on the wall a woman's voice spoke, calm and soothing. "Doctor Warden, Doctor Warden, you are wanted in emergency. Doctor Warden to emergency, stat."

"Oh, God," said one of the nurses, "some nut with a carving knife probably wants to hijack us to Cuba."

"How's his pressure?"

"Falling slowly."

"Order more blood."

"*Ulcus veneria*, do you think, doctor?"

"In this old geezer? He hasn't got it up in years. *Ulcus rodens*, I'd say. Where's he from?"

"Fifteenth and South," said a nurse, reading from a chart.

"Fifteenth and South. Definitely a rodent ulcer."

A nurse giggled.

"Any word from the O.R.?"

"They said it would be a while."

"We haven't got a while. How's the pressure?"

"Falling."

"Blood?"

"On the way."

"Must be bleeding like a fountain in there."

Two men in uniform appeared behind Brown, grasped him by his upper arms. "You'll have to leave this area, sir," one of them said.

"How's his pressure?"

"Ski slope."

"That's my friend," Brown said.

"Yes, sir, we know. But you'll have to leave."

"He's dying," Brown said. "And they're making jokes."

"I wouldn't know, sir."

"All right," Brown said dully. They led him back to the reception area and sat him down in a chair. The nurse regarded him reproachfully.

"I told you you couldn't go back there." She looked at the guards. "I think he'll be all right."

"Are you sure? He looks pretty weird."

The nurse looked at Brown sitting braced against the shiny white wall, a white towel draped around his shoulders, a bloody shirt clutched in his hand. "Weird," the nurse agreed, "but harmless." The guards went away. Brown started to shiver. "Would you like a blanket?" the nurse asked. Brown said nothing. The nurse took a thin blanket, worn gray and smooth from many washings, and placed it around his shoulders.

Brown looked up at the touch of her hands. "Thank you," Brown said. The nurse nodded. "They were making jokes," Brown said. "Sick jokes in lousy Latin."

"That's why you're not supposed to go back there," the nurse said. She finished wrapping him up. "You speak Latin?"

"No," Brown said, "but I once played Marc Antony in *Julius Caesar.*" The nurse looked at him sharply. "Friends," Brown said, "Romans, and countrymen. Lend me your ears. I come to bury Caesar, not to praise him. The evil that men do lives after them. So let it be with Caesar. I forgot some." The nurse swallowed heavily. "Don't worry," Brown assured her. "It's just that I've been under a strain. I got blood all over a perfectly good shirt."

The nurse looked down at him. "You carried him from Fifteenth Street?"

Brown nodded.

"You should have taken him to Graduate Hospital," she said gently. "It's closer."

"Didn't you know?" Brown said. "South Street's one way downtown." The nurse gave him a wary look and left him propped against the wall, shivering.

Vanessa woke from a light doze when Brown opened the door. She stepped into the kitchen, looked at him. "Oh my God!"

"Don't you like pizza?" Brown said. He closed the door, stripped off his bloody shirt, and threw it in the corner.

"Leroy's?" Vanessa said calmly.

"What?"

"Whose blood is it?"

"Jake's," Brown said. "I found him in the alley. He bled to death."

"Somebody knife him?"

"No," Brown said bitterly. "His guts turned to—Swiss cheese." He walked over and set a bottle of wine on the table.

"What's that?"

"A bottle of wine. His last bottle. He told the doctor to tell me where to find it. In the alley."

Vanessa regarded the bottle with distaste. "It's all yucky." Brown took the bottle over to the sink and began washing it. "What are you going to do with it?"

"I'ma drink it," Brown snapped. "What the fuck you think I'ma be doin' with it?"

"I don't know what the hell you brought it up here for. Here I am worryin'—"

"If somebody died an' left you a million dollars, wouldn't you spend it?"

"That's sixty-cent rotgut, not a million dollars."

"It's moren a million dollars," Brown said. "It's all his worldly goods."

"Are you drunk?" Vanessa demanded.

"Not yet," Brown said. He cut off the water, dried the bottle.

"You sound drunk."

Brown looked at her. He twisted the cap off the bottle and took a swig. "I am not drunk," he said carefully. "But it is none of your fucking business if I am drunk. If I am drunk it is because I want to be drunk or because I need to be drunk. Right now I am going to get drunk because there is not much else I can do right now."

"I'm sorry," Vanessa said. Brown smiled, reached out, and squeezed her arm. "Can I have some?" Brown nodded, reached into the cabinet, and took down his two mismatched jelly jars, poured them full. He sat down at the table.

"In Africa," Brown said, "when someone died they would throw spears at the moon. A missionary told them it didn't do any good. They told him they knew it didn't do any good, but they had to do something. So the missionary taught them to give the Last Rites instead." Brown raised his glass, drank the wine down, and poured the glass full again. "I hope they ate him."

"I thought you was dead," Vanessa said.

"No," Brown said. "No, I'm not dead." He got up and turned out the light. The chair creaked as he sat down again, in the darkness.

"Leroy's out to get you," Vanessa said. "Mostly on account a me."

"Leroy," Brown said.

"He'll let you be after I go back to him." Brown looked at her. "He said he'd kill you. He means it." Brown threw back his head and laughed. "He will," Vanessa insisted. "He's for real."

"I know," Brown laughed. "I know he is. It's just too damn real. People dyin', an' killin' people, an' runnin' away from their husbands. It's just like a goddamn soap opera. Any second now some fool's gonna come tippin' in to try an' sell us some Ivory soap. Only what we need is D-Con."

"What you need is some sense," Vanessa snapped.

"If I had any sense I'd a jumped off a bridge a long time ago," Brown said. He drank some wine. "You know, outside that damn hospital there's this old watering trough. You know what it says on that fuckin' horse trough?"

"Maybe 'No Parking'?" Vanessa said tiredly.

"Not bad," Brown said. "But what it really says is better. It says"— Brown raised his hand as if he were writing a message on the darkness—" 'A merciful man is merciful to his beast.' How 'bout that?"

"What's so great about that?" Vanessa said.

Brown smiled sadly. "Nothin'. Drink your wine." He emptied his own glass and poured in the rest of the bottle. Vanessa peered at him through the darkness, raised her hand toward the dim outline of his face. Brown pulled his head away.

"People die," Vanessa said softly.

"Sometimes," Brown agreed. "And sometimes someone kills them. And sometimes someone lets them die. But they all go sooner or later."

"So what's the point—"

"You have to do something," Brown said. He got up and carried the empty bottle to the window, raised the sash, leaned out into the chilly night. He dropped the bottle. It fell into the darkness, banged against a garbage can, shattered on the cobblestones. Brown pulled himself back inside, closed the window against the cold. "Blood frightens me," he said.

Vanessa stepped up behind him. "I'll go back to Leroy tomorrow."

"You shut the hell up about that."

"Take your choice," Vanessa said. "I can leave tomorrow mornin', or I can stay until Leroy gets around to killin' you. Might be a whole day's difference."

"I'll take the day," Brown said.

Vanessa wrapped her arms around him. Brown turned and kissed her, forehead, cheeks. She pressed her face against the cold skin of his chest. Brown laid his hand against the back of her head. For long minutes they stood motionless, then Brown bent his head and kissed her. His hands worked against the bulge of muscle where her shoulders met her neck. Her hands moved to his belt, his to her blouse. They freed each other from their clothes, slow fumblings in the darkness. Brown's hands beneath her buttocks raised her, lowered her slowly, with straining creaks of muscle, short gasps. She hugged him with her legs, her arms. As he kissed her she tasted salt. Her tongue flicked out, licked at the tears, and suddenly she felt a sudden looseness in the pit of her stomach. She cried out, clutched at him, shuddered, felt her body shaking as if it had a mind of its own, and then she forgot it, forgot herself, went drifting on a dark cloud, almost unconscious. Brown held her so tightly her ribs ached. Suddenly she felt frightened. "Baby?" she whispered.

"Shh," Brown said. "Shh."

11 Saturday

The Reverend Mr. J. Peter Sloan awakened in his broad bed and smiled with satisfaction as he regarded the ripe outlines of Sister Fundidia Larson, who lay beside him, invitingly draped with a satin sheet. The Reverend Mr. Sloan sighed as he recalled the details of the seduction of Sister Fundidia. The Reverend Mr. Sloan had taken it slowly, moving from dry martinis to a dry sauterne to a dry brandy and then on to Sister Fundidia, who by that time was rather wet. Mr. Sloan had congratulated himself on once again surpassing Christ's Last Supper. Having supped, Mr. Sloan had moved on rapidly to the Crucifixion. He had been somewhat astonished by Sister Fundidia's state of innocence, and a trifle disgusted at the bloody nature of the sacrifice, but he had managed to rise to the occasion. Sister Fundidia had proven quite athletic, and one of Mr. Sloan's most vivid recollections was of her sitting astride him, spurring on to the Glory River, her breasts bouncing like chocolate volleyballs.

Mr. Sloan glanced at his wristwatch and saw that there was plenty of time to get to the airport. He relaxed and reviewed his itinerary. The only problem with the Caribbean tour was Sister Fundidia, whom, in the heat of the chase, he had promised to take along. Now Mr. Sloan's thoughts turned to all the West Indian women who would challenge him with their heathenness, and he shivered as he anticipated plunging the sword of Christian faith into a pagan mass of caramel thighs. Witchy-women, beaded and bangled, danced across his vision, shoved their bellies in his face, and Mr. Sloan wondered if his penis, in closer proximity to the headwaters of Black Power, would grow to enormous size. Speculation gave rise to fact, and so the Reverend Mr. Sloan peeled back Sister Fundidia's satin wrapper, filled his fists with Sister Fundidia, dug his heels into her meaty thighs, and, riding high, gave her her head. Just as they galloped to the wire, neck and neck, destined for a photo finish, possibly a dead heat, Sister Fundidia's eyes popped open. The Reverend Mr. Sloan spurted into the lead. Sister Fundidia failed to finish. "My Lord!" exclaimed Sister Fundidia. "Reverend Sloan, what are you doing?"

The Reverend Mr. Sloan dismounted and lay on his back with his slowly softening member pointing toward heaven.

"Oh, Lord," wailed Sister Fundidia, grasping at her sopping pubic hair, "I'm ruined!"

"You can't be ruined," Mr. Sloan assured her, "you've only just opened for business." Sister Fundidia flopped over on her stomach and watered the mattress with her tears. "Sheet," muttered the Reverend Mr. Sloan. He rolled out of bed, stomped into the bathroom, and began to brush his teeth, pausing from time to time to spit out a hair. Sister Fundidia wailed away, shaking the big round bed with her sobs. "Keep it down," the Reverend Mr. Sloan ordered.

Sister Fundidia rolled over again and glared at him. "You're *horrible*," she told him. "You—forced me."

Mr. Sloan strode out of the bathroom and presented his back to her. "You wanna tell me how I forced you to bite me?"

Sister Fundidia gazed in horror. "I did—that?"

"Indeed," Mr. Sloan told her. "Why, just as I was gettin' ready to take you home, when I was puttin' your sweater around your shoulders"—Mr. Sloan moved up behind Sister Fundidia and grasped her shoulders—"you caught my hands and forced them to your *breasts!*" With a convulsive motion Mr. Sloan grabbed a rubbery handful of Sister Fundidia.

"*I* did *that?*" cried Sister Fundidia.

"That ain't all," declared the Reverend Mr. Sloan, working away like a Wisconsin dairy farmer. "After that, you took one hand . . ." Mr. Sloan grabbed Sister Fundidia's left hand and pressed it firmly against his scrotum.

Sister Fundidia's hand trembled. "I did *that?*"

"And *that*," thundered Mr. Sloan, "ain't all. When you had aroused me beyond all hope of control, you ripped your clothes away, fell onto your back, and pulled me down upon you!" Mr. Sloan demonstrated the final phase, paying pious attention to detail. Bouncing up and down on Sister Fundidia, he glared sternly.

"Um, um, um," said Sister Fundidia. "I did all that!"

"And you've done it again!" shouted Mr. Sloan. He stopped in mid-stroke and made to pull away.

"Oh, Reverend, I'm so sorry!" cried Sister Fundidia, grasping him convulsively.

"Release me, hussy," Mr. Sloan shouted. He wriggled strenuously. Sister Fundidia's eyes glazed over and she began to do some strenuous wriggling on her own.

"Jesus and Mary," screamed Sister Fundidia. "I see Jesus and Mary!"

Sister Fundidia wriggled so much she pushed the Reverend Mr. Sloan out, and he banged himself painfully against her thigh. "Thou vile whore!" screamed Mr. Sloan. "First you ruin me as a Christian, and now you destroy me as a man."

"Oh, Reverend," panted Sister Fundidia, "I didn't mean it."

Mr. Sloan clutched himself and moaned, carefully observing Sister Fundidia through half-closed eyes. Sister Fundidia hesitated, then bent over and gently pried his hands away from his groin. "Ahhh," moaned the Reverend Mr. Sloan.

"Don't worry, Reverend, I'll make it all well," said Sister Fundidia. She bent to kiss him. Mr. Sloan grasped her firmly by the hair and shoved himself halfway down her throat. "Ughcmlumphmmkhck," said Sister Fundidia.

The Reverend Mr. Sloan moaned in divine release and let her go. Sister Fundidia came up for air, looked around dazedly, and then planted a soupy kiss on Mr. Sloan's lips. With a horrified shout Mr. Sloan applied the back of his right hand to his mouth and the back of his left hand, with considerably more force, to Sister Fundidia's face. Sister Fundidia vanished beyond the far edge of the bed. "Don't ever do that," said the Reverend Mr. Sloan.

"Yes, Reverend," whispered the invisible Sister Fundidia. "I'm sorry, Reverend."

"Go brush your teeth," Mr. Sloan ordered. Sister Fundidia got up off the floor and scurried into the bathroom. "And wash yourself while you're at it," Mr. Sloan called after her. "You smell like last month's chitlins." He climbed out of bed and went into the bathroom, where Sister Fundidia stood brushing her teeth with one hand and, with the other, energetically mopping herself with a washcloth coated with Ivory soap. "Y'oughta use Lava," grumbled Mr. Sloan.

"Eychgh guchgh ehchgh alhmochgh lichgh wchee wachs marichgh," said Sister Fundidia, looking doe-eyed at the Reverend's reflection in the mirror.

"Spit that out and talk right," snapped Mr. Sloan.

Sister Fundidia obeyed. "I guess it's almost like we was married," Sister Fundidia sighed. "Goin' away is almost like a honeymoon."

"Umm," said Mr. Sloan. He reached out and took the washcloth from her. " 'If you gonna steal yourself a lamb, might as well have yourself a ram'—John 3:16."

Sister Fundidia smiled happily. "And when we get back we can get married for real."

In the mirror Mr. Sloan gave her a saintly smile, while congratulating himself on having had the foresight to buy Sister Fundidia a one-way ticket.

"Good morning," Brown said, grinning.

Vanessa opened her eyes, blinked. "It's still the middle a the goddamn night," she complained. Brown, still smiling, licked his finger and touched the tip of her nose. "Ugh," Vanessa said, rolling over.

Brown bounced out of bed, dropped to the floor, and squeezed out seventy push-ups. Then he straightened up, sweat shining on his skin, and padded into the kitchen. He set up the coffeepot, turned on the stove, picked up the bag of garbage, and went to the window. Below him, in the alley, broken glass glinted in the morning sun. Brown swallowed heavily, dropped the bag, watching as it fell and burst. He turned away from the window. He sat at the table while the percolator perked, drumming on the tabletop with his hands. A bouncy rhythm—Brown wondered what it was. Then he remembered: Jake's "pome." Brown smiled wistfully, then stopped smiling and looked thoughtful. He took out paper and pencil and scribbled a few lines. Then he beat on the table some more.

"That coffee I smell?" Vanessa called.

"No," Brown said absently, "what you smell is the collected sweat of several million exploited niggers an' spics."

"Smells good," Vanessa said. "Bring me some when it's ready."

"Yes, missy," Brown said. "Anything else you'd like? A ripe bird? A singing melon?"

"Just the coffee."

" 'Just the coffee,' " Brown muttered. He beat on the table some more, scribbled a few lines. "You want some eggs?"

"I don't like eggs."

"You don't mind exploitin' niggers, but the hens is safe."

"I used to be one a them bitches lays them golden eggs," Vanessa said sourly.

Brown sighed, put down his pencil, went to stand in the doorway. Vanessa lay on her back, her eyes closed. "Don't you go thinkin' it meant nothin', Brown, 'cause that's exactly what it meant—nothin'."

"It happened once, it'll happen again."

"That's what they keep sayin' about Jesus. We're still waitin'." Brown looked at her for an instant, then burst out laughing. "An' just what is so goddamn funny?" Vanessa demanded. Brown, grinning, hummed a few bars of "Adeste Fideles." "That ain't what I meant," Vanessa snapped.

"Well, you was talkin' about the Second Coming," Brown said, and ducked back into the kitchen. He heard her give a low chuckle, but when he carried a cup of coffee to her she was frowning again.

"What time is it?" she said, taking the cup.

"Ten-thirty." Vanessa groaned. "Ten-thirty," Brown repeated firmly. "Ten-thirty on payday. I gotta go an' get ma money."

Vanessa set the cup down, got out of bed, and followed him as he went back to the kitchen. "You can't go out till I find Leroy," she said.

Brown finished pouring himself some coffee, and added milk and four sugars before he spoke. "I don't want to hear any more about that."

"But I—"

"I *said* I don't want to hear any more about that. You ain't goin' nowhere."

"You don't own me," Vanessa snapped. "I do what I want. Don't you be tellin' me when to come—" Brown snorted. "Shut up." She glared at him with eyes dark and smoldering.

Brown sat down. "I don't want to give you orders. I don't want to tell you what to do or what not to do. If you want to leave here now and never come back, you go ahead. If you wanna peddle your ass up one side a South Street an' down the other, you go ahead. You wanna kiss Leroy's backside, you go ahead. But you do it because you want to, not for me. I ain't no damn pimp, got to be sendin' somebody out to do for me. Now, are you goin' lookin' for Leroy because you want to be with him? You want to go, or you want to stay?"

"You know," Vanessa said.

"I don't know nothin' if you don't tell me."

"I want to stay. An' I want you to stay alive."

"All right," Brown said. "You stay, an' I'll try an' stay alive. An' if I fuck it up, then you can call me names."

"You really could get killed," Vanessa said. "You know that?"

"Yep. Truck might get me. Might have World War Three, or eat a can a tuna fish that some unhappy wage slave shit in to show his contempt for the Great Society. You expect me to worry about pissin' off Leroy when I got God to worry about? Leroy'll probably forget all about me sooner or later, but God got pissed at Adam an' Eve an' the joker ain't got over it yet."

"You're a jackass," Vanessa told him.

"Now the deal was you was supposed to wait until I was dead 'fore you started callin' me names."

"Jackass," Vanessa shouted. She leaped at him. Coffee splattered all over the place as they rolled around on the floor. Vanessa got Brown's head in a scissors and put on the pressure. Brown, half-laughing, half-crying, twisted at her big toe. When that had no effect he slid his hand on up her leg. "You're cheatin'," Vanessa protested.

"That's what Liston said every time Patterson hit him on the fist with his face."

"That ain't ma fist."

"That ain't ma face, neither, but it will be if you're not careful."

Vanessa relaxed the pressure on his head. "I'm always careful. Ma mama always told me, if you can't be good, be careful."

"Yeah," Brown said, "an' if you can't be careful, please don't name it after me." Vanessa looked at him, jumped up, and ran for the bathroom. Brown stared after her, mystified. He shrugged and got up off the floor. In a few minutes she came back. "You're good, anyway," Brown said, with exaggerated blandness.

"That was an accident," Vanessa said. "Ain't nothin' changed."

Brown sighed. "You're beginnin' to sound like a cross between Barry Goldwater and William F. Buckley."

"And who the hell's William F. Buckley?" Vanessa sat down across from him, glaring.

"William F. Buckley is one of the principal masters of the Tai Tass or Hung Oop school of moral and political philosophy, which maintains that what did not happen yesterday ought not to happen at all. Practically speaking, Mr. Buckley would love to send all the niggers back to Africa, but he can't find enough clipper ships."

"Sometimes," Vanessa said, "you sound like educational TV. I wish I could change the channel."

"What you want, a soap opera?"

"Maybe I just want to turn you off altogether."

"Click," Brown said. He slurped loudly at his coffee. Vanessa got up and went to look out the window. Brown rocked back in his chair. Vanessa walked into the bedroom, came back with a cigarette, and leaned out the window, smoking. Brown let the chair come down onto all four legs, went to the sink, and rinsed out the cups. Vanessa hummed softly. Brown turned off the water with a violent twist that rattled the plumbing. Vanessa looked over at him reproachfully, then turned her attention back to the window. · Brown stalked through to the bathroom, slammed on the water, climbed beneath the iceberg coldness. He smiled grimly as he soaped himself, his face turned into the frigid spray. He felt Vanessa's breasts against his back. He rinsed himself off and got out of the shower. She followed him. Brown made a large production of drying his face. Vanessa pulled the towel away.

"Don't you hide from me, muthafucka!"

Brown looked at her. "Who," he said carefully, "is hiding from whom?"

"You is hidin' from whommmm, dammit!"

"No," Brown said. "You are hiding from you. You *want* to just lay there like a goddamn whore."

"I *am* a goddamn whore!" Vanessa shouted. "I'm a goddamn H, O, R, E whore. I ain't no college professor—"

"Lotsa college professors are whores," Brown said. "There's more to bein' a whore than not knowin' how to spell it."

"Here we are, the world's fuckin' expert on fuckin' whores—"

"No," Brown said, "actually, it's a new thing for me. I never met a whore I wanted to fuck before."

"Shit," Vanessa said. "Why can't you just leave me be?"

"I care about you," Brown said.

"Oh, yeah," Vanessa said. "I knew that was comin'. What else is there to try?"

"If I didn't care about you, I wouldn't care if you came or not."

"Onliest reason you do care is so you can think you're big shit—Dr. Brown, who came on down to South Street an' scared the shit out a the tough guys an' taught the hookers the meanin' a true love."

"That's right," Brown said. "Matter of fact, that's the only reason I even touch you. You're so ugly, if you was a dog I'd shave your ass an' teach you to walk backward. That make you happy?"

"Lemme outa here," Vanessa said. She ran into the bedroom and began putting on her clothes. Brown stood watching. "Don't you try an' stop me," Vanessa said dangerously.

"Wouldn't dream of it," Brown said.

Vanessa stepped into her shoes. "You can forget all about me."

"Forget who?" Brown said. He turned to the basin and ran water, lathered his face, started shaving. A minute later he heard the door slam. Brown went on shaving, ignoring the blood that reddened the white lather where, in a moment of inattention, he had cut himself.

Willie T. swaggered into the lobby of the Elysium Hotel, stopped just inside the door, and cleared his throat loudly. The Muslim desk clerk continued his diligent perusal of *Muhammed Speaks*. Willie T. glared at the lowered head, cleared his throat once again. The desk clerk looked up very slowly, glanced at Willie T. for the barest second, then wordlessly returned to his paper. Willie T. strutted over to the desk and banged on it. "What?" said the desk clerk without looking up.

"What, what?" retorted Willie T.

The desk clerk raised his head and examined Willie T., like a zoologist studying a strange new creature. "What you mean, what, what?"

"I mean what, what?" Willie T. snapped. "Don't you be givin' me no plain what, nigger."

"Well, what you want on it, fried onions?"

"I want a little respect around here," Willie T. declared. "I don't want to be walkin' in an' have some silly fool sayin' 'what,' that's what."

The desk clerk looked heavenward in a silent appeal to Almighty Allah. "All right, Willie," he said patiently. "What can I do for you?"

"What can I do for you, *sir*," said Willie T.

"You can't be doin' nothin' for me, 'ceptin' maybe get on outa here with your foolishness."

"Sir!" roared Willie T.

"Leroy's still asleep," the desk clerk said mildly.

"Sir," repeated Willie T. in a hoarse whisper. "You call me sir."

"I don't call nobody sir. An' if I was gonna be callin' anybody sir, it sure ain't gonna be you." Willie T. reached across the desk and grabbed the clerk by the front of his shirt. "The Prophet trains his men to resist the infidel," the clerk said softly. "I am a 'Fruit of Islam.'"

Willie T. let go in a small hurry and retreated a step. "I don't know nothin' 'bout no Islam, but you is a fruit for sure." The clerk smiled benignly. "You better show some respect, or your X is gonna get turned into an O." The desk clerk snorted and went back to his paper. "X, shit," said Willie T. "Your mama just didn't *know* your daddy's last name." The desk clerk sighed. Willie T. reached out and plucked the corner of the paper. "Why don't you fools ever change the back page a that paper? 'What the Muslims Want.' Shit."

"We ain't changed it 'cause we ain't got it yet," the desk clerk said.

"An' you ain't never gonna get it, neither. Only a crazy fool'd trade in pork chops an' wine for a newspaper an' a fuckin' bean pie." The clerk gave Willie T. a tolerant smile and went on with his reading. "Damn if I'd want a God that hung out in Chicago," said Willie T.

"The Prophet is in Chicago," said the desk clerk. "Allah is everywhere."

"Um, humph," said Willie T. "Y'all in great shape. You got a nigger Al Capone for a prophet, a bunch a fruits for followers, an' a God that lays around everywhere like a pile a cat shit."

The desk clerk put the paper down. "We got somethin' else, too. Only we just about run out of it."

"Oh yeah, what's that?" said Willie T.

"Patience, brother, patience."

"Uh huh," said Willie T. "Well I guess it's easy to wait when you can't come anyways."

The desk clerk shook his head sadly. "Willie, please. It's just too early in the mornin' for your mouth to be out diggin' your ass a grave."

" 'Ass!' " exclaimed Willie T. "I thought you fruits didn't use bad words."

"Ass," said the desk clerk, "is found often in the Koran. It is not a bad word. It is a noun indicatin' a familiar beast of burden. This animal is usually brown in color, havin' big ears, a big mouth, a big nose, small eyes, a particularly tiny brain, an' no sense whatsoever. Asses usually live to the age of ten or eleven before bein' beaten to death. How old are you now, Willie?"

"If I was you—" Willie T. began. He was interrupted by a heavy thump on the ceiling. "What's that?"

"Sounds like Leroy's gettin' up," the desk clerk said. Willie T. stared up at the ceiling. The desk clerk settled back with his paper. From above came a sound like a 747 on takeoff. "Yep," said the desk clerk, "he's up all right."

Footsteps banged across the ceiling, which bounced slightly with each heavy thud. A door slammed. There was a sound like a Mack truck revving up, followed by a series of cannon shots. "What's that?" said Willie T., his voice trembling.

"Sounds like Leroy's takin' a dump," said the desk clerk without looking up from his paper. There was a metallic screech and rumble like Niagara Falls. "Yep," said the desk clerk, "he's takin' a dump all right."

The footsteps pounded back across the ceiling. There was a moment of silence, followed by a sharp crack, a sound like a screeching cat, and a heavy thump. "What in Jesus' name was *that?*" said Willie T.

"Sounds like Leroy's in a poor mood," the desk clerk said. Light footsteps pattered across the ceiling. Leslie appeared at the head of the stairs with blood all over her face. The desk clerk looked at her, sniffed, and returned his attention to the words of the Prophet. "Yep," he said, "he's in a bad mood all right."

"Lord," said Willie T. He pulled out his handkerchief and extended it toward Leslie. She came down the stairs, took it, and held it to her face. "Lord," said Willie T. again.

The front door opened and Cotton strolled in. "*Salam alaikum,*" Cotton said. "What's happenin'?"

The desk clerk looked up. "*Alaikum wa salam.* Not much. Willie T. almost got hisself wasted, I almost got a medal for exterminatin' a public nuisance, an' Leroy, as you can see, is in a poor mood."

"In other words," Cotton said, "not shit."

"*Bismellahi,*" said the desk clerk.

"How come Leroy's in a bad mood? Didn't he get all his mean out yesterday?"

"Brown," said Leslie

"He been around here again?"

"Nah," Leslie said. "Leroy went lookin' for him."

Cotton chuckled humorlessly. "Leroy get his ass whipped or somethin'?"

Leslie took the handkerchief away from her face. "Cotton, Leroy ain't lookin' for no rumble, he wants a shoot-out."

Cotton stared at her. "A shoot-out? You mean Leroy went lookin' for Brown with a gun? With a fuckin' gun?"

"That's exactly what you call it," Leslie said, grinning sourly.

"Oh, Jesus!" Cotton said.

"Whatsa matter with you?" said Willie T. "He's been gettin' his shit together to go after Brown for two weeks."

"Yeah, sure. He was gonna kick the dude's ass or beat him up, or bust his legs or somethin'. Gino might not get too upset about that, Gino ain't fond a niggers anways. But even Gino can't afford to be lettin' people shoot his men down."

"You a worry-ass," Willie T. said. "We don't even know for sure the cat works for Gino."

"So when we gonna find out, after Leroy turns him into hamburger?" Cotton looked at Leslie. "How come Leroy didn't kill him last night?"

"Leroy didn't say," Leslie snapped. "But if he was in the same shape when he tried as he was when he come back, he's lucky he didn't shoot his own damn dick off."

"You shouldn't be talkin' about Leroy that way," Willie T. said.

Leslie regarded him sourly. "While he's killin' folks, I hope he gets you, too. An' Rayburn, too," she added. "Put the poor bastard out a his misery."

Cotton shook his head. "I'll say this for Leroy, he don't go pickin' up no second-class cunts." Leslie shot him a threatening look and opened her mouth.

"If I was you," said the desk clerk, "I'd just keep it closed."

Leslie kept it closed.

"Leroy still upstairs?" Cotton asked.

"Yep," said the desk clerk, "he's up there all right."

"All right, Willie, when he comes down, you tell him not to go killin' nobody until I get back." Cotton turned and trundled out the door.

"This I have got to see," said the desk clerk. "You tryin' to tell Leroy he can't kill somebody when he feels like it."

"I'ma tell him," Willie T. snapped. "I ain't afraid a no Leroy."

"Uh, huh."

"I will," Willie T. insisted. "I'll tell him."

"Tell who what?" asked Leroy from the top of the stairs.

"Tell Cotton he can kiss his own damn rattlesnakes," Willie T. said promptly.

Leroy descended the stairs like a lowering storm. He stopped above the step where Leslie was sitting, tapped her spine with the toe of his shoe. "Move it," Leroy said.

"Walk around," Leslie said.

Leroy bent over and whispered something in her ear. Leslie moved it. Leroy continued his descent. "Now, Willie, what's this shit about rattlesnakes?"

"Oh, nothin', boss, nothin'," Willie T. said. The desk clerk snickered. "Boss, why don't you get rid a this Arabian asshole?"

"Well, I was gonna let him keep you in line, but it's probably a bad idea. He won't touch pork."

"In his case," said the desk clerk, "I will make an exception."

"All right, now, we got us some work to do," Leroy said. "Les, you go get cleaned up. You look like you fell off the roof on your face. Willie, T., you comin' with me. We goin' Brown huntin'."

"But . . ." said Willie T.

"But what?"

"But what if the character really do work for Gino? Ain't Gino gonna be mad, you killin' one a his men?"

Leroy stuck out his lower lip and considered the proposition. "Most likely. But if he do get upset, I know what to do to calm him down."

"You do?" said Willie T. "What's that?"

"I'll let Gino kill one a mine," Leroy said. Smiling, he strode out the door.

✎

The banging had been so furious that Mrs. Fletcher half expected to see white-sheeted forms bearing burning crosses when she opened the door. But the only white she saw was in Sister Fundidia's eyes. Sister Fundidia dropped to her knees and hugged Mrs. Fletcher's legs for dear life. Sister Fundidia's breasts formed a fulcrum, and Mrs. Fletcher was nearly levered to the sidewalk before she managed to grab the doorjamb to hold herself up. "Oh sweet Jesus!" wailed Sister Fundidia, "oh sweeeet Jesus!" She clung to Mrs. Fletcher like a boa constrictor. Mrs. Fletcher kicked at her, leaped away. Sister Fundidia pursued, still on her knees. Mrs. Fletcher retreated hurriedly. Sister Fundidia pursued doggedly. Mrs. Fletcher took refuge behind the coffee table. Sister Fundidia, in hot pursuit, lost her balance and fell on her face. She began to kick the floor. "Oh Jehoshaphat," wailed Sister Fundidia.

From down the hall came the sounds of a squeaking roller, a clanking belt buckle, a flushing toilet. Brother Fletcher came through the door buttoning his shirt. He took one look at Sister Fundidia and decided he'd better zip his fly first. Sister Fundidia looked up, saw Brother Fletcher, struggled to her knees, and charged, bellowing like a cow elephant in heat. Brother Fletcher, both hands on his zipper, backed away. Mrs. Fletcher intercepted Sister Fundidia with a passable open-field tackle, slapped on a half nelson, and had her pinned in seconds.

"What—?"

"Don't ask me," grunted Mrs. Fletcher. "She's one a yours."

Brother Fletcher shrugged. He got down on his knees so he could look Sister Fundidia in the eye. "Now calm down, Sister," Brother Fletcher said gently. Sister Fundidia's deranged canary wails degenerated into sobs. Mrs. Fletcher cautiously released the chicken wing she had prudently slapped on Sister Fundidia's left arm, but retained the half nelson. "Let her go," Brother Fletcher said. Mrs. Fletcher looked doubtful, but she let go and rose to her feet, groaning. "Where did you learn that?" said Brother Fletcher.

"I had seven brothers and four sisters," Mrs. Fletcher reminded him. "I *had* to learn that."

Brother Fletcher returned his attention to Sister Fundidia, whose sobs had become hiccups. "Now, Sister," said Brother Fletcher, "how can we help you?"

Sister Fundidia raised her face from the floor. "It's hic Je hic hoshaphat hic," Sister Fundidia said. "He's in hic jail." Sister Fundidia gave Brother Fletcher a pleading look. "Hic," she added as an afterthought, before letting her head sink back to the floor.

"Jehoshaphat," breathed Brother Fletcher. "Who's Jehoshaphat? I don't know any Jehoshaphat."

"Looks like you're gonna be gettin' acquainted," observed Mrs. Fletcher. "Come on, honey," she said, reaching down and hauling Sister Fundidia to her feet and conveying her to the sofa. "Coffee?"

"Hic," said Sister Fundidia.

"Coffee," said Mrs. Fletcher, and went to make it.

Brother Fletcher sat down next to Sister Fundidia and patted her gently on the arm. "Now, Sister, I'll certainly try to help your friend, ah, Jehoshaphat, but—"

"Well, hic," said Sister Fundidia, "I sup hic pose I shouldn't really hic call hic him by his hic first hic name. But we *are* in hic love." She looked at Brother Fletcher woefully. "Hic."

Brother Fletcher sighed. "Would you bring us a glass of water?" he called. The pipes banged briefly. Mrs. Fletcher appeared in the doorway holding a glass of water.

"Hic," said Sister Fundidia.

"Water won't help," Mrs. Fletcher said.

"Of course it will," said Brother Fletcher, taking the glass. "Here you are, Sister, drink this, all at one time." Sister Fundidia drank the water all at one time. They waited for a few minutes in expectant silence. "There you are," said Brother Fletcher triumphantly. "Feel better now, Sister?"

"Yes, thic you," said Sister Fundidia. Mrs. Fletcher snorted and returned to the kitchen.

Brother Fletcher cleared his throat. "Now, Sister, about your friend—'

"I just don't hic know hic what to hic do," moaned Sister Fundidia "We were going to get hic married hic and he can't hic marry hic me hic if he's in hic jail, can hic he?"

"No," said Brother Fletcher gently, "I wouldn't think so."

"An' if he hic can't hic marry hic me," said Sister Fundidia, "I'm hic ruined!"

"You mean—"

"I hic raped him hic," Sister Fundidia confessed.

"I see," Brother Fletcher said gravely.

"Hic," said Sister Fundidia.

Mrs. Fletcher entered carrying sugar, milk, and three steaming mugs on a painted tray. Under one arm she held a brown paper bag.

"What's that for?" asked Brother Fletcher.

Mrs. Fletcher set the tray down and looked at him haughtily. "Anybody with good sense knows there ain't but one cure for the hiccups."

"A paper bag?" demanded Brother Fletcher scornfully. "Pshaw."

Mrs. Fletcher looked at him, smiled knowingly, and turned to Sister Fundidia. "Don't you pay no attention to him, honey, he's a *man*. Now you just blow into this bag. Fill it right up an' don't let the air out."

"Hic," said Sister Fundidia. She accepted the bag, plastered it over her mouth, and began to blow into it with great enthusiasm.

"Jehoshaphat," mused Brother Fletcher. Sister Fundidia completed her task, and Mrs. Fletcher took the bag carefully and strolled around behind the sofa. "You say his name is Jehoshaphat, Sister?"

"Hic," agreed Sister Fundidia.

"I told you that wouldn't work," Brother Fletcher said.

"Hic," said Sister Fundidia apologetically.

Mrs. Fletcher slammed her free hand against the bottom of the bag which she was holding three inches from Sister Fundidia's left ear. Sister Fundidia let out a howl like a strangling cat and leaped two feet into the air. She landed back on the sofa and bounced heavily. Her breasts bobbed like balloons in a high wind. "It's the only way to get rid of the hiccups," Mrs. Fletcher explained to her startled husband.

"Hic," said Sister Fundidia.

" 'It's the only way to get rid of hiccups,' " said Brother Fletcher.

Mrs. Fletcher ignored him and sat down on the other side of Sister Fundidia. "Sugar, dear?" she said.

"Yes hic please," said Sister Fundidia. "Only . . ."

"Only what?" said Mrs. Fletcher.

"It just hic don't seem hic right, us drinkin' hic coffee while the hic Reverend's in hic jail hic."

"What?" exclaimed Brother Fletcher. "You mean Jehoshaphat is—"

"He hic *said* it was hic all hic right to call him hic Je hic hoshaphat hic," Sister Fundidia said quickly. "But hic," she added, "maybe he hic meant hic only hic when we hic was hic a hic lone."

"I think maybe he did, honey," Mrs. Fletcher said softly. She looked at Brother Fletcher. Brother Fletcher looked at her. Mrs. Fletcher began to giggle.

"Harriette, this is serious," admonished Brother Fletcher. "The man's in prison."

"Sure is serious," agreed Mrs. Fletcher. "They might make a mistake an' let him loose."

Brother Fletcher glared at her. Mrs. Fletcher covered her mouth with both hands and giggled more quietly. Brother Fletcher turned to Sister Fundidia. "Now, Sister, I want you to be calm. Are you calm?"

"Hic," said Sister Fundidia.

"Good, good," said Brother Fletcher. "Now I want you to tell us everything."

"Every hic thing?" said Sister Fundidia uncertainly.

"Yes," giggled Mrs. Fletcher, "every hic thing."

"I don't see what's so funny about a man being in jail," Brother Fletcher snapped.

Mrs. Fletcher stopped laughing instantly. "You're right," she said. "It's not funny. It's not funny when a chicken is in a hen house, so it isn't funny when Sloan's in jail."

Brother Fletcher shook his head and turned back to Sister Fundidia. "All right, Sister, go ahead." Sister Fundidia launched into her story, punctuating it with hiccups. "He was taking you to the Caribbean?" interrupted Brother Fletcher.

"Hic," nodded Sister Fundidia. "See, hic, it was all my hic fault about the hic other, but he hic said we could get hic married as soon as we hic got hic back hic. He was real hic good about it. Hic."

"You say you raped him," said Mrs. Fletcher bluntly. "Just how did you do that?"

"Well I don't hic remember for hic sure," admitted Sister Fundidia. "I was hic unconscious at the hic time. I wouldn'ta hic known at hic all but the Reverend hic told hic me."

"Oh," said Mrs. Fletcher. "I hic see."

"All right," said Brother Fletcher, "now you said you were just about to leave for the airport when the police came?"

"That's hic right," said Sister Fundidia. "An' then I hic ran right hic here."

"Didn't the police say anything?"

"Oh hic yes," said Sister Fundidia. "They hic said a hic lot. They hic said somebody had hic tipped them hic off and that hic they were hic taking him hic back hic."

"Back?" said Brother Fletcher. "Back. Well, Sister, what did he say?"

"I hic wouldn't wanna repeat it, hic, but he was mighty hic up hic set."

"I'll just bet," Mrs. Fletcher said, standing up. "Sister, I think you should come on in the bedroom and lay down for a while. You've had a hard time." She took Sister Fundidia firmly by the hand.

"But what about hic Je hic Reverend hic Sloan?"

"Don't you worry," Mrs. Fletcher said. "I'll make certain the Reverend gets all the help he's got comin'." She smiled grimly and led Sister Fundidia off to the bedroom.

Brother Fletcher got up and went to stare out the window at the clot of winos gathered in front of the liquor store. "Back," he said musingly. "Back."

Mrs. Fletcher returned from the bedroom and sat down on the sofa. "I wonder what they caught him for. Is there a law against sellin' you mother?"

Brother Fletcher turned away from the window. "The question is," he said, "what to do about it."

"Why do anything?"

"Well I've got to do *something.*"

"Why? Seems to me somebody already did something. You're always sayin' God moves in mysterious ways. Now what could be more mysterious than the Philadelphia Police Department?"

Brother Fletcher looked at her. "They that hunger and thirst after righteousness shall be filled," he said softly. "Maybe it does work."

"Of course it does," Mrs. Fletcher said. "All you got to do is figure out what it did. This time it gave you a church."

"I suppose so," said Brother Fletcher. "But that's not really important. What's important is that it works."

"Fletcher," Mrs. Fletcher said, "you know half the time I don't understand you at all." She got up and went over and planted a soupy kiss on his cheek.

The fan in the ceiling cast floating shadows over the lobby of the Elysium Hotel. A few feet away the evening's festivities were well under way in the cocktail lounge, and the doorway that led from lobby to bar exhaled tobacco smoke, music, laughter, and the odor of alcohol. The desk clerk, bent over an Arabic edition of the Koran, wrinkled his flat nose in pious distaste.

It was a few minutes after ten when Cotton came in. "Where the hell's Leroy?" Cotton said without preliminaries.

The desk clerk looked up. "Mr. Briggs is out."

"Where'd he go?"

"He went, quote, Brown huntin', unquote. He left shortly after you this morning."

"Oh, Jesus! Didn't Willie T. tell him what I said?"

"In the words of the Prophet—"

"Fuck the Prophet," Cotton said.

"—never trust an infidel to behave with honor." The desk clerk smiled serenely.

Cotton moved closer and peered suspiciously at his eyes. "You been into the camel shit again, ain't you, Mohammed?"

"I have not—"

"Shut up. I gotta think." Cotton paced the lobby for a few minutes. "That Willie T., didn't he even *try* an' stop Leroy?"

"He said, quote, Cotton can kiss his own damn rattlesnakes, unquote."

"Well, why didn't you say somethin'?"

"If it is the will of Allah—" said the desk clerk. He stopped when Cotton tapped him firmly over the belly button.

"Now you listen here, Mr. Hophead X, if I don't get ahold a Leroy before he gets ahold a Brown you best be worryin' about your will, 'stead a Allah's." The desk clerk smiled serenely. "Where's Willie T.?" Cotton barked.

"I have been immersed in the waters of Truth and can pay no attention to the comings and goings of minnows."

Cotton stared at the ceiling, grinding his teeth. "How much a that shit did you smoke?"

"Only a fool attempts to count the sands of the desert."

"My God," Cotton groaned.

"Were I to guess," the desk clerk continued, "and I would only guess under duress, but were I to guess, I would surmise that Willie T. is somewhere like the North Carolina Bar-B-Q, busily reserving his place in Hell by feasting on pork chops."

"If you don't quit monkeyin' around an' give me some straight answers, I'm a shove a pork chop up your ass an' send you to Hell backwards," Cotton told him. "Now, do you know where Willie is, or don't you?"

"He went out. With Leroy."

"Oh, shit."

"He returned, without Leroy."

"So he's here?"

"No." Cotton ground his teeth. "He went out again."

"Where?"

"I don't know. But"—the desk clerk raised a finger—"he came back But"—he lowered his finger—"he went out again."

"Did he stay out?" Cotton asked.

The desk clerk wrinkled his nose. "He went out with Charlene. In the words of the Prophet, a man who will sup on unclean animals will also—"

"Yeah, yeah, yeah," Cotton said, "an' ain't no damn prophet never said that."

"You don't know what the Prophet said," the desk clerk said. "You can't read English, let alone Arabic."

"Two courses at Community fuckin' College don't make you the Sheik a Araby," Cotton snapped. "Now you listen. If Leroy comes back you keep him here, you understand? Keep him here. If you don't, this place is gonna be one big pork roast, you dig?" Cotton started toward the door.

"Allah," said the desk clerk, "will protect his own."

Cotton shook his head, snorted, and trundled out the door.

"Hey, Leo, how about a lil drinkee-drink?"

Leo, his features already twisted into a mask of distaste, glanced as briefly as possible into the simpering face of Elmo. "Y'already had too much," Leo said.

Elmo looked hurt. "Whatsa matter, doncha like Elmo?"

"Sure he does," Big Betsy broke in. "We all like you. Course," she went on thoughtfully, "we'd like you a lot better if you was someplace else. Like Texas. Y'oughta go out west, Elmo. They got lotsa rattlesnakes out west. It ain't good to be separated from your own kind." She turned to Leo. "Don't give him nothin'," she advised.

"I gotta serve him," Leo said in disgust. "It's the law or somethin'. Sometimes I think them segregationists got a point. What you want, Elmo?"

"Beer," Elmo said, pushing money across the bar with a grubby hand.

Leo drew the beer, set it up. "Now you listen, Elmo, I don't wanna hear one damn word outa you. 'Specially not to Rayburn."

"Rayburn's here?" Elmo gulped.

"Sure is," Betsy said. "Now ain't you got an urgent appointment in Timbuctoo?"

"No," Elmo said.

"Well I do." Big Betsy lowered herself from the stool and, holding her nose, waddled away.

"You know, Leo," Elmo said, "I don't care too much for the way you treat me. Every time I come in here you be shovin' me out 'fore I even get in the door. Makes me feel like I was on a merry-go-round. Ma beer don't settle right. I get a belly full a gas."

"Aww," Leo said. "That's too bad. Don't hardly leave enough room for the shit. Try puttin' it in your head, 'cause that's stone empty."

"Well," Elmo said, "that may be, but ma empty head has the idea that maybe if you was to treat me a little better, I might see ma way clear to not doin' ma duty, which is to tell Rayburn where his run-off wife done run off to. You see what I mean?"

Leo gave him a look of grudging admiration mingled with acid disgust. "Elmo, I got to hand it to you, you had everybody fooled. They all said you was a prick, but what you are is a cunt. With crabs." Elmo glared. "But," Leo continued, "I do see your point. Only I wouldn't want to stand in the way of a man doin' his duty, so I tell you what you do. You tell Rayburn where that bitch is. Then he goes chargin' outa here to get Leroy, an' he might just do it, too. Rayburn moves real nice with that razor." Leo paused to suck in air through his teeth. "Or maybe Leroy beats the shit outa Rayburn. Now that's bad for Rayburn, but it's all right for me, 'cause then I'll have the best excuse in the world to split you open from the top a your head to the crack a your ass. Either way, there's gonna be one less muthafucka on South Street. You, ah"—Leo pitched his voice high to imitate Elmo's whine—"see what I mean?" Leo grinned and turned away.

Elmo smiled evilly and waited until Leo had taken a few steps. "Ain't you got enough funerals to go to?"

Leo stopped and turned slowly. "Elmo, I'm tired a your shit."

"You don't act like a man in mournin', Leo," Elmo giggled.

"What are you talkin' about?"

"Aw," Elmo said, "ain't you heard? Your buddy the wino kicked off this mornin', early. Died of an overdose a livin'. You can't imagine how I hate to be the one has to tell you." Elmo grinned at Leo's stricken face and took a sip of beer.

Leo put his side towel down and leaned on the bar, seeming to shrink slightly. The noise in Lightnin' Ed's rolled on unabated, although a few faces turned to look at Leo's bent form. Brown came through the open door and took a seat next to Elmo. "What's wrong with Leo?" Brown said.

"Leo just got some bad news," Elmo said.

"Jake?"

Elmo nodded solemnly. "I think it mighta hit poor Leo pretty hard."

Brown got up and went over to Leo, put a hand on his arm. "Leo?"

"It ain't true," Leo mumbled.

"It's true," Brown said. "I'm sorry, Leo."

"Are you *sure?*"

"I'm sure."

"I can't believe it," Leo said. He swallowed heavily, looked at Brown, shook his head. "I don't know what to do. What should I do, Brown?"

"I don't know, Leo, I don't think there's anything you *can* do."

"There's gotta be somethin'," Leo said. He wiped his big hands on his stained apron, looked around. He nodded to himself, bent over, and pulled the switch that controlled the jukebox. The music died.

"What the hell, Leo?" demanded Big Betsy, seconded by an annoyed chorus.

Leo looked around. "Jake died this mornin'. I sorta feel like closin' up for the night."

Brown shook his head slowly. "I don't . . ." He stopped.

"What?" Leo said.

"It don't seem right closin' a bar when a wino dies."

"He's right, Leo," Big Betsy said. "That's the last thing Jake woulda wanted."

Leo sighed, nodded, and turned the jukebox on again. He drew himself a beer and stared into the darkness at the far end of the bar. Brown looked at him, hesitated, then resumed his seat. Big Betsy came trundling down the bar. "Move," she said to Elmo.

"What for?"

"To give your seat to a lady," said Big Betsy.

"You ain't hardly no lady," Elmo snapped.

"Uh huh," said Big Betsy. "Well in that case, there ain't nothin' keepin' me from kickin' your balls so hard you'll have to fuck with your nose. Now move your ass, nigger, I wants to talk to Leo."

"Bitch," said Elmo. Big Betsy raised a foot. Elmo got up.

"Thank you, sir," Big Betsy said. "Now fuck off." She turned to Leo. "You all right?"

"It ain't gonna be the same, Saturday nights," Leo said. He looked at Brown. "Every Saturday night Jake sleeps in the storeroom."

"I know," Brown said softly.

"Slept," Leo amended. A plump tear escaped from his right eye, meandered along his nose. Leo sniffed powerfully. The tear disappeared. "Every week."

"I know," Brown said.

"Christ's sake, Leo," said Big Betsy, "you almost make me believe you was queer for him or somethin'." Leo ignored her. Big Betsy looked at Brown, shook her head.

"You know," Leo said, "I been thinkin'. Maybe I oughta take me a vacation."

"Vacation?" said Big Betsy. "What the hell for?"

"To get away from some a these goddamn hookers," Leo said. "Think maybe I'll go on down to Florida. Sposed to be pretty nice in Florida. I hear you don't do nothin' all day but set around drinkin' orange juice an' playin' shufflabode."

"What the hell's shufflabode?" demanded Big Betsy.

"It's a game. Ain't it, Brown?"

"Listen to him," crowed Big Betsy. "Wants to go to goddamn Florida to play somethin', an' he don't even know what the hell it is."

"It's a game," Brown said.

"Ain't no such thing."

"You heard Brown."

"He don't know everything."

"Knows moren you. Knows what shufflabode is."

"An' what about us? What the hell we sposed to be doin' while you go off to play some simple-ass game?"

"We?" said Leo. "Just who is we?"

"Me," said Big Betsy. "Ain't that enough?"

"Oh yeah," said Leo. "That's enough, all right. That's plenty. Matter a fact, that's too much. You hear that, Brown? I can't take ma first damn vacation in fifteen years 'cause some damn whore might have to peddle her ass on the street 'stead a parkin' it on a nice soft bar stool. Damn!" Down the bar someone waved for service. With a parting glare at Big Betsy, Leo trucked away.

"Gotta keep his mind offa Jake," Big Betsy said to Brown. "Leo, he likes t'act tough. He is tough. But him an' Jake was real close."

"Maybe he should take a vacation," Brown said.

Big Betsy looked at him. "I thought you was supposed to be so smart. What's he gonna do, go to Florida for two damn weeks or whatever an' then come back to this shit? The only way to take a vacation is to do it like Jake done it—cheap an' permanent." Big Betsy looked at Brown fiercely. "You don't take no two weeks, Brown. You do like Jake. You last as long as you can. Then you rest."

"What for?" Brown said.

" 'Cause you're tired," snapped Big Betsy.

"No," Brown said, "I mean, why do you last as long as you can?"

Big Betsy glared at him. "I ain't got time to be thinkin' about shit like that. I gotta keep Leo's mind off Jake. Poor Jake." Big Betsy snorted heavily and turned away. "Leo, you black bastard," she shouted over the noise of the bar, "there ain't no such thing as shufflabode."

The moderate mass of Willie T. was accelerated out of Charlene's embrace by an irresistible force which, Willie T. saw from his rest position on the floor, had been administered by the sole of Cotton's shoe. "What the fuck?" said Willie T. Cotton launched another place kick. Willie T. executed several rather unorthodox bounces, like a somewhat underinflated football. "Awfghlumphgh," said Willie T.

"You sure is," Cotton said.

"Leave him be," Charlene shouted, waving a stained doily, which had lately adorned the back of the sofa upon which she and Willie T. had reposed, around in front of her in an unsuccessful attempt to conceal both her mammary glands and her pudendum from the eyes of a disinterested Cotton. "Leave him be an' keep your goddamn eyes to yourself."

"Shup," Willie T. gasped, protecting his testicles with one hand and his face with the other.

"Shit, Willie," Cotton said amiably, "you'd be better off coverin' your belly to protect what guts you do have."

"You let him be, now," said Charlene, who had solved the modesty problem by rolling over to face the back of the sofa and holding the doily over her behind.

"Quiet, bitch," snapped Willie T. "I'll deal with this."

"You couldn't deal a game a slapjack," Cotton told him. "Now where's Leroy?"

"How the hell should I know?"

"I don't know, Willie," Cotton said sadly. "All I know is, you better come up with some idea, or I'ma have you eatin' pabulum an' fuckin' jello for the next six months. If you live that long."

"Why can't you let him be?" Charlene demanded.

Cotton looked at her back. "Charlene, now, we're talkin' a little business here, an' I'd appreciate it if you wouldn't keep on interruptin' me that way. It upsets me." Charlene's cheeks quivered slightly and she made small whimpering sounds, but she said nothing at all. "Now, Willie, you tell me where Leroy is. Since you let him get away."

"I tried to make him wait, Cotton, honest to God I did, but you know Leroy, when his mind's made up it'd take moren me to change it."

Cotton looked down at him in disgust. "I guess it would, Willie. I guess it would. It'd take moren you to walk a fair-sized poodle. Now where'd you leave Leroy?"

"He left me. He said he didn't want me jogglin' his elbow when he killed Brown. He just—"

"Just what?"

"He just told me to be around later to help get rid a the body." Willie T. swallowed heavily and closed his eyes.

"Aw," Cotton said, "whatsa matter, Willie, don't you like dead bodies?

'Fore long you gonna be havin' one a your very own, so you better start lovin' 'em. Now put your damn clothes on." Willie T. got up, rubbing his backside with one hand and his ribs with the other. "Move it, nigger," Cotton snarled.

"I'm movin'."

"You don't move fastern that, you gonna be needin' another hand." While Willie T. struggled into his clothes Cotton backed up to the sofa and sat down. Charlene squealed. "Oops," Cotton said, and got unhurriedly off Charlene's head. She took a swipe at him. Cotton caught her hand and snatched the doily out of the other. " 'Sides bad manners, bitch, you got a fat ass. You ready, Willie?" Without waiting for an answer he released Charlene and headed for the door. When he looked back Charlene was bidding Willie T. a soulful farewell. Cotton sucked in air, threw his head back, and bellowed. "Move!" Willie T. broke away from Charlene, grabbed his stingy-brim, and scuttled toward the door, wiping saliva from his chin. Cotton grabbed him by the elbow and propelled him down the stairs and out onto the street. Willie T. escaped from Cotton's grasp and took refuge on the other side of a garbage can.

"All right now, nigger," Willie T. said toughly, "I want to know what this shit is all about, an' it better be good."

Cotton looked at him, snorted. "Now, Willie, I don't know where it come from, but I got this feelin' you don't want to die. Am I right? Now, I went on over an' waited around outside a Gino's place. You do remember Gino, don't you? Anyways, I was settin' around there for a while an' here comes that Brown fella. You remember him? Well, he walks into the front damn door a Gino's little front operation over there, you know what I mean. You, ah, gettin' the picture, Willie?"

Willie T.'s jaw started to quiver.

"I see you're gettin' the picture," Cotton said. "Now what I did was, I went on around to a pay phone, an' I called up this white dude I know an' got him to come over there. I sent him on inside to see what's happenin'. By this time Brown's been in there, oh, half an hour. You dig?"

Willie T. started to drool.

"You dig," Cotton said. "Now the paddy told me when he got inside, there was Brown callin' Gino a fat greasy wop. An' Gino was laughin'."

Willie T. grabbed a light pole and began to shake and whimper.

"Uh huh," Cotton said. "Paddy says Gino bought Brown a drink an' they talked for a while, an' then Gino asted Brown to have dinner with him."

Willie T. stopped drooling, whimpering, and shaking. He was absolutely still for a few seconds, and then he sank to the pavement in a dead faint.

"Shit," Cotton said with a sigh. He stood Willie T. up against a wall and slapped him until he came to.

"Oh, Jesus," moaned Willie T. "What we gonna do?"

"We gonna look in every damn joint on South Street until we find Leroy," Cotton said.

"Right," said Willie T., nodding his head, "right." He stood there nodding his head. "Right."

Cotton sighed again. "Willie," he said gently, "we ain't got all night."

Willie T. nodded one last time, whirled jerkily, and set off down the street like a deer afflicted with a mild case of polio. Cotton trundled after him, shaking his heavy head.

He was watching somebody named Rayburn Wallace. He felt an incredible sorrow rising within him as he watched Rayburn Wallace talk earnestly with a fat, undesirable whore. The pity turned to acid and burned big holes in his stomach. He rose quickly and ran for the men's room to bend, to sway, to vomit out the acid into the bowl, or onto the floor, or anywhere. Arriving, he found Rayburn Wallace there, too, bent over the bowl. He bent beside Rayburn and they vomited in unison, together feeling the relief, the painful tightening beneath the scrotum as the liquor and the pity gushed out into the cracked white bowl. He saw Rayburn Wallace in the mirror as he had seen him in the barroom: face strained and ashy, shoulders slumped.

"Rayburn, man," he said, "you looks like a piece a shit the cat left out for the crows." He giggled painfully, was pleased to see that Rayburn giggled too. It gave him a sense of connection, a feeling of unity. He pulled the crumpled beret out of his back pocket and set it on his head at a rakish angle. Suddenly the sickness welled up inside him again. He pulled the hat off, leaned over the bowl, feeling the tightening below his balls as the foulness inside him came reeking roaring upward. He prayed it would not go on when his stomach was empty. He rose, dunked his head in the sink and wet his face and hair, dried himself with a rough paper towel. He opened his eyes. Rayburn looked at him again. He put the beret back on his head, pulled it down over his eye, tried to look mean and badass. His stomach heaved. He grabbed the hat off his head and bent over the bowl, but it was a false alarm. He straightened. The room swayed. He stuck the beret in his pocket and turned toward the door.

Rayburn moved slowly on rubbery knees. The barroom swam before his eyes, from the far end where Big Betsy held lonely court beside the stool he had vacated, past the row of faces, all shades, all smeared, as if some master artist had portrayed them with painstaking care in infinite detail and then, in a moment of passionless carelessness, had smeared it all with his elbow. Rayburn's vision crawled over them. The room went out of focus, jiggled, twisted, sharpened again as Rayburn's eyes fell on the solid, massive shape of Leo, caught in the familiar motions of drawing a beer from a tap, wiping the bottom of the mug with his side towel, setting it in front of a round head and white-shirted back. Rayburn moved toward Leo, his feet shuffling across the hard floor, his velocity increasing until his motion became a fall that was arrested only as he fetched up against the bar. He grabbed a stool and managed to lower himself onto it.

"You okay, Rayburn?" Leo asked.

"Course I'm okay," Rayburn said.

"You don't look too damn good."

"How about a drink?"

"All right, but don't you be botherin' nobody."

"How'm I gonna bother anybody? Spit on 'em?"

"Lean on 'em, maybe," Leo said. Rayburn realized that he had been leaning heavily against the occupant of the next stool.

"Lord," said Rayburn, straightening up and almost falling in the process. "I'm sorry." He looked at the man. "Hey, don't I know you? It's all right, Leo, this here's ma goddamn buddy. Right, brother? Say, what's your goddamn name?"

"Rayburn, I think you done had enough," Leo said. "You're botherin' folks."

"He didn't say I was botherin' him. Hey, bro, am I botherin' you?"

Brown looked at Leo, then back to Rayburn. "No. You ain't botherin' me. You want a beer?"

"Sure," Rayburn said. Leo shrugged, drew the beer, and ambled away. "That Leo," Rayburn said, "has got his damn nerve. Had enough, shit. There *ain't* enough." Brown smiled tightly. Rayburn leaned against the back of his stool and discovered that his stool had no back. Brown caught him before he fell. "Thanks, bro," Rayburn said. Brown nodded and raised his beer. "Say, bro," Rayburn said, "this stool ain't taken or nothin', is it? I mean your woman ain't—"

"No," Brown said.

"Oh," Rayburn said. "Ain't you got a woman?" Brown ignored him. "I ain't got no woman." He looked at Brown. Brown's eyes were fixed on the ranks of bottles on the backbar. "She run off," Rayburn said. "She run off on account—"

"On account of you was messin' with some white woman," Brown said.

Rayburn stared at him. "How the hell you know that?"

"I heard the story before," Brown told him. "It's a legend."

Rayburn glared at him. The silence between them stretched out, a thin thread in the general clamor. Rayburn finished his beer and gave Leo a poorly coordinated wave. Leo planted himself across the bar. "'Nother round, Leo," Rayburn said.

Leo raised his side towel and removed the drops of Rayburn's spittle from his face. "I think you had enough, Rayburn," Leo said calmly.

"Awright," Rayburn said. "But I owe ma buddy here a drink."

Leo looked at Brown's still-full glass. "It don't look like he's ready just now," Leo said.

"I'll drink it for him." Leo shook his head, bent over and drew two beers, and walked away. Rayburn picked up one glass and maneuvered it toward his mouth. Brown turned his head and watched as Rayburn's lips protruded grotesquely to embrace the foamy white head. Rayburn slurped the beer and set the glass down. "Where's your woman?" he said to Brown. Brown looked back at the bottles behind the bar. "They're all the same," Rayburn said. "Every one. Bitches. Every one. Sisters, you know what I mean? You get right down to it, they're all the same."

"Yeah," Brown said, "you and Rudyard Kipling."

"Yeah," Rayburn said. "You married? Don't get married. Mistake. Marriage is just like one a them western movies: the good guy marries a woman an' pretty soon the bad guy comes 'long an' off she goes. Ain't her fault. The bad guy, he got clothes an' cars an' money. Women just naturally goes for them things. So then the good guy's got to go beat the shit outa the bad guy an' bring the bitch on back. That's marriage."

"What if the good guy loses?"

"He don't lose," Rayburn said. "Nigger, don't you watch TV?"

"What if he does?" Brown insisted.

"He *can't*," Rayburn said. "Listen, brother, the good guy, he don't never lose. Now me, I'm a good guy. If I knowed where ma woman run off to . . ." He stared at his beer for a few minutes, then pushed himself swaying to his feet. "Hey, you goddamn muthafuckas," he bellowed, "any y'all know where the cunt I married got to? Hey!" Leo moved quickly and clamped a hand over Elmo's mouth.

"C'mon, man," Brown said, getting up. He took Rayburn's arm, forced him back onto the stool.

"Won't none of 'em tell me," Rayburn muttered. "They know I'd go get her back, kill whatever muthafucka she's with, too. They know I'd go do it if I knowed where she was."

"Sure," Brown said, holding Rayburn steady on the stool.

"She'd have to come. I'm a good guy. The good guys, they always come out on top. Get right up there, right to the top." He looked at Brown. "That's right, ain't it? It can't be no other way, can it?"

Brown closed his eyes and swallowed.

"If it was any other way," Rayburn said, "nothin' would make no sense."

South Street danced in the humid darkness, drinking the liquor of Saturday night, twisting hatred into anger, grinding anger into lust, battering lust into frustration, diluting frustration with watered gin. Blinking neon wrote the lyrics, mercury vapor hummed the tune, Vanessa's feet beat out the rhythm, scuffing across the broken concrete, her heels on pavement conjuring fire. A thousand dreams went up in smoke, making the dark a little darker, the dripping neon more like blood. The door of Lightnin' Ed's was open. Vanessa paused outside it and tried to dab the perspiration from her face without ruining her make-up. Then she stepped inside.

The bar was not quite full. She surveyed the backs along the bar, found the back that belonged to Brown, went over and stood behind him. She moved her hand toward him, hesitated, drew it back, moved away. Brown turned around and smiled at her. "I don't bite."

Vanessa smiled weakly. "Are you—busy?"

"No," Brown said, "I ain't—busy, 'cept maybe for listenin' to drunks tell me how marriage is a cowboy picture, 'fore they go off to get sick. You want a drink?"

"I want to talk," Vanessa said.

"Well, you wanna drink while you talk? Because I definitely want to drink while I listen." Vanessa nodded. "Leo," Brown called. Leo came scuttling up the bar. "Could we have a . . ." Brown looked up at Vanessa.

"Sling?" Leo said. Vanessa nodded. Leo went to work on it.

"Well, hell," Brown said. "You come here often?"

"Only when I'm tryin' to make ma mind up about somethin'," Vanessa told him. Leo set her drink in front of her. "I'm sorry 'bout Jake, Leo."

"Yeah, well," Leo said, "Jake was just an' old wino. I 'preciate it, 'Nessa, but you know Jake wasn't nothin' special to me."

"I know Leo, I know," Vanessa said. "Hey, Leo?"

"What?"

"How come you so full a shit?" Leo looked shocked for a moment, then grinned ruefully. He waved away the money Brown offered, and trucked away. Vanessa looked at Brown. "There an empty booth?"

"We'll empty one," Brown said. He led her to the back, found a spot.

Vanessa sat down. Brown started to slide in next to her, then moved around
to the other side, facing the door. Vanessa lowered her head. "Shit," Brown
said, and moved around again.

"You don't have to be settin' next to me if you don't want," Vanessa
said.

"I don't have to talk to you if I don't want. I want."

"Lucky me."

"Yeah, lucky you. An' lucky me. I'm glad you came."

"I just came to deliver your mail," Vanessa said quickly. She opened her
purse and took out a small buff envelope. "I found it outside the door when
I left this mornin'." She reached into her purse again and took out her
cigarettes.

Brown looked at the envelope. There was no stamp or postmark, just his
name written in ink—not ball-point. "It's from Alicia," Brown said.

"I know that," Vanessa said sullenly. "Why the hell you think I took
it?"

"How did you know? I recognized her handwriting but—"

Vanessa blew smoke in his face. "The bitch's *name* is on the back,
Brown."

"Oh," Brown said, turning the envelope over. It was unsealed. "What's
it say?"

"How the hell should I know?" Vanessa flared. "I don't go around
readin' other people's mail."

"No, just stealin' it," Brown said, grinning.

"I *didn't* read it."

"All right, I believe you," Brown said. He opened the envelope, read the
note.

"You goin'?" Vanessa asked. Brown looked up at her and laughed. "All
right, so I did read it. That a crime or somethin'? You didn't believe me
anyways."

"Nope," Brown agreed, "I didn't believe you anyway." He put the
invitation back in the envelope and the envelope in his hip pocket.

"Well?" Vanessa said.

"Well, what?"

"Are you goin'?"

"Goin' where?"

"Don't play them games with me, Brown. This bitch done invited you
to a party, an' I want to know if you're goin'. I got a right to know."

"What right?" Brown said. Vanessa glared at him. "What right?"

"You owe it to me."

"Why?"

"All right, I just want to know, okay? I just want to know."

"What difference does it make?"

"Damn your black ass," Vanessa said, "you know what difference it makes."

Brown smiled faintly. "I'm going."

"Yeah," Vanessa said, looking away and puffing hard on her cigarette, "I guess you are. I guess you tired a talkin' to drunks an' whores. You tired a drinkin' gin, you want dry martinis."

"You don't just change your whole life overnight," Brown said. "It takes time. Like lots a things."

Vanessa snorted.

"You catchin' cold, or is that just some a your goddamn nosiness comin' out?"

Vanessa ignored him. She stubbed out her cigarette, blew out the last lungful of smoke. "You get over there with her, you ain't never comin' back."

"Shit," Brown said.

"Shit, yourself. You'd be crazy if you did. Ain't nothin' worth comin' back to, is there?"

Brown looked at her. "Finish your drink," he said. He stood up. Vanessa looked up at him in surprise. Brown leaned over and kissed her on the nose. She got up awkwardly and followed him as he walked toward the front of the bar, stumbling slightly in her high heels. She caught up to him and hung onto the back of his belt. Brown turned to wave to Leo and ran right into the oscillating form of Rayburn.

"I wanna talk to you," Rayburn said.

"Later," Brown said.

"Not you, nigger, *you*," snarled Rayburn, looking beyond Brown to Vanessa. "Bitch, where's your littermate?"

"Only bitch I know is your mama," Vanessa snapped, stepping out from behind Brown.

Rayburn took a step toward her, but Brown shot out an arm and blocked him. "Just take it easy, now," Brown said.

"I'ma ask this whore some questions."

"Her name's Vanessa," Brown said.

Leo came out from behind the bar, working the thong of his billy club onto his wrist.

"You don't move that arm, nigger, you gonna be dead." Rayburn's arm moved and the razor flashed. Brown blocked the stroke with his forearm and gave Rayburn a hard shot over the breastbone with the heel of his hand. Rayburn stumbled backward into Leo's arms, gulping and gasping.

Leo grunted in disgust and shoved him against the wall. Brown leaned over and picked up the razor. Rayburn moaned and looked at Vanessa. "Tell me where she is."

"You know," Vanessa said.

"Shup, 'Nessa," Leo said urgently.

"I got a right," Rayburn said.

"You know," Vanessa said. "You pretend you don't, but you know."

"Tell me," Rayburn said.

Vanessa looked at him, pity and disgust mingled on her face. "She's with Leroy." She stepped around him and out the door.

Brown looked at Leo, then at Rayburn. He held out the razor. "You keep droppin' this," Brown said.

🖼

Leroy Briggs sipped a cold Ballantine ale and peered through the halo of street lights at the dark rectangle that was Brown's door. Below him, cars sped down South Street on whispering wheels, winos wandered, ladies of the evening loitered in purplish clots. Young men clumped at light poles, talking jive and drinking cheap wine from bottles cloaked in brown paper. Leroy looked down on it all, hearing nothing but the hum of the air-conditioner that pulled in air, cleaned it, cooled it, and left the odor of the street outside. Behind a closed door a thin, saffron-skinned prostitute named Doris practiced her trade on firm and silent springs. Leroy looked down at the dark doorway while he loaded and unloaded the gun.

The bedroom door opened and Doris came out, wrapping a thin nylon robe around her. "You still here?"

Leroy turned. "No."

"You're makin' ma friend nervous," Doris complained. "He thinks you're gonna roll him."

"Tell him only gumshoe niggers an' greedy honkies works on Saturday night, not me."

"Then what's the gun for?"

"Pleasure," Leroy said. "Pure pleasure."

"Well, I do work on Saturday night. Can't you go someplace else to get your rocks off?"

"Where the hell you go to get your rocks off 'cept a whore?"

"Call girl," Doris corrected.

"Shit," Leroy said. "I like your view. An' you got air-conditionin'."

"How about some music?" Doris said sarcastically.

Leroy turned back to the window. "That's a good idea. Put on some Sam an' Dave."

"Jesus," Doris said. She shook her head and went into the kitchen.

Leroy turned. "Hey, how 'bout that music?"

"I ain't got no Sam an' Dave."

"What you mean, y'ain't got no Sam an' Dave." Leroy stalked into the middle of the room and stood, arms akimbo.

"I *mean*," Doris said, coming back carrying a tray covered with a small, oddly-shaped loaf of bread, several cuts of cheese, a bottle of good red wine, and two glasses, "I ain't got no Sam an' Dave. I ain't got no Temptations, neither. I ain't got no Supremes. I ain't got no Motown at all. Berry Gordy can kiss ma ass."

"Who?" said Leroy.

"Never mind." She eased open the door to the bedroom, slid inside, closed it behind her.

"What is this shit," muttered Leroy. He stomped over to the stereo and examined the record jackets. "Damn," he growled, "who the hell is this?"

Doris reappeared. "Keep it down, will you? He's nervous enough without thinkin' I got one a Tarzan's apes hangin' around in ma livin' room."

"Who the hell is this Batch?" Leroy demanded.

"Bach," Doris told him. "It's baroque."

"I don't want to hear it anyways," Leroy said, putting the record down.

"Ma customers like it," Doris said. "I got a very sophisticated clientele."

"What the hell's that mean? They use scented rubbers, or do they just eat you out with a knife an' fork?"

"You're gross." Leroy smiled, stuck the gun in his belt, and headed for the bedroom. "Stay out a here," Doris screamed. Leroy pushed her out of the way.

There was no one visible in the bedroom, but there was a big pile of blankets in the middle of the bed that quivered slightly. Leroy went over and lifted a corner of the pile. "Peekaboo, I see—Jesus!" Leroy flipped the covers back and stared in amazement. "It's a honky! Doris, why didn't you tell me you was fuckin' a fuckin' honky in here?"

"What damn difference does it make," Doris snapped. "You prejudiced?"

"It makes a lot a difference. Why here I thought you had some simple-ass nigger in here, an' here it's a white gentleman, a member of the master race." The gentleman member of the master race was huddled in a tight fetal ball. Leroy spread the covers over his pinkness. "Beg pardon, sir,"

Leroy said deferentially. "Didn't nobody inform me you was payin' a little visit to the cabins. I hope you'll forgive me." Leroy waited a minute, then drew his gun and prodded the pile of covers. "You do accept ma apologies, don't you, bwana?"

"Yes," said the pile.

"Let him be, Leroy."

"I ain't hurtin' him," Leroy said. "I was just tryin' to apologize. I got to be on ma best behavior. I feel bad. Ma man here came down to get laid, an' I done spoiled some a his fun. I want him to have a good time. You hear that, boss? I definitely want you to have a good time. I want you to go on back to your fuckin', an' I'ma go on outa here an' let you be. But you know, if you wasn't to fuck all night, I might think you didn't have a good time. You wouldn't want me to think that, would you?"

"No," said the pile.

"Fine," said Leroy. "I tell you what. You get on this hook—a young lady, here, an' you have a good time. I wanna hear some screams a pleasure comin' outa here. Ain't no soul on the stereo, so I want you to take this fine black woman an' make me some soul music. No fakin' it, now, Doris. We gotta give our visitors the real thing." Leroy paused to give the pile a last poke. "Nice seein' you. Sorry we can't spend more time together." Leroy turned and strolled out into the living room.

"You know I ain't gonna be comin' for no john," Doris whispered as he passed her.

"Sure, I know," Leroy said, resuming his vigil at the window. "Whores never do." He turned and looked at her. "That's why I hates whores."

Brown and Vanessa strolled along the sidewalk, holding hands, an equal-opportunity version of Barbie and Ken. They drifted past the open doors of taprooms, Christmas-tinseled watering holes, leaning away from the sounds and smoke that rolled out. They didn't say much of anything. Brown hummed softly, a song that had once been blues, that might get back to being blues someday, striding along with his head up, his shoulders moving too much sometimes, sometimes not enough. Vanessa walked beside him, her head down, not looking where she was going. Her strides were a few inches shorter than Brown's, and every few steps she took a little stumbling hop to catch up, throwing them either in or out of step. They paused at Nineteenth Street to wait for the light, then stepped off the curb and across the street. Brown slipped his arm around her, cupping her hip with his palm. Outside a bar on Seventeenth a covey of Saturday-night drinkers loitered, laughed, whistled at Brown and Vanessa—"Um, um, ma man has got hisself a live one! In-deed! That fox gonna be turnin' him every damn way but a-loose!" Brown grinned. Vanessa lowered her head and smiled faintly.

They climbed the stairs out of heat and darkness into hotter heat and darker darkness. The walls of the stairway enclosed them. Vanessa's knees sagged; she held onto Brown's belt as they climbed. Brown half carried her inside, not bothering to bolt the door. "You okay?" Brown said.

Vanessa pulled his head down into the powder-sweet valley between her breasts. His tongue tasted talcum and salt. Vanessa dropped her arms and moved away from him. "You want a beer?"

"Later."

"I want one."

"*Now?*"

Vanessa grinned, leaned in and kissed his nose, danced away from his grasping arms like a picador toying with a bull. She went to the refrigerator, took out the beer, poured it into the jelly jars, gave one to Brown. "Anybody ever tell you you're a weird broad?" Brown asked conversationally.

"I ain't never met nobody who didn't tell me I was a weird broad," Vanessa told him.

"I can see why," Brown said. "Who ever heard a drinkin' beer after a Singapore Sling."

"It's a new drink. It's called a Singapore Screw." She went over to the window, leaned back against the sill, her face outlined against the skyglow. Brown kicked around until he found a chair, sat down, and sipped his beer. "When we was kids we useta play this here game," Vanessa said. "We'd go up to Pine Street an' get us some empty pop bottles, an' then we'd go down to the store an' get us some candy. I 'member these coconut candy things, sometimes they was yellow an' pink an' brown stripes, but mostly they was made to look like slices a watermelon. Three of 'em for two cent. One pop bottle. We'd get us some a that candy an' go set on the doorstep an' see how long we could look at that candy 'fore we just *had* to eat it. Then we'd set around an' wait some more 'fore we ate the second one. Ma one sister, Lindalee, she useta start talkin' an' forget what she was doin' an' have hers gone. Les, she couldn't hardly play. She spent all her time waitin' to see who was gonna come in second. I almost always won. Same thing with Christmas. 'Fore Daddy went to hell he useta tell us he could make it any day we wanted. Les, she'd say make it her birthday so she could get a present. Lindalee'd say she wanted it to be Christmas, so everybody could get a present. That simple fool had us believin' he could change the world."

"What day did you want it to be?" Brown said gently.

"Me? I wanted it to be Christmas Eve, 'cause then no matter what happened, the next day was gonna be Christmas. If it already was Christmas, the next day was December twenty-sixth. Who gives a damn about December twenty-sixth?"

"The British," Brown murmured. He put his beer down, stumbled through the darkness, and put his hands on her bare shoulders. Vanessa shivered. "Maybe you ain't so weird after all," Brown said. He brushed her lips lightly with his. Vanessa closed her eyes. Then she pushed him away and almost ran into the bedroom.

"Ho, ho, ho," Brown said as he drained his beer and followed her.

Cotton and Willie T. dragged despondently into the Elysium and came to rest against the bar. Cotton waved vaguely in the direction of the bartender before joining Willie T. in a slump of utter defeat. "What you havin'?" the bartender asked.

"Poison," Willie T. said.

The bartender looked at him and sniffed. "Straight up or on the rocks?"

"Nemo," Cotton said, "remind me to put you up for the Emmy Award."

"Yeah," Willie T. said, "posthumous."

"Past what?" Nemo demanded suspiciously. "Don't you be comin' around here with none a them fifty-cent words from the Temple night school. I done had me a hard day."

"Community College," Cotton corrected, "an' he means after you're dead."

"You startin' trouble, Willie?"

"Hell, no," said Willie T. "Pretty soon we gonna have so damn much trouble around here, they gonna be haulin' it away in garbage trucks."

"When was the last time you seen a garbage truck around here?" Cotton demanded. "They gonna use paddy wagons."

"What kinda trouble?" Nemo asked.

"Chef Boy-ar-dee trouble," Cotton told him.

"Yeah," said Willie T. "Spaghetti an' minced niggers."

"Dry niggers," Cotton corrected. "What about them drinks, Nemo?"

"I can't give you no drink 'less you tell me what you want."

"Somethin' strong. Give us some a Leroy's private."

"Leroy's private? I don't know—"

"Shit," Cotton said, "we gonna be dead so soon it ain't gonna make no difference."

"Huh?" Nemo said. "How come you gonna be dead?"

"Not just us. You, too. Give me that drink an' I'll tell you."

Nemo brought up a sealed bottle of Wild Turkey bourbon and two glasses. Cotton broke the seal and poured two healthy slugs. "Now, what's this shit about dyin'?" Nemo demanded.

Cotton leaned back against the bar and belched heavily. "Ma man, you see that door over there?"

"Yeah," Nemo said.

"Well, when Leroy comes through that door you better lean over an' grab ahold a your ankles an' kiss your ass good-bye, 'cause about half an hour later they gonna declare World War Three, Little Italy against Little Africa, an' the suckers got us outgunned."

"Uh huh," Nemo said. "Well in that case we been fightin' for an hour an' a half, 'cause Leroy come in about midnight."

"Leroy's *here?*" Willie T. gasped.

"Aw, shit," Cotton said. "Here I coulda been enjoyin' ma last few minutes a life—"

"Wait a minute," said Willie T. excitedly. "Maybe he didn't do it."

"Do what?" asked Nemo.

"Course he did it," Cotton said.

"He didn't do it last night," Willie T. argued.

"Do what?"

"That's 'zactly why he done it tonight," said Cotton.

"Done what?"

"You're right," Willie T. said morosely.

"I ain't got time for you silly-ass niggers anyway," Nemo said angrily, and stumped away.

Cotton poured another round and regarded the closed office door. "Maybe he didn't do it."

"Yeah," said Willie T. "An' maybe there really is a Santa Claus, an' maybe Jefferson really was a nigger, an' maybe—"

"All right, all right, I was just thinkin'."

"Thinkin', hell, you was prayin'."

They drank a few shots in silence. "Hey," said Willie T. suddenly. "There's Les settin' over there. If he'd a done it, he'd be fuckin' her someplace, wouldn't he? Guess that means he didn't do it."

"I don't know," Cotton said. "Maybe the last thing you want after killin' somebody is a woman."

316 ((*South Street*

"Oh," said Willie T. "Guess that means he did do it, then."

"Hell," Cotton said, "I don't know."

"I wonder if I'd want me a woman after I done killed somebody," Willie T. mused.

"I wonder if I'd want to kill somebody enough to do it," Cotton said.

Willie T. stared at him. "You mean you ain't never killed nobody?"

"Sure," Cotton said, "but it ain't like I ever hated anybody to go huntin' 'em like they was an animal. Shoot 'em 'cause they're tryin' to shoot you, or 'cause they're in your way, or 'cause they pissed you off right then an' there, that's one thing. Trackin' a man down, that's somethin' else. Takes somethin' *strange* inside." Cotton drained his glass, poured another slug.

"You think Leroy's got somethin' strange like that inside him?"

"Who the hell knows what somebody else got inside 'em? Got enough trouble with ma ownself. Maybe you got it inside a you."

"Oh no," said Willie T. "No, I couldn't never kill nobody."

"Y'ever done it?"

"Hell, no!"

"Then how you know you couldn't?"

"What?" said Willie T. "That don't make no sense."

"Sure don't," Cotton agreed. He picked up the bottle, examined the label. "Good bourbon."

"Yeah," said Willie T. "Cotton?"

"Whahuh?"

"How long you think it'll take 'fore Gino sends somebody down here?"

"Who the hell knows."

"Maybe we could get outa town?"

Cotton slammed the bottle down. "I ain't runnin' from no goddamn white man."

"Even if he's comin' to kill you?"

" 'Specially if he's comin' to kill me," Cotton snapped.

"Maybe he'll only kill Leroy."

Cotton sighed. "Willie, sometimes you're so damn dumb there ain't no words for it. I don't know why I'ma spend some a ma precious last minutes explainin' this to you, but I guess you got a right to know why you're gonna die. Gino gonna send somebody to get Leroy. We gotta stop 'em. Gino's gonna keep sendin' people until they get us. It's that simple."

"Oh," said Willie T. He took the bottle and poured himself a drink, downed it. "Well, how come we don't just let 'em *have* Leroy?"

Cotton sighed. "We gotta protect Leroy 'cause soon as he's gone every two-bit hustler on South Street is gonna be takin' pot shots at us, all at the same time. It's just like when they shot Kennedy. Five minutes later them Russians an' everybody else was pushin' us around."

"I still don't see why *I* got to die," Willie T. said.

"It's the rules," Cotton said. He picked up the bottle and took a long drink.

"Maybe he didn't do it," Willie T. said, without much hope.

"Well," Cotton said, "there ain't but one way to find out."

"Go in an ast him?"

"You got it, brother."

"I don't wanna know," Willie T. said.

"I do," Cotton said. "I wanna know it if he didn't do it, an' I don't wanna know it if he did."

Willie T. took the bottle away and sucked at it. "I know. We'll get Nemo to go in an' ask him, an' only tell us if he didn't do it."

"Hey," Cotton said. "You are pretty smart. You ma main man from now on."

"That there was easy," Willie T. said modestly. "I can figure all kinds a shit out, you give me a minute."

"Yeah," Cotton said. "That was pretty good thinkin', Willie. Onliest thing that bothers me is, when Nemo comes back an' don't be tellin' us nothin', how we gonna not know that what he ain't tellin' us is what we don't want to know?"

"Um," said Willie T. "That's right. If he didn't tell us what we told him not to tell us, that'd be the same as him tellin' us. That's no good. Lemme think a little more. Gimme the bottle."

"I got it," Cotton said, trying to snap his fingers and missing. "What we do is we get Nemo t'only tell us the truth if it's good news an' lie if it ain't. He goes in an' asts Leroy, but no matter what Leroy says to Nemo, Nemo tells *us* that Leroy didn't do it."

"Hey," said Willie T., "that there's great. Slap me five." Cotton slapped him five. "You pretty smart, Cotton. Even if you can't read, you oughta be in the State Department or somethin'."

"Well, yeah," Cotton said modestly, "I coulda had that Vietnam thing over months ago."

"Yeah?"

"Sure," Cotton said.

"Only thing," Willie T. said, "only thing is, 'bout your plan, now, only thing is how we gonna know if Nemo's lyin' when he tells us Leroy didn't do it?"

"We don't *want* to know if he's lyin', Willie, we wants to know if he's tellin' the truth."

"Oh. Yeah, that's right. Well how we gonna know if he's tellin' the truth?"

"Damn, Willie, how you think? We gonna ast him."

"Wait a minute," said Willie T. "We gonna tell him to lie so we don't know an' then we gonna ast him if he's lyin' or not so we do know? Why we goin' through all that?"

"Because," Cotton told him, "we already do know."

"Oh," Willie T. said. "Yeah. I guess we do." He picked up the bottle and took several healthy swallows. "Well, then," he said finally, "I guess one a you has got to go ast him."

"I guess I will."

"You gonna tell me afterwards?"

"You want me to?"

"No."

"I'll tell you."

"Thanks."

Cotton pushed himself away from the bar. He looked around. He hitched up his pants. He coughed.

"Will you go on?" Willie T. said.

"I'm goin'. I'm goin'." Cotton stumped across the room, slow and bandy-legged. He paused before the door to the office, knocked. There was no answer. Cotton pushed the door open and went inside. The room was dark, the only light the Band-Aid shaped block with Cotton-shaped shadow that came in through the door. Cotton stepped into the darkness, sniffing like a bloodhound—whiskey and cigar smoke. He saw a sudden red glow near Leroy's desk. "Leroy?"

"Close the door, Cotton," Leroy said tiredly. "The light bothers me." Cotton closed the door. He waited until his eyes adjusted a little, then made his way to the pool table and half sat, half leaned on the edge of it. He looked toward the slumped shadow in the midst of shadows that was Leroy, seeing the slow blooming of tobacco embers, hearing the harsh crackle of burning leaves, smelling the smoke. In a few minutes there was a grating sound as Leroy ground out the cigar. "You want a drink?" Leroy asked.

"No thanks. I had enough."

"Me too," Leroy said.

They sat in silence for a while. Leroy shifted his weight. The chair springs creaked in mild protest. "I hear you went coon huntin'," Cotton said finally.

"Yeah," Leroy said. "You sure you don't want a drink?"

"Nah," Cotton said. "I had enough. But you go ahead."

"Yeah," Leroy said. "I think I will." The springs complained as Leroy moved. Cotton heard a drawer open and close, heard the flat rattle of thin metal on glass as Leroy opened the bottle, the gurgle as he poured, the musical tinkle of glass on glass as the bottle tapped the rim of the tumbler.

"You have any luck?" Cotton asked.

"What with?"

"The coon hunt. You find him?"

"Oh yeah," Leroy said bitterly. "I found him all right. Found him with ma woman." Leroy gulped his drink. "Oh, I found him all right."

Cotton pushed himself off the edge of the pool table and stumbled to the desk. "I do believe I'll take that drink after all."

"Bottle's right in front a you," Leroy said. "You know, you sit here in the dark for a while, you get so's you can see real good."

"You better hand it to me," Cotton said. "I might knock it over." Leroy took his hand and guided it to the bottle. Cotton raised it and drank deeply.

"Don't you be spittin' in ma gin, now," Leroy said. Cotton grunted and put the bottle down. He wiped his mouth with the back of his hand and made his way back to the pool table. "Man," Leroy said, "I'll never be able to figure that cat out. Comes tippin' down here like he owned the place, touches ma balls like he done up to Lightnin' Ed's, walks up an' down the street, *ma* street, like he was God Almighty, takes ma woman out from under ma nose, an' then he don't even lock his goddamn door. Jesus! Almost like he didn't know what the hell he was doin'. Almost like he didn't understand—oh, hell, I don't know. Door unlocked an' her right there with him in the bed. I heard it squeakin'. An' you know what else I heard? I heard her makin' them sounds, you know? She wasn't screamin' or nothin', just makin' them little sounds, like she had the hiccups an' couldn't stop. She never made no sounds for me. Bitch just laid there till I was through an' never made a goddamn sound."

"Maybe she was fakin'," Cotton said.

"She never even faked for me. Just waited until I was finished an' got up an' wiped herself off, right in front a me, like I made her dirty or somethin'."

"Well," Cotton said uneasily, "it don't matter no more."

"Nigger left the door unlocked," Leroy said. He raised the bottle and drank.

"Maybe you oughta get laid," Cotton suggested. "Les's outside. She'll fix you up."

"Yeah," Leroy said.

"There anything you want me an' Willie T. to, ah, dispose of?"

"Yeah," Leroy said. "Here. It's empty."

Cotton took the bottle. Leroy stood up, groaning. "Maybe I better tell you—"

"Not now," Leroy said.

"It's business."

"Not now."

"It's important."

"Later."

"Might not be no later."

"Then it ain't gonna make no difference." Leroy shook himself, cleared his throat, tucked in his shirt, and walked out into the barroom. Cotton followed, grasping the empty bottle, blinking his eyes in the sudden brightness. Leroy spotted Leslie and started in her direction. Cotton went to the bar.

"Gimme another bottle, Nemo."

"I can't sell no more, it's closin' time."

"I ain't buyin'," Cotton snapped. "An' I ain't astin', neither. Now give me that drink. Where's Willie T.?"

Nemo nodded to indicate the corner where Willie T. sat, silent and alone. Cotton grunted, picked up the bottle, and went over. "Don't tell me," Willie T. mumbled. "I'ma go to church on Sunday an' pray."

"It's Sunday right now."

"Lord Jesus have mercy," Willie T. responded.

"Amen," Cotton said softly. He watched absently as Nemo came around the end of the bar and went to lock the street door as an unsubtle hint that the bar was closing. Nemo reached the door, reached out for the fastening, then backed quickly away as if he had seen a rattlesnake. Blood dripped from his arm. Cotton blinked, clawed for his gun. "It's started!" He kicked the table over and hauled Willie T. to the floor. "Get your gun out, get your gun out!"

"I want ma mama," wailed Willie T. He wrapped his arms around Cotton's legs. Cotton kicked himself free and cautiously raised his head over the edge of the table. Rayburn Wallace stood in the doorway, a razor glinting in his hand.

"I'm lookin' for Leroy Briggs," Rayburn said. "I don't want nobody in ma road." There was a general scramble to get out of his way. A broad avenue opened up to the table where Leroy sat with Leslie. Cotton lined his gun up on Rayburn's chest.

"Put that away, Cotton," Leroy called. Cotton lowered the gun but kept it ready. Leroy got up and moved toward Rayburn. He stopped ten feet away, smiled into Rayburn's sweat-shining face. "How you doin',

Rayburn? How's your, ah, job?" Rayburn advanced a step. Leroy held his ground, smiling, relaxed. Cotton brought his gun up again. "I told you to put that thing down," Leroy said. "I ain't gonna be tellin' you no more."

"I ain't puttin' nothin' down," Rayburn said.

"Oh, no, brother, I wasn't talkin' to you. I was talkin' to ma man over there. See, he was gettin' ready to blow your ass to kingdom come. Wasn't you, Cotton?" Leroy looked in Cotton's direction, but Rayburn's gaze was steady on Leroy's belly. The razor twitched slightly.

"Sure was," Cotton shouted.

Rayburn's gaze held steady.

"Me too, boss," yelled Willie T.

Rayburn's eyes did not flicker. "I don't care 'bout your men. I come to get ma woman. She's ma wife, an' I want her back."

"Oh yeah?" said Leroy. "Well, help yourself." He stepped back out of the way. "There she is. Big as life an' twice as beautiful. Great condition. She works fine. She's all yours. I ain't got to be hangin' onto no woman if she don't want to stay."

Rayburn wet his lips nervously. "Les? Les, honey? Daddy come to take you home."

"Shit," Cotton muttered, and put his gun away.

"Go home, Rayburn," Leslie said. "You're drunk."

Rayburn took two steps toward her. "Come with me."

Leslie arched her eyebrows. "You givin' me *orders*, Rayburn?"

"Please, baby," Rayburn said.

"That's better," Leslie said. "If there's anything I hate, it's takin' orders from a toilet cleaner."

"I want you to come with me, baby," Rayburn said.

Leslie got up and stepped over to him, leaned against his arm, rubbed herself against his hip. "I know you do, honey. An' I would, 'cept for one thing. You make me sick." She smiled sweetly and whirled around. Her short skirt spread, showing a blaze of orange panties against pale skin. "You useta make me laugh," she said. "You was so damn funny, comin' in smellin' like white folks' shit." She looked around at the few people left in the bar. "You shoulda seen him. He'd come home an' point to a spot on his knee an' he'd say, 'See this, baby? This here's the shit a the executive vice-president.' An' then he'd point to a spot on his sleeve an' he'd say, 'See that, baby? That there's the shit a the president.'" She smiled at Rayburn. "An' then he'd point to his nose an' say, 'You see this right here? That, baby, is nothin' else but the shit a the chairman a the board.'"

"I never said that," Rayburn said.

"He useta call me up an' say, 'Guess what, baby? I just finished moppin' the president's private crapper. Got it real shiny. I mopped the floor with ma wooly head, an' then I shined the tile with ma liver lips, an' then I cleaned the toilet seat with ma tongue.' "

Rayburn took a step toward her. "I never done that."

"But the best part," Leslie said, giggling, "the best part was what he useta do when he got ready to fuck."

"Shup up," Rayburn said.

"Leroy? You know what this big nigger useta do when he got all hot? He useta—"

Rayburn grabbed Leslie's arm and slung her across the room, following quickly, the razor slicing the air. Leroy moved to stop him. Rayburn brushed him aside.

"Oh yeah," Leslie shouted triumphantly, "that's just *exactly* what he done."

Rayburn grabbed her by the hair, laid the razor against her throat. "I'ma kill you!"

"Shit," Leslie said. Rayburn pressed the razor against her skin. A thin line of blood erupted along the blade. "Mmmm," Leslie said. "That feels good."

Rayburn snatched the blade away. Leslie snickered. Rayburn laid the blade flat against her cheek. "I'll mess you up. I'll mess you up so bad won't nobody want you!"

"Nobody?" Leslie said calmly. "You mean nobody, or you mean nobody but you? Folks that cleans toilets can't be too proud. Now put that thing away, I'm gettin' tired."

"I oughta kill you," Rayburn said.

"You oughta kill yourself. Go home," she said, as if she were talking to a dog.

Rayburn turned docilely, walking as if in a daze toward the door.

"Oh, Rayburn," Leslie called sweetly. Rayburn stopped. "I just wanted to tell you, you got to be a pretty good fuck there toward the end. 'Bout once a month I got so I wasn't even pretendin' it was somebody else."

Rayburn stumbled on toward the door.

"Oh, Rayburn, I left some dirty panties in the drawer. Case you get lonely, take 'em out an' have a sniff." Her laughter pushed him out into the night. Leslie got to her feet and looked around. "Well, Leroy, ma hero, where was you when the shit hit the fan?"

"Watchin'," Leroy said. "Just watchin'. Cotton?"

"Yo."

"You go an' get some money out the safe, an' then you an' Willie T. take this cunt out to the airport an' put her on the first thing goin' beyond

Chicago. Give her some money. But not enough to get back." Leslie's grin vanished. "Sorry, baby," Leroy said. "I ain't got time to be sleepin' with cobras."

"Fuck you," Leslie snapped. "The trouble with you niggers is that you're all goddamn janitors. You all cleans toilets. Every one a you."

"Leroy?" Cotton asked, coming back with the money. "A thousand enough?"

"Make it two. Send her to Alaska."

"Amen," Cotton said. "While we're goin' out to the airport, over the river, past the junk yards, all that shit, maybe we oughta be gettin' rid a some other trash at the same time?"

"What trash?"

"Well, you know, just, trash."

"Cotton, what the hell—"

"Guns," Cotton said. "Bodies. That kinda trash. Your gun an' Brown's body."

"Huh?" Leroy said. "Brown ain't dead."

"But you said—"

"I said I went up there, an' they was in bed. I didn't kill him."

"Well, why the hell not?" demanded Cotton.

"Well, how the hell should I know? Maybe I didn't feel like shootin' a man while he was fuckin'. Maybe I just wasn't in the mood." Leslie snickered. "Get her outa here," Leroy said.

"Sure, Leroy, sure," Cotton said, and hauled Leslie unceremoniously out the door.

Brown sat silently at the table, sipping coffee from a cracked cup. He made a face, reached for the sugar, and dumped in two more spoonfuls, tasted the coffee again, and nodded. "You gonna make yourself sick, takin' all that sugar," Vanessa told him. "All that sugar's bad for you."

"You're always so concerned about ma health," Brown said. "You ma insurance company or somethin'?"

"Or somethin'," Vanessa said. Brown chuckled. Vanessa sighed. "I'll get you some brown sugar tomorrow. Brown sugar ain't as bad for you." Brown grinned at her lecherously, reached out a hand. "Quit that, now," Vanessa snapped. "How you want your eggs? Straight up or over easy?"

"How 'bout one straight up an' one over easy?"

"I tole you to quit that," Vanessa said crisply. She broke the yolks and pan-scrambled Brown's eggs, slid them onto a plate, and put them in front of him. Brown looked at them. "What's the matter?" Vanessa demanded. "Somethin' wrong with them eggs?"

"No," Brown said quickly. He began to eat.

"Can't be sendin' you up there to that woman with an empty stomach." Brown paused, glanced at her, then went on eating.

"I guess she cooked all kinds of fancy shit for you, huh?" Vanessa said.

"No," Brown said. "Most a the time I cooked fancy shit for her. Her family had hired help. She never learned to cook."

324

"Oh," Vanessa said acidly. "She had hired help. I'm sorry I never had no hired help."

"That's okay," Brown said charitably. "You can't cook any bettern her."

"I ever tell you you was a bastard?" Vanessa inquired.

"I do seem to recall," Brown said. Vanessa opened her mouth. "I also," Brown cut in, "recall what comes next: fifteen seconds of angry glances followed by two and a half minutes of tears followed immediately if not sooner by a quarter hour's dissertation on how you ain't good enough in bed or smart enough in the head an' had to quit school at fifteen an' screw everybody that had the price an' how I'm wastin' maself with you an' how you know deep down inside that I can't hardly wait to get away. Excuse me, ma'am, but I am a little bit tired a that stale bullshit." He grinned. "I even prefer your eggs."

"It ain't bullshit," Vanessa snapped. "You're goin', ain't you?"

Brown sighed. "Yes. I'm going. I'm going to a cocktail party. You want to come?"

"No," Vanessa said. "I just want to know why you have to go."

"I don't *have* to go," Brown said.

"You want to go."

"Not exactly."

"Then what the hell you goin' for?"

Brown looked at her for a minute, looked down at his plate, pushed it away. "To get a decent meal."

"You're full a shit," Vanessa said.

"I don't want to talk about it."

"Tough shit, babycakes," Vanessa said. "*I* want to talk about it."

"Well, I don't."

"But I do."

"Well then, you just go ahead an' talk about it," Brown snapped. "I ain't figured out how to shut you up anyways."

"You ain't hardly taken the time. Shit, I don't know why I want to bother. You know, nigger, you're beginnin' to make me mad. Who the hell you think you are? You know what you are? You're one a them outside agitators—"

"Oh, Lord."

"—come down here stirrin' up people's lives—"

"I didn't do nothin'."

"You done somethin' to me."

"Yeah," Brown said, "an' you even got so you liked it."

"Yeah," Vanessa said. "An' don't that make your ass proud? Makes you the best cocksmith on South Street, man that finally made 'Nessa come.

You gonna be a fuckin' legend, Brown. You can write it yourself, you'd like that. You go on up there an' do that, Brown, now that you finished your goddamn research."

Brown got up and went over to her. He took her by the shoulders. Vanessa turned her head away. Brown caught her chin, tried to turn her head. She twisted away. "Look at me," Brown said. Vanessa glared at him, her nostrils flared. "Is that what you think?"

"I don't know," Vanessa said. She swallowed, lowered her eyes. "I don't know. All I know is, you started somethin' an' you ain't hardly finished it. You walked in one end a somethin', an' now you wanna walk right out again. Ain't gonna let it touch you."

"I'll be back," Brown said. "I told you that."

"You're lyin'. I know when a man's lyin'."

"Damn, you act like I was goin' to the other side a the moon."

"That's where you are goin'."

"Well, I'll be back this evenin'."

"How come you got to go in the first place?" Brown sighed. "I'll wait," Vanessa said. "I'll wait until tomorrow mornin'. You ain't back by then—"

"I'll be back."

"If you're worried about Leroy, I'll handle Leroy."

"*You're* the one worried about Leroy."

"You started somethin' with Leroy, too," Vanessa said.

"It wasn't nothin' important."

Vanessa stepped back away from him. "Dammit, there you go again. It is important. It's important to Leroy. You scared him. Man like Leroy can't afford that."

"Lord," Brown said.

Vanessa turned away. "You're an idiot, you know that?"

"Right," Brown said. He got up and stomped into the bedroom.

Vanessa took his cup and plate from the table. She scraped the cold eggs into the garbage, washed the cups and dishes, filled the skillet with water and left it to soak. Brown came out of the bedroom dressed in tan slacks, a white shirt open at the neck. Vanessa glanced up. "You look good. You can have any woman you want up to that party."

Brown smiled faintly. He went over and laid his arm around her shoulders. She pushed him away. Brown went over and looked out the window. "Wonder who sleeps down there now?"

"Brown?"

"What?"

"You ever write a poem 'bout Jake?"

"No," Brown said.

"Why don't you? Jake woulda liked it. Or just write one with him in it."

"You don't write poems *about* people," Brown said. "You write poems about rats and roaches and garbage. Sometimes you write poems for people. But mostly you write poems because of people. Jake'll be in every poem I write from now on." He turned. "So will you."

🦶

Cotton lounged in the deserted barroom of the Elysium Hotel, his stubby legs propped up on a chair, the air-conditioning turned up high, the latest issue of *Playboy* magazine lying unopened on his knee, a frosty beer in his hand. Cotton sighed his contentment and sipped the beer. He opened the magazine and flipped through it, glancing disinterestedly at the pictures. The door to the office opened and Leroy emerged like a reluctant dragon, jowls unshaven and sagging, shirt stained and aromatic, eyes red and unfocused. Cotton looked up in astonishment. "Leroy?"

"Yeah," Leroy growled in a gravelly voice.

"I ain't seen you up this early on a Sunday in a long time. Never. Monday, neither, for that matter."

"That's true," Leroy allowed, taking a chair. "I always figured if God needed one day's rest I was entitled to at least two. Maybe three."

Cotton looked at him suspiciously. "You gettin' religion or somethin'?"

"What? Hell, no."

"Just wonderin', just wonderin'," Cotton said.

"Well, quit wonderin'. What's that you got?"

"Beer."

"Think I'll have me one," Leroy said. Cotton stared as Leroy got up and went behind the bar.

"Opener's there on the left," Cotton said.

Leroy grunted. The bottle hissed. Leroy came back and dropped into the chair. He took a long, loud swig. "That's pretty good. That's pretty damn good. You know, Cotton, I ain't had me a beer in a long damn time. Real long time." He took another swig, then held the bottle up, examining it carefully in the dim light. "A man oughta drink beer," Leroy said. "Somethin's wrong with a man if he don't drink nothin'. Somethin' wrong with him if he drinks too damn much. Or messes around with them pills an' dope an' dust an' all that shit."

"Humph," Cotton said. "You'd be in pretty bad shape if all them junkies decided to guzzle beer. You wouldn't have a Volkswagen, let alone a goddamn Cadillac."

"Well, I ain't talkin' about junkies. I ain't no junkie. I ain't no pill freak, neither. Not no more." He looked at Cotton. "You know I been takin' pills? Pills to get up, pills to get down, pills for every fuckin' thing. Ruins your goddamn appetite. Shit." He sucked disgustedly on his beer.

"You, ah, been 'up' all night?" Cotton inquired delicately.

Leroy looked at him. "I been awake all night. I ain't been up. I'm finished with that shit. That's all right for them fools out in the street." Leroy raised his beer again, but stopped with the bottle only halfway to his lips. "You know how old I am, Cotton?"

Cotton lied with an exaggerated shrug. "What's the difference?"

Leroy lowered the bottle. "There's lotsa difference. I'm too damn old—"

"Oh, damn, you ain't startin' in with that retirement shit again, are you, 'cause if you are I'ma look at ma magazine here."

Leroy glanced over. "I didn't know you was into starin' at white pussy."

"I ain't," Cotton said. "There's supposed to be a black girl in here somewheres, only I can't see her noplace. They probly got the whitest-lookin' black woman they could find."

"Well, hell," Leroy said, "it's hard to tell the difference when you're lookin' up at it."

"Yeah," Cotton said. He examined the front cover. "Damn if I'd want me a woman done had her ass on every newsstand in the damn country."

"What the hell," Leroy said. "Get right down to it, it don't hardly make no difference what she done. Onliest thing that matters is what she's doin'."

"Or what she ain't doin'," Cotton said.

Leroy looked at him sharply. Cotton did not drop his eyes. "Yeah," Leroy said, "or what she ain't doin'. Now gettin' back to what I was sayin'—"

"Not killin' somebody don't make you ready for the boneyard, Leroy," Cotton said.

"I know that, Cotton," Leroy said. "I ain't ready for the boneyard, but if you interrupts me one more time, you will be."

"Sorry," Cotton said.

"Umph," Leroy said. He drained his bottle, rose, and went back behind the bar. When he returned he had a fresh bottle for Cotton, too. Cotton stared at him. "What's the matter with you?" Leroy demanded.

"Nothin'," Cotton said, accepting the bottle. "Not one thing."

"Keep it that way," Leroy said. He sat down and stared thoughtfully at the wall. "Cotton, I been livin' a long time." Cotton made a large production of drinking his beer and did not reply. "Yeah," Leroy said, "I've been livin' a long time, an' every minute of it I been a nigger. I'm gettin' tired of it."

"What?" Cotton said. "Maybe you'd better talk that retirement shit. Lest I'll know what kind a shit it is."

"This ain't shit," Leroy said. "I'm talkin' about bein' a nigger. I been a nigger all ma life. Ain't no accident rats an' niggers go together. They both live on crumbs."

"Shit—"

"It ain't shit. It's true."

"You run this whole damn street," Cotton protested. "Every nigger—"

"Every *nigger!*" Leroy exploded. "That's right. That's just exactly right. Every nigger. Every black face had better be smilin' at me. Damn right. I run South Street. Amen. I'm the biggest nigger around. Only just let me *step* on Market Street, you let me *try* an' send one a ma girls up to the Sheraton, or the goddamn Ben Franklin. Then you wait an' see how long that shit is gonna last."

"That's life," Cotton said. "You only get what Charlie wants you to have."

"Shit if you do. You only get what the muthafucka don't even care about. Or what he don't know about. An' you only get to keep it so long as he don't start wantin' it, or don't find out about it. You got to lose sleep for fear the muthafucka's gonna find out you got a little piece of gold somewhere. An' I'm tellin' you, Cotton, I am through with that kinda shit. I'ma buy me a congressman."

"Huh?"

"You heard me. A congressman. Senators is too expensive. We get us a congressman, an' then we get it together an' go on up an' pay a call on Gino, 'cause the way I hear it, that muthafucka buys Christmas turkeys for half the city government. I'm talkin' 'bout power, baby."

"A week ago we was scared a Gino. Now how the hell we gonna talk to him?"

"Brown," Leroy said. "You say he's buddy-buddy with Gino? Good. We be buddy-buddy with Mr. Brown. We'll kiss that sucker's ass so much he's gonna save a cool million on toilet paper. We gonna send him presents. He wants a piece a the Street? Sure, baby. He gets some a ma asphalt crumbs an' I'ma get some a his fuckin' *soul*. He wants 'Nessa? Sure, Mr. Brown. When he pulls his pecker out we slip some handcuffs on his balls. An' when we're real good friends an' I got ma congressman, we go see Gino."

"But what about—"

"What about nothin'. Go get me a beer. Have one yourself."

"I don't want no more," Cotton said, getting up.

"I don't recall astin'," Leroy snapped. Cotton grinned to himself, and went to get the beer.

Vanessa waited in the kitchen, nervously sipping at an unwanted cup of instant coffee and watching a cigarette, untouched since the first puff, burn itself to white ash. When she was sure Brown would be well on his way she stood up and looked around her. The room seemed empty, barren. She went to the door and stood with one hand on the knob, the other grasping the doorjamb as if the door were a hole she was trying not to fall through while she looked around once more. She took a deep breath and stepped into the hall, closed the door carefully, and went down the stairs.

The street was hot, bright; she paused to take out her shades and slip them on her nose. The hard white glare softened and darkened. Beneath the brightness, shadows lurked. Her feet carried her away from Brown's door. She walked slowly in the heat, smelling the odor of the street mingled with her own perfume-sweetened sweat. The heat made her head itch, as if tiny sparks arched at the roots of her hair. She felt tired as she pushed open the door to the Elysium's lobby. The lobby was deserted. Vanessa looked around it with distaste, moving on to the door that led to the barroom with the exaggerated care of a whole man running a gauntlet of lepers. She pushed the door open, stepped inside. The barroom was dark, except for the whisper of an air-conditioning unit. She went to the office door. Through it she heard muffled curses, the click of billiard balls. She pushed the door open. Leroy and Cotton looked up from the game, straightened quickly. "I wanna talk to you," Vanessa said.

Leroy smiled broadly. "Why, 'Nessa! Good to see you, sugah. I believe you know Cotton, here, an' Wilbert Tatum." Leroy gestured expansively at Willie T., who was seated behind the desk devouring Cotton's *Playboy* with voracious eyes. Leroy glared at him. "Get to your feet, nigger, an' put that honky shit away. There's a lady present."

Willie T. stood up in amazement. "What kinda shit—"

"An' mind your tongue, fool." Leroy turned back to Vanessa and shrugged apologetically as Willie T. knocked the chair over getting to his feet. "Some of us just ain't ready," Leroy observed sadly. "Now what can I do for you?"

"I want to talk to you."

"Why a course. What about?" Vanessa glanced at Willie T. and Cotton. "Take a walk," Leroy said. Cotton put his cue down and left with the ponderous dignity of an obese undertaker. Willie T. stumbled all over himself as he tried to accomplish the near-impossible task of keeping the *Playboy* out of sight of both Leroy and Vanessa. "Now," Leroy said, when

Willie T. had managed, not without considerable difficulty, to close the door, "what can I do for you?"

Vanessa smiled sweetly and stepped close to him, insinuating her hand between the third and fourth buttons of his shirt. "What can I do for you?"

Leroy looked down at her hand. "How's your gentleman friend?" Leroy inquired.

"Fine," Vanessa said. "An' I'd do damn near anything to keep him that way."

"I'm sure you would," Leroy said.

"I'd do just about anything to make sure nothin' happened to him," Vanessa said.

Leroy looked puzzled. "Is somethin' gonna happen to him?"

"Oh, well, you never know," Vanessa said. "Accidents do happen. He might be walkin' down the street an' slip an' cut his throat on a busted switchblade. He might be in the wrong place when somebody was cleanin' their gun an' get shot right between the eyes."

Leroy looked shocked. "Are you trying to tell me that somebody might have it in for Mr. Brown?"

"I've heard whispers," Vanessa said drily.

"Who?" thundered Leroy.

"Shit, Leroy," Vanessa said, "I don't know what kinda game—"

"Me?" said Leroy, in tones of outraged innocence. "You think that I— 'Nessa, I am shocked."

"Shocked, shit. Now listen, Leroy, I come down here to tell you you can do anything you want with me, but you just let Brown be, you hear? You want me to stay away from him, fine, we'll both stay away from him."

"Vanessa, I surely don't understand you. I would *never* want to come between you an' Mr. Brown. I was hopin' you could introduce us. We've met, but not formally."

"What kinda shit—Leroy, all I want you to do is to let the man be. He ain't nobody gonna do you no harm, I can guarantee that, so why can't you just let him be?"

"I'm tryin' to tell you—"

"You're tryin' to sell me a whole truckload a cat shit, an' I ain't hardly buyin'."

Leroy spread his hands. "Vanessa, you have got to believe me. I'm as concerned with Mr. Brown's health as you are. I done give the word. Ask anybody. Won't none a my people lay hand number one on him. They won't rob him, they won't cheat him, they won't shortchange him, hell, half the time they won't even *charge* him. An' if any nigger so much as looks at him sideways, that black-assed bastard is gonna have me to deal with, an'

I'ma be doin' ma own light work." Leroy looked at the suspicious expression on Vanessa's face and sighed. "Front!" he shouted. The door burst open and Willie T. sprang in like an eager recruit. "Now," Leroy said. "Will you please tell this lady what our policy is with regards to Mr. Brown?"

"Mr. Brown gets whatever Mr. Brown wants," Willie T. chanted. "Free protection. He wants to play, he wins three times outa eleven. Free girls—"

"That's fine," Leroy said quickly. "You see, 'Nessa? Any friend a Gino's is a friend a mine."

"Gino," Vanessa said.

"Oh, but that's not important," Leroy said. "We just want to be sure that Mr. Brown is happy. You tell him if there's anything he needs, we'll be happy to supply it."

"Yeah, well," Vanessa said. "He ain't gonna be needin' no girls."

"Of course not," said Leroy, shooting a glare at Willie T. "But you tell him the bar at the Elysium is always open to him. Does he play pool?"

"No," Vanessa said, "he don't play pool."

"Pity," Leroy said. "Anyway, as I was sayin', if he needs anything, furniture, stereo, you tell him I got some a the baddest boosters in the *world*, an' I'd be honored to get him anything, even if I got to send somebody out to Mount Airy to steal somethin' special. You too. Willie, you take down 'Nessa's size. I got me a line on some mink, 'Nessa, truck ain't even got a tailgate."

"You already gave me a mink, Leroy," Vanessa told him. "I wore it one time an' damn near took a fall for receivin' stolen goods. Had to tell 'em I was a hooker 'fore they'd believe I could afford it."

"Oh, yeah," Leroy said, "I do recall. How about air-conditioning? I'm gettin' in some great units."

Vanessa looked at him coolly. "Brown's got you pretty shook, ain't he?"

"I just want to be friendly."

"That's what the snake said when he screwed Eve." Leroy smiled tightly but said nothing. "I don't know what you're after, Leroy," Vanessa said, "an' I don't much care—"

"Peace," Leroy said serenely, "just peace." Vanessa shook her head and went to the door, turned back as if to say something. "Peace," Leroy said, making a V with two fingers.

"Jesus Christ," Vanessa said. She hurried out onto the street, shades on, feet tapping the pavement. Sweat sprang up on her back as she half ran back to Brown's place, up the stairs into the oven heat. She sank into a chair, shaking her head in bewilderment. A smile stole across her face, and suddenly she was laughing loudly, almost hysterically. The chair creaked as her body shook with laughter. " 'Mr. Brown,' " she giggled. "Oh my Jesus, 'Mr. Brown.' " She laughed until her ribs began to hurt and then she sat there thinking of Brown and looking around at the barren room, smiling at the dirty corners, smiling at the dingy walls. She imagined the walls painted, the corners scrubbed. She imagined Brown sitting where she sat, pen in hand. She smiled and opened the drawer where Brown kept his poems. The smile died on her lips. The drawer was empty.

Brother Fletcher stood sweating into his clerical collar on the hot sidewalk in front of The Word of Life Church, graciously accepting the congratulations of the departing parishioners on his ascension to the pastorate. They had always, they assured him, preferred him to the Reverend Mr. Sloan. It was, they were certain, God's will that Mr. Sloan be removed and that Brother Fletcher replace him, and God's will would, of course, be done, on earth as it is in heaven. Amen. Those members who had held positions of power in Mr. Sloan's administration hastened to assure Brother Fletcher that they were just as willing to serve under him. Those members who had not held positions of power hastened to apprise Brother Fletcher of their ability, availability, and approbation of his assumed intention to inaugurate a new order. Those members who neither held power nor desired it hastened to surround him because everybody else had. Brother Fletcher was the only one who was not hastening anywhere; he stood amidst the hastening hordes, giving the appearance of attention to every petition, nodding his head, and occasionally smiling as the account of the first game of a doubleheader between the Philadelphia Phillies and the New York Mets came to him through the earplug that all the parishioners, who had never really paid much attention to Brother Fletcher before, assumed was connected to a hearing aid. Brother Fletcher had moved only once—to fight his way through the maelstrom to shake the hand and kiss the withered cheek of Sister Lavernia Thompson, who had been standing beyond the edge of the inky whirlpool surrounding Brother Fletcher gazing at him hopelessly, as if he were somehow beyond her reach.

The crowd thinned slowly. The Phillies were leading, three to two in the third. Brother Fletcher's thoughts were turning to the iced tea and roast-beef dinner that Mrs. Fletcher would be preparing when he saw Leo coming down the street. Brother Fletcher advanced to meet him. "Afternoon, Reverend," Leo said as they met on the corner. "Special duty today? I don't recall seein' you out here before."

"Well, the Reverend Mr. Sloan is indisposed," Brother Fletcher said.

"Tut, tut, tut," said Leo, shaking his head. "I hope it ain't nothin' that's gonna be fatal right away. He can use this heat to get in shape for Hell."

"He's not sick. He's in jail. Turns out Mr. Sloan is an escaped convict. He's already on his way back to California."

"Do tell," Leo said. "That means you the big man now, I guess. Make lotsa changes."

Brother Fletcher shook his head. "No," he said, "no, they don't want any changes. They want circuses. Who knows, maybe it does some good." He shrugged and smiled. "But there'll be religion here for anybody that wants it, and help for anyone who needs it. Sloan's circus is gonna pay for it. You tell Jake I said that any wino needs a place to sleep—Leo! What's wrong?"

Leo raised his head and wiped a tear from his eyes. "Jake's gone home, Rev. Passed away late Friday night."

Brother Fletcher stared at him. Leo lowered his head again. "I'm sorry," Brother Fletcher said. "It's hard to believe."

"Yeah," Leo mumbled. He looked up again, smiling around the tear streaks. "You know, I was halfway up here this mornin', comin' to let him outa the bar like always, 'fore I remembered." Leo wiped his face with the back of his hammy hand.

"When's the funeral?" Brother Fletcher asked.

Leo looked surprised. "You know, I never even thought about that. You think we oughta have a funeral for him? Will it hurt him if we don't?"

"Hurt him how?"

"You know, gettin' into heaven an' all that."

Brother Fletcher smiled. "I don't think so, Leo, but then I'm not even sure there is a heaven."

"What?"

"Nope," said Brother Fletcher. "But I do know if there is a heaven an' they don't let him in, there's somethin' wrong with the management."

Leo nodded. "You're right, there." He shifted his weight. "Lord, it's hot out here. I was on ma way down to the bar to watch the ball game. Too hot up to home. You wanna come along? That bar's real cool when there ain't nobody much there. Me an' Jake useta watch the games all the time." Brother Fletcher hesitated. "On the other hand," Leo continued, "I guess maybe now that you're in charge maybe you can't be goin' into bars no more."

Brother Fletcher laughed. "No, it's not that. God knows what happens in bars is nothin' compared to some of the things these Christian folk can do in the name of Jesus. No, I was thinking you could come on home with me an' take a piece of dinner an' watch one game, then we'd go on down to the bar for the second."

"That sounds all right. If you're sure it's not gonna be no trouble."

"Lord, no! Just let me call ma wife. She'll want to yell at me for a minute."

"Well if she's gonna be mad—"

"Nah," said Brother Fletcher. "She's not gonna be mad except because she won't have time to make a big fuss. She complains about all the trouble she goes to, then looks for more. You wait right here." Brother Fletcher disappeared inside The Word of Life and Leo lounged against the wall, basking in the warmth, not all of which radiated from the sun. In a few minutes Brother Fletcher reappeared, grinning. "Man, you shoulda *heard* that woman! 'What you mean, Fletcher, callin' me to tell me you bringin' somebody home? Don't you know this house is a mess an' we ain't got nothin' for dinner?' " Brother Fletcher chuckled. "She was up this mornin' gettin' that roast ready, an' that place is so clean the cockroaches starve. Come on." Brother Fletcher and Leo ambled up South Street, the volume of Brother Fletcher's transistor turned to high. Just after they crossed Nineteenth Leo stopped and waved to someone on the far side of the street.

"Brown," he bellowed. Brown looked over, checked the traffic, and crossed.

"Leo," Brown said.

"Brown, this here's the Reverend. Rev, this is Brown."

Brown smiled and nodded.

"Mr. Brown," said Brother Fletcher.

"Brown," Leo said, "I been thinkin'. Seems to me we oughta have a funeral for Jake. I think we oughta get together an' finish off that bottle a wine I kept for him. Terrible stuff, but it's what he used to like."

"That sounds like a good idea," Brother Fletcher said.

"This afternoon, 'bout five?"

"Well . . ." Brown said. Leo looked at him. "I'm on my way somewhere, an' I don't know if I'll be back. . . ."

"Exact time don't matter," Leo said. "We'll be there watchin' the ball game. Where you off to?"

Brown jerked his head toward the Schuylkill. "Other side a the river."

"You're headin' the wrong way," Leo said.

"Yeah, well, I just wanted to walk down the street, you know "

"In this heat?" said Brother Fletcher

"Sure," Brown said.

Leo shrugged. "It's your brains. We'll see you later."

"Sure," Brown said. "Nice meeting you, Reverend."

"Mr. Brown," Brother Fletcher said. He and Leo resumed their stroll. "Brown's a strange man," Brother Fletcher observed.

"Oh yeah, he's strange all right. I ever tell you 'bout the night Brown fronted off Leroy Briggs?"

"Who?" said Brother Fletcher.

"Never mind," Leo said. "Turn that radio up 'fore we miss all the action."

Brown watched them go, shadows swallowed by the loud blaze of white air that shimmered over South Street, then turned and wandered east. Brown's feet burned with reflected heat, scuffed a concrete sidewalk marred with grassless cracks, tripped on pebbles, kicked at trash, carried him deeper, beyond Broad Street, into the blocks where no one lived, where building shells stood raped and gutted, where lean dogs prowled in boneless alleys, where tomcats howled over tuna cans that were emptied days, weeks, months before. Brown's legs moved through the strip of heat that hovered just above the ground, sweat swiftly soaking his inner thighs and making his body sticky-warm. South Street passed before his eyes, a knife cut slicing across the city, a surgeon's incision, oozing pus, stitched with numbered streets. Brown walked along it until the playgrounds of Society Hill intruded. Then he turned north, to Lombard Street, and waited in the shade of an ancient oak.

A bus came rumbling up Lombard Street on a jet of hot, dirty air. Brown stepped into air-conditioned coolness, paid his fare. The doors closed but the bus idled, waiting for the light to change. Brown looked around. An old lady dressed in black was seated on one of the front seats. She looked at Brown with a disapproving gaze, clutching tightly at her purse. Brown moved on by her. Toward the other end of the bus a thin, well-dressed black man sat reading *The New York Times Book Review*. Brown took a seat next to him. "How you doin', Earl?" Brown said.

"Hey, Adlai, how you makin' it, brother?" Earl folded the book review and tucked it under one arm. The bus pulled away from the curb, trundled across the trolley tracks on Fifth Street, and picked up speed.

"Not so bad," Brown allowed.

"Solid," Earl said. "Hey, brother, I hear you been way down in the jungle, as the sayin' goes."

"Huh?"

"Yeah, man, Alicia, she been tellin' everybody 'bout how you decided that the only way one can be with the People is to be with the People, you dig? She says you been hangin' out on South Street, right in the *middle* a the shit."

"Oh," Brown said, "yeah."

" 'Course I know better. Soon as I heard that shit I said to myself Adlai has got himself some stuff down there, that's why he's there all the time. Pokin' himself some real jungle fire. Indeed. How you run that number, Adlai? I mean, don't Alicia get a little bit upset, you not comin' home at night?"

"I don't live with Alicia any more," Brown said shortly as the bus stopped for another light. "I got my own place."

"You mean you left that foxy broad behind? With all that bread? Damn, I heard a sacrificin' yourself to your art, but that, brother, is takin' that shit too far. Uh, excuse me, brother, but does the sister realize that you are, as the sayin' goes, no longer in residence? The reason I ask is she's been layin' the story, at least to me, that you been on what you might call a sabbatical. Like I do believe she expects you to come to your senses an' haul your little ass on home."

Brown looked out the window, caught a glimpse of South Street through a gap between two expensively restored townhouses.

"This, ah, new place you've acquired, is it on South Street?"

"Yeah," Brown said.

"Heavy," Earl said. "Uh, excuse me for askin', but I heard you was kinda, well, what you doin' for bread, brother?"

"I work for it."

"Umph. I didn't know they were hirin' poets these days."

"Sure they are," Brown said. "If they can tend bar."

"Umph," Earl said. "You must forgive me, brother, but I do believe you have got to be the craziest thing since that black astronaut thought they was gonna send him to the moon. I mean, there you are with a foxy woman, a fancy pad, a bad car—"

"Yeah," Brown said, "an' I didn't even nave to push dope.' He looked out the window.

"It's your life," Earl said. He started to unfold the book review. "Ah, where you goin' now?"

"Alicia's," Brown replied absently. He hitched himself closer to the window. The bus eased across Juniper Street, stopped at Broad.

"Well you'll have to excuse me, brother, if I sound a little confused, but I thought you said—"

"I did." Brown turned away from the window. "I'm going to Alicia's little party. You wanna see my invitation?"

"Easy, brother."

"You want me to explain it to you?"

"Oh no, brother, it ain't none a my business."

"You don't want to know why?"

"*Ours*," Earl quoted, "*is not to reason why.* Tennyson."

"You know that, Earl, or you just read Bartlett every damn night?"

"I know it, Adlai, I know it all. Do you?"

"Yeah," Brown snapped.

"Damn," Earl said, "and to think there ain't but one of you." He opened his paper.

The bus grumbled and growled, lumbered across Broad Street belching smoke like a tubercular dragon. The driver hauled at the wheel, hit the brakes, brought the bus to a halt at Fifteenth Street. A man got on, slowly, unsteadily, hung onto the fare box, fumbling for coins, dropped them into the fare box. The man stood, hanging onto a stanchion. "You're gonna have to siddown, buddy," the driver said.

"I want ma transfer."

Brown's head snapped around at the sound of the voice. He peered through the golden glare of sunlight lancing through the windshield. To Brown's eyes the man was a swaying shadow in a hazy halo.

"Transfer's another nickel, buddy," the driver was saying. "Now, will you move back behind the line so I can see the mirror."

"What about ma transfer?"

"Rayburn," Brown breathed.

Earl looked at him. "Friend a yours?" Brown did not reply. Earl looked toward the front of the bus.

"Look, buddy, the base fare is twenty-five cents. Transfer's a nickel more. You want a transfer, you owe the box a nickel. Now, will you get behind the line."

"Box, shit," Rayburn said. "I don't owe nothin' to no damn box."

"Shees," the driver said. He tromped down on the pedal and the bus rumbled away from the corner. "Here—" he ripped off a transfer coupon and handed it to Rayburn. "Now, will you get back behind the line?" Rayburn stumbled across the yellow restraining line and hung onto a grab bar like a hulking ape, peering at his orange transfer.

"Driver!" said the lady in black. "Can't you make this man move to the rear? He smells."

"Shees," said the driver.

Brown turned away, stared at the cross streets as the numbers climbed.

"He smells," the lady in black said again.

Rayburn staggered the length of the bus, took a seat facing Brown and Earl. "Brothers," Rayburn said. Brown smiled. Earl nodded uneasily. Rayburn looked at Brown without recognition. "I hope y'all ain't gonna mind me rappin'," Rayburn said. "I love to rap. I sure do. I can rap in ten languages." He counted on his fingers. "English. 'Merican. Nigger. Spic. Wop. Jap. Hell, that ain't but six. I'll remember the rest in a minute." Brown looked at him, his face blank. Earl studied the back page of the book review. The bus crossed Seventeenth Street. "Useta live down there," Rayburn said, pointing. Brown looked south. "Me an' ma woman. I left the bitch. Me, I got to keep flyin'."

The bus slowed as it approached Eighteenth Street, but the light changed, and it rolled on across, picking up speed as the street sloped down toward the Schuylkill. Brown turned to the window. South Street passed in strobe-light flashes, glimpses down the passing streets.

"That's what I useta do," Rayburn said. "Fly. Air force. I could fly any goddamn thing they had. Fuckin' fighter planes, jets, helicopters, any goddamn thing. Rockets. Speed, baby. I was the fastest thing in the world. Broke the sound barrier a hundred times. Broke the damn light barrier. Broke every damn barrier them honkies *had*. They got so they was worried there wasn't gonna be no barriers left for them white boys. Them goddamn generals, they'd set around all fuckin' week long tryin' to think up new ones. Then I'd go out on Saturday afternoon an' blow 'em away." Brown was staring out the window. South Street passed in glaring glimpses. Rayburn touched Earl's knee. "Saturday afternoon. Spare time. You dig?"

"I can't take this," Earl said. He got up and went to the front of the bus and took the seat across from the lady in black, who turned up her nose.

"They couldn't figure out if they was gonna send me to the moon or not, but they was afraid I'd be so damn fast gettin' up there wouldn't nobody believe it."

Brown looked at him. "You might as well be fast," Rayburn said. Brown looked back to the window, but the bus had reached the end of Lombard Street. It curved around slowly, climbed a slight rise, paused at a blinking yellow light, then swung up onto the South Street Bridge. Brown twisted in his seat, tried to look out the back window, but smoke and grime had coated the glass. Rayburn touched Brown's arm. "I'ma get outa here," Rayburn said. "I gots to be flyin'. I got ma transfer." He held it up. "You see, I'm on ma way."

"I see," Brown said. He got up quickly and swung to the front. The bus slowed, halted at the traffic light controlling the entrance to the Expressway, hanging on concrete over the river. "Let me out," Brown said.

The driver looked up. "No stop here."

"I want out here."

"Stop's on the other side." The light changed. The driver pressed the accelerator. Brown grabbed him by the throat.

"I want out here," Brown said.

The driver jammed on the brakes. "Sure, buddy, sure, anything you say." He hit the release lever. Air hissed. The doors popped open. Brown stepped down onto the pavement. The door closed quickly behind him.

"Shees," said the driver, rubbing his neck.

"They should never have let them use the public busses," said the lady in black. "It's just not safe."

"Shees," said the driver. "Sunday afternoon. Same goddamn story. Drunks an' nuts."

"The light's green," Earl said.

The driver turned and glared at him. "That friend a yours is sick. Sick, you know what I mean? Sick."

"Never saw him before," Earl said.

"All belong to the Black Muslims or somethin', an' you're all sick. Goin' around chokin' folks. Sick."

"You don't move this piece a shit off this bridge, I'm liable to choke you myself," Earl snapped.

The driver turned hurriedly. The light had gone red, but he pulled the bus away from the curb anyway. One hundred and sixty-two yards beyond the western bank of the Schuylkill the bus crossed Thirty-third Street, and South Street quietly, almost gratefully, became Spruce.